BREAKAGE

To Anne,
Best of Luck! — [signature]

FROM PEN INTERNATIONAL PRIZE WINNER
DAVID-MICHAEL HARDING

[signature] 8/'24

Black Rose Writing | Texas

ISBN: 978-1-68513-248-4 (Paperback); 978-1-68513-292-7 (Hardcover)
PUBLISHED BY BLACK ROSE WRITING
www.blackrosewriting.com

Printed in the United States of America
Suggested Retail Price (SRP) $22.95 (Paperback); $27.95 (Hardcover)

Breakage is printed in Minion Pro

*As a planet-friendly publisher, Black Rose Writing does its best to eliminate unnecessary waste to
reduce paper usage and energy costs, while never compromising the reading experience. As a result,
the final word count vs. page count may not meet common expectations.

For Kate

BREAKAGE

1

"I want you to remember four words. Apple. Coin. New. Gray. Okay, Mr. Chariot?"

The doctor's voice was pleasant and gentle. The examination room was spic-and-span clean, comfortable, and the staff courteous, but none of it eased the sickness Donnie Chariot was feeling. "Got it," he answered nonetheless.

"All right. Why have you come in today?"

"Something's wrong with me."

"How so?"

"I'm forgetting things."

"Such as?"

"Things I should know. Little things. Big things. But it's more than that. Way more."

"Give me an example."

"I do...." There was a pause that instantly felt too elaborate and Donnie tried to shed it. "I do a lot of accounting work. I've gotten so I can't do my job. I can't seem to get the numbers to cooperate like they did. I'm making mistakes. Those are the big things. They're expensive mistakes."

"Have you talked to your boss about it? He knows what's happening?"

"Oh, he knows all right."

"That's good. It's important to be honest about such things."

Donnie grimaced. "He's not happy."

"Perhaps it's time to give yourself a break from work. Step away for a while."

"That's unlikely. We're in…um…this is our busy season. Can't you just give me something? Maybe Adderall. I heard that's the rage on campuses. Does that really help with concentration? That's what I need, doc."

"We can talk about it. What other symptoms can you tell me about? Any headaches? Balance concerns?"

"No. None. It's just the numbers. They don't fit like before."

"What do you mean, fit like before?"

Donnie squirmed on the edge of the examining table. "There was a time when I could do some pretty advanced math in my head. I can't do that now."

"That's not abnormal. You're only doing what most of us can do. It doesn't mean you're ill."

"It does for me. It goes beyond math."

"Try this. Count backwards from one hundred by seven."

Donnie didn't flinch and rattled off numbers like a machine-gun. "Ninety-three. Eighty-six. Seventy-nine. Seventy-two. Sixty-five. Fifty-eight. Fifty-one. Forty-four. Thirty-seven. Thirty."

"That's enough. You're remarkable. Not one of my patients can do that as easily as you just did."

"Thanks, but it's not addition and subtraction I'm talking about. It's probability. Coherent odds…I mean ratios. Coherent ratios. Operational subjectives. It's looking at a map of equations and seeing a clear route through all of them. That's what I used to do. And I can't anymore. Not anymore." Donnie's voice trailed off and his eyes fell to the floor. "I'm sick, doc. I need help."

"I know you do."

Donnie's gaze broke with the floor. "You do?"

"What were those words I asked you to remember when you came in?"

They were lost to him, but Donnie searched the doctor's face, his own mind, and the ceiling before his eyes fell to the floor again. "I don't have a clue. Green? A color maybe? Cat? I think one was cat."

The doctor turned a card on the examining table face up. On it were the words, *Apple, Coin, New, Gray.*

"Didn't do very well, did I?"

"The same."

"The same as what?"

"The same as you did three weeks ago."

"Three weeks?"

"When you came in last time."

Donnie stood up and rubbed his face hard with both hands. "Is that true? I was in here three weeks ago?"

"Yes."

"God damn it!"

"Did you fill the prescription I wrote you?"

"I don't know."

"Donnie, this has been going on too long. It's early onset Alzheimer's. I'm as certain of it as I can be, short of an autopsy."

"Don't waste all your bedside manner on me, doc."

"This is serious, Donnie. I can't sort it all out. Every case is different, and how you present isn't in any textbook. You can do things most people would need a calculator for, but then there's these classic signs. I don't know all the answers, but I do know it's getting worse."

"You're telling me."

"You're still a relatively young man. You can enjoy a very successful retirement. Back off on working all hours. Keep up with your medicines, watch your diet, exercise. You need some help. The sooner the better. I need you to come in and see me next week."

"What will that change?"

"Probably nothing, but I want you to bring your daughter. You need help with this. You can't do it alone any longer."

"I'll bring my maid into the fold."

"Not this time. It's too important. You need to tell your family."

"That probably isn't going to work very well."

"When's the last time you spoke to Donna?"

"Li'l Donnie? A couple years anyway. Maybe longer."

"You're not sure, are you?"

"A long time."

"You can't remember."

"I remember. I remember an ungrateful girl, that's what I remember."

"You're no bed of roses either. You know that?"

Donnie locked eyes with the doctor for a long count.

"What do you remember, Book?"

The name startled him. It was a handle hung on him decades ago for his skill and predilection with illegal gambling and bookmaking.

"I know you, Donnie. I've been your doctor for thirty years. I knew your wife. I know your daughter, Donna. I know your granddaughter. And I know you. Thirty years you've been coming in here and you don't remember coming to see me a few weeks ago. What's that tell you?"

"Tells me I've been coming here too damn much."

"Get in touch with Donna. If you don't, I will. You need her."

Donnie considered the suggestion for just a moment. Whatever afflicted him, it didn't stop him from thinking ahead to the racehorses and odds already swirling around the upcoming "Run for the Roses" at Churchill Downs.

"You might be right," Chariot said as he explored the doctor's face and his own uneasy mind. He compared what he found with what he knew he needed to produce for the gamblers of Las Vegas. "I believe I do need her."

2

"The Most Exciting Two Minutes in Sports" had not yet ended. Sleek horses, bleeding sweat down coats of chiseled black, chestnut, and dappled gray, were still pounding down the stretch where the crowd's roar was rising to meet them. Behind the entries lay the touted turn for home; ahead waited the wire. The eventual winner of The Kentucky Derby had a furlong yet to cover, but Donnie Chariot had seen enough races to know the horse's lead was insurmountable. He also knew the place and show horses had settled into locks. The next horse's connections would have to settle for fourth.

Though Donnie had already put the finish up on the tally board in his mind, on the track, the jockeys' whips bit into their laboring horses' flanks in what Donnie knew would be a failed attempt at a better finish. Unless one of the horses broke down, the "Run for the Roses" was as good as over. Before it ended for real, Donnie calculated the payouts would cost him north of seventeen million dollars, his reputation, and perhaps even his life.

Chariot didn't see a broken foreleg coming in the next twenty seconds. It wasn't in the genes of these four particular thoroughbreds. Though anything was possible, it was not probable. A breakdown among this quartet was against the odds. Odds and probability—by the numbers, Chariot's numbers—was what Donnie knew better than anyone else.

Genetics was only one piece of a living, breathing dimensional puzzle that was a horse race. Forelegs genetically prone to snapping were more difficult to see than unicorns. Finding winners was easier. Professional handicappers, weekend warriors, bookies, and dreamers each had their method. Donnie Chariot's gift—a blazing quick-strike mainframe of a mind that crunched statistics as easily as other people breathed—dissected the puzzle with a scalpel made of numbers. Past performances, weight, weather, track, trainer, time, distance, and competition calculations were dumped into his head. He reviewed all the horses' bloodlines in the time it had taken to turn the pages.

The process was repeated with trainers, tracks, and jockeys. The sets of numbers were then overlaid in his mind. Ten million synapses fired in a nanosecond and winners, losers, and "also-rans" trickled out his fingers as checks next to horses' names on Daily Racing Forms. Other handicappers used their own processes, even if it was only a dart board. The difference is that Chariot's worked. It had made him rich, but what he did when he didn't handicap a race is what made him powerful.

When the numbers on a tote board winked at Donnie in a singular fashion only he could discern, the supercomputer between his ears whirled. The tallying odds gave him a peek behind the certainty curtain of numbers that ebbed and flowed as bets. Courtesy of his unusual genius, Donnie pegged results that were immune to the outcome of the race. He called these races "Specials." They were rare to his eyes and invisible to others'.

What brought Specials to light was a peculiar algorithm that tilted the amount wagered per horse and subsequent odds, versus the total pool, or dollars, bet on the race. A Special exposed a circumstance where monies placed delicately on the scale of a horse race, in certain places on certain horses in certain amounts, forced a yield that was like compounded interest to a banker. If there was such a thing as a sure bet in gambling, Donnie's Specials were it. In the maelstrom of numbers that continually raged in his brain, this perfect storm of unbalanced odds presented the surprisingly quiet eye of a hurricane where his thoughts could settle and find a respite.

This is what made Donnie Chariot powerful and also what gave him that nickname, "The Book." He fed the furnace reputation of The Book on his usual flare for handicapping and odds setting, but in the orgy that came with a Special, Donnie Chariot became an icon. He was an oracle of betting that scooped the pool of smaller tracks and lighter races, emptying the coffers previously stuffed with cash, two-dollar wagers at a time.

Donnie had the power other people wanted. Money came and went and could be recovered, lost, and gained again in a day. Power endured and Donnie Chariot had power in spades. It was money that bought the mansion in New York near his home track at Belmont Park. Money also paid for the jet that brought him to Churchill Downs, but it was power that had gotten him his usual private box and it was power that brought disciples to that box to symbolically genuflect and kiss the ring.

But right now, lost beneath the climaxing wail of 160,000 spectators, Donnie Chariot was alone with his torrent of thoughts. Today had been unusual for a myriad of reasons. A Special had presented itself, but it was vastly more extraordinary than any other. Today the numbers had tickled Donnie's mind from the tote board for the running of The Kentucky Derby.

"It's never happened before," Donnie heard his voice in his ears, perhaps talking about the simultaneous arrival of both the Derby and the Special. Or perhaps it was something else whispering as numbers reset, stopped, and started again in his head.

From the time the top horses entered the stretch, Donnie knew the outcome, but that result was the most peculiar thing of all peculiar things to happen. As horses streaked below the wire of Churchill Downs and glided into easy canters, the winners didn't match Donnie Chariot's picks. The Book was wrong.

3

The roar of the Derby throng was far from settled. Flamboyant hats and empty mint juleps in their commemorative cups were still being jostled about. The jubilant sea around Donnie seemed oblivious to the fact that most were holding losing tickets. For them, it had merely been enough to be there.

The Book held no tickets—winners or losers—and to "be there" had lost its fascination twenty years ago. There was normally little appeal for Donnie in the race itself, apart from the historical significance and the impact he would see materialize in the breeding sheds. That changed when the Special in the esteemed race had revealed itself. Until then, he was here to fulfill an expectation, a step shy of an obligation.

With the presentation of the Special at Churchill Downs, handwritten notes, texts, and whispers flowed out from the guarded box seat he had occupied beneath the Twin Spires now for his thirty-fourth Kentucky Derby in a row. The stream of information had peaked at the bell when the last of his "beards"—secretive betters and punters for Vegas—approached betting windows the world over and discreetly placed the last bets based on what Donnie had seen in the numbers. Even with the closing of the windows, none of Donnie's money was in the till. His business had evolved to the point where he handled the money of others for the vigorish.

Donnie's cut kept him flush, but more importantly, kept his mind engaged. Without the daily odds making, the energy in his head conspired to prevent sleep at best and cohesive conversation at worst. His mind was an under-loaded circuit that, try as he might, endless games of fiendishly difficult sudoku couldn't abate.

As winning owners ran the gauntlet of glad-handers and backslappers toward the Winner's Circle to be captured forever by a hundred photographers, the losers eked toward the paddock where pundits would pine in hopes of discovering what went wrong. For his part, Donnie tried to see the numbers again in his mind, but they were gone.

He held a racing program for Derby Day and absently noted he was leafing through it with an uncommon regularity. Years before, the box on millionaire's row would have been witness to him holding the decorative souvenir program outlining the day's races simply as a prerequisite prop. Today, rather disturbingly he discovered, he returned to the assorted undercard races to remind himself of trainers, barns, owners, and who would be in the irons.

His eyes lowered and he gently scratched an itch on his cheek. While the crowd waged pandemonium and stood on their feet with phones pressed into service as cameras, Donnie Chariot turned the page to the next race of the day and touched the sleeve of the bodyguard standing next to him.

"Do you have my racing form?"

His voice and action were swallowed in the chaos of crowning a new champion. Unintentionally rebuffed, Donnie took note of the empty seat next to him and this time swatted at the burly attendant.

"Hey! Jimmy? Where's Li'l Donnie?"

The big man was startled and looked down, but through eyes that were uncommonly confused. "Frank, Mr. Chariot. I'm Frank. Jimmy's...you know...Jimmy's away."

"With Li'l Donnie?"

"Your daughter, sir?"

"Yes, my daughter! Donna. Where'd she go? She must have my Daily Racing Form. I need the DRF."

"LD didn't make the trip, Mr. Chariot." There was a pause that drowned the cheering crowd from Frank's ears. The drowning was spurred on by a vacant and desperate look coming from Donnie's eyes that unnerved the big man. "She hasn't come to the track in a long time, Book."

Frank reached into the inside pocket of his sport coat and inadvertently revealed the resting place of a Glock .45 pistol. The pocket yielded a folded Daily Racing Form. He handed the booklet, crowded with tracks, races, horses, and past performances to his boss. "Here you are, Book. Use mine."

Donnie Chariot uncharacteristically snatched the booklet. "Damn it! She doesn't have the picks for the twelfth race yet."

Frank followed the DRF to Chariot and cautiously dropped into the empty seat beside him. He shot a pleading look to his own underling standing in the aisle at the edge of the luxury box, then returned to his boss. "Mr. Chariot? LD, I mean Donna. She isn't here." He shot another glance to the aisle and then around as if someone might be listening. "She didn't make the trip. She's probably still in New York."

Donnie was leafing through the souvenir Derby program again while the Daily Racing Form had taken up a lesser position beneath it. "What'd you say?" There was more than a little menace in Donnie Chariot's voice as he came away from the programs and stared tight in Frank's face.

"Li'l Donnie isn't here, Book. She's in New York."

"Did she call in the picks?"

Frank was more confused and becoming anxious. It didn't fit a man whose thick arms tested the seams of his light-colored sport coat. "She doesn't call...I mean, Donna don't pick anymore. Not for years. Not since she was a little girl."

Focus came back into Donnie Chariot's eyes as plainly as if a cloud had passed from his face. There was a moment's hesitation as he physically felt the shroud being lifted. He searched a moment for something in his mind, then smiled and patted Frank's heavy thigh.

"I know she doesn't, Frank. I was testing you. What's the matter? You look tense. You want a mint julep or something?"

Frank relaxed, but not completely. He got up from the seat and took his place at the aisle. "Naw. I'm good. Must be the sun."

"Maybe we could get you one of those Derby hats that block my view now and again." Donnie leaned around his protector to Nicky, Frank's second in the aisle. "Hey, Nicky? Frank needs a hat. He's getting too much sun. Find him one with steeples on the top and maybe a pony running around the brim. A couple flowers too."

"I'm good, boss."

"You'd look good in a hat like that," Nicky grinned. "It'd show off your eyes."

"You'd like that. Probably ask me out."

"You wish."

Donnie broke the coarse banter. "Nicky, go bring the car up."

"Sure thing."

Nicky was bounding down the steps, leaving Frank looking at his back then to his boss. "We leaving, Book?"

"Yes." Donnie was stuffing his program and Frank's DRF in his pocket.

"The card's not up, Mr. Chariot. There's a couple more races. Then the party. You gonna bail on the party?"

"I need to get home."

"Tonight?"

"Yes. Tonight. What's the matter with you?"

"Well, nothing, I guess. I got a few bucks on the twelfth race, but—
"

"You know I'd rather you didn't gamble."

"I'm just playing around. Makes the races worth watching. A little skin in the game to keep me awake, is all."

"I'd hate to see you fall on your face at a betting window. You'll have some skin in the game then and it'll keep you awake, too. Let's go."

Frank was moving slowly. "I heard Mr. DeSeti mention that Baron was coming in from Vegas for the big race. You want to see him before we go back to New York?"

"Baron's here?"

"I thought you knew."

"I must've forgot. Are you certain?"

"That's what I heard from DeSeti."

Donnie motioned to the steps. "I'll talk to him later. He'll be calling."

Vehicle traffic was already picking up outside the grandstands. The VIP walking lanes, behind their velvet ropes, were filling as well, and apart from the oblivious celebrities, seasoned big-time gamblers occasionally caught Donnie's eye and nodded their respect. Frank saw each one, as well as any quick movements. He was always happy when they settled in the car. He was happier still when the jet lifted off as he reclined in the furthest back seat—weight to help balance the plane. With no one onboard but The Book, Nicky, and the pilots, Frank would sleep away the quick trip back to New York. He wouldn't wake up until the wheels touched down at JFK.

Across the aisle, Nicky surfed the net and dozed. Toward the front, Donnie Chariot couldn't close his eyes. He stayed hunched over a leather-bound binder of sudoku games working a vintage fountain pen until the jet landed.

"We're home, kiddo," Donnie said as he set his booklet beside him in the plush seats, got up, and pulled an overnight bag from a narrow closet.

Frank was slowly coming to life. "Leave that bag, Mr. Chariot. I'll bring it."

"You mean, you'll tell me to," Nicky said, collecting his own carry-on.

"I mean, I'll have Nicky bring it. She's strong."

Donnie glanced down the aisle at his two-person entourage, nodded, and went forward. The plane stopped rolling and the copilot was already opening the door.

"How was the race, Mr. Chariot?"

"Fine. They're all fine. No one got hurt."

"I see all the jocks wear flak jackets now and the rails have catchers built in if they fall off. Sounds like it's working."

"I was talking about the horses."

"Oh. Of course," the copilot said as he lowered the steps.

Donnie smiled. "The riders all got off on their own accord. That's good too."

Relieved and relaxed, the copilot went too far. "Did one of those jockeys bring home a winner for you?"

"I don't gamble," Donnie said as he descended the steps and walked away toward the terminal.

Behind the bemused copilot, Frank and Nicky were gathering The Book's luggage. Frank pointed into the plush seat and the forgotten sudoku binder. "Grab the boss's book."

As Nicky picked up the leather-wrapped volume, he flipped it open. The book was a thick collection of inked-in, finished sudoku games.

Nicky touched Frank's arm with the open book. "Hey. Check it out. The boss plays crossword puzzles."

"I said, pick it up, not search the man's things, you nosey shit."

"It's a book."

"It's *his* book. Mind your business if you want to keep working and stay above ground."

"What's that mean?"

Frank stopped his unloading. "Are you stupid? If you don't know who you're working for, you better run while your knees still bend in the right direction. You turnip-truck-riding—"

"I know who I work for. I was just saying—"

"No, you don't know, 'cause if you did, you wouldn't be going through the man's stuff. You might see something that you're not supposed to see. You do that, it's like taking poison. Might as well put a gun in your mouth."

"Relax, Frank. You're paranoid."

"No. I'm smart. And those aren't crossword puzzles, Turnip. It's sudoku. Tough ones. I'd go blind just looking at them. The Book fills them in with a pen by the fistful. No mistakes. The guy's like a computer with numbers. He gets new inserts now and again for that book from an old trainer he knows in Japan. We used to go over to a big track— Fuchu, or some Japanese shit like that—once a year or so. Not so much anymore. Something's changed. He's slowing down maybe."

"Probably thinking about retiring."

"I dunno. I don't think you can retire from his kind of life."

"How come?"

Frank stopped again and stared. "See that? You're showing your ignorance again, Turnip."

"Don't call me that."

"Okay, Turnip."

"Aww, move your ass, will you?"

4

Frank bounced up the wide stone steps of the mansion—light on his feet for a big man—and opened the door for his boss. Nicky was pulling the Bentley away toward the back of the estate and the garages.

"Always good to be home, hey Book?"

"Right you are." Donnie stopped just inside the doorway, froze, and looked around at his bags and across the floor, patting his pockets. "Where's Mr. Nakamura's book? I just had it."

"I slipped it in your bag. You left it on the plane."

"Did I?"

"Yes, sir. Right here." Frank pulled the finely tooled leather-covered booklet from a bag and handed it to his boss.

"Oh, good. I need another set of inserts. I knocked these out coming back from Baltimore." The phone in Donnie's jacket pocket rang. "I think I have a few yet. Maybe in the office." He glanced at the phone and put it away without answering. "Probably in my desk."

"You mean Churchill?"

"Churchill?"

"We just got back from Louisville, not Baltimore."

"Yes, I meant Kentucky. Pimlico needs a facelift. You can only put so many coats of paint on an old rail and it starts looking like an old rail with lots of coats of paint on it."

"Yes, sir. Are we headed there?"

"Where?"

"Pimlico."

"For what?"

"The Preakness."

"Hell, that's a lifetime from now."

"They run two weeks after the Derby."

"Two weeks. Like I said, a lifetime."

The house phone rang in a distant room.

"You want me to grab that?" Frank asked as he poised for a quick dash.

"Let it go. They'll call back."

Frank glanced at his watch. "Pretty late to be calling anyway."

"It is late. I'm headed up. Leave the bags until morning."

• • •

Donnie had just closed the door to his bedroom when his cell rang again. This time he didn't bother to see who was calling and left it unanswered. Less than a minute after the cell stopped ringing, the house phone by his bed rang. He knew who it'd be. There was little to be gained in avoiding the inevitable. He'd been in ticklish spots like this before. Maybe not as deep a hole as this one, but he'd work it out. He figured that honesty, in any enterprise—even one that was criminal— was still the best policy.

"Hello?" Donnie said softly into the receiver.

"Good evening, Book. Have you retired for the night?"

"Getting ready. How are you, Baron?"

"Broke."

"I rather doubt that."

"I might have a few nickels to rub together, but it's not for your lack of trying."

Chariot balked.

"You still there, Donnie?"

"Still here."

"I was planning on seeing you at the track. Someone said you left about the same time I took a bath on the Derby. You were calling in a lot of action at post time. Sold me short, Chariot. Real short."

"Just south of seventeen million."

"Like I said, real short. You want to tell me what happened with that?"

"It was a horse race, Baron. That's why they race. You can't tell who wins if they don't race. You know that."

"What I know is that I dropped $17 million in two minutes. That's not good business. Not for me and certainly not for you."

"Agreed."

"But the true rub is that it was my money—"

"And my reputation," Donnie cut in. "You can make money any day—"

"Except today."

"It's harder for me to recover what I lost."

"You spend much reputation lately, Book?"

"I live on it."

Both phones fell quiet.

"You left the track early. How come?"

"I was done."

"Seen enough, huh?"

"Yes."

Quiet.

"You know that when you make a call like that, Donnie, we load up pretty heavy."

"I've told you not to do that. You can impact the odds with big money."

"Yes, well, it happens. Everybody wants to get a piece of the action when you say jump, especially on a high-profile event."

"I've always advised against it."

"And when things don't turn out, a lot of people get caught in the wringer. That doesn't make people happy—"

"I've always advised against—"

"—and pissed off people are dangerous people."

"This isn't my first rodeo, Baron."

"I know. I know. I'm just talking here."

"And I'm just listening. Is there something further?"

"I've asked twice already, but haven't got an answer. Are you going to tell me what happened today?"

It was the third silence.

"So that's how it is, Donnie?"

"It's a horse race. These things hap—"

"Not when you drop the hammer they don't! Not once. Not ever! Have you taken to betting against the house, Chariot?"

"Don't be—"

"If a little bird whispers in my ear that you were laying off my seventeen mill so you could—"

"I wasn't. *I wasn't!* I wouldn't do that."

"No, you wouldn't. Not back in the day. People change, Book. Things change. Maybe somebody's giving you a better deal. A bigger cut. That it? You want more of the pie?"

"No. Nothing."

"And that's my answer as to what happened, too? Nothing. Just a race."

"Yes."

"All right, Donnie, but I'll be looking for you to help recoup my bad day. Any more bad days like today and I'm apt to take it rather personal. I'd eat my grandchildren before I'd part with another seventeen million on one race, and I love my grandchildren."

"I love mine, too."

"That's good, Book. All right. Sorry to keep you up. I'm on Vegas time. The party's still going strong here at the track. You should have stayed. Might have enjoyed it."

"It's not my thing."

"I know. One last piece bears mentioning. Find me a good race to pull the trigger on before the Belmont. Get back in my good graces. Fair enough?"

"I'll see what comes up."

"Do that. Maybe help it along a little. For all our grandchildren's sake. Goodnight, Chariot."

5

Donnie was in his cavernous office ahead of the first light. On the oversized desk, four wide computer screens provided a glowing early breakfast of data. It streamed through The Book's eyes and applied a salve over the restless mind that was forever seeking something to numerically digest. He touched one screen and it jumped to another bank of data. A mouse click away he was scanning racing results from the weekend and cards that would be run over the days to come. He saw horses' names, followed them to bloodstock agents, noted pedigrees and racing histories of sires and dams, siblings and offspring. It was a colossal, uncontrollable morass of information and numbers. But it settled him and occupied his mind. The data poured through his eyes in a drowning rush—a firehose into a mason jar—but nothing spilled. It was taken, distilled, digested, and stored in nanoseconds.

An hour later the sun was breaking through the late spring clouds over New York and Donnie was in his gourmet kitchen pouring a second cup of coffee. Decaf. Frank came in for his first—caffeinated from a second pot.

"Morning, boss."

"Frank," was all Donnie said by way of a greeting as he weaved his way through the first floor of his mansion back to his office.

In a few moments, Frank followed him in with three morning newspapers. He set the *New York Times* and the *Wall Street Journal* on the corner of Donnie's desk and took the *NY Post* with him to a big chair. The chair had been strategically placed years earlier so he could see the door to Chariot's office and out the floor-to-ceiling wall of windows to the entrance of the estate.

Frank settled without a sound. For almost two hours he sipped his coffee and turned the pages of his paper in total silence. When Mrs. Glass, the housekeeper and cook, brought in a small plate with toast, peanut butter, and fresh coffee at precisely nine o'clock for The Book, it was not an interruption. Instead, it was a continuation of the mandated morning. As he always did, Frank followed Mrs. Glass back to the kitchen. He would get his own coffee and as ever, find Nicky bent over breakfast.

"Morning, Frank," Nicky said. "You want an omelet? I just made a doozy."

"That's right. You're a cook now instead of a driver."

"In my day job, I'm a bodyguard. Like the secret service. A trained assassin."

"Here we go," Frank said as he filled his cup.

"But at night, I'm a *commis*."

"A what?"

"Like a chef-in-training."

"You can practice here any time," Mrs. Glass said. "Save me the bother."

"I keep forgetting that night school gig," Frank said. "How's that working out?"

"Excellent. Last night we made—"

"I don't give a shit," Frank said between blowing over hot coffee. "Don't let it interfere with this house. That's all I want to know."

"Ease off," Mrs. Glass said. "It's a fine thing he wants to do something besides what goes on here."

"Nothing wrong with this job," Frank said as he continued cooling his coffee. "If the boss taps your shoulder, you better have your mind right—be ready to step up. That's what's important."

"You're a dinosaur," Mrs. Glass snapped. "He don't want to be a bone breaker his whole life. Good for you, Nicky. Stay in that school."

"Thanks," he said before turning his attention on his mentor. "Is the boss going out today?"

"I doubt it. They're racing next door at Belmont this afternoon. He'll be into that board, no question, but I doubt he goes over."

Mrs. Glass pried. "How'd he do at the Derby?"

"I dunno. He's always been a tough read. Keeps the cards close to his vest, but the phone was ringing last night. Somebody—"

"Probably Vegas," Nicky volunteered.

"Probably so. If they're calling that quick, I don't think it's a good sign. These guys don't call to congratulate each other. They call to collect."

"Ouch."

"You never know," Frank continued. "Could be a little, could be a lot."

"I don't think The Book handles a little."

"Nope. He don't. Either way, you both better look busy. Do some dishes or mop a floor somewhere. Nicky? Go wash the car or something. Walk around like you're a secret service agent. Put on your shades and talk into your sleeve."

Frank smiled at himself as he refreshed his coffee and headed back to his station and his paper.

Nicky didn't smile a bit.

"Don't mind that one," Mrs. Glass said. "He misses the old days. The rough and tumble. I don't."

"The rough and tumble?"

"Back when. It was different. Now, everybody uses the internet to gamble. Back in the day, it was all cash. Piles of it. There'd be tables in the basement. Men counting all day long."

"I'd like to see that. Piles of cash."

"Well, there's other things you wouldn't have wanted to see in that basement."

"Like what?"

"Never you mind." Mrs. Glass stopped, but enjoyed having an audience too much to close the show just yet. She took up where she left off, scarcely missing a beat. "Frank would drag in some schmuck who didn't pay. Back then, Mr. Chariot wasn't the calm, quiet gentleman he is now. If you had his money, you'd count it out on the table to him, or the fingers you counted with would be on that table, but not connected to your hand. I scrubbed blood out of that man's shirts more times than I care to remember."

"Mr. Chariot?"

"The same."

"You'd never figure him that way."

"It was twenty-five years ago. Maybe thirty. It got real bad after his wife was gone."

"You been here a long time?"

"A very long time. I seen it all. The parties. The big crowds. People all over the lawn. Too much work. Way too much for the pay. It's better now. Quieter. Not so much work."

"The boss liked to party?"

"Like a rock star, as they say. That's why his wife left him. That, the bloody shirts, and the craziness in his head. The numbers. The edginess. He always had to be busy. Busy, busy." Mrs. Glass pointed to her head. "Up here. He'd be pacing at night. Walking all over the house. Outside on the grounds. The guards almost shot him more than once, I can tell you that.

"Then that damn game of his. I used to find books all over the house. All filled out. Hundreds of them. That Chinese puzzle, number thing. You know it?"

"Sudoku," Nicky said as though he'd known it forever.

"That's it. There—"

"I think it's Japanese."

"Whatever. There isn't as many as there once was, but I'm still picking them up. I don't even look any longer. Zip! Right in the trash. Silliness."

"He played with one of those books all the way back from Kentucky."

"You like as not don't know how he made out at the Derby, do you?"

"No."

"That's the way of him. You'd think in all these years, he'd offer up a tip now and again. Nary a word. And after all I've done for him and his family. I near raised his daughter—especially after his wife went round the bend. She topped herself, you know."

"I hadn't—"

"They said it was a car accident, but everybody knows better. Might not have even been suicide. One gambler or another gets in deep and needs a way out. Cap the ex- and The Book saves a fortune in alimony. Can't prove it by me, but I've always had my doubts. No matter.

"His little girl—cute as a button, that one—Donna, or Li'l Donnie, LD she was called then—came back here to live after her mother passed. And who do you suppose takes on the task of raising her? For no extra pay? And still, like I say, never a tip for reliable, steady Mrs. Glass. I work for the biggest bookie in New York and I'm tearing up tickets and tossing them in the air at Belmont just like ten thousand other idiots. We're all flunkies. You included. It's not right."

"I wouldn't mind a tip or two myself."

"Fat chance. Frank doesn't even get any. Nor Li'l Donnie for that matter, though I doubt she'd play. Her and her father don't get on."

"No?"

"Not since she came back the second time."

"A second time?"

"She followed in her father's footsteps when it comes to matrimony. Divorced. She moved back here. Her ex? Nowhere to be found. You're a smart kid. Figure it out."

"Really?"

Mrs. Glass crossed a finger over her heart. "God's honest truth. This can be a dangerous place. If you mess with this house, you better have all your T's crossed and your bags packed for someplace warm.

"And it was the same as when Mrs. Chariot died, except this time I got to take care of LD's baby—the grandbaby. She's another cutie pie just like her mom. People around here—the help—we called the baby, 'D Three,' but not around LD. She hated that name. She hated being called Li'l Donnie, too. I guess that tells you all you need to know about how good her and her father make out."

Nicky pushed up from the counter. "That's too bad. The old man must want to see his grandkid, don't you think? She's never been here as long as I have."

"Oh, he dotes on that one. At least he used to. Apple of his eye. He weaned her at Belmont Park, same as her mom. Sharp as a tack too. Just like her mom. Chariot had her reading by the time she was three, I think. Course, it was a Daily Racing Form and not no nursery rhymes. She must be eight or ten now. Probably reads a DRF faster than you.

"But she don't come around much. It's Li'l Donnie who's the wedge." Mrs. Glass held her arms out to the house. "He'll leave her and her baby girl all this and Donna won't even come to see him. Not even Christmas. Heartbreaking. All this to gain, but me? I can't get one tip on a race. Isn't that awful?"

Nicky was growing bored with the gossip. "I better get moving. Pretend I'm doing something."

"Yep. Like I said, you're a smart young fella."

6

At the entrance to the estate, the gate began to move and announced an arrival with its clamor. Big German shepherds strained against their chains on either side of the vintage iron behemoth and barked an echo to the gate's clanking. Nicky was headed out the front door and recognized the driver as his boss's daughter, Donna Chariot. Alexis, Donna's seven-year-old daughter, craned her neck to look around the manor. Nicky had seen Donna a couple times, but the two hadn't met. He thought she was pretty but wondered how she'd look if she smiled. Always in a rush to drop off some papers or get her father's signature then get away, she often never went in the house. Today looked like more of the same.

The car rolled near the stone steps and stopped as the passenger window went down. Donna leaned across the seat holding a large envelope up to Nicky.

"Would you see he gets this?"

"Sure," Nicky said as he begrudgingly moved down the steps. "Good morning to you, too."

Behind the car, a small truck pulled in the still open gate and likely averted a sharp exchange. The dogs didn't bark at the truck but pointed their sharp ears toward Donna's car when Alexis piled out of the back seat.

"There's Mr. Abreu! I bet he has flowers!"

"Stay away from those dogs!" Donna yelled as she pivoted in her seat and jumped from the car herself in the draft of her daughter's spirited rush.

Nicky tapped the envelope on his palm and watched until the door of the mansion opened behind him. Frank came out and walked by.

"This ain't gonna be good."

"What's wrong?" Nicky asked as he caught up and walked alongside.

"The Book wants to see LD. A C-note says she won't even go in the house."

"No thanks."

Ahead of the pair, Mr. Abreu had already tossed Alexis up into the back of the truck where she found it full of flowers for spring planting. When Donna got to the truck, she gave the old gangster-cum-gardener a warm hug. It caught Nicky's eye.

"She's pretty cozy with the help, don't you think?"

"You're 'the help.' You should live so long to be cozy with a woman as sharp as her."

"Hi, Mr. Frank," Alexis hollered and waved. "Me and Mr. Abreu are going to plant all these flowers. Want to help?"

"Not today, you're not," Donna chided as Frank and Nicky walked up. "Hop down. We've got to go into the city."

"I'd rather plant flowers," Alexis said. "I'd like to be a part-time gardener when I grow up."

"I know that, kiddo," Mr. Abreu said. "And I know what you want to be full-time."

"You do?"

"A jockey would be my bet."

"You should go right to the pay window," Alexis smiled. "We have a winner."

"Excuse me while I cash," Abreu grinned as he reached for her.

Alexis backed up further into the truck bed. "I'm staying."

"Not likely," Frank said as he reached into the flowers and held a thick arm out in front of the little girl. "Grab on before your mother hauls you off to the woodshed."

"Nope. I'm staying here."

"Lexy, get out of that truck," Donna said. "Now."

Frank turned toward the directive. "Hey, LD. How you doing?"

"Real well except for an obstinate seven-year-old whose convinced she's smarter than the rest of the world."

"Probably is," Abreu said as he took down a flat of flowers.

"Your father wants to see you," Frank said. "I'll get smarty britches here while you—"

"Another time. Tell him I had to go. C'mon, Lexy. No fooling around. We're late for—"

"Grandpa!" Lexy was over the side of the truck into Frank's arms and down him as if she were dropping from the limbs of a tree.

Donnie didn't break stride as he scooped up his granddaughter. "How's it going, kiddo?" he said as he carried her back to the truck and sat her on the tailgate. "That might be the last time I can do that. You getting too big. Are you going to be able to make weight? This isn't a handicap race, you know? I need you at weight or I'll have to get another rider."

"I can make it, Book."

"Don't call him that, Lexy," Donna snapped. "I've told you before."

Without looking at her mother, Alexis continued the game with her grandfather. "Who's my mount? Don't set me on a dog. I need to pad my poke going into Belmont. We gotta run in the money."

Donnie thought a second and looked around before his eyes settled on Frank. "You're aboard Frank's-a-Faker. Real strong horse. Don't let him push you around. Keep a tight rein on him and don't let him unseat you." Donnie was staring at his granddaughter, but the look on his face was suddenly vacant. He kept talking as his thoughts waged a battle to catch up to him. "Hold on tight and finish strong. No matter what, you always have to finish the job. Don't fail and always finish. Stay high and tight in the irons. Never welch on a bet. Keep your word over everything. Finish and keep your word."

Frank stepped into the fragmented diatribe. "Riders up!" He sat down hard on the tailgate, bouncing like a temperamental stallion in its starting gate. It was all to buy his boss time to recover.

Lexy had hold of Frank's jacket on his broad shoulders. Abreu silently cupped his hand for Lexy's ankle as she knelt into it and then was raised up and straddled Frank's back.

"Where am I running?" Alexis half whispered to her grandfather.

"C'mon, we have to go," Donna tried.

"One of my favorite tracks," her father continued, as his focus began to return.

"Then it's either Belmont, because it's our home track, Churchill for the history, or Tampa Downs in February for the weather. Since it's not February, can't be Tampa. You just came back from Kentucky, so I'll bet Belmont Park."

"We've got a winner," Donnie said. "Pay the girl, Nicky."

Nicky smiled at the game but didn't move. Everyone, including Donna, looked at him, but he still didn't make the right connection. Behind the pretend jockey on the back of the thoroughbred, Frank's-a-Faker, Abreu made a spectacle of pretending to count out money. Only then did Nicky stuff Donna's envelope under his arm and dive into his pocket for cash. He held out a five for Alexis.

She looked at the five, then to Nicky. "I went off at four to one. Tell him, Mr. Frank. We went off at four to one."

"We went off at four to one."

Nicky fumbled for a ten and Alexis took it with a smile.

"Okay, you ran your scam," Donna said as she firmly unsaddled her daughter from Frank's back. "Perfect teachable moment, Dad. Why am I not surprised?"

"Come in the house," Donnie said, his mind clear again. "I need to talk to you."

"We have to go."

"It's very important."

Donna was disgusted and it showed, but her father persisted. "Lexy can breeze Frank around the driveway then help Mr. Abreu. Five minutes."

"Five minutes, Mom," Lexy begged.

"Fine. Five minutes. Against my better judgement," Donna said as she pulled her phone from her back pocket. "I have some calls to make. You help Mr. Abreu. Don't get in the way and don't get dirty."

"I won't."

Donna punched up a number and shot her father that same disgusted look. "I'll meet you in the office," she said as she drifted away on a circuitous route to the house with the phone to her ear.

"I shoulda bet," Nicky said to no one in particular.

"I better put tea on," Donnie said, unable to hide his genuine surprise at having won a small battle. He gave Lexy a hug and kissed her on the top of her head. "You work on the posies. Li'l Donnie's in charge, men."

"I'm Alexis."

"I know that," Donnie smiled. "I'll try to get your mother to stay for lunch."

"No peppers, Grandpa. Remember, I don't like them. You neither."

"That's right. Let's you and me swear off peppers for life. Whaddaya say?"

"Deal!"

"I'm all in. Now, get your chores done."

Abreu pulled a tray of flowers from the truck as Donnie headed for the mansion. "You want to lay them out?" Abreu asked Alexis as he pointed. "All around this tree here. Hold the plastic. You won't get dirty. Space 'em out a little."

Alexis started to carry the flowers, dropping them sporadically, but also looked across the yard at the big dogs.

Mr. Abreu motioned at Frank and Nicky then whispered, "Give this a listen." When Alexis came back for another tray, Mr. Abreu was ready. "Hey, kiddo. I'd like to lay them flowers out nice for your grandpa. All around that tree. How many flowers do we need?"

Lexy abandoned the black plastic tray and stared at the big circular flower bed. "Do you know how big the flower bed is?"

"Just what you see there. That big."

"I mean in feet and inches, silly. Or use metrics. I can convert that."

"How big around would you say that flower bed is, Frank?'

"I don't know shi—nothing. I don't know nothing about flower beds."

"I'd say about sixty feet around," Abreu toyed. "Let's call it fifty-eight feet. Fifty-eight feet, three inches exactly."

"Okay. And what concentration do you want the flowers?"

"Concentration?"

"Density. How close do you want them?"

"I dunno. A foot or so. They'll fill in."

Alexis drew a circle in the air and began silently jotting down an equation in the air.

"Hey, kiddo? Can you do the ciphering out loud? Maybe Mr. Frank can pick up a couple a pointers."

"Sure. We change the circumference to decimals—that's 58.25. Pretty simple. Divide that by pi. We'll use 3.14159, to make it easy."

"To make it easy," Abreu smiled and winked at Frank.

"You get 18.5415 plus a little bit. That's called the diameter, Mr. Frank. Divide that answer by two. What do you get?"

Frank was caught but came close. "Umm…nine and change?"

"Good. 9.2707. That's the radius. The rest is easy."

Abreu winked again at Frank and Nicky. "The rest is easy."

"You multiply 'pi' times the radius and multiply the answer by the radius a second time. It's two hundred and seventy. We need two hundred seventy flowers. Do you have two hundred seventy flowers?"

Mr. Abreu looked at the wealth of plastic containers in the bed of the truck. "Well, I got about twenty-eight flats of eighteen plants each left."

"Oh, you have lots."

"How many is lots?"

"Five hundred and four," Alexis said as though everyone should know.

Abreu looked at Frank and Nicky. "Thanks, kiddo. Five hundred and four. Ain't that something?"

Frank shook his head. "Amazing." Next to him, Nicky's jaw was slack.

"Before the starting gate opens," Lexy asked them all. "Can I go pet the dogs?"

"Yep, but move slow," Frank said.

Before she'd gone far, Frank motioned for Nicky to go with her. "Keep her away from the house. It's apt to get loud. Usually does."

Nicky jogged to catch up to Lexi and got acquainted in the short walk.

"Make sure they get a good whiff of you so they know who you are," Frank yelled. "If you get bit, your mother will skin me alive."

Abreu chuckled. "That's a damn poor choice of words around a Chariot."

Frank looked at Mr. Abreu hard. "I wouldn't play them games with her. Li'l Donnie don't like it. She's got a temper."

"She's cut from the same cloth as her old man."

Across the driveway, Donna ended her phone call and headed toward the house.

"She won't be here ten minutes," Frank said as he started walking away. "I better get in there in case they start swinging."

He caught up with Donna on the stone steps and jogged past her to hold the door. "Always good to see you, Donna. Lexy's getting tall. You making out?"

"All right. You?"

They were walking through the mansion to Donnie's office.

"Good. Your father treats me well."

"You'd be the first."

"Awww, c'mon, LD. Cut him some slack. Things are way different. He's like a new guy. You should see him."

"I'd have to be here for that to happen."

They were in the office. Through the windows Donna could see Nicky and Alexis at the gate petting the big dogs.

"Who's the new guy?" Donna asked as she gave herself permission to notice Nicky was both handsome and athletic before dismissing him as another hired thug.

"Nick Colletta. Local. Real good guy."

"Good guy? Then why's he working for my father?"

Frank ignored her. "He just drives. He don't do anything else in the business."

"My dad will corrupt him before long. Or get him killed. Not killed. Sorry, Frank. He'll 'move away' or just go 'missing' out of the blue."

"Not this one. He goes to school at night."

"Trying to get his GED, no doubt."

"No, he's studying to be a chef. He makes things in the kitchen here that are damn tasty. Nice fella. You two would make a cute couple."

Donna ignored the suggestion but looked at Nicky again through different eyes before turning away from the windows. "Speaking of the kitchen, where's Broom Hilda?"

"If she ain't in the kitchen, grocery shopping, I think. At least that what she says, but I know she goes to the track when the weather's decent. Your father knows it, too."

"I'm surprised he hasn't chopped her thumbs off for stealing from him—even if it's only time."

Frank was at the collection of decanters and glasses along a far wall. "Make you a drink?"

"Yes, please. I'll need it to talk to him. Would you mind going to find him? Let's get this over with."

• • •

When The Book stepped in, he went to the windows. There wasn't the slightest glimmer of a salutation. A hug or peck on the cheek was beyond the pale. Donnie watched Alexis talking with Nicky and laying out plants for Mr. Abreu. The sunlight back lit him to his daughter, but

Donna negated that gunfighter's advantage by moving to the far side of the room, drink in hand.

"What's this all about?" she said as she tapped her tumbler with a manicured nail, looking more through her father than at him. "You said it was important. It better be. I don't enjoy coming to this old hovel."

Donnie glanced up into the deeply coffered ceiling. "She's hardly a hovel, Donna. Do you dislike your own home that much?"

"This isn't my home."

"It was. Could be again—"

"No thank you."

"—if you weren't so stubborn."

"I'm stubborn? Is that what this— Oh, forget it. I should have known this was some ploy." Donna set her drink on the desk and headed for the door. "Tell Frank to call me when it's time to read your will."

"That won't be necessary. You're not mentioned."

She was almost to the door. "That's a good approach. You almost won me over."

"Alexis inherits everything I don't give away. She'll have enough to do anything she puts her hands to, but not so much as to do nothing. Much like what I've given you."

Donna stopped. "Oh, please. Is this where I'm supposed to break down and thank you for everything you've done for me?"

"That's not my intent."

"I could start with…what? Thanking you for driving my mother mad and out of the house? Thank you for her supposed *accident*? Lexy's father—he's still missing. Do you want me to thank you for that too? Or do you want to stand Lexy up in your pillory until you hear it from her own mouth?"

"Where does that vitriol come from?"

"I presume all those things I'm supposed to thank you for. Let me know where Lexy can pick up her check."

"How is she?"

"Fine. She's fine, Dad. I'm leaving now."

"I'd like to see her more often."

"Why?"

"What do you mean, why? I'm her grandfather."

"What are you going to say to a seven-year-old? The same stuff you said to me? 'Primrose Dancer looks like a lock in the third at Saratoga.' 'Hey kiddo, what's the difference between a claiming race and an allowance?'"

Donnie looked away from his daughter. "It wasn't all like that," he said.

"It wasn't? I remember thinking going to Florida for vacation meant Disney World, not Gulfstream and Hialeah. Every other kid went to a *real* park—like Central Park. Dad, we went to *Belmont* Park."

"They have swings."

"And booze and cigars and betting slips—"

"You sound like your mother."

"You ever think she might have been right? Christ, I took a racing program for show and tell."

"What's wrong with that? How many other kids had one?"

"You never got it, did you? You used to drag mom around until you drove her crazy and she bolted; then you had me to take."

"I only wanted you with me. That's all. The tracks were my job."

"It's not a job. It's a sickness and I don't want my daughter exposed to it."

"It's not like the flu. It's not something you can catch. Besides, I used to take her. She loves horses and she has a mind for them."

There was a sudden quiet that sucked the air out of the room. They looked at each other, wondering who would say it and if either one dared.

Donnie walked from behind his desk with his daughter's half-empty glass. He went to his makeshift bar and poured two fingers of Scotch for himself and held the bottle up as a question for his daughter.

"No," she said.

His tumbler went with him back to the windows where he continued to watch his granddaughter. He sipped and Donna waited, hoping he'd go in another direction. He didn't.

"How is she at math?"

"You sonofabitch…."

Donna was headed for the door again. This time she wouldn't balk.

"Donna, wait. I'm sick!"

"I'll say."

Donna slammed the door behind her, but Donnie was on it almost as fast. He yanked the door open and caught a glimpse of his daughter flying down the main hall to the big doors.

"Donna, wait! We need to talk."

"No chance."

"Hold up! You're the only one who can help me."

Donna stopped just inside the doors. "No, Dad, I can't. No one can help you. I've seen your act. Remember? I know I sure do. Almost every night I remember."

"I'm sorry, Donnie. You know I am," her father pleaded. "I've apologized a thousand times. I can't take it back. I'd give anything if it didn't happen like that. Anything if you hadn't been there."

"Do you remember it though? Like I do?"

"That's the thing. I don't remember—"

"Let me help you. It paints an unforgettable picture."

"Don't do that, kiddo."

"Why? Why not?"

"Don't do that to yourself."

"I remember it! You should remember it, too! There's a little girl—screaming her brains out. Running. Crying. She runs to her father to protect her. He reaches for her, but his hands are all bloody. Then the blood's on her! That bring it back for you?"

Donna went out the doors. "*Lexy! Get in the car.*"

The youngest Chariot came running and was stuffed in the back seat. The car door slammed as Donna yelled to her father. "Don't call me again. And stay away from Lexy."

. . .

"You okay, boss?"

The query came from Frank and was uncharacteristically tender. The Book was seated at his desk but hadn't even heard the big man come in the office. Donnie's head was wound in a tangled knot he couldn't find the end to. With no end, no beginning, he couldn't even begin the unraveling process.

"Yes. Fine, Frank. What is it?" came The Book's socially acceptable, automatic reply.

"Nothing, boss. Just. You know…you could hear LD all over the house."

"She can be loud."

"You're not kidding. Though…I kind of miss her being around, you know? I seen her grow up. Then you don't see her anymore. Well, you know…."

"I do at that."

"Yep. You need anything, boss?"

"Thank you, no."

Frank was in the frame of the heavy office door. "She's a good kid, Book. She's been through a lot."

Donnie didn't answer, but Frank read in his eyes that he didn't need reminding. Donna had done a fine job of that in the hallway.

"Okay, boss. You sure you don't need something?"

"I'm sure. Why do you keep asking me?"

"Because I guess you must have needed something pretty bad to ask Li'l Donnie to chat, and, if you don't mind my saying so, it's pretty easy to tell her coming over didn't work out too well. So, I'm thinking whatever it is you needed, you probably still need. Am I right?"

"Yes. Thank you. You're a good man. I appreciate your concern. I truly do."

"I'm more than that. You're my boss and I've tried to never cross over the line, but I'm your friend, too. We seen too much together for way too long to not be. So, you need some help, I suspect you should ask your friend. Know what I mean?"

"I do. I do and I will. But there's nothing you can help me with at the moment."

"Okay. I'll leave it alone."

Donnie smiled. "Leave what alone?"

"Nothing, Book. We're good."

"Okay. Let's do that," Donnie said, but thought otherwise. If something was amiss with the business, Frank would have already told him. The smile faded. Maybe he had already told him and it was gone from his mind. What else had he forgotten? This was bad. Very bad. But what he hadn't forgotten was Baron's threat. He also remembered that the Belmont Stakes would go off in a month or so. Donnie had to have a special kind of help and the only one who could give him that was his daughter, but it was clear she hated him and would never budge. He thought for a moment that maybe it was the way she'd been raised.

7

The shadows were stretching long and low as Nicky finished waxing the Bentley. Nearby, Mr. Abreu was picking up empty black plastic flower packs and stacking them in the back of the truck. He'd had a good day despite losing his helper early on. The estate showed his efforts. With the new plants lining the driveway, spring had officially come. The flowers always went in following Derby weekend. The threat of frost was past and the bright colors either joined in the celebration of a successful day at the races or provided a poultice to ease the sting.

Nicky's soap and water melting away on the warm blacktop was another sure sign that spring had reached New York. Sprucing up a car that didn't need it made the pretend scrubbing and buffing easy and served a valuable purpose. He had parked the big car out front in hopes that Mr. Chariot would see him working from his office windows. Nicky couldn't see through the heavily tinted, thick Lexan, but he knew the boss was there. He was always there.

"Nicky's going to wash the paint off that car," Donnie said as he held his hands behind his back and looked out the windows as Nicky predicted.

Frank set his iPad to the side. "Maybe it was dirty. It's good he's staying busy."

"He might scrub the chrome off the bumper," Donnie offered as he stood staring.

Frank joined him. "Does that car even have bumpers?"

"Plastic ones, I suppose."

They watched Nicky picking up the tools of his impromptu trade and Abreu blowing any remnants of dirt off the driveway.

"Things are pretty quiet," Frank said, his pace revealing a measure of disappointment. "You want me to let Nicky go?"

"Probably should. Go ahead."

"Is there anything I can have him do for you first?"

A sleek Corvette announced its arrival at the gate with a deep throated roar that set off the guard dogs. Nicky walked over, touched a button near the thick columns, and the gate, clanking an argument, gave way to the visitor. The 'Vette revved again, jumped through the still moving gate, and wheeled toward the house.

"Who's that?" Donnie asked the world outside his windows as much as Frank, who was still watching with his boss.

"DeSeti's kid. Junior. That's his new toy. He had it here last week. You saw it."

"What's Julian doing here?"

"It's his boy. He's dropping off the pickups for the week. Same as always."

The Corvette rolled its fat Michelins off the driveway over Abreu's new plantings as it came to a stop.

"You see that, Frank?"

"I'll take care of it."

Frank was out of the office like a shot. He came out the front door to meet Junior DeSeti on the steps.

"Get that car off them flowers, DeSeti. Mr. Chariot don't like people disrespecting his property."

Junior tossed a laundry bag at Frank's feet. "There's three hundred large in there. He can buy new ones."

"That's not how he works."

Nicky had wandered over and was looking at the flashy car. Mr. Abreu appeared to be ignoring the building fracas.

"You tell him that's how I work," DeSeti cracked as he headed back to his car.

"You can tell me yourself, Mr. DeSeti," Donnie said as he came through his doorway onto the portico. "It seems you've ventured off the driveway onto my flowers. That's not a pleasant thing to do."

DeSeti snatched a wad of cash from his pocket and ripped a pair of twenties off up into the air. "Here. For the flowers."

"That's not necessary," Donnie said as he descended the stone steps and picked up a twenty. Nicky left the car and grabbed the second bill for his boss. "Thank you, Nicky. An apology would suffice. I'm sure it was a simple lapse in judgement."

Junior DeSeti came back for his money, snatched it from Donnie's hand, but stayed by his host. "That's right. I didn't see them."

"See that, Frank. Just a—"

"But maybe you should keep this money," Junior said. "I hear you had a bad day at Churchill Downs. Real bad. What's in that bag won't touch it." Junior held the twenties out between his fingers. "You need this worse than me."

"You're outa line, kid," Frank threatened as he came down the steps. "Shove off."

Donnie stopped Frank with a touch on his sleeve. "How about you, Mr. DeSeti? Did you do well in Lexington?"

"Better than you," DeSeti laughed.

"Better than me.... Blind courage. So you like to gamble. I'm not much for it myself, but I'd play along with you if you'd like." The Book had walked back up the stairs and turned, the laundry bag at his feet. He pointed across the courtyard to a pair of barn swallows sitting quietly courting on a wire. "See those two birds, Mr. DeSeti? Your car against the money in this bag. Which one leaves first? All you have to do is pick which one leaves first. Do you have the courage for that action, Mr. DeSeti?"

Everyone searched for the birds. Junior found them and looked at Donnie while everyone else stared at him. "Yeah, right."

"Which one leaves first? This bag. Your car. I calculate that's four, five to one in your favor."

"You sure about that?" Junior laughed. "Remember, you're not used to betting your own money. I hear you only lose other people's money. Or do you plan on not paying anyway? This or the Vegas money either?"

"Are you saying I wouldn't pay?"

Nicky answered for DeSeti. "Mr. Chariot's never welched. Everybody knows that. You want his action? Yes or no? If you're in, toss your keys to Frank. If you're a stone-cold wasted bitch, get your punk ass out of here before I turn the dogs on you."

"You know who you're talking to?"

"Do you know who *you're* talking to? Mr. Chariot was making his bones before—"

"Thank you, Nicky," Donnie said as he kicked the bag down the steps to Frank. "There's my ante. I'm in. Better hurry, little girl. Two hundred fifty-six thousand, four hundred eighty dollars might take flight any moment."

All eyes were back on Junior. Even Mr. Abreu was drawn across the drive, but he was watching the birds.

"So?" Frank asked. "Play or go home."

Junior pulled a keyless fob from his pocket and tossed it at Frank, but looked at Donnie. "I'll take your money, Book. One on the right leaves first. If you don't pay, they'll know in Vegas before I'm through the gate."

Every eye was on the birds.

Other birds chirped and sang around the manor, but the swallows were quiet and still. Soon they'd dart off to a mud nest they'd built somewhere. Perhaps they'd make the short trip to Belmont Park and snatch the flies that were pestering thoroughbreds as they cantered for exercise riders.

Junior DeSeti was anxious. He looked from the birds to Donnie and back again.

Donnie Chariot watched Junior, taking no apparent notice of the birds that held so much money in the balance.

Junior DeSeti tried to joke. "Are they even alive?"

"Hope you like walking," Nicky said, trying to encourage and convince himself.

The bird on the right flapped its wings as though it had lost its balance but didn't let go of the wire.

"Ah! Ah! There he goes! Get ready, Chariot," Junior began.

Then the swallow on the left launched itself. It was a dark feathered blot streaking head high across the driveway in a dive-bombing attack on some unseen bug. Then the bird disappeared around the big stone house and left its partner alone.

Donnie Chariot smiled. "Thank you, Mr. DeSeti."

Any thoughts of easy money vanished from Junior's face. "Hold up, Book. That was stupid. It's a couple of birds. That's not a bet."

"Was that a bet, gentlemen?"

"It was a bet," Frank answered as he walked up the steps and handed the key fob to his boss.

Nicky grinned. "Try Uber."

"This is bullshit! I wouldn't have taken your money over a bird!"

"Mr. Abreu?" Chariot asked with a gentleness in his voice as he looked over the fob. "Would you like a new car? This one seems to have run over your flowers."

"No. Thank you, Book. I like the truck you got me."

"I'll take it, boss," Nicky volunteered.

"You touch this car," Junior spit, "and you'll never touch another." Nicky was in his face. "Bring it."

"Everyone relax. Nicky? That means you," Donnie more than suggested. "Frank? Would you give young Mr. DeSeti a ride home?"

"Glad to."

Donnie whispered to Frank as he handed the fob back. "Nicky stays on. Find something for him to do."

In the driveway, Junior DeSeti was fuming. "Are you kidding me?"

"Not at all. Frank would be happy to accommodate." Donnie pointed to the bag at the base of the steps. "Nicky, bring the bag please. Thank you for dropping that off, Mr. DeSeti. Oh, and sign the title over if you would. You can drop it in the mail if that's easier for you. Please extend my best to your father."

The Book had turned his back and was headed in the mansion. Nicky bounced up the steps, snatching the bag of cash as he did. He went up the last step backward and flipped Junior DeSeti the finger.

"That'll do, Nicky," Donnie called from beyond the heavy wooden doors.

Nicky smiled at Junior, grabbed his crotch, mouthed, "Fuck you," and disappeared inside with the bag.

"You ready, Junior?" Frank asked as he smiled at Mr. Abreu and stepped around the car. "I never drove one of these things. I hope I don't wreck Mr. Chariot's new car."

Junior opened the passenger door and caught a smile on Mr. Abreu's face. "You think this is funny, old man?" DeSeti stomped and kicked several flowers underfoot and flipped the gardener off before becoming the passenger in what had been his own car.

Mr. Abreu's smile vanished as he looked at the disheveled flowers, then watched as the fancy car—in lurches, fits, and starts—inched out the gate.

It was after dark when Donnie heard the big gate open. He glanced out an upstairs window to see the truck Mr. Abreu had been using earlier pull in. Frank and Nicky got out and drifted away into the shadows of the estate.

8

"And so?" Baron said as he leaned back in his desk chair, surrounded by the opulent hard comfort of marble columns and Brazilian wood that defined his expansive Las Vegas office.

"So, I'm just saying. I think he's become a liability," Julian DeSeti said as he made his case in a conversation he'd begun a half hour earlier. "We weren't whole yet from that debacle at the Derby. Now he's dropped the ball again at the Preakness. The gates for the Belmont open in two weeks and we're slipping badly."

"What do you mean, slipping?"

"Our book. The word is spreading that we're missing our calls. The opening odds on the boards are off. And getting worse. It's not just the marquee races. He's handed over millions since the Derby in claiming races, allowances, stakes—you name it—all over the country."

"Are you certain of this?"

"You're damn right I am! Belmont's in two weeks. That's my home turf, same as him. I have an office on the clubhouse turn. I see what goes on. The odds are so screwy, he might as well be picking numbers out of a hat."

Baron was up and out of his chair, but slowly. He walked with his hands clasped behind his back to his monstrous windows. Beyond them stretched the Las Vegas strip, reaching out toward the desert. Even in the relentless Nevada sun, the Strip glowed and pulsated below him with a heartbeat powered by millions of lights. Far off in the distance, he could see heat waves rising from invisible sand.

"I told him," Baron said to the windows, the Strip, and the desert as his shoulders twitched and his fingers fidgeted. "I told him after Lexington. If he was working me over to leverage another book…I told him."

"I'm sure you did."

"Do we know where he's laying off? He's making a killing somewhere."

"No. I've been looking. He's good—"

"I know that."

"Wherever he's loading up, it's heavily camouflaged. It's not showing up. But it will."

Baron ignored the windows and returned to his desk. "I can't wait. As you reference, the Belmont's in a couple weeks, then Saratoga."

"Then my fall meet and the Breeders' Cup."

"This will be resolved long before then. I'd like to see something first." Baron looked at his thick gold watch. "What's post time at Santa Anita?"

Julian checked the chunk of bullion on his own wrist. "They're already running."

"Good." Baron spun the monitor around on his desk and handed Julian a remote keyboard. "Bring up the tote board for the next race."

The room was silent except for the whispered clicks of the keyboard. In seconds, Julian DeSeti had the odds for the upcoming race scrolling on the screen.

"Bring up the morning line from today," Baron instructed with a chubby finger studded with another chunk of diamond-encrusted gold.

A few more clicks and it was done. Baron motioned at the opening odds with his chin. "Are those our numbers?"

"Yes, sir."

"So those are Chariot's? What he sends us?"

"Exactly."

"Okay. Go back to the current tote."

DeSeti did just that. Neither man saw much.

"The flock is following the favorite," Baron noted. "No harm, no foul. We keep a percentage of winners and losers regardless."

"Right. But when the morning line is way off, we take a shot in the mouth. And when The Book triggers a full-court press, we load up. When he's wrong, we get our throat cut."

"And you think Chariot's holding the knife?"

"Has to be. I've known him forever. He's too proud to make mistakes."

"And too good."

"If he's missing, he's missing on purpose."

Baron picked up a remote from his wide desk. He pointed it at a huge screen on the wall. In a moment, the starting gate at Santa Anita raceway was on the screen. Eight horses were being jostled into place. Handlers hung from the gate next to the mounts and tried to point the horses' heads down the track.

• • •

There was a bell. The horses tensed from a Pavlovian response to the sound. In an instant, the gates flew open and the horses broke away onto the track. Jockeys were chirping, clicking, and cursing each other as they maneuvered into what they thought might be the best position to have a go at the wire come the finish. Before the horses reached cruising speed, many strategies were already obsolete. Muscled equine athletes purposely bumped each other and tried to crowd the favorite out of his comfort zone.

The two front-running jockeys were chatting from the irons as though they were commuting to work.

"He's strong now, but he'll be toast at the quarter pole. Save yours."

"*Si.* I'm on Goldencoin in the eleventh. Great draw and he's due."

"Got it. Enjoy the trip. I have to put on a show."

At that, the favorite's jock eased the reins and his bay colt pushed out ahead by a neck. Then a head and a length. The crowd cheered. But at the quarter pole he slipped into reverse—woefully out of gas and totally spent.

• • •

The horses clipped the wire to end the race. The men in the office didn't speak as they waited out the returns. When they came up, DeSeti pointed at the screen. "Doesn't tell much, does it?"

"Get the total payouts. See if anybody scooped that pool."

"I don't think he's going that way. I think Chariot's juggling your numbers, then laying off in someone else's book."

"A Dutch book?"

"He's in a great position. Plus, he's the only bookie I know smart enough to read odds that well."

"Especially if he's setting mine."

"He has time to look over a few books, balance the odds against each other, and back bets in both that'll pay him either way."

"How much am I down?"

DeSeti huffed. "Millions. That we know of."

"But it could be turned around just as quickly."

"Just as quickly."

"I'm going to talk to Mr. Chariot once more. He's too valuable to lose over this."

"Have a 'come to Jesus' talk with him."

"I don't think that'll be required. But still, this isn't a topic to be litigated, is it?"

"Not hardly."

Baron smiled. "I am licensed to practice law in New York, Florida, Nevada, and a few other places, but a courtroom is no place for this."

"Funny how all those states are horse or gambling States."

"Not funny, planning. Design and convenience. And yet, I can't seem to place what Chariot is after."

"Money. Same as everybody."

"I think not, Julian. Mr. Chariot is not like you and I."

"Well then, if Benjamin Franklins don't do it for him, you better stick a gun in his mouth or he's going to destroy your pony book and it can spread. This thing is like a cancer. Next week it could be college hoops. That would hurt."

"Hurt? That would shake the foundation of the world. It won't come to that. No. Money doesn't motivate Mr. Chariot. He wants the power. But you can't have weaknesses if you want power. No. This nonsense will end. The Book will make me whole and then some. You'll see."

"What's the plan?"

"I'll speak with him. You'll learn more as I need your intercession. Go back to New York. Don't upset Mr. Chariot. Don't allow anything to upset him. Things will have returned to normal for the Belmont Stakes."

"If this isn't fixed soon, that's apt to be a couple of very expensive weeks."

"More so for Mr. Chariot than us."

"A moment ago you said he doesn't care about money."

"The value of some things is not easily quantified when it's in the hand. But take it away, and its worth is impossible to calculate."

"You're deep, Baron. I'll say that."

"Yes. Deep."

9

The big car was up to speed as Nicky steered casually through traffic. He kept his place—both in traffic and with his employer. He'd learned from Frank to talk little. Mr. Chariot preferred the quiet.

In the back, Donnie was leafing through a sudoku book purposely kept in the car for occasions such as this. As he went through the book he suddenly came to the realization that he wasn't entering any numbers. The blocks didn't fill in magically behind his eyes. He perched his pen over a square, but the subtle priming brought nothing to the digital pump in his mind. Donnie waited, fidgeted, stretched his fingers, and shook the ink down in the pen as though it was somehow to blame. Nothing happened. The pen refused to move.

The book snapped closed. "Nicky, swing over to the track, please."

"It's kinda early, Mr. Chariot. It'll be a couple hours until the gates open."

"Pull up to the horseman's gate. I shouldn't be too long."

"You got it, boss."

• • •

Nicky didn't have time to be the perfect chauffeur and open the rear door of the Bentley. Donnie was out before the car stopped.

"I shouldn't be long," The Book said as he walked away.

Though the smallish horseman's gate was restricted to horses' connections, Donnie Chariot was not even stopped when he signified his intention by merely pointing through the gate.

Once clear of the gate, Donnie drifted straight ahead by the paddock that had seen thousands of horses and thirteen Triple Crown winners saddled. He stepped through the walking ring himself and sat on a white bench beneath a three-hundred-year-old white pine tree that had heard the call, "Riders up!" for all those champions. Over his shoulder was a bronze statue of 'Big Red' - the other worldly Secretariat. Ahead of him were the ivy-covered arches of the grandstands and the tunnel beneath them that led to the Big Sandy.

"Who won the Triple Crown?" Donnie said out loud to his hands as a test that seemed more personal and fitting than some damn math quiz from a sawbones.

Horses came into Donnie's mind's eye. Ink drawings and artist's renderings of the early winners—Sir Barton, Gallant Fox, War Admiral. Grainy black and white photographs of the champions of the Roaring Forties—Whirlaway, Count Fleet, Assault, and the great Citation. Then the drought. The explosion of the Seventies with Secretariat, Seattle Slew, and Affirmed. "I missed somebody. How many was that?" he asked himself. He counted out loud on his fingers. "Sir Barton was first. One, two, three. The three early ones. Four. Five—"

Donnie's hands and mind locked tight. He heard and saw it all at once. Something he'd felt creeping up his throat and tightening around his neck for over a year was crystalized there beneath Belmont's pine. Donnie Chariot—The Book—the odds maker for Vegas and horse tracks from coast to coast—the greatest natural talent who ever handicapped a horse race, was counting using his fingers.

Those same hands began to tremble and wouldn't stop. Donnie clenched his fists and pushed them against his thighs to arrest the fear. Like a horse, nervous in its maiden race, Donnie tried to walk off the anxiousness. He moved out from the comforting shade of the great pine and away from the walking ring where on stakes day the crowd would be thirty deep. The dark, quiet tunnel beneath the grandstand was inviting. Beyond it, bright sunlight suggested the promise of a reprieve out from the shadow, but Donnie held up in the coolness to collect himself.

It proved a poor escape. The bricks, sand, and loam floor of the tunnel that spread out and over the main track and gave The Big Sandy its nickname, had no answers. The best Donnie could glean from the vintage portal to horse racing immortality was a deep breath of cool, but stale air. At least his hands had stopped shaking.

The Book emerged from the tunnel like all those winners and also-rans before. He turned his back on the track and meandered up the grandstand into the cheap seats. Deep in some anonymous row, three-quarters of the way up the echoing theater, Chariot lowered himself into a seat. He sighed and leaned forward, resting his chin in the palms of his hands. The gargantuan oval looked even bigger than its mile and half pitch of dirt. Everything seemed overwhelming when seen beneath the spotlight of his diagnosis. He knew little of Alzheimer's apart from what any person gleaned through osmosis in the present world of rapid-fire advertisement and occasional movie topics. Predicting the length of time left would be difficult, but the outcome was surely not. What would life be like in a year? Two? Would there even be life?

Donnie watched the grand old track a while longer and decided that if his numbers flashed on the monstrous green tote board in front of him, they would likely read that he'd be dead or entombed in a long-term facility eating baby food and wetting his pants in short order. And that was if Las Vegas let him stick around that long. Given his recent mistakes, the odds on the latter scenario occurring were improving.

In ten days there'd be a hundred thousand people around this track looking at what Donnie was watching almost alone. Ten days to bring home some big winners, pacify Vegas, and tee up retirement.

The doctor had been right, though Donnie had agreed for different reasons. He needed help and he knew there was only one place to get it. If she wouldn't help him, there'd likely be no retirement.

The phone rang in his pocket. He recognized the coded name. It was Las Vegas.

"This is Chariot."

"Good day, Mr. Chariot."

"Hello, Baron."

"I don't wish to be disrespectful of your time, but I believe this is a conversation that's due. You agree?"

"It's not a surprise, if that's what you mean."

"Of course. Mr. Chariot, we had this conversation several weeks ago and you assured me my business would be making a significant course correction. That hasn't happened, as I'm certain you must know."

"It's been a rough patch, but that's why—"

"—they run the races. Yes, I know. You've reminded me of that on prior occasions. I'm afraid that will no longer be sufficient."

"I can't run the races myself."

"Let me tell you what I know, Mr. Chariot. You're kiting a Dutch book somewhere. Oh, I'll find out where you're laying off eventually."

"I'm not doing that. What would be the point?"

"I've been reminded by mutual friends that money is at the root of all evil."

"Money? You and I will never spend what we already have."

"So why, Donnie? Why are you feeding me lousy numbers? If not for the money, why? Power? You want to control the book?"

"I made mistakes. Pure and simple. They're just mistakes."

"You don't make mistakes! You never make mistakes! If you give me bad odds, it's part of a plan. It's no mistake."

"It is. I'm telling you. Baron, listen to me. I'm struggling, I admit it. I'm sick. It's caused me to make mistakes."

"You're sick? What do you mean?"

"It's complicated, but I can turn it around."

"How, especially if you're ill? Will you be well at any moment?"

"All that's important for you to understand is that I can."

"You told me after the Derby you'd have this fixed. Now I'm supposed to take you at your word again? Because of a mystery illness? I don't think this will do. Apparently I thought much too highly of you. I would have considered this type of play beneath you. It's unbecoming.

It has the desperate tone of a grifter who's unable or unwilling to pay his debts."

"I'll pay, Baron. I've never welched."

"But this is no bet. It is much worse than that. This is the type of thing that, among lesser men, leads to all manner of acts of indiscretion, even violence. It's important for you to understand. Do you?"

The first pause since the call began gave the men a moment to silently voice the severity they both already understood. Donnie got up and uncharacteristically paced down the long row and up the steps of the empty aisle.

"That won't be necessary," Donnie said to break the silence.

"I'm afraid, I'll have to be the one who determines what is and what is not necessary."

"I need until Belmont."

"That's ten more days of unfettered access to my till. That's potentially millions. I'll need something beyond your reassurance that whatever you're gaming—your short money scam, your alternative book—whatever you're doing, stops now. Today. Can you do that?"

Donnie paused at the top of the grandstand. He turned and looked out on the manicured big track.

"I need to talk to someone—"

"Ahh…, that'd be the other book, no doubt."

Donnie let a weak smile escape. Fortunately Baron couldn't see it or his threat might grow teeth immediately. "The other Book…there is no other book, but in a manner of speaking, you might be right."

"You're talking in riddles."

"I'll need until Belmont."

"You say you *need* until Belmont. You say you *need* to talk to someone. I believe what you *need*, sir, is incentive—"

"Give me until the Belmont—"

"—and you also need to get busy. Good-bye, Donnie."

10

Julian DeSeti Sr. punched the doorbell of the Chariot mansion and heard the bells of Westminster chime with authority inside. Mrs. Glass opened the door and, knowing the local kingpin, launched into her delivery minus formalities.

"He's not to home. Left with Nicky. Taking him over town, I suppose."

"Do you know when he'll get back?"

"Anybody's guess. He doesn't check with me when it comes to his social calendar. You should have called first. Don't you usually call?"

"It's Mrs. Glass, correct?"

"The same. I'll give you credit for remembering. I don't think his Holiness here even knows it. Not even after thirty-some-odd years."

"Chariot doesn't forget anything. He knows you all right. He knows what a find you've been for him as well. You can be assured of it."

"He hides it well. You'd never guess the depth of his admiration by my pay. I've changed diapers on two generations in this house, cleaned up bloody—cleaned this big old place more times than you can shake a stick at, for the good it's done me. Answering the door and making coffee. You want a cup, Mr. DeSeti?"

Julian physically looked over Mrs. Glass's shoulder into the empty house, then over his own as if to gauge witnesses.

"Yes. That'd be very nice of you."

"Not my coffee. I don't have a nickel invested. I'd as soon give it all away."

In the kitchen, Mr. DeSeti was soon perched at Nicky's breakfast station. "I've never seen this part of the house."

"He don't let most people beyond the foyer, but he's known you a hundred years. What's the harm?"

DeSeti had taken in everything on his walk and now plied everything to his advantage.

"Good coffee, Mrs. Glass. Thank you."

"I don't work for you. You call me Margaret."

"Thank you, Margaret. Does Chariot take good care of you?"

"Not by a damn sight." Mrs. Glass had her own cup now and took a seat near DeSeti. "Funny you might ask. You know what I've looked for the whole time I've been working here?"

"What is it?"

"One good tip on a horse. And for a man like that. It'd be a trifling, I tell you."

"Stop it. He doesn't give you tips?"

"Nary a one in all these years. I'm not starving, mind you, but a gentle nudge on a race goes a long way."

"Doesn't seem right, does it? I'm sure he gives the high sign to lots of people."

"And well I know it! But does the loyal Mrs. Glass get a taste? I shouldn't think so."

"You know, Mrs. Glass—"

"Margaret."

"Margaret. I spend a certain amount of time around the track myself. I'd be happy to float a few pointers your way if something should cross my path."

Mrs. Glass clasped DeSeti's hand. "You'd find me forever in your debt."

"No need. It's only something between friends. Good coffee, Margaret."

Donnie Chariot rolled his shoulders—first forward, then back—trying to relax. He hadn't been to his daughter's luxury apartment in years. The reason being that he'd not been invited. Today was no exception. She wouldn't be happy to see him, especially after their most recent encounter. It occurred to him that he'd be hard-pressed to make it in the door, but he had to try. In truth, he had to succeed. Anything less would likely be detrimental to his health which was already under assault. Before he rode the elevator up, Donnie had considered that getting offed by Baron might not be so bad in comparison to taking Alzheimer's hand and embarking on a prolonged battle destined to be lost in darkness.

There were other losses to consider and other people. Donnie had never purposely left someone else holding a bag with his name on it and despite the nature of their relationship, he knew that Baron's recent losses were his fault. He couldn't let that stand without making every effort to right the wrong. It was the type of grist ground on the Chariot mill.

He listened for the curse he was certain would follow the recognition of his face through the viewfinder. The voice was muffled beyond the door, but he wasn't disappointed. The door burst open and Donna stepped outside, holding the door ajar with her foot.

"What are you doing here?"

"An apology?"

"For?"

"A lot of things. But I've tried that. I'd like a couple of minutes."

"Again, for what?"

"I need a favor. I need help. I don't know how to word it so you'll listen."

"You mean, so I'll do it? You're right, there probably aren't any words for that."

"I'm sick, Donna. No games. I'm really sick."

"Again with the sick routine. Come inside, but keep your voice down. Lexy's doing her homework. She doesn't need to hear this, but I don't need the neighbors calling the cops." The pair stepped inside and Donna closed the door behind her father. "Don't get comfortable."

"Homework? She's four years old. What's she doing having homework?"

"She's seven, Dad."

"So?"

"So she has homework. It's a progressive school. I don't know. I guess they want her to be able to read something besides a racing form."

"You could already read and do advanced algebra when you were five."

"Here it comes. Two steps past the front door. Do I need to call security or will you just go?"

"Okay. Not a word. I've been sick, like I said."

"What is it? Cancer? How long have you got?"

"That's awfully cold. It's your mother's voice. You didn't learn that from me."

"I'm calling security."

"Wait. Wait! They say…maybe I have some kind of Alzheimer's."

"There's more than one kind?"

"I don't know." Donnie's tone allowed him deeper into the apartment. "Alzheimer's then. Whatever."

"Is this real? You've had tests? Been examined?"

"Yes. Yes! Is it so hard to believe?"

"Not that someone, even you, has a disease, but hard to believe you? Yes."

"I'm a lot of things, but a liar isn't one of them."

"You have convictions for perjury!"

"What of it?"

Donna tallied on her fingers. "And gambling, and larceny, evidence tampering, extortion, assault, racketeering—"

"That was a hundred years ago."

"A conviction follows you around, Dad. C'mon. Give me a break."

"There's a difference…."

Obviously not convinced, Donna summed up the futility of the last several minutes. "Whatever you say."

Her father's own weariness reared its head. "You win. Okay? You win. I'm an ass. I'm no good. Been a rotten father. Agreed? But I'm in trouble and you're the only one who can help me."

Donna paused, but only for a breath. "What do you mean? You can buy and sell me in a heartbeat. Anyway, you can't be broke. That old safe in the basement is probably ready to split its sides for all the gold you've stuffed in it. But I wouldn't know as I don't go near that basement. You probably could have guessed that."

Donnie didn't take the bait his daughter dangled, and she was left to field her own tainted question with something well short of any power swing she'd hoped for.

"So, unless you've picked up more bad habits I haven't heard about, you can't be bankrupt. Like I said, even if you were, what I can access wouldn't amount to much in your circles. Here in the civilized tax-paying world, it's considered really good, but—"

"I don't need your money. I need you."

"To do what?"

Donnie took another unfettered step into his daughter's apartment. He was hoping, against the hope of his only child salvaging his reputation and perhaps his life, for another glimpse of his granddaughter.

"I need you to come work for me."

Now it was Donna's turn to pause for real, but hers was in exasperation as she strained for a gasp of stupefied air.

"You have really gone around the bend this time. Maybe you *are* sick. Let me see…can I say this any clearer? For the hundredth time, absolutely no-fucking-way-José, no. Are we clear?"

"Donna, please. Honey, I need help. I've made mistakes. I've made mistakes and people are…are disappointed in my performance."

"And that is my fault how?"

"It's not your fault. But I need you to help me."

"By coming to work for you?"

"Just for a couple of weeks. Then I'll be out from underneath this and I'll retire. I promise."

"Wow," Donna said as she dropped into a decorative side chair in the foyer. "We've finally gone full circle. You told me that exact thing when I was fifteen. And again when I went to college. Then you promised you'd retire on my wedding day."

Donna leaned forward and rested her elbows on her knees. She rubbed her face and talked through her fingers. "I've told you a hundred—maybe a thousand times. Even back when we sort of got along. I'll never do the kind of work you do."

She stood as though it pained her. She drifted to the door as though opening it for her father's exit was a foregone conclusion. "I have a five-star accounting firm that is very successful. I don't want to lose it or my license by cavorting with criminals. I've worked hard to make my business a legitimate concern."

"Oh, bullshit. Bullshit!" Donnie's cool façade slipped and he stomped into the apartment and away from the door. "How many employees do you have?"

"What difference does that make? My firm netted almost a million last year—that's *net*—and it's growing."

"Without any employees."

"Employees? What are you talking about? Jesus, you *are* sick!"

"You netted a million last year with no employees apart from a Girl Friday at the front desk. And I doubt you need her."

"What? You make no sense," Donna said, though it was clear from a fleeting but discernable twinge in her voice that she knew what her father saw.

"Your firm—meaning just you—nets a million," Donnie continued, but gently. "That's a lot of accounting. Even if you only charged one percent, that's a hundred million dollars gross of other people's corporate interests you're documenting. Doing their bookkeeping. Their accounts receivable. Invoicing. Taxes. Corporate taxes. That must be arduous. I imagine even a smallish company's taxes are a hundred pages thick. Times that by a hundred million dollars. That's a lot of accounting for one person. But you seem to manage. How is that?"

Donna was trapped. Like any cornered animal, she could fight. It would vent some more anger and frustration. Maybe it would get her father out of the apartment sooner than diplomacy, but after she'd slammed the door, it wouldn't change anything. She could avoid and deny. That would work a little, but it wouldn't turn the truth of her life into something else.

Her father was dawdling at her kitchen counter, awaiting an outburst. She only half saw him flip open a cheap spiral notebook she'd left there. He looked at the first page then turned another and still another. They were pages jammed with rows and rows of numbers, written margin to margin as neat as a pin. Donnie offered a momentary reprieve and pointed at the notebook's pages.

"You ever try sudoku?"

"What?"

"Sudoku. The game. Not like this stuff. I recognize '*pi*.' I did that for a while, but really, Donna—an equation with no end? Doesn't that get boring?"

"Isn't that the point?"

"Occupying. Engaging. Burning off that energy. That's the point. Not boredom."

"I have my work. I stay busy."

"And I'm certain your clients love you."

"They seem happy."

"They should be. No team of ten accountants could give them the level of perfect detail they get from you. Just you. But even calculating every nuance for them isn't enough. For that million, I bet you didn't raise a sweat."

"You'd *bet*. That's funny. I thought you gave up gambling."

"A long time ago."

"Not long enough."

Donnie let the pause linger and tried to find a toehold in the stillness. At least she wasn't screaming.

"I am sick, kiddo. You'll be disappointed to know I'm not suffering much, but Alzheimer's isn't a good fit given what I do for a living."

"I don't imagine it's a good fit for anybody."

"True, but it's especially bad for me—right now—thick of the summer meets. The Belmont's coming up."

"I can see the circus is in town. It happens every year there's a gamer for the Triple Crown. And I'm not glad you're going through this. Being that way would make me as wicked as you and I'm not. I'm not like you at all."

"Keep telling yourself that."

The ice between the two had enjoyed its momentary thaw but was refreezing quickly.

"Whatever you want, Dad, the answer's no. I have a good job, a great kid. We have a great life. We're whole without you. You…Dad, you break things. I don't want that life for us."

"I'm not like that now. I'm ready to completely walk away."

"And do what? Play sudoku games around the clock to keep from going nuts?"

"I don't think I'll need that. In fact, I don't think I'll have a choice. See, the…whatever it is—blessing, curse, gift, talent—whatever—"

"Curse."

"Whatever we call it. It's not there. Not all the time. Not like it used to be."

"Lucky you."

"Well, the timing hasn't been very tender. I've made a number of errors in my book. Lost a great deal of money. Other people's money. They'd like to see me make it back and I do feel a degree of obligation."

"Honor among thieves."

"Well, yes, maybe. There's that. And also a little pride. I admit it. I don't make these mistakes."

"Dad? You're a bookie. You're not working on national defense here, for Christ's sake."

"There's still a sense of pride. In any work—"

"See that? That's what separates you and me. You're a bookmaker for a slew of itinerant gamblers. They go from track to track, following the seasons like barkers and carnies at a side show. Yet, somehow, you seem to think there's a redeeming quality to the hustle. I don't."

"Horse racing is a multi-billion-dollar entertainment industry."

Donna shook her head and held up her hands in resignation. "It's not worth the old argument. Tell me what, exactly, you want, so I can say no and you can leave."

"I need you to help me set odds for Vegas. Just two weeks. Until after the Belmont."

"No."

"And hopefully find a couple of perfect setups where we can recoup what I've lost recently."

"No."

"Donna, please."

"I can't do that."

"Yes, you can. You've been doing it since you were a little girl—"

"And I was treated like a freak for it!"

"You weren't a freak—"

"How many first graders can multiply four hundred thirty-six by seven hundred eleven in their head? When the shock wore off, they put me under a microscope. It wasn't fun."

"I'm sure it wasn't."

"I finally said it was a trick. That I'd lied. That really endeared me to everybody. Wow. I wasn't a freak, I was a liar."

"It endeared you to me."

"No, it didn't. You didn't help me. You didn't help me hide it or manage it."

"I tried."

"Not even close. You were never around. Forget it. Just go."

"I'm sorry, kiddo, but could you see your way to help—"

"No, I can't. Just go."

Donnie made no move toward the door. "Donna. These men...I know what they're like. What they're capable of."

"You mean they're like you?"

"Not like me. They're worse. Much worse."

"No one is worse. I've seen your handiwork up close."

"I changed a long time ago after I lost you and your mother."

"*Lost*? Playing on my sympathies won't cut it."

"Then not for me, for yourself. They know you're my family."

Whether it was the intent or not, the truth was taken as a thinly veiled threat.

"Unbelievable." Donna could no longer look at her father. "Get out."

"No one else can do what we do!"

"No! People win, people lose. Apologize. Pay them out of your own pocket and retire. I don't know and I don't care."

"They won't let me retire. They want access to what we have—"

"I said no! *Get out!*"

Alexis appeared in an archway to another room. "What are you shouting about? I'm trying to study." She saw her grandfather. "Oh, hi, Grandpa! I didn't know you were here."

Donnie squatted down at the counter. "Hi, yourself, kiddo. I wasn't certain you'd remember me."

"She saw you just the other day," Donna said coldly.

"I remember all kinds of things," Lexy said as she hugged her grandfather.

"I'll bet you do. I doubt you forget anything."

"That's enough, Dad. Lexy, Grandpa has to go. He's in a hurry."

"How are you, kiddo?"

"*Très bon. Et vous?*"

"Impressive. What is that?"

"French. I'm practicing. I told you a while ago. I told Mr. Frank and Mr. Nicky about it the other day at the big house."

Donna was using Lexy's shoulders as a tiller and steered her away from the kitchen. "Say good-bye in whatever language you prefer, but Grandpa has to leave. Right now."

"Hey, kiddo? What's four hundred thirty-six times seven hundred eleven?"

"Don't answer that."

"I bet she knows. I'll bet you an ice cream you know, huh, kiddo?"

"Leave now."

Donnie was idly moving. "I will, but think about what I asked you. The working. And Lexy, you think about the answer to that equation. You probably know already."

"Get *out*," Donna said to her father as Lexy was unceremoniously ushered out of the kitchen.

"Bye, Grandpa. Come back when you can stay and play."

"In the other room, Lexy. Right now."

"What's wrong?"

"*Go!*"

Donnie was at the door as his granddaughter was shuffled out.

"I'll be back another time, kiddo. Take care. I love you."

"I love you too, Grandpa, and three hundred nine thousand, nine hundred ninety-six."

Donna was screaming at both of them. "Go! *Go!*"

Alexis escaped her mother's voice and Donnie his daughter's wrath as each darted from the kitchen. Donnie left empty-handed of help, but burdened with a new, far heavier care he had long suspected. Behind him, left alone in her kitchen, Donna shared the same concern.

11

"Pull out back," Donnie directed Nicky. "I need to stop in the kitchen and have a word with Mrs. Glass."

"Sure thing," Nicky said as he wheeled the Bentley through the open carport and around to the four-bay garage. As the car rocked to a stop, Nicky hit the button to the overhead door. Donnie let himself out and would go in before the car. "Thank you, Nicky."

"Anytime, Mr. C."

Donnie ducked beneath the clamoring garage door, Donna and Alexis still heavy on his mind. A much fainter memory distracted him. There was something missing. When he could not recall what it was, he was instantly angry with himself. He stood in the garage looking around, back and forth, for something lost that perhaps had never been.

"Sonofabitch," Nicky heard him mutter as the door completed its trip and exposed The Book standing rather awkwardly in the middle of an empty bay.

Nicky lowered his window. "Drop something?"

"What goes in here?"

"In the garage?"

"Yes, in the goddamn garage."

"Uh, the car?"

"That car?"

"Yes, I guess so."

Donnie jerked himself around. The move was enough to pull Nicky from the car.

"You okay, boss?"

"Of course. What's missing?"

"Umm, from right here? The car. I'll pull it right in. I got this, Mr. Chariot. Go ahead to the kitchen."

Donnie nodded and took two steps, stopped, and turned back toward the empty garage. "That's not it. Not my car. Where's that little shit Junior DeSeti's car? The one from out front with the flowers and the birds?"

"Um, damn, boss, I don't really know where it is. Not exactly."

Donnie had heard guarded fear in men's throats most of his life. "Nicky, if you took it out somewhere, its fine. Next time ask, but where's the car?"

"You maybe should ask Frank, Mr. Chariot. I don't want to blow up the spot behind this. Really, I don't."

"What are you talking about? Where is it?"

"I don't really know and that's the god's honest truth. Frank does though."

Frank came from the house as though on cue.

"Frank does what? What's he throwing me under the bus for this time?"

"The whereabouts of my newest acquisition," Donnie said. "Young DeSeti's car."

"Okay. Yeah, that."

"Wherever it is, I don't really care just now, but I'd like it put back in this garage. That shouldn't be an issue, should it?"

"No, sir, it shouldn't. But it sort of is."

"Sort of?"

"It never made it to the garage," Frank explained. "But I'll get it for you. There was a problem that day I took Junior home, but I'm working it out."

"A problem? What kind of problem?"

"I don't suppose you'd just let me handle it? I'll get it straightened out."

"What was the problem, Frank? Tell me the problem—I need another—then we'll decide who's going to straighten it out. What happened? It get wrecked?"

"No, sir, the car's fine. At least it was the last time I saw it."

Donnie was distracted, bored, and out of patience. "Frank?"

"Junior stuffed a pistol in my ear and had me get out of the car."

"Just like that?"

"He's a doper, boss. Heroin. Bigtime habit. Might go off like a bomb. I didn't want to try him under them circumstances. Nicky picked me up. But I'm working to get it back. He'll see the error of his ways."

Donnie walked by Frank and patted his shoulder. "You showed remarkable maturity. I'm happy you demonstrated restraint. I agree, DeSeti will see his mistake."

"I'm sorry, Mr. Chariot. I'll get it back."

"Not to worry. It doesn't mean a thing."

"It does to Junior," Nicky said. "He's psycho about that ride. And his dope."

"He's going to get over that car," Chariot said as he stepped to the door to the house. "I can't speak to his other vices."

"I'll square with him over pulling the gun," Frank added. "But is the car worth a problem with the DeSetis?"

"A bet's a bet, Frank. You know that. Everybody pays. Even me. Especially me."

• • •

Julian DeSeti was almost stomping through his house looking for his son. When he found him, he was in their garage waxing his Corvette.

"That doesn't need waxing, does it?" Julian asked.

"Keeping it nice."

"Donnie Chariot will appreciate it."

The words stopped the buffing for a moment, then Junior began again, rubbing harder.

"To hell with Chariot."

"You think I wasn't going to hear about this?"

"I took care of it."

"How do you figure?"

"I have my car, don't I?"

"For five more minutes you do. When you finish waxing it, you're going to take it back to Chariot along with your apologies."

Julian turned to leave.

"No way."

"What'd you say to me?"

"I'm not giving that old bookie my car."

"You'll do what I tell you to do."

"I'm not giving him shit!"

The senior DeSeti slowed his delivery in an attempt to keep his blood pressure and his temper under control.

"Did you make a bet with Chariot?"

"It was bullshit. Everybody knew it was bullshit. We were messing around."

"Chariot doesn't, 'mess around.' Now, did you bet?"

"No."

"That's not how I heard it."

"You heard wrong then."

"Take the car back, Junior."

"No! Let him send that bitch of his over! He couldn't get out of the car fast enough when I stuck a pistol in his ear."

"So, we can add armed robbery in addition to being a welcher. Hurry up with that car wash, boy."

"Ain't happening."

"Listen to me. There's things going on you know nothing about. I'd like to have a son I could give more—take into the confidence of the business—but I can't. You're always pulling one dumb stunt or another.

Like this thing with Chariot." Julian pointed hard. "You get your head out of your ass and that needle out of your arm."

"What are you talking about?"

"You think I don't know about that either? The whole town knows!"

"Nobody knows shit."

"Well, here's something you need to know and know quick. Chariot's more valuable to us than this car. You take this over, beg forgiveness, and hope it disappears. If he throws this in our faces because of you, the whole family could suffer. I'm not telling you again."

"It's *my* car!"

"You made a bet! The worst thing you can be in this business is a welcher. Or an addict."

"It was two *birds*!"

"It don't matter! If I have to put my hands on you, I will. Now, get that car out of here."

"I can't hear you."

"How's that?"

"I won't do it."

"I guess you will."

"Or what?"

Julian moved with surprising quickness. He had his son by the throat up against the 'Vette. "I'll put you in the trunk of this car you love so much and throw the both of you off a bridge!"

"It doesn't have much of a trunk," Junior garbled around the fingers at his throat.

Julian tossed him to the side and went to the driver's door. "Fine! You won't listen. Typical. That's fine. I'll do it myself."

Julian was behind the wheel and fired up the big engine. He purposefully over-revved it and made the exhaust roar.

"Dad, wait!"

"What did you say? I can't hear you!" Julian shouted over the motor.

"It's *my car*!"

"Sorry, *I can't hear you!*"

DeSeti pulled the door closed and screeched the tires backing out of the garage. Junior followed, livid, but pleading at the driver's door.

"It was a bullshit bet!"

DeSeti put the window down and continued the fight. "There's millions of dollars at stake, you idiot! I'll talk to Chariot and do what I can to keep you alive, but I'd shoot you if you reneged on me."

"You take this car and I'll make you and Chariot both suffer!"

"You think men like us are scared of a drugged-out punk like you? Only thing I could trust you with was making deliveries. Now I can't even let you do that! Go see if your mother needs help in the kitchen."

Julian smoked the tires away from his garage then really lit them up when he hit the street.

• • •

A couple of hours later, Julian was riding in the back of a cab when he returned to his tony neighborhood. Manicured lots overlooked rubber laid in the road at every corner and intersection as the cab retraced Julian's earlier route in the Corvette. The trail pointed the way home to his own mansion and made him smile. After the last corner, the smile vanished. Up ahead, a police cruiser was pulling out of his driveway and unknowingly driving over the tire marks Julian had laid down as he'd peeled out of his own driveway.

"Keep going," Julian said to the cabbie.

"How's that?"

"I changed my mind. Don't stop. Keep going."

"Where to now, Mac?"

"Anywhere. Nowhere. I don't give a shit. Drive. *Drive!*"

Julian nervously speed dialed his son. There was no answer. He called again. And a third time. Still no answer. Julian called his wife.

"Hi, honey. Whatcha doing?"

"Nothing. What's the matter?"

"Nothing. I don't know. Why?"

"Why what?"

"Why'd you ask if something was wrong?"

"Because you don't call unless you're in trouble. Have you been picked up again?"

"That's not true. I'm okay. How's things at the house?"

"All right, I guess. Except for Junior. He's in a state."

"What happened to him? Was he arrested?"

"Why would you say such a thing? You always think the worst of our boy. If he does get in trouble, I blame you. You're the one that sets him up with your no-account friends. 'Business partners.' I doubt that very much. My mother told me you'd amount to no good. You think a big house and a little money in the bank means—"

"Shut up! Jesus, shut up!"

"Don't you talk to me like that, Julian Anthony!"

"I'll talk how I wanna talk! I saw a cop car at the house. What's going on?"

"That's what I was trying to say. Junior's in an awful way. You'd better come home. I don't know what he'll do."

"Tell me about the cops. Can you do that? This one time. Why were the cops at the house? Can you do that, please?"

"The cops came to take a report. Someone stole Junior's car. That pretty red one. He—"

"Say that again. I heard you wrong."

"I said, some dirty sonofabitch stole Junior's new car! Why don't you ever listen to me? If you'd been home, maybe it wouldn't have happened. You're always running around the city doing god knows—"

"Is he there? He wouldn't answer his phone. Now I know why. Let me talk to that stupid— Put him on."

"He's not here. Someone picked him up after the cops left. He's very upset. If he finds who took his car, there's going to be real trouble. He has your temper and believe you me, I can—"

"Oh, there'll be trouble. Call him. See if he picks up for you. Tell him to get his ass home."

DeSeti hurled his phone into the dirty Plexiglas partition of the cab.

Across town the Corvette was rolling smoothly into its new stall in the Chariot garage. Frank was to the side, motioning Nicky with universal hand signals to come ahead, slow down, and stop. Nicky revved the engine a few times to feel the horsepower until Frank's slicing hand across his own throat took on too prophetic a zeal. The car was instantly quiet.

"Hey, partner," Nicky asked as he clamored from the car. "You're not mad, are you?"

"At you? Naw. You weren't looking to flip the script on me."

"The boss asked, you know? Wasn't much I could do. I can't lie to him. I won't. He's good to me."

"I know. You did the right thing. Always step up for him and tell him the truth. He's a guy who won't steer you wrong. Believe that. If you cross him, he has a way of making people wish they hadn't, but treat him good, he'll treat you better."

"He didn't seem mad at you. That's good."

"Yep. That's good."

Frank hit the button and the garage door began to close behind the latest addition to the Chariot fleet.

"At least he got it back," Nicky said as he looked back at the machine. "What a cool car."

"Yep."

"I wonder if Mr. Chariot called—"

"Nicky? Let it go. We're cool. The Book isn't mad at you or me. I just look like an ass because I let that little shit get the drop on me."

"He had a pistol in your face. Nothing you could do."

"And I had one under my jacket. Back in the day, I would have let hell loose in that car."

"Forget that. You heard the boss. He likes, you know, restraint. Tough to miss a shot inside a car."

"Yeah…tough to miss."

The 'Vette was locked away for the night. The men drifted through the laundry room and the kitchen's pantry. The entire mansion was quiet.

Nicky pulled leftovers from the refrigerator and turned them into something that both looked and tasted great. Frank ate, then buried his hands in his pockets and was pacing. "They teach you that in cook school?"

"*Chef* school."

"I think you got a future."

"Hopefully, but whatever I end up doing, I'm not forgetting how that little shit DeSeti disrespected the boss or put a gun in your face."

"Thanks, killer, but don't say anything like that around Li'l Donnie. I was talking you up the other day. Tried anyway. I told her you weren't a gangster and only drove. Don't make me out a liar."

"Just a driver? She'd never go out with a guy who's just her dad's driver."

"Quicker than she'd go out with his lawyer. She hates anything to do with her father's business. You'll do better as a cook."

"She's pretty. I could go for that."

Frank stopped short. "Here's something to think about. I've been around LD since she was born. It's like she's my baby sister. She ain't some pole dancer. Do the right thing by her or you answer to me. If you ever have guts enough to ask her out, remember that her father was real hardcore in his prime and I was holding most of those guys down when he introduced them to Chariot justice. *Capisci?*"

"Whoa, big fella. Okay. I doubt she'd go out with someone like me anyway."

"I ain't trying to be no matchmaker, but from where I'm standing, she needs a good friend more than a hot date. If she could ease off her father—give him some slack—and you man up when your time comes, you could both do worse."

"Thanks. I think."

"You're welcome. I'll put in a word, but first I got to get Junior DeSeti right with Jesus."

"I'll break him up for you for nothing. Call it a thank you for putting in a good word for me with Donna."

"Naw…when we're done there won't be enough left of Junior to fill a bucket. You won't even be able to find him."

"Sucks to be him, you know it?"

"It sure does."

12

A weekend passed and with it, more racing. The run-up events for the high dollar races were long over. The point getters had been loaded in the Kentucky Derby's gates on that first weekend in May for their run at immortality. The winner and a few friends had gone on to Baltimore and ran at Pimlico for the second jewel of the Triple Crown. Now a mish-mash collection of runners and resters were eyeing the Belmont Stakes along with gamblers of every stripe. Vegas had been watching as well and not liking what they'd seen.

"You see a change?"

"Do the math. No change. Maybe worse."

"Do we know where's he's laying off?"

"Not a hundred percent, but we think Dubai—at Meydan Racecourse. It's got to be Dubai. They're the only one who has the right pieces—enough money to back the play, a big enough book to hide it, and a willingness to shove it up our ass."

"Can't someone find out for certain? You know, follow the money."

"It's almost impossible. There's so much money passing through their book, millions can disappear. Hell, a hundred grand to win is common. They piss platinum and crap gold in the Emirates."

"That's great. So we have nothing on the back end."

"Can't find it."

"What else have we got?"

"Nothing. Got to be there, though. I say we ratchet up the pressure on Chariot."

"I'm open to suggestions."

"We could rough him up. Read him the riot act."

"Do you know who we're talking about?"

"Absolutely. Donnie Chariot."

"That's right. And Chariot has been cracking heads and knees so long he gave Jesus himself the come-to-Jesus talk. You gonna scare a guy like that? He'd laugh in your face. No way. Plus, you can't put the screws to the golden goose. He'll stop laying entirely."

"What's the plan then?"

"Same as in any good play—leverage."

"How you going to work it?"

"How isn't as important as who. I know somebody who can help us."

"Then get him and tee this up fast. We need Chariot to get his mind right before Belmont."

"It'll be reaping benefits before then. Jesus or not, Donnie Chariot is about to see the light."

●　　●　　●

Donna jumped between yelling at the top of her lungs for her daughter and muttering curses aimed at her father as she burst through the front door of the Chariot mansion. Frank had come out of his chair when he saw her pull in. Donnie remained behind his desk. He had been hopeful at the sight of her car, but any rise vanished as soon as he heard his granddaughter's name being yelled from the vestibule.

Donna headed for the kitchen, thinking Alexis would be availing herself of Mrs. Glass's or maybe even Chef Nicky's sweet treats, but stuck her head and an accusing finger into her father's office on the way.

"This tears it," Donna barked from the door. She glanced over her shoulder to gauge if Alexis was coming. "This really does. Even

DAVID-MICHAEL HARDING

77

knowing you like I do, I didn't think you'd sink this low. I'll get a restraining order. You come near her, you're going to jail—again!"

Donna disappeared like a rabbit ducking down a hole, leaving Donnie and Frank staring at each other and shrugging their shoulders in her wake.

Donna's voice, still rising, but controlled, faded from the office as she scoured the first floor and on to the kitchen. By the time she'd darted up the wide winding staircase and shouted down every hall and darted into most of the rooms, Donnie was up. He came around his desk straight into Donna's unflinching assault.

"Where is she, you sonofabitch? At the track getting ice cream? Going to see the ponies—that's the same shit you used to sell me on. Leave it to you to farm her out the moment you've got her. I knew you never really wanted to see her."

"Alexis isn't here."

"I can see that! Call Broom Hilda and get her back here or I'm calling the cops!"

"Lexy hasn't been here. Why do you think she is?"

"Oh, *bullshit*! When's it end with you?"

"She's not here and hasn't been. Frank, has Lexy been here?"

"I ain't seen her, LD, and—"

"Don't call me that!"

"Sorry, Donna. I've been looking out that window all day. She didn't come in that gate."

"You'd say whatever he told you to. Where is she, Dad? I'm through screwing around. You mess with me if you want, but not her! Do you understand? Tell me you understand."

"She's not here! What makes you think she is?"

"Mrs. Glass picked her up after school. The only people on that list are me, her father, you, and Glass. It wasn't me and I doubt her father came back from the grave. So that leaves you and the wicked witch. Well, the witch signed her out around three o'clock. Where'd they go?"

Donnie knew any answer was pointless. He had his phone out and was dialing. "I'm calling Mrs. Glass."

"I tried her. She doesn't answer."

"Frank, get Nicky. See if he's seen Mrs. Glass."

"I'm calling the cops," Donna said as she ripped her own phone from a back pocket.

"Wait two minutes."

"Why?"

Donnie's phone rang to Glass's message and Donnie disconnected.

"Let's talk to Nicky first. He may know."

"Another henchman? He'll be dependable."

"Nicky's a good boy. He won't lie."

Nicky hustled in, followed by Frank. "Boss, I saw her at lunchtime, but not since."

"Her car's gone, Book," Frank added. "It's a little early. She usually makes up dinner for you first. I don't see nothing ready."

"Then she'll be back," Nicky said, relaxing. "She's not going home for the day without fixing you a plate." He turned to Donna. "She wouldn't do that. She'll be back."

Donna ignored him and pressed her father. "I'd like to know why you had her pick Lexy up anyway."

"I didn't," Donnie answered, drifting back behind his desk. A curious look came over him. He was clearly thinking through something profound, and it appeared he didn't understand or like the result.

Likewise, Donna's own words were catching up to her. "If you didn't have her picked up, and these guys don't know about it—providing they're telling the truth and not just your version of it—why would Glass pick her up? And where would they be?"

If there was an answer about to be offered, it would have to wait. Donnie's phone was ringing in his hand. He looked at it and saw Mrs. Glass's name as the caller.

"This is her."

"Tell her get her ass back here with my daughter or I'm calling the police."

Donnie was curt. "Where are you?" served as his hello. Then he fell into protracted silence. The phone was pressed hard against his head. He dropped into his chair, hunched over, totally immersed in listening, saying nothing while the others stared and waited.

Donna came closer.

"I understand," Donnie said into the phone. "But there is something you should understand just as clearly. When this is over—"

Chariot took the phone away from his ear when he heard the caller disconnect and set it on his desk. He motioned for Frank. "Let me see your phone."

Bewildered, Frank handed it over as Donna watched, words caught in her throat.

"What's up, boss?" Frank said as Donnie made a call.

"Lexy's been taken."

"What?" Donna said in the softest voice she used since she came in the house. "Where?"

"Not where. Who," her father said as he snapped into response mode. "I know someone who can help."

Nicky was looking at everyone, trying to catch an eye that would explain what was happening. While Donnie began his call he pointed from Frank to Nicky.

"Use Nicky's phone. Call in some extra bodies. Good men. People we've used before. The very best."

"Dad?"

"How many, boss?"

"I don't—six. Make it eight. Get eight. And Nicky, go close the gate." Nicky was moving. "Chain it!"

"What are you doing?" Donna asked. "We need the police."

"I'm calling them," Donnie said before he broke away into his conversation with the phone. "This is Chariot. Listen to me closely. I'm going to text you a phone number. Someone just called me from it. I know who's supposed to have it, but it wasn't her. They called my phone...good. Triangulate it back or whatever it is you do...get as close as you can. Call me as soon as you know then get over here. I'll likely need you."

Donnie ended the call and handed the phone back to Frank. "Dad? Where's Lexy? What's going on?"

Donnie stood up as his daughter came around the desk.

"Frank, we need a few minutes. Collect your men in the basement. I'll be down in a while. Have Nicky stay out front. Tell him a man named Gabriel is coming."

"Gabriel? He's worse than—"

Donnie held up his hand and cut him off. "The cure is as bad as the disease, I know. But that's what we need."

Before Frank had closed the door behind him, Donnie planted Donna in his chair and pulled up another until father and daughter sat knee to knee. They were clutching each other's hands and looking hard, eye to eye.

"Dad?"

"She's not been harmed and won't be. We need...we must be calm—"

Donna's body began to tremble—visibly shake as though she had a high fever. She leaned back, away from her father, pulling her hands free and brushing his hands off her knees.

"No. No...not again."

"Lexy's safe. Very safe."

"Kidnapped isn't 'safe.' I know. They'll torture her. Torment her."

"No, Donna. This isn't the same."

"It is," Donna said as she struggled to breathe. "They'll do things. Put her in a closet. Dark. Scare her. Scream at her."

"Nothing like that. I swear to you. She's with Mrs. Glass—someone she knows. She's safe. That's the main thing."

"I want her back. Now. Get her back! We need to call the police."

"Not now. I know what they want."

"How much? I don't have a lot of—"

"They don't want money, Donna. They want me."

"It *is* the same! It is. Just like before."

"It's not. Lexy's safe. They don't want money nor me, really."

"What? Why Lexy?"

"It's not me so much as what I can do, or what I used to be able to do."

"I want her back, right now," Donna said as her mind cleared and began whirling through probabilities of rescue.

"We'll get her back. She's with Mrs. Glass so she's okay. She's safe and comfortable, eating ice cream and watching cartoons."

"Who was on the phone?"

"I don't know," Donnie said as his eyes drifted away and he got up from his chair. He began to pace his own office with an unusual anxiousness brought on by a mind that was struggling to make pieces fit.

"But you know something. Do you know who's doing this?"

"No."

"Are you sure about that? You seem awfully calm. Almost, not surprised. What's happening? Is this some sick joke?"

"It's not a joke. I don't know who took her, but I do know what they want, and I do know who it profits if I deliver."

"Shouldn't we give it to the police? They'll trace that call, find them, and maybe Lexy's there. We have to call them. The FBI, too."

"They won't find Alexis. The people I'm talking about are two thousand miles from here, if they're in the country at all. Lexy's close. If we get nothing else from the disappearance of Mrs. Glass, we have that. It's doubtful they've had time to get out of New York. Nor is there any need."

"This is too much. I can't *not* call the police."

"That's a very bad idea, Donna. Before. Back then. Did the police help?"

Donna's face and voice stalled amidst her thoughts, then reversed away from the memory. She came out of her father's chair and moved to a far corner of the office still trembling.

"I understand that's the knee-jerk reaction," Donnie continued. "But it would be wrong. Very wrong. Perhaps dangerous."

"What do you mean? You said she was safe."

"She is. She is. For now. And I already contacted the police, after a fashion. Gabriel is a detective in the city. He works for me from time to time. For now, we have to do as the caller asks."

"What do they want?"

Donnie walked a little more. He was as certain as he could be that his next statement would knock the fragile legs out from beneath his daughter and likely turn her on him once and for all.

"You remember how I asked you to come work with me, to help me?"

"That has nothing to do with Lexy."

"It does now. People in Las Vegas have the idea that I'm giving them bad numbers when the odds are set for races. They think I'm running a second book somewhere to lay off bets and scoop the difference."

"Are you?"

"Absolutely not. I've never done that, and I wouldn't."

"What's Lexy have to do with it? I need her back." Donna joined her father in the room. Nerves wouldn't permit her to stay away. "I can't do this. We need the police, the FBI—everybody! You tell them what you know about the gambling and who's behind it and let them sort it out. I can't stand here and do nothing."

"You're not doing nothing. We'll do everything that's possible. The police can't do better and they can do a whole lot worse. If this is a ploy to get at me, the people involved aren't concerned with stopping at kidnapping."

"You said she was safe!"

"She is! For now. That's why we have to be smart. If we call the police, it could go south very quickly."

"This is madness! Who *doesn't* call the police?"

"We don't. Not yet."

"This is crazy."

"We're already ahead of the police. I have an idea—though not a sure bet—who might be behind this. I'll settle that score when the time is right. For the moment, our only concern is getting Alexis home."

"At least we agree on that. So what are you suggesting we do? And what's this about odds?"

"I told you I've been sick. I've been making mistakes. It makes it look as though I'm running that second book—it's called a Dutch book—against bad odds I give Vegas. They want perfect numbers. And they want the magic races where you can nearly run the table if the odds are just so. I thought I saw a couple of those, too, and it proved not to be the case.

"I've made very expensive mistakes. People I work with are disappointed. They want things fixed. That's why I came to you. I can't do it like I once did. I knew you could."

Donna was quiet only for the time it took to digest what her father was saying. Some of the words were not said at all, but she heard the inference as clear as the bell before the clang of starting gates bursting open. In the ringing, the bell's clapper cracked her square in the face.

"Did I hear that right? This is my fault for not helping you fix horse races?"

"I don't fix races. Not anymore. I lay odds. You know that. And I never said any of this was your fault. It's no one's fault."

"Yeah, yeah, it is. It's someone's fault. Try, yours!"

"I didn't know they'd use Alexis to leverage me."

"If they're like you, they're capable of anything. I've seen your handiwork up close."

"You better remember that."

"Remember what, that my father used to carve people up for fun?"

"No, no! You said, they're capable of anything. That's something you should remember when you start to phone the police."

"I don't trust you and I don't believe you."

"You'd better start."

"Is that a threat? What are you going to do to me? My daughter's been kidnapped! There's nothing you can say or do that would bother me one bit at this moment."

"I want to bring her home and I can, but I need your help. If you say no, then you *will* be to blame if you don't see her again."

"You sick sonofabitch."

"Think what you want. It's clear I can't make you feel differently. But if you want her home safe, you'd better start trusting me—at least a little—and pronto. There's no other sure thing. Anything else—including the cops—is a long shot. A real longshot."

"Why? Why trust you?"

"Because I'm half of the only equation that adds up to her coming back safe."

"And the other half?"

"You. I still need your help, and now Lexy does, too."

"If…and it's a big if. If I was to help you, would they let her come home now? If you promise to make the numbers right?"

"But I can't."

"If I were to help you. If you promised, they'd let her go now. Today. Tonight, right? You're The Book. Everyone knows you don't go back on your word. That's your whole game, am I right?"

"Partly."

"Would they let her go?"

"I don't know, kiddo. I truly don't know."

"Will you try?"

"Of course I will, but how? I can call back, but you have to admit, it's unlikely they answer."

"But you'll try."

"I'll call right now."

And he did. Several times while Donna dropped into his chair and rested her head on the desk, she could hear the faint ringing captured in several attempts. The plan was stymied. She wouldn't see Alexis tonight.

• • •

"I'm sorry, Donnie," her father said as he laid his phone down. "There's still no answer."

Donna raised her head only slightly. She perched her chin on the back of her hands. One of the many monitors was now less than a foot from her face. She didn't even see the scrolling reams of data flickering by. Tears had collected on her father's leather desktop and her hands. They continued to run, and she wiped at them as though they burned.

"I guess that was my big plan. Shot to hell."

"It was a good plan. Still is. We just have to be patient. They hold the cards."

"And my baby."

Donnie wandered away from the desk and rubbed his face hard.

"What now, Dad? What do I do?"

"Try to rest? Be ready? I don't know really. Wait for another call."

They were both quiet for a time. Donna pressed up from the desk. She wiped drying tears and others less so from her face with the heels of her hands.

"I'll have that drink now," she said as she came out of a stretch, got up, and went to the makeshift bar. "You want another?"

"Yes, thank you."

The cut glass decanter clinked against the tumbler. "My daughter's been taken and I'm pouring a drink. It doesn't seem right."

"It's smart."

"Says you."

"You came up with a sound idea. They'll call and I'll talk to them. My associates will trace that call and find a location. Other calls will help."

"They must know that too," Donna said as she took a long drink. "What if they don't call?" She took a second deep pull from her glass.

"That's high-octane stuff, kiddo."

"I don't feel a thing."

"No, I don't imagine you do. We'll get her back. They'll contact me. They'll want to press their advantage. There's big races coming up."

"What about that? The odds and the special races? How many tracks do you set the odds for?"

"Depends on the season and who's open. Winter slows down, but the Florida tracks close in the heat of the summer. It balances some."

"Ten races a day at each track. What, ten or twelve horses per race? That's a lot of odds setting."

Donnie smiled faintly. "I'm glad it's just thoroughbreds. Somebody else has to do harness racing, the quarter horse tracks, on and on. Not to mention Europe, Dubai, and Japan. I go over them after they're in, but I don't set them up. I leave that to some other poor fool."

"Dad, there's no other 'poor fool.' There's a room full of mainframes and three hundred techs entering data and working spreadsheets throughout the night."

"Right now, I'd rather they were here. It would be a great help."

Donna finished her drink and poured another as she rambled to ease the tension. "Belladonna is an early scratch in the first race at the Park tomorrow. That's one less to odds up."

"Belladonna? At Belmont?"

"Just caught my eye at the desk," she shrugged. "The *Donna* part of *Belladonna*. Hope it's not a sign. Being scratched."

"With that handle, he has to be sick."

Donna huffed a stifled laugh. "Right? GreenSleeveDream will pick up his action. He'll bump to four to one."

"Think so?" Donnie said from beneath a raised eyebrow.

"GreenSleeveDream is coming off some solid work and he's got a clever trainer behind him. He's run him up for the new distance perfectly."

"GreenSleeve what?"

"GreenSleeveDream. Are you going deaf too?"

"No, I'm not going deaf. I'm just asking."

"You can't remember one horse's name? Especially something like GreenSleeveDream. For two minutes? Are you playing around?"

"I got it," Donnie said without making any actual note of the horse's name. "That's two down." He moved a glass on the serving sideboard in front of his daughter. "Three fingers, if you please?"

The decanter clinked again, then the pair meandered with the liquid pain killers to the desk and the bank of monitors. Another tear escaped Donna's eye. She attacked it with her hand, still holding the tumbler of Scotch, then pointed with the glass at the mass of scrolling screens.

"How's all this work?"

"Lots of feeds. A mile of cable. Dedicated mainframes. Software of my own design."

"Dad?"

"Yes?"

"What was the name of that horse I said would pick up Belladonna's action?"

Donnie stared at the screens on his desk. He was quiet. She let him stay that way and waited.

In a few moments Donnie began to talk slowly, softly, but distracted. "I have this monitor…scrolling blood stock. It's tied directly to…past performance of horses that—"

"GreenSleeveDream, Dad. GreenSleeveDream."

13

"You see, Alexis, that's the real beauty of surprises," Mrs. Glass explained. "There's lots of pleasant things that come about, and you don't even see them coming. Not having to go to school is one such a thing. You get a little vacation, you might say."

"But can I call my mom?"

"Well now, she caught a plane yesterday and a second one while we were asleep. It was a sudden trip or she wouldn't have darted off like that. She'll be gone a week or so, but we'll make out. Far as school goes, you got your iPad there to fool with. Your mom said you ain't to try to get to email or make phone calls with it. Bad guys can get through that to your mother's banking account."

"Not through this one. My mom put layers and layers of security on it. I don't even have an email account or access to Twitter. She made it so I can't make phone calls either. My mom's really smart. She says there's lots of time for that when I'm older."

"That's true enough. Here's something though. I brought you one of your grandfather's number puzzle books to work on. That can count towards arithmetic class."

"I don't take arithmetic class," Lexy said as she happily took the sudoku book and scanned several ink-filled pages. She was certain she recognized the flow of her grandfather's pen. "How come we're at a hotel? Can't we stay at the big house?"

"This is a right smart place, don't you think?" Mrs. Glass said, motioning around the expansive adjoining suites. "We each got our own rooms and little parlors. We're hooked together. I'm right through that little door. And since your mother told me you get out of 'tending school, it's even better. We can call room service and order our breakfast. No cooking for a change. If we were at your grandfather's, I'd have to cook and clean all day. I don't suppose you'll mind if I get a few days off alongside of you, do you? Plus, with no cooking, we have more time to go off anywhere you want, or near so."

"Anywhere?"

"Or near so. Where'd you like to go?"

"Belmont Park. Let's go see the horses!"

"Bel—. My, you are your grandfather's filly, aren't you?"

"Maybe we'll see Grandpa there. He goes there a lot. He loves horses. Like me."

"Is that so?"

"They're beautiful."

"That they are. Say. Listen," Mrs. Glass stumbled, piloting away from possibly the worst place in the world to take a kidnapped bookie's granddaughter. "I'm not for sure there's racing today. We might have to go someplace—"

"They race today."

"How do you know that?"

"I saw the schedule."

"Did you?"

"Yep."

"No, you didn't. When did you see a racing schedule? I don't think your mother would allow it."

"I read the DRFs on my iPad. I mostly like looking at all the numbers—they call them odd numbers, but that's not really right because they're even numbers too. I like the ratios best."

"Do you?"

"There's a pretty horse running in the very first race. He's gray. Not a lot of thoroughbreds are gray. Some turn gray when they get older. Like Grandpa's hair has a little gray because he's older."

"You're right knowledgeable about horses, aren't you?"

"My grandpa is. He used to take me to the Park at Belmont when I lived at the big house. He taught me how to read past performances, weights, trainers, tracks—"

"I wish he'd tell you who's going to win that first race. Being the pretty horse is nice, but being first is better."

"We could ask Grandpa. He knows."

"Probably does, but he won't give it up to the likes of me."

"Why?"

"I can't say. He's never given me a tip in a race. But that doesn't matter anymore. Doesn't bother me a smidge."

"Did you ever ask him about horses and numbers?"

"Nah. If he don't want to just toss a coin my way and help a body out, far be it from me to go begging. Your Mrs. Glass don't beg. I'll not be beholding to no one."

"If you said please, he would tell you all about horses. He used to tell me all about them and I didn't even ask. He's real good with all the different numbers. I like them too. They make headaches go away."

"How's that?"

"My head sort of hurts sometimes. It gets…like, fuzzy, I guess. Then it's hard to do other stuff. If I look at all the numbers about Grandpa's horses, it goes away."

"Is that so?"

"Yep. I'm pretty sure my mom's head hurts sometimes too. She writes down lists of numbers. One after another—full pages of numbers."

"You know your grandfather puts numbers in those puzzle books," Glass said as she pointed to the sudoku book. "He does it all the while."

"Maybe his head hurts, too. I'll ask him."

"Maybe it does. If your head commences to hurting, you try that book of his and see if, you know, maybe it gets rid of the fuzzies in your noggin."

"Thank you. I will. So, can we go see the horses? I know they're there."

"Let's kick that around a bit. It's too early anyway. The Park's not even open."

"Grandpa walks in whenever he wants."

"Well, I ain't your grandfather. God knows. I can't pick a winner if it kicked me in the head."

"Who'd want to be kicked by a horse?"

"I'm just saying, it'd be a pleasure to know who was going to trip the wire. You know—win the race."

"I didn't look at all the races, but my gray horse will win that first race."

"You an expert, are you?"

"I don't think so, but the gray horse is going to run faster than the others." Alexis slid off the bed and danced to the window. She pulled back the curtain and looked out into Manhattan. "He's the only horse to run six furlongs twice before. He doesn't have the fastest time, which is why his ratio has bigger numbers. But he went five furlongs in fifty-nine and three in his last work. He's ready."

"How old are you?"

"Seven."

"And you think this gray horse of yours will win because he is practicing better?"

"The real reason he'll win is because that's what his trainer does."

"His trainer does what?"

Alexis came away from the window in a quick start, bounded across the floor, and hopped onto the king-sized bed. "When he has a horse ready. He works them at six furlongs twice, then five twice. Then six. Then five. Always five days apart." Lexy was on her knees bouncing on the big bed as she chattered away. "Then the horse is due."

"The horse is due?"

"Yep," Lexy was on her feet now, bouncing higher. "He's due to win at six. He'll win. My gray horse. He's due. I looked at the others. They're not due."

"The others aren't due?"

"Nope."

"I tell you what let's do. We'll watch the race on the computer. On your iPad, see. If what you say goes, we'll look into getting over to the track. How's that sound?"

"If the gray horse wins, we can go see the other horses?"

"No promises, mind you, but I'll say this—if you didn't fall far from the tree—your pretty little head will never get the fuzzies again. I'll see you get your fill of horses and numbers every day Belmont's gates open."

Alexis fell backward and bounced her entire body on the bed. As she settled, she stretched. "It's a deal. Did you know horses can be sound? But not like the sound of a bell."

"I did know that, as a matter of fact."

Alexis squirmed around and picked up the remote for the television. "My gray horse is sound. Very sound. The favorite wasn't. He scratched. My horse will pick up his action."

"You and me are going to get on just dandy," Mrs. Glass smiled as she sat on the edge of the bed. "I do believe it. So, by-the-by, what's your gray horse called?"

"His name is GreenSleeveDream."

14

It was early for Baron to be crossing the vestibule of his office. An initiated ear could discern an anxious tint coloring his voice as he barked his directives.

"But the real order of business is I want to see the odds laid in for today's races."

"Which races?"

"The thoroughbreds. Send me Santa Anita and Belmont first. Let's see if things are turning around. Let me know as soon as they're locked."

"They're locked now. They came in last night."

"The odds are laid out for all the tracks?"

"All the thoroughbred racing. Yes, sir. They came in early."

"That's better. At least the timing is better. Cue up Santa Anita live when they open. They had better be flashing some better numbers. Then Belmont's. I want a crack team of bean counters reporting on every race at those venues before the horses step off the track. Let's go! Let's go! Turn this around! We need a good day today!"

Fifteen hours later, numbers reported to Baron that he had gotten his good day. GreenSleeveDream went four wide at the top of the stretch to win going away in the first race at Belmont Park, jump-starting the juggernaut of the day's action. The volume generated by the odds balanced payouts across the boards. Assorted horses, jockeys, connections, and punters won, but the overall gambling pool didn't take notice. What the pool felt was only the ebb and flow of balanced money. The odds set to entice both conservative and daring bettors did exactly that with an invisible tug, nudge, and pull. The payouts at dozens of tracks from the highbrow and high profile to the backwaters were met with a comfortable ease that regardless of who, how, or what, won and lost, the business of racing stayed snug and low, spinning in its greased groove. All was right in the world of thoroughbred gaming and Alexis was a day's racing closer to coming home.

In the short cycle of another day, it would all be placed on the line again. In New York, the Chariots would fold together the results of training breezes, gallops, and run-outs, versus distances, veterinarian's reports, past racing performance, trainer's cues, and the weather. In shockingly short order, the odds for the next day's races would be massaged into place.

• • •

Donnie didn't offer the customary morning salutation to his daughter when she came dragging into the kitchen. Her eyes were red and puffy, and she was wearing badly wrinkled clothes from the night before. In time Donnie learned she'd slept in them, despite being surrounded by closets of her mother's clothes which would have fit nicely. Her father silently poured a cup of coffee, left it black, and set it in front of her. The best he could do was suffer a quick smile. Behind it was a jumble of strained emotions.

He had strangely enjoyed the tense evening working alongside his daughter. It was a glimpse at something he had longed for. Together they could distill and decipher information at a rate of speed, efficiency, and accuracy that was exponentially greater than he could do alone. It would only get better. Donna would get faster—faster even than he had been in his prime. Donnie's smile grew then vanished. The specter of dementia tapped him on the shoulder. There wasn't time for doing more, faster, or better. Mere survival was hardly a guarantee.

"Is this decaf?" Donna said.

"No. I had to do some rooting around, but I found regular. I thought we could both tolerate a little caffeine after yesterday. Turned into a long one."

"Is that how it usually goes?"

"It'll get quicker."

They each braved hot sips

"I could use a shower," Donna said.

"Help yourself. You know where everything is."

"Everything except my daughter."

Donna took another taste of the early morning elixir while her father leaned against the counter and gently blew the heat away from his.

"She can't be far and she's with Mrs. Glass. She misses you, no doubt, but she's not afraid or in danger."

"So you keep saying."

"She's their leverage. They're angry. At me. There's no profit in hurting her."

"Will last night help?"

"I should think. I'll keep my phone handy. We'll hear from them."

"Them. Are you going to tell me who 'them' is?"

"I can't say with certainty. It'd be impossible to prove, but with results like we gave them yesterday, this will end quickly."

"It still doesn't sit right not bringing in the police, the FBI— somebody with a badge."

"I understand that. It's reasonable."

"What are the extra men—the ones you had Frank get. What are they for?"

"For you. For now. For me later."

Donna didn't ask for clarification.

"You want to do something," Donnie said. "Anything to get her back. I know that. I had a friend locate where the call originated. It's in the city, but it's a big city."

"That was the Gabriel character?"

"Yes."

"And that's somehow for my benefit?"

"To a degree. I want you to know we're trying. Gabriel will keep at it and when he gets closer, Frank's people will start watching and knocking on doors."

"What's the part that's for you?"

"When they find her and whoever's holding her, they'll call me."

Donna let that fall to the floor. She knew exactly what he meant. For all the disparaging comments, criticism, and worst she had heaped upon him through the years, her father's past no longer stuck in her throat. It still drew the same hot breath and left the distinctive bloody wake, but now Donna was prepared to dip her own hands in that sticky crimson bucket. She'd pass a blade neatly across the throat of the one who'd taken her daughter without a second thought.

Donna went for a warmer and topped off her father's coffee. "What's Glass's connection?" she said as she poured. "Don't tell me you haven't thought about it because I know you have. I'm sure you're already several steps out in front of this and you're waiting to dole them out to me in pieces you think I can manage."

He was in his coffee, lingering for the extra preparation the sip allowed. What he knew of Mrs. Glass, or thought he knew, was not quite ready for dissemination. In that respect, Donna was right, but as her father considered the right words and the extent of his explanation, he felt the shudder that precipitated the vagueness of something forgotten.

Mrs. Glass. Something about Mrs. Glass. Her involvement? What was the threat? Where did it come from? Did she have Lexy and what was he doing to bring her home? Something once so carefully orchestrated was now a spinning kaleidoscope of disjointed thoughts.

"Dad?"

"Yes?"

She touched his arm for the first time in years. "Are you all right?"

"Yes. Good coffee. Thank you." He took another sip—one purposely too big—in the hopes the burning in his mouth would rekindle a fire in his mind.

"Glass. What's her connection?"

"I'm working on her," was all he offered until another scorching drink jolted him enough to respond, though he was certain some of what he was saying wasn't right.

For her part, Donna took his evasiveness as protection or part of the process. Knowing her father as she did, it was possible it was all a lie.

"The tie is blatant," Donnie said. "There's no hiding that or any attempt to. They want us to know Alexis is with Mrs. Glass. That fact would serve to placate us—keep us from screaming for the cops. Beyond that much, Mrs. Glass is a problem for them."

"How so?"

"She's the connection to them. Plus, you know how she is. You've seen her pluses and minuses. If I was operating from their position—a position of strength at present—I would view Mrs. Glass as a horrific liability. For the moment, she suits the purpose, but there'll come a time when she will be expendable. And it goes without saying, she'll find no quarter from us. I would not want to be in her station."

Donna had no argument, but weighed every word.

•　•　•

One floor below, Nicky was carrying two cardboard carriers of coffee cups into the basement. He set them, along with a bag of creamers and sugars, on a bar that would have been too elaborate in almost any other basement.

"Coffee," was his simple announcement.

Big men in zippered sweat suits and sagging socks rolled off couches and single cots from the far corners. Some looked up only to roll back beneath their blankets for another forty winks. Others staggered away for the morning ritual in the bathroom. Frank came down the stairs and met a couple at Nicky's coffee.

"What's up, Frank?"

"Same ole. You?"

"Same shit. Different day."

"I see you're still with The Book."

"Never gave me a reason to leave. Treats me good."

"Making any money?"

"Some."

"Not like the old days though."

"Nothing is like the old days."

"We made a lot, but we paid a lot. In a lot of ways."

"I wouldn't trade for them. No way."

"Probably so. It was never boring though."

"Dying is real exciting. I can wait."

"Smart man. Who's your coffee jockey?"

Frank pointed a lazy finger at Nicky. "He'll answer to Nick."

"Hey."

"Hi, ya," one of the men said over hot coffee, but held back his hand as did Nicky. "Thanks for the eye opener. Frank teach you anything useful?"

"I teach him to keep his mouth shut," Frank said. "Do as he's told and stay out of trouble."

"So what happened this time? Somebody put the snatch on The Book's grandkid right in front of you? How's that happen and you not be dead or at least shot to hell?"

"Didn't happen on our watch," Frank said before coffee.

"We don't watch her," Nicky snapped. "If we did, she'd be here and you wouldn't."

"Fair enough. Only trying to figure the score. We ain't been told much. If I gotta back your play, I'd like to know I'm not backing a dickhead."

Nicky grabbed his own crotch. "Back these. Nobody gets near Mr. Chariot. That's what I do. The kid is not my problem."

"Jesus, Frank, keep your pit-bull on a chain. We're only trying to get the lay of the land. Relax."

"You relax."

"Okay. Okay. It's your house. But here's a wakeup call for you, Nick. To go with that coffee."

"What's that?"

"Looks like that kid is your problem now, don't it?" and the sweat suit wandered away with his coffee.

Behind Nicky, a neatly pressed suit walked in the basement. One of the big men touched Nicky's arm, whispered, and pointed discreetly. "I've got a twenty says that guy's a cop. You want it?"

"No cops are getting in this house. I'll take it."

"Damn it!" Frank said as he choked on his coffee. "I couldn't stop you in time, partner."

"Stop me from what?"

"You got played." Frank motioned for the suit to join them. "Nick, meet Gabriel."

The suit just tipped his chin. Nicky pointed to him and spoke as if he wasn't there.

"This is a cop? Ain't happening."

"Pay up, kid."

"I get half," Gabriel said as he reached for a coffee.

"See there, Nick? He wants a piece of everything. That proves he's a cop."

"Blow me," Gabriel said as he tore open sugars and spilled most on the bar.

"Not on your best day, needle-dick."

"Why? You tired of giving discounts to public servants?"

"Your wife ain't."

Gabriel laughed as he looked around the basement. "Christ, Frank, your boss must be pretty desperate to hire this dreg. Where'd you find these guys?" Gabriel said as he motioned toward the big guy who'd taken Nicky's money. "This one was holding a cardboard sign on a corner last time I saw him."

Frank was smiling. "I had to go his bail at Riker's."

"I don't doubt it. I hope they didn't hit you too hard. First chance he gets he'll steal the old man's silver and leave you holding the bag."

"What'd I tell you, Nick?" the big man said. "A cop. Talking shit. Always letting their mouth write a check their ass can't cash. Get him in an alley some night and he'll be on his knees crying for his mommy."

"You'd know all about being on your knees." Gabriel stirred his coffee. "Frank, you got any of that special creamer around?"

Without a word, Frank pulled a bottle of whiskey from under the bar.

"Here," Nicky's gambling partner said as he motioned to undo his pants. "I got some special creamer for you."

"Christ, keep your pants on!" Gabriel said as he pointed at Nicky. "There's children present."

"If there's children around, they ain't safe. You still like little boys or you trying to cut back?"

"Go ask your son."

They laughed as the man pushed his cup under where Frank was preparing to pour a shot of liquor into Gabriel's coffee that instead went into his.

"Thank you, Frank."

"You two haven't changed," Frank said as he made a second attempt at Gabriel's coffee. "Degenerates. You're still disgusting."

"Thank you," Gabriel and his sparring partner said in unison as they raised their doctored coffees and bumped the cups.

"To the sunny slopes—"

"—of long ago."

"Wait a second," Nicky complained. "You two know each other?"

Gabriel held a finger to his lips. "Don't tell anyone. I have a reputation to think about."

"You still owe twenty, kid," the guy reminded, then pointed with his cup at Gabriel. "Frank, what we got going that we need her?"

"That was the boss's call. Some tech stuff."

"Triangulating a phone call," Gabriel said between sips made hotter by the whiskey.

"You find it?"

"Close."

"Close? You cops. Always a maybe. You ever catch a real honest-to-goodness bad guy? You can't do shit. Couldn't pour piss out of a boot if the directions were on the heel. Tell The Book he's wasting his money."

Gabriel poured another shot into his coffee. His banter companion held out his own cup for another shot. "You've a fine steady hand, Gabe. If the city ever finds out you ain't shit for a cop, you can put your skirt back on and start waiting tables."

Instead of pouring, Gabriel set the bottle down. Nicky pushed it toward the waiting cup and followed it with what he thought was an obvious question.

"So Gabriel is running down the whereabouts of a phone call. What are these other guys for?"

"Whatever our boss says."

"Shouldn't they be out looking for Lexy?"

"Where do you suggest? New York's kinda big. Maybe you hadn't noticed."

"You find that kid, you'll be her mommy's hero," Gabriel said between sips. "A regular knight in shining armor. Young stud like you, that'd be convenient. Every morning when you show up, there'd be a blow job waiting—"

"Hey," Frank snapped along with a rough bump that spilled Gabriel's coffee on his hand.

"What the—"

"Li'l Donnie's off limits. I seen her grow up. The little one too. Not word one. *Capisci?*"

Gabriel licked the coffee off his hand as Frank tossed a bar towel at him. "What? You sweet on her? Kinda old, aren't you to be—"

"Shut up, Gabe. I ain't, but Nick is. Cop or no, he'll cut you from stem to stern—gut you like a fish—if you say anything about his girl."

Gabriel looked at Nicky a little differently. "That makes sense. A knife guy. He looks like a knife guy, don't you think? I can see The Book's interest in that quality." Gabriel raised his cup in a toast. "To the House of Chariot—few dull moments and no dull blades."

"Didn't I ask you to shut up?"

The veterans shared a knowing look and returned to their sweetened coffee, leaving Nicky wondering how Frank always seemed to be right. Nicky did like Donna—more than a little. Of course, she was attractive, but what Nicky saw beneath her curves was a real bleeding need. She wasn't vulnerable—certainly no damsel in distress. Instead, he saw her as a showpiece doll fallen to the floor. Nicky wanted to help her back to the center of a gilded shelf—safe, secure, and free from falling again.

Before he drifted further away into his daydream, Nicky forced himself back to the bar. "Seems like we ought to be doing something besides drinking up Mr. Chariot's booze."

"I'm doing something," Gabriel said.

"What?"

"Waiting for the terror to start."

"What terror?" Nicky asked as Frank and Gabriel nodded and sipped their coffee.

"Our job. Gabe's job," Frank offered. "They're the same. Twenty mind numbing days of absolute bone-crushing boredom followed by twenty seconds of stark naked, soul-burning terror. That's the job. I'm holding up my end just fine."

"What's that even mean?"

"You ain't been baptized yet. You'll see."

Gabriel picked up the whiskey and touched Nicky's arm with the bottle. "Here. The boredom or the terror. This helps with either one."

"No thanks."

"Suit yourself, but if you go looking for the kid, start down on the Deuce. The call came from Manhattan."

"What's the Deuce?"

Frank took over. "It's not so much a 'what-sa' as a 'where-sa'. Forty-second Street. There was a time when that was the place anything went. Gabriel here, was born in the gutter on 42nd Street. No one knew who his father was, but his mom thought she had it narrowed down to the third shift at The Brooklyn Navy Yard."

"You're an asshole."

Frank ignored him.

"The Deuce," the big man said, thinking back with the help of the whiskey. "There was this little grinder theater we hung out—"

"Save the war stories," Frank said, cutting off the story. "Manhattan's a start, but 42nd is a big-ass street. Sit tight until The Book tells us what's what."

"I will, but maybe I'll swing down 42nd on my next coffee run," Nicky said. "You never know."

Gabriel sipped his Irish coffee. "Yep, you never know."

15

"So? What's that mean to me?" Junior DeSeti was saying to his father as he dropped into a wingback chair. "I don't give a shit about that sonofabitch."

"It's only a question."

"One you should ask yourself. You have more to lose than anyone except maybe that fat bastard in Vegas."

"You don't like Baron either? What is it with you and authority? I imagine I'm on your list as well."

"You're too old school. You, Baron, Chariot. It's time you all retired. Chariot first. Permanently."

Julian DeSeti laughed. "You'd like that. Answer the question. Do you know anything about Chariot's granddaughter?"

"How would I know?"

"Answer the question!"

"*No!* I don't know anything."

Julian was pacing off the energy he was ready to use on testing his son's jaw. "There's a great deal at stake."

"You keep saying."

"And I'll keep saying it until you understand! You're pissed about that damn car of yours. I get it. But we're all in. Chariot needs to be left alone or it costs us a shitload of money." Julian put one finger against his son's head like a pistol. "Can you get that through your doped out, thick skull?"

Junior swiped the hand away. "Don't take it out on me if Baron's pet monkey's slipped his chain! The whole street knows the numbers are messed up. Chariot manages the numbers. You manage Chariot. Or at least you're supposed to. So Baron's on your ass over it. You know what I think?"

"I don't care what you think."

"Then get off my back! What if I did have something to do with the kid getting snatched, so what? I hear the numbers ran real good yesterday. You and that Vegas pimp ought to be happy as hell someone grabbed the kid. Looks like it shook Chariot up." He came up out of the chair. His body was telling him he was ready to cook up another fix. His nerves were paper thin. "I'm glad! Make the sonofabitch sweat."

"You don't get it, do you?"

"No! I guess I don't! You should be laughing your ass off that someone put enough pressure on Chariot to bring him around."

Julian stopped wandering and sat down in the chair his son had just vacated. It was hot. "You're right. You're right. I should be happy about that, but I'm not. Do you want to know why?"

Junior was exasperated and flopped onto a couch as far from his father as he could get. "Go ahead," he said as his head, aching and hungry for heroin, lolled backward over the top of the couch's back.

"You're right. I'm supposed to monitor The Book. Keep him happy. Keep him working. Keep him making good calls. When I can no longer do that, I'm expendable."

"But he picked good—"

"One day. Even a broken clock is right twice a day. Remember that."

"Dinosaur bullshit. So old school...."

"That 'old school' bought that car you gambled away."

"That you made me give away!"

"I'm sorry I brought it up. Forget that car. You can buy another if the Belmont breaks our way. And while it's true, Chariot had a good day, if he continues—"

"It would be perfect."

"*Shut up*! It would not be perfect. If he's been pressured through this grab, who controls Chariot?"

"Who cares? The numbers are good again!"

"I should go punch your mother right in the mouth. No way you're my son. Try to listen, Junior. Whoever has that kid controls Chariot. Whoever is giving that girl her breakfast, runs a billion dollars' worth of gambling whether they know it or not. And I know it's not me."

"Fine. If it's not you and I know it wasn't me, then it has to be Baron. Who else wants Chariot?"

"Who knows? Could be anybody. Could be Dubai. A tent full of gold might have turned his head."

"Not Baron?"

"I think he'd have told me."

"Unless he thinks you're in on it with Chariot. Maybe he's trying to out you."

"Christ. Maybe so. That damn Chariot. Everybody is going to want a piece of him before this is over." Julian laughed a little. "Even that cook of his hates him. I had her teed up pretty well to keep an eye on him, but that ship has likely sailed now. Or sunk. I hear she's AWOL."

"The cook?"

"Same day the kid got snatched. She probably got capped in the process."

"Maybe she was in on it."

"How's that?"

"You said she hated Chariot. Maybe she was in on it."

Julian looked at his son hard. "That's an idea. You sure you don't know anything more about this mess?"

The younger DeSeti smiled. "I already told you."

Julian pulled out his phone and Junior saw a pistol beneath his jacket. "When'd you start carrying?"

"Since you decided to get in a pissing match with a skunk," Julian said. "I gotta call a couple guys who might have some more info on Chariot. Don't go anywhere."

"How am I going to go any place? I don't have a car, remember?"

16

"This is not a good idea, Alexis," Mrs. Glass said as she looked around and took the girl's hand a bit too tightly.

"Sure it is. It's always a good idea to see the horses." Though Glass held one of Lexy's hands, the little girl's other one clutched her grandfather's sudoku book as if it were her private talisman.

"What I mean is that I don't think your mom wants you to come here."

Here, was Belmont Park.

Mrs. Glass tugged down the brim of an odd baseball hat on her head and fidgeted as she walked. Lexy wore a similar cheap hat that was sized for an adult.

"Let's call her and ask."

"She's busy. She's busy all day. I talked to her late last night when you were asleep."

"Aw. You're lucky. When can I talk to her?"

"She'll call as soon as she can."

"Can I go home after we see the horses? I miss my apartment."

"Not yet. Your mom said to keep you at the hotel. I think they might be painting your place or something."

"Well, can I at least get some of my clothes? These new things don't fit very well."

They were walking across the wide parking lot toward the main gate.

"I'm doing the best I can. Don't get sharp with me. You look fine." Mrs. Glass reached over and pulled the oversized baseball cap a little lower on Lexy's head.

"I can't see."

"Leave it be. It protects you from the sun. You don't want skin cancer, do you? Your nose will fall right off. Your mother said no sun. Keep that hat on, Missy."

"I won't even be able to see the horses when we get there."

"Never mind the horses, all you have to see is a DRF and the tote board."

The two paid at the main gate, picked up the requisite Daily Racing Form along with a program, and slipped into the track unnoticed along with the small weekday throng.

"Oh, let's go to the playground!" Alexis said as she bumped her temporary guardian in a quick pivot.

"Don't run into me like that! That's a foul," Mrs. Glass said, snapping what could have been a fine joke in another tenor. "I'll have you drawn up before the stewards, I will."

"Aw, come on. We won't miss anything. The race you want is the fifth anyway."

"How do you know the odds are still the same? You haven't seen the board on it yet."

"And we won't until after the fourth race. Not much will change until it goes up. I saw the morning line in the hotel. A little move in the right direction and that race is a winner every which way."

"You best be right, little sister. But that still don't get you no playground. Let's grab us a couple seats up high and you go over the next races. If you pick some winners for me, I'll take you to the playground after the fifth. Deal?"

"I don't want to sit up high. You can't see the horses."

"I guess you'll sit where I say sit." Glass looked out from beneath her hat for any faces she knew, or more importantly, who might know her. "Besides, I like to sit up high so I can see the whole track. If you're low, sure, you can see the horses good, but races is won and lost on that back stretch."

"You're no fun."

"You spout off and I'm apt to get a lot less fun. You'll see."

Stressed by boredom and charmed by GreenSleeveDream's win the day before, Glass was ready to launch the biggest gamble of the day. She dressed Lexy like a boy and slyly limped off to the track. Following their spat, when they'd settled in their high seats, Glass thrust the DRF and the day's program into Lexy's hands.

"Work your magic. Give me that puzzle book. We got no time for foolishness." Glass dropped Donnie Chariot's book at their feet.

"I can hardly see the horses."

"You want we should go back to the hotel room? You missing reruns of *Sesame Street*?"

"No, thank you."

Glass tapped the program with a slightly arthritic bent finger. "Hard at it now. What's that next race look like?"

The race and Alexis delivered Mrs. Glass the first winner she'd cashed in longer than she could remember. Flush with success and up thirty-six dollars, she put twenty on the following race at her little handicapper's direction. The rush of the win far outpaced the payout and prompted her to go all in on Lexy's quinella in the third pick of the day. When it came home, Mrs. Glass was beside herself. It wasn't until she saw people jealously staring at her celebration that she quickly settled back in her seat.

"Look at that," Glass said as she held the ticket under Lexy's nose. "That's four hundred dollars cash right in my pocket."

"Four hundred thirty-four dollars to be exact."

"I dunno how you do it, but it works. We're gonna take this place for all it's worth. They owe me plenty. Your grandfather could have tipped me one of these now and again. Wouldn't have hurt a thing, you know what I mean?"

"Not really."

Alexis didn't know—not completely. Still, she put this suggestion together with ones from the other day and concluded that Grandpa Chariot must have had a reason for not showing Mrs. Glass the winners. She concluded that she should follow his lead. When the horses for their fourth pick hit the wire, Mrs. Glass was left stunned and stammering.

"Hey, hey, hey! What happened? Our nag was an also-ran. That ain't how we play. C'mon now. That cost me forty dollars. Here's the next one up on the card. This is our big one. How's it looking?"

Alexis looked from the DRF to the tote board. If she had to answer Mrs. Glass's question then and there, she'd have said, "Pretty close." Odds were moving slightly in the right directions. Horses were being numerically positioned so that if bets were laid in on the right numbers at the right times, a payout, maybe a healthy one, was assured. But she was quiet and waited, for the numbers and also to gently torment Mrs. Glass.

Lexy stared at the board as if by a psychic will she didn't possess, she could move the number that needed a bump. As she watched, the numbers began to grow clearer and larger, but it was in her mind's eye and no one else's. The odds flashed and connected with other numbers on the board. To Alexis it became a perfect rhythm. The flashing and connecting of the numbers sped up until they were racing by in a blur. The alternating brilliance and fading were like flashes from a camera as the odds began to communicate with one another and find footing among themselves. Their instant influence on neighboring numbers was forced by trips to betting windows from a few yards away within the park, to electronic wagers placed halfway around the world. While the system fought to stay abreast, Lexy absorbed it all with a new-found fluid ease. In that instant, a new challenge outweighed the desire to cut off the greedy Mrs. Glass.

"How much money do you have?"

Glass dug in her purse and counted awkwardly. "I got…four hundred eighty-four dollars."

Alexis eyed the total pools. The dollars bet on the horse headed to the number seven hole were ridiculously small, even for a no-account race of maiden claimers. She closed her eyes a moment. The numbers were still there, whispering to her.

•　•　•

Less than five miles away, Donnie Chariot was at his desk. He let a small smile come across his face when he saw—across the country—that thus far they had teed the odds up perfectly. Vegas would be pleased.

Always holding an affinity for the local track, he began scrolling through Belmont's board. He stopped and watched the numbers for the upcoming race. "Donna? Come look at this."

She had been standing in a distant window with another cup of coffee. The second half of the odds-setting team for the nation's thoroughbred race tracks—inhabited by sprinters and closers, all of which were fleet of foot—moved painfully slow. Each step did in fact pain her. She had slept little and when her eyes closed for real, it was after substantial encouragement from a dangerous combination of pills and alcohol.

She only half-trusted her father and trusted even less her decision to not get the police involved. If there was solace, it was in the notion that Mrs. Glass—herself loaded with disparaging faults—was with her daughter and hopefully rendering a measure of comfort. Taken as a whole, the package was riddled with concerns.

"Show me something that says Lexy is coming home today."

"It'll come. Every day, she's closer to home." Donnie rested his hand on his daughter's hip and patted it as though reassuring a nervous two-year-old running her first race. Whether it was working or not didn't seem to matter as he pointed from her hip to one of the monitors.

"See this? Look at this board and tell me what you see. It's the race due up next door. Maidens looking, hoping, to be claimed. You could probably buy the entire card for twenty thousand. What do you see?"

Donna looked at the electronic version of Belmont's tote board, but offered nothing.

"Take it all in. You'll see it."

"Sorry, I don't see anything." Donna turned away, but her father caught her arm.

"Look again and stop lying to yourself. These are the races that can get Lexy home quicker. Look at the odds—how they're lining up against each other. Watch the board."

Her father's direction was part instruction, part challenge, but if this sped up Lexy's return, Donna would play along. She set her coffee on the desk and rubbed her face to life. With both hands now on the desk surrounding the coffee cup, she leaned toward the screen. It was just a breath and she saw it all. The numbers glowed and did everything but twinkle. They sent flashing lines to other odds and swelled and shrank like a beating heart. She watched a few changes, then touched the screen as though it may have been hot.

"If this horse, number seven…if he were to pick up some action at the right time, the needle for the entire race moves into a subtle alignment that…can that be right? The payouts are—"

"Guaranteed and universal," The Book said proudly. "Payouts will always come, but when the stars are aligned—or in this case, the numbers—they will pay off nicely on bets laid in all over the board."

"That's unfathomable."

"It requires tremendous luck with timing though. There's still a balance to be achieved and maintained. If we were to put a grand on that horse right now, the odds would move to that sweet spot, but its four minutes to post. That's too early. John Q. Public would see the board move and think the smart money was coming in late. They'd jump on it and the dream would shatter."

Donna was still enraptured by the monitor. "I see it. Remarkable."

"What is remarkable is that you and I are the only people who can watch a board and see it percolate like this. It doesn't happen often, maybe once a week across the entire country. Sometimes less. To manipulate it into happening is impossible. I've tried it. Almost succeeded. The amounts required to move the needle can be pretty staggering and when you lay that kind of money in, it shows up too easily. The wagers in the everyday races from casual players are the only way."

"Is this what got you in trouble?"

"The lion's share. My daily set-ups had been lacking. That was showing up in the tallies as well. If the street tried to bring my odds in line, people took that market correction as either positive or negative depending on whether it took a horse up or down. It all impacted the overall board rather adversely. Oh, that little bit of an overage, the breakage for the house, and the vig, they were always there, but any type of disruption in the cash stream is a negative. Then when I thought I saw races like this one," Donnie said as he pointed to the screen, "and it turned out not to be? Or I missed the amounts to lay in? Or screwed up the timing? Everything took a bad turn. Very bad."

Donna eased up from the desk and brought her coffee with her. "What's changed? What if this race isn't what you think it is?"

"But it is. I'd say for a few hundred dollars we could lock it in. It's right, but not because I saw it. I don't trust myself anymore, but you saw it. People with this gift—"

"Curse."

"All right. Curse. They're the only ones who can see these things. You saw it. So it's there." Donnie pointed again to the totals. "You can see it here in the total amount in the wager pool." As Donnie touched the screen, the number went up by exactly three hundred dollars. Both he and Donna stared at the point of his finger. Then their eyes drifted to each other and back to the screen.

17

Alexis was standing near a trash can against a support column beneath the grandstands. Around her feet, the scattered betting slips of a hundred dreams collected spilled condiments and dirty shoe prints. She was nursing a bottle of water and watching Mrs. Glass coming across the wide foyer from the betting windows.

"Did you get it in?"

"Yep. All three hundred. You better be right. That's the day's kitty."

"And the sides?"

"All bet. Just like you said. They weren't very big. Wasn't much left over. We might have to eat ramen noodles for the rest—"

"You can have steak every night. I want chicken and biscuits with mashed potatoes."

"C'mon," Mrs. Glass said as she looked far too nervously around the wide betting parlor. "Let's get back upstairs. You should have stayed put like I told you."

"It has a lot to do with when the numbers change. I had to send you to the window at the right time."

"Says you."

The pair headed back up the grandstand stairs. Glass walked without thinking what she'd do if someone saw her. Though she'd been promised otherwise, it was possible all of New York City was looking for this girl.

"Can I get a hotdog?"

"What?"

"A hotdog."

"A hotdog? Goodness' sake! How can you eat at a time like this? Hurry up to the top there."

Alexis moved up the stairs but looked over her shoulder at the big board. The numbers went dark as a bell rang in the distance. The clanging of the metal gates sprung the horses free and they bolted.

• • •

The door of her father's office served as Donna's starting gate. That three-hundred-dollar uptick was her bell. She was in the main hall of the mansion yelling for her father to hurry when he came to the same door, nearly caught in a vacuum created by Donna's rush.

"Donna, we don't know—"

"Yes, we do! You said no one can see that set-up but us. Someone put down that three hundred and we know it wasn't us. It was her! C'mon!"

The Book reluctantly followed his daughter, but she left both him and his plea behind.

"Wait a minute. That doesn't mean she's at the track. She could be any—"

Donnie Chariot came to the door of his mansion to see Donna sprinting across the courtyard to where Mr. Abreu was unloading bags of mulch from the truck.

"We need the truck right now," she said as she jumped inside.

For his part, Mr. Abreu said nothing, but smartly got out of her way. Behind him, Chariot was at the base of the stone steps. Donna wheeled the truck across the courtyard to her father as he continued to try and make a case. "That bet could have been placed from anywhere in the world."

"But it wasn't. I know she has it, but she's not good enough to figure out that timing unless she was there watching the board and someone was running up to the window with that three hundred. They've got her at the track! Get in!"

Donnie was still hesitant, but got in the truck. "Honey, take a breath—"

The words were choked off by the truck's lurch toward the gate. Donna rocketed through and fishtailed as she throttled away toward Belmont.

• • •

Mrs. Glass was long up and out of her seat as the horses hit the top of the stretch. "C'mon. C'mon! There it is. *There it is!*" she screamed as the horses crossed beneath the wire. Hands clutching tickets and waving in the air, she began to run down the high steps of the grandstand.

"Don't forget my hotdog!"

"Are you crazy? Get your nose in them papers and your eyes on that board. We're gonna clean them out!"

"But you said!"

"Later!" Glass shouted as she ducked out of sight, headed for her payout.

Alexis wasn't having it. She didn't open the DRF and looked at the board only because it was in her way as she jogged down the steps. But where Mrs. Glass made a bee line for the betting windows, Alexis continued down through the grandstand to Belmont's apron. She breezed up the apron and waited by the main tunnel. The horses for the next race were at the other end, still in the paddock. If someone was supposed to be watching for little girls ducking into the tunnel, they weren't doing a very good job. Alexis sneaked through in a blink.

Straight ahead was the paddock proper with its busy runners and riders. Horses had already begun stepping into the ring and their riders were being given the leg up and settling on broad backs in the summer New York sunshine. While the horses circled beneath Secretariat's bronze gaze, Alexis circled the entire affair and jogged away toward the playground.

"Mrs. Glass can pick her own horses."

• • •

Donna whipped into a limited access parking lot and bailed from the truck. She was running for the restricted horseman's gate with her father lagging badly.

"I know you're trying to do the right thing, but the best thing we can do is to be home working up tomorrow."

Donna was stopped by security. "Miss, I'm sorry, but this entrance is for—"

"Dad! *Hurry up!*"

The verbal crop did little to speed Donnie along. Donna would have used a real crop on her father's flank if she'd had one, and it would have helped her find Lexy quicker.

"Hello," The Book said almost apologetically. "We're looking for someone—"

"We need to get inside as quickly as possible."

"I can see that, but this gate is only for trainers and—"

"Do you know who this—" Donna stammered. "This is Donnie Chariot. He practically pays for this place to operate. Could you let us through, please?"

"I'm sorry, Mr. Chariot. Please, go right ahead, sir."

"Thank you," Donnie said. "You're most kind."

Donna had already cleared the narrow gate and was running across the lawn toward the grandstand. Her father was hustling behind her, but was tardy, as before. The luck that had seen them through the gate was about to run out. Whereas a little girl was invisible to the security men intent on keeping the tunnel free from humans and open to equestrian talent only, a man running after a pretty lady proved a magnet. Two guards met Donna as she tried to circumvent the rail and go up the tunnel to the track.

• • •

Mrs. Glass was still playing with her cash as she drifted back up the grandstand stairs to her seat in the nosebleed section. She pulled out a five and wadded it up as she tucked away the rest of her roll.

"Here's a fiver for that hotdog, but it's a trade. No dog until I get the next—" Glass looked up at the empty seats in a sea of empty seats then spun away from the obvious and hurriedly scanned what she could see of the park. "Oh, you little shit, you!"

• • •

"Whoa! Hold it, Miss," the security guard was saying to Donna. "Where do you think you're going?"

"My daughter's here somewhere. I'm trying to find her."

"What's she wearing?"

"I'm…I'm not certain. She came with someone else. I'm trying to find them."

"If your daughter's with a friend of yours, that's no reason to jump the rails. They're here to protect you and the horses."

"Yes, I know they are, but—"

"All good, Donna?" Donnie said as he came alongside.

"These guys are stopping me from going through the tunnel."

"The horses are headed to the track. These gentlemen kept you from getting stepped on," he said smiling. "Thank you, boys. This way. We can go around."

"No, I can't—"

"She could just as easy be over this way," Donnie said as he led her away. "Let's not make a scene. Thanks again, fellas."

Donnie tried to steer his daughter through the paddock.

"I should ask them for help," Donna said.

DAVID-MICHAEL HARDING   119

"No, you shouldn't. If she's here, and you show our hand, we've lost the element of surprise. No theatrics."

"God, Dad! This is Lexy!"

"I know who it is. I'm not completely off my rocker yet."

"Then keep up at least. She's in the seats. She has to be somewhere where she can see the tote board." Donna bolted from the paddock and began to run.

· · ·

The grandstand and the clubhouse were undergoing a survey by Glass for a little girl with a big hat pulled low. She was looking left and right as she descended the step when she heard the call begin for the next race. "And me without any skin in the game. On a day when I've got the oracle sitting next to me."

The sight of the same pair of security guards who had spoken to the Chariots gave her pause. She felt for the wad of cash in her pocket. Suddenly she felt as though everyone was watching her. She was trying to see everywhere at once and walking with purpose out from beneath the stands and away from the Big Sandy all the while straining against looking obvious.

Ahead of her was the sprawling, poorly attended picnic area. Beyond that, she saw a few children at the small playground. In the midst of the running kids was one with an oversized hat.

"You little shit. I'll—"

Mrs. Glass looked behind her at the sprawling complex as though someone had tapped her on the shoulder. If The Book himself wasn't in one of those fancy rooms or private box seats, she thought, it was a safe bet some of his friends were. It was time to fold 'em, as Kenny

Rogers sang, and get outa Dodge, but first she had to snatch her handicapper off the back of a merry-go-round pony.

· · ·

The Book caught up to Donna at the base of the grandstand. She was scouring the seats, coiled like a spring. Donnie turned and joined her, asking the obvious question that had an equally obvious answer. "Anything?"

"No."

"It was a long shot."

"Let's split up. Do you have your phone?"

"Yes."

"I'll take the clubhouse. You go through the apron and the stands."

Before he could offer an opinion, Donna was gone.

Donnie took one flight of the stairs down and spilled out on the wide asphalt that was the cheapest seat in the house. The apron held a collection of the stereotypical suspects one expected to find meandering about the rail of a horse track amid the flotsam and jetsam of discarded tickets and dreams. The incredulous looks of disbelief that bounced from the tote board to the bettor's notes on racing forms and back again were universal as grieving players saw their picks melt away. Eyes moved: from the board, to their programs, to the tickets in their hands. Repeat. Board, notes, tickets. Repeat. The action was a ritual, both symbolic and predictable, as if done with enough effort and concentration, the number on one of the stops would change and show a winner overlooked on the pass a mere three seconds before. It never did. But an inch down the page—only minutes into the future—a chance at redemption beckoned, holding out the gleaming promise of treasures and glory to be found at the payout window.

Donnie weaved about the apron and looked up and across the thousands of mostly empty green seats in the stands. He didn't see Alexis. Instead, he saw wrinkled and worn dress shirts, frayed at the collars. He noted that if gauged by racetracks, an observer would discern that fedoras were making a comeback in men's fashion.

The apron was soon cleared. No Alexis. While Donna finished off the clubhouse and worked around the expensive and empty box seats, Donnie went back up the stairs and on to the highest reaches of the grandstand.

•   •   •

Mrs. Glass had Lexy's hand, plenty tight, and was making her way briskly across the grass toward the exit.

"Left me scared to death thinking some pedophile had kidnapped you. What's the matter with you, running off like that?"

"I was looking for a hotdog."

"Oh, you misplayed that one. I had a hotdog for you—a snow cone too. I gave them to another kid when I had to go looking for you. She appreciated them. Not like someone else I know."

"Can I get one now? Now that you've saved me from kidnappers?"

"I should hardly think not! I ought to drop you right off at reform school. Save your poor mother the aggravation."

"Can I call her now? I want to call my mother."

"You can talk to her tonight. Right now, we have to catch the train back to the city."

"I barely got to see the horses! We could at least have sat on the apron so I could watch them at the rail."

A few newly-broke early retirees from the sport of kings were the only witnesses to a little girl in apparent need of a nap going out the gate.

"My, but you are a sassy bandit. Here I take you out of the hotel, like you wanted, and what's the thanks? Sass!"

"This isn't fair!"

"Well, life ain't fair. I'll tell you all about it someday. I'm an expert."

• • •

In the upper grandstand, Donnie had his hands buried in his pockets and was wandering up the stairs though it was clear no one was there to be looked over. A few rows from the top he saw evidence that at least one person had taken the crow's nest view of the afternoon's races. A program and a DRF was on the floor in front of a seat along with something else that caught his eye. He nudged the program with the toe of his shoe and eased it off a book of sudoku puzzles.

He had the book, the program, and the DRF in his hands before he realized. In that same instance, he spun away from the top of the grandstand and began looking for Lexy with a rejuvenated interest. As he jerked back and forth, looking everywhere at once, he snatched out his phone and began to call his daughter, but stopped.

Instead, Donnie looked through the groups of people below him on the apron and others well up the track, milling about in anticipation of the next race. Beyond the white rail in front of them, horses were walking and prancing the parade to the starting gate. If Alexis was nearby, she'd be staring those horses down. Donnie couldn't find her, and if he did, what then?

If Alexis was found, the ruckus generated trackside would draw an obvious and ugly close to his working with Donna. The numbers would go back to being errors, money would be lost, and Vegas would once again be looking to The Book for answers. The result could put Alexis at the point of the spear again. For now, it seemed she was enjoying the horses on a pleasant summer afternoon.

He was still holding Lexy's book when he went to the far end of the grandstand and looked over the railing. Below him was the roof of the covered walkway that ran from the park to the nearby Long Island Railroad station. The station was at the end of a spur dedicated solely to Belmont Park. The trains ran when the horses ran. When the racing meets ended, the trains stopped.

Like everything associated with a city of millions, the depot was huge. Eight sets of rail lines converged around four massive concrete loading docks. Even on a non-stakes day like today, a little girl would be tough to pick out, especially if her handlers didn't want her to be.

Donnie was obliged to share what he'd found. If he said nothing, the day might pass with only an improbable possibility that Alexis had sparked the wager they'd seen from right here in the grandstand. Conversely, drawing Donna's attention to the puzzle book could alleviate, momentarily, a mother's concerns that her daughter was alive and well, as Donnie had promised.

Then again, Lexy's confirmed presence at the track might encourage a continued search that could culminate in a short-lived happy reunion if she was found. The real results of a premature reunion of mother and daughter wouldn't reveal its ugly side until the numbers began to fail again. Then the leverage of what Alexis, or even Donna, represented, might carry them into a deadly situation where they were no longer able to enjoy Belmont on sunny days.

It was complex, but Donnie was good at complex. He leaned on the railing and looked at the people getting on and off the trains in the distance and considered his choices. Whether it was to be a decision with endless variables and incalculable ramifications that might test his own strange skill, or a head-in-the-sand no decision, the stakes were about to get ramped up considerably. On the sidewalk well below him, walking away from the racetrack toward the trains were Mrs. Glass and Alexis.

The list of reasons to either yell or hide were instantly tallied and found to be balanced. Donnie neither ducked nor hollered. He continued leaning on the railing and watched as Mrs. Glass led Alexis away from the horses and her mother, to the station and the invisibility that waited when a person stepped off a railroad platform in a city of eight million people.

When Alexis went up a covered stairway and was momentarily out of sight, Donnie dialed his daughter again, but this time let it go through.

"Do you have her?"

"No, but she was here."

"How do you know?"

"Meet me in the upper level of the grandstand."

Donna was already moving.

"How do you know she was there?"

"I found a book that I think belongs to her." Donnie was looking for his daughter instead of Alexis. When he saw Donna come into the section, he waved. "To your right and up. Near the top."

"I see you," Donna said and disconnected.

Donnie held up the sudoku book as his daughter came up the last steps two at a time. "Remember sudoku? I mentioned it the other day."

Donna took the book as though she might feel her daughter's aura or pick up a vibe on where she was.

"I have those all over the house," Donnie continued.

"Okay, but these are for sale everywhere. They might even sell them here."

"Look inside."

Donna did just that. "Done in ink. No mistakes."

"And my printing. This was mine. Mrs. Glass must have taken it."

Like her father had done, Donna spun away and scanned the park as far as she could see. "I've been through all the restaurants. It's not that crowded. Where'd you go, Lexy?" Donna went to the end of the seats where her father had been and leaned out as far as she could over the railing. "Can you see the playground from here?"

Donnie didn't answer the question but walked in Donna's footsteps up near her on the railing. He was looking ahead to the train station platforms. "If they cashed out after that special, we could have missed her," he said as he surreptitiously glanced at his watch and also measured Mrs. Glass's steps to the train.

The thought led Donna to look off toward the trains.

A couple hundred yards away, standing on a platform with a dozen other commuters they could make out a woman with a girl, both wearing big baseball hats that, though intended to disguise, now made them stand out.

"Do you see the woman with the hat?" Donnie asked slowly as he pointed. "With the little girl? Getting ready to board? That look like Mrs. Glass to you?"

"And Lexy. Lexy! *Lexy!*" Donna was shouting with her hands as a megaphone. "We're too far."

Donna shot from the railing like she'd been whipped coming into the top of the stretch. Her father was in tow, keeping up better than before. Donnie didn't waste much needed breath trying to stop his daughter. They went down to the lower grandstand and out the doors onto the covered bridge to the trains. Donna's sprint would have made any speed horse proud. When she came to the rotunda halfway to the platform, she yelled back over her shoulder. "Which track was it?"

"Second stairs on your right!"

Donna vaulted down the long staircase to the platform, but was only in time to see the tail of the train moving away up the track. She chased it out of frustration to the end of the platform and stopped there, jumping, flailing, fretting, and nearly leaping on the tracks in a pointless attempt to run it down.

18

"Heartbreaking," Frank said as Donnie recounted a fragmented version of the story from Belmont over Scotch in his paneled office.

"That sucks," Nicky echoed. "Another minute and you'd have had her."

"Looks that way."

Gabriel had been quiet throughout but spoke up respectfully. "What's the plan, Book? Any changes?"

"No, stay the course. That train was headed to Penn Station. Does that help with tracking that phone call?"

"It doesn't hurt, but it doesn't help much either. We have it in Manhattan. It's a fifteen-, twenty-minute walk from Penn Station to Grand Central—the Manhattan bullseye."

"From Grand Central, you're anywhere in the city," Frank added. "Or you could grab a bus or a hack from Penn."

"True enough," Gabriel continued. "But I've been leaning hard toward the Deuce somewhere since the beginning. Big hotels. Lots of foot traffic. Five thousand cabbies. The Deuce has always been a good spot to hole up and get lost in. It was true back when, and it's true today."

"Boss?" Nicky said with some hesitation. "We sent some of the fellas from the basement to 42nd. They've done a once-over on all the big places. I know it's a reach. Who knows what name the rooms might be under, but we have to look, don't you think?"

"That's good, Nicky. Thank you."

"The tougher part is getting a look at everybody," Frank added. "Through the tracks and the book, we've got eyes in most places already—bellhops, desk clerks, waitresses. If someone matches Lexy's description, we'll know about it."

Donnie took a deep breath and examined his desk, as though sincerely looking for something. "What else? What else do we have?"

Other eyes followed Donnie's around the desktop.

"What else, boss?"

"To locate Donna. Are we looking at anything else?"

The men in the room eyed at each other and back to Chariot. No one had anything to offer, and they delicately told him as much.

"That's all right, men. Keeping your ears open will suffice. Something will break."

"Nick's idea will keep the guys we brought in busy," Frank said as he settled in his usual perch. "You want me bring in more for the house?"

"What guys?"

Frank looked around the room for help. There was none coming. "The guys you had me get. You wanted a few extra warm bodies around. Nick's got them downtown. You want more?"

Donnie was lost, knew it, and tried to hide it. "That's fine. Something will break."

Frank fidgeted in his seat. "I'm sorry, boss. Is that fine, as in, 'get more,' or fine, as in 'we're straight?'"

Chariot didn't have an answer. The room stayed quiet, but eyes were jumping and wondering. Something had to be said, even if it was wrong.

"Sit tight," Donnie blurted. "Something will break. Something will break."

"Sure thing, boss."

Donnie tried to ease away from the abyss and straightened papers on his desk that didn't need it, but he was in trouble. He looked at Gabriel, lost for a name. Nicky's face was a stranger. Only Frank was familiar, but the look on Donnie's face hid the fact and men afraid of little were suddenly anxious.

Unencumbered in youthful ignorance, Nicky went out on the thin ice. "You all right, Mr. Chariot?"

"Quite. What is it?"

"Nothing. I was wondering if you were feeling okay. You looked—"

"Hey, boss," Frank jumped in. "I had a thought. I haven't run it by Gabriel here, but what's your take on seeing if we can tap a few phones? Can we tap a couple of phones, Gabe?"

"Maybe. Not easy. There might be a tech geek who could be bent in our direction for a price. Who do you want to give a listen to?"

"What do you say, Book? It'd be nice to know what Baron is up to these days, wouldn't it? And his flunky, DeSeti. I've liked him for this from day one. What do you say?"

"Say?"

"To tapping phones."

"Tap phones?"

Frank tried to give Donnie room to recover, but it was immediately clear there might not be that much room available or the ability to capture the chance that was offered.

Nicky didn't realize it, but he was hurting the cause. "That dope, Junior DeSeti, I like him for it more than his old man. That kid hates you, Mr. Chariot, for that car squeeze."

Donnie looked around his desk and the room, questions all over his face. "What's wrong with the car?"

"Nothing. That thing is sweet, but you can bet that jackass Junior's still pissed. He'd do something dumb like this. He's an addict. His brains are fried."

"Junior's too damn dumb to pull this off," Frank said.

Donnie echoed for no other reason than to echo. "Junior's too damn dumb."

"Maybe, but he's high most of the time and always jacked up."

Gabriel pointed at Nicky. "The kid makes an interesting point. We were all young once. Impetuous. So, Junior DeSeti isn't the brains of the scheme. That's where his old man comes in. Julian gains a lot of favor with Vegas if he can reel you in, Donnie. He cooks up this snatch-grab stunt and his punk kid is the muscle. You said you liked the old man for it, Frank. What do you think? Both of those DeSetis. With the blessing of Vegas."

"Works for me. What do you say, Book?"

"Works for me," came another subdued echo.

Frank was up like a shot. "Okay. Gabe, put your foot in somebody's ass on those taps. Start with Julian. Nick, you and me are headed back to Belmont and see some people. You should meet them anyway. If anybody takes the girl there again, we're gonna know about it.

"Book, we'll leave you to work your magic on tomorrow's numbers. Sound like a plan?"

Donnie's eyes were glazed over. "Sound like a plan," he mumbled.

Frank was herding his two partners to the door. "Let's go, girls. We got shit to do." At the door, he snapped his fingers. "I'll be right out, Nick. I forgot something. Hey, find Li'l Donnie and send her in, would you?"

"Will do," Nicky said as he looked over Frank's shoulder into the office. Donnie Chariot had his hands in his lap looking like he'd fall asleep if he wasn't so scared. "Frank?" Nicky whispered. "The boss don't look—"

"I know," Frank whispered as he pushed Nicky out the door. "Keep your mouth shut and get Li'l Donnie. Quick."

• • •

When Nicky went toward the kitchen, Gabriel followed him. Donna wasn't there. Nicky went by the platters of sliced sandwich meat, trays of ziti and meatballs, and mountains of rolls, to maintain his search.

"Never thought you'd pass a sandwich with your name on it," Gabriel jabbed.

"I'm good. We got a lot to do."

"We do at that. And it's no easier with the old man struggling like he is."

That brought Nicky up short. "You saw that?"

"Couldn't miss it. He been drinking hard?"

"I don't think much. He likes the high-octane stuff, but I've never seen him falling down hammered, you know?"

"Well, no one could fault him if he did now."

"What do you guys think? I mean, as a cop? Will they get the little girl back?"

Gabriel was making a sandwich as he talked. "Normally, I'd say no. Kidnappers don't like witnesses. This being a kid, though, could work to her advantage. Kids are flighty, like yearlings. Never know what they're going to do next. Flighty, but not too big a threat. The people who put the snatch on her are probably just giving her ice cream or whatever she wants to keep her entertained and quiet."

"Like taking her to the races."

"But now, that's a funny thing. The racetrack."

"Why?"

"Going out in public like that."

"It's not like there's posters on every corner," Nicky said. "No one even knows she's missing."

"Chariot sure knows and where's his business? That track. Risky move taking that kid there. I haven't figured out why they'd do that. I sure as hell wouldn't."

"What I don't get is that damn cook. I talked to that bitch every day. I never thought she'd get wound up in something like this."

"Maybe nobody wound her up. Maybe she wound herself up. What if she did all this on her own? The kid knows her. She'd go along, no problem. Nobody calling the police or recording it on their phone. Easiest kidnapping ever."

"Why would Glass do that?"

"Who knows? People get strange ideas. But I doubt she pulled this off by herself. If she did, and was looking for ransom, there'd be a demand already. No, this is tied to the horses. Glass is likely just a patsy and history tells us how things work out for patsies."

"Oswald?"

"Glad to see you read some."

"Being a patsy makes for a short career."

"You called it," Gabriel said as he bit into a massive sandwich.

"Oh well," Nicky shrugged. "Then don't grab The Book's granddaughter. Hey, I gotta find Li'l Donnie. See ya later."

19

"Are you sure, Dad? You look...tired, I guess. It's been a tough day. Why not go lay down a few minutes?"

Donnie didn't answer, but Donna was right about his look. It was hard to place. Even a neurologist would have struggled.

Donnie's eyes were not a vacant, unseeing, unknowing stare. They were capturing the world as ever, but after sight, a breakdown was taking place. Running with what little he had told her, Donna looked deeper, slightly fearful of the specter that walked a closing distance behind her father's eyes. She was absolutely certain her father knew her. Beyond that however, Donna sensed he did not know exactly what to do with the fact that he had indeed recognized his daughter.

Donnie's eyes were slightly wider than normal. It wasn't the pupils, but the eyes themselves. Wide, as if to see more, even if what was seen couldn't be fully processed. They were also slightly jumpy if you could catch it, and set in a face that, like the eyes, was wide awake. He was taking in everything he possibly could, as if to compensate with more information for the inability to understand any of it.

For the first time since her recent reentry to his home and life, Donna looked closely at her father. Days before, she couldn't see him if she stared right at him, such was the virulence clouding her eyes. Now she set aside everything—including Alexis—and looked at him clearly. What she saw was fear.

"Dad? Do you want to go lay down? C'mon. I'll help you."

"I think he's having a stroke," Frank whispered.

"Come lay down, Dad."

"No."

"You don't want to lay down?"

"No."

"I think you're tired. It's been a long week."

"I'd like a cold beer."

"You don't even drink beer."

"Can I have a cold beer, or not?"

"You can have a beer." Donna looked to Nicky, but he was already headed to the door, happy for the reprieve from watching a strong man falling.

"What are you two staring at?" Donnie lashed out.

Frank headed for the door.

"Where are you going?"

"I need to get a drink, is all."

"Get me one, will you?" the Book said. "You want a drink, Donnie?"

"No, but thank you."

"We're good, Frank," Donnie continued. "You know what? We're going to be working in here for a while. Close the door, would you please? No interruptions."

"Sure thing, boss."

Frank stepped out and closed the door as Nicky came up with the beer. Rather than give way to Nicky and the delivery, Frank took the beer and helped himself to an immense taste that drained half the bottle.

In the office, Donnie echoed his daughter. "We've had a long day. We still have to put together the numbers for tomorrow's races. Happy we don't do harness or cricket. You know why people don't bet on those much?"

"Too crooked?"

"Too crooked," Donnie kept on and focus crept back in his eyes over his voice. "Most have the fix in. Holy Christ, jai-alai is the worst. I took action on jai-alai a hundred years ago. They were out of control. Made me look like a choir boy. But I'm no choir boy, am I?"

"Few people are."

"I was once. I ever tell you about it?"

"Many times."

"I liked to ring those little bells. They had a real pretty sound."

"I can do the numbers tonight. You should rest," Donna said as she felt her father regaining himself. She went to the couch and sat down a bit too hard.

"Maybe it's you who needs a nap," Donnie said.

"I'd take one."

"Go ahead. I'm feeling pretty good. You can go over my numbers after."

Donna dropped her head back on the couch. "I'm going to call your doctor."

"No need."

"Yes, there is. There's lots of need. My daughter's been taken. My father's losing his mind—"

"I'm losing my memory, not my mind."

"That's a subtle distinction, I should think. What's your mind if not memories?"

"I'm fine. That is, I'm healthy. It's strange though. Sometimes I can feel it. It's the disease. Then I try to think or remember something and it's gone. Just gone. Like it was never there or it's behind a curtain I can't quite get to stay open."

Donna's head was still back. Her eyes were closed and words trickled out unthinking. "There's plenty I wish I could forget."

If she thought her father was no longer lucid, was over the hill, had gone around the bend, was a candidate for an old folks' home or ready to be institutionalized, she was wrong.

"No, you don't. Don't say that. Good and bad. You are today what the past has made you. When the disease has a hold of me, it is the greatest fear anyone could have. It's indescribable. Beyond fear. Terror.

A terrifying aloneness that separates you from the world and even from yourself.

"When you're alone, kiddo, you still have your thoughts, plans, dreams, and those memories—the good ones and those bad ones you want desperately to lose. When I'm alone, and this thing slips up on me, there's nothing. I can breathe and see, but that's all. I don't know where I am, who I'm with, where I've been in life, or where I'm going. And the worst thing is I don't even know myself. I'm a stranger surrounded by strangers in a strange place. You don't know it, or them, or if even you are good or bad. Everything is a sluggish, damp fog you can't see through. There's no way to measure any of these things—people, places, yourself. No yardstick of memory to put the present against. You're only alive, and barely.

"No, honey, keep the bad memories. When you have nothing, not even yourself, a bad memory would be a gift."

Donna lifted her head. "But is that numbers thing we have, is that what you really want to have? When things, you know, sort of slip sideways?"

"Maybe. Once, I thought yes. I don't know. My work has always been important to me—more than important."

"More important than family."

He wouldn't and couldn't disagree.

"That's fair. You're right. It sounds misguided, but those are the facts. I never mistreated you or your mother. You never wanted for anything. And I did spend time with you."

"At the track. Card games in the back of some seedy social club." She dropped her head back to the couch. "I knew all the casinos in Atlantic City." She laughed. "My friends would reel off stories of the fun they had at Disney and Epcot. I regaled them with tales from Harrah's and Ceasar's."

"C'mon. Whose stories were better? Who really cares about a six-foot rat? How many of your friends ever got to see a casino? All those bright lights? All that action?"

"None did, and for good reason. It's illegal to take kids in those places! How did you get me in anyway?"

"You weren't on the casino floor very often."

"Always the master at justifying whatever suits you."

Donnie dodged the barb. "Plus, you got to see all the top shows. How many kids can say that?"

"Yes, I did. I saw Sinatra. It's surprising how little that can mean to an eight-year-old."

Donnie turned his palms face up as he resigned his last defense. "It was front row."

They both laughed a little and waited. Each was content to let any discussion on their mutual past that contained the semblance of a smile bask in the fleeting sunshine a few moments longer. Donnie broke the spell by vigorously rubbing some color back into his face. "We need to get started."

"How are you feeling?"

"Fine."

"I'm going to make an appointment with your doctor anyway."

"Suit yourself. I saw him a short time ago. Nothing's changed."

"How do you know?"

"It's *my* brain."

"When did you see him?"

"About a month ago."

"When?"

I don't remem—Oh, bad answer."

"I'm calling."

"Whatever you say," Donnie said as he reached out and pulled a chair closer to his and patted the seat.

20

After cruising around Manhattan for almost an hour—back tracking, running red lights, and cutting through parking lots to lose any tails—Gabriel jumped up on the FDR headed south, crossed into Brooklyn, and got on the Expressway to Bensonhurst.

He parked in a narrow street near the DeSeti home and yelled to Julian when he saw him in his driveway. "When you going to move uptown?"

"You sound like my wife. She wants to go to Staten Island."

"It'd be better than this," Gabriel said as he got out of his car and casually crossed the street.

"You're both crazy. I live in heaven. This was my father's house. Long paid for. I'll leave it to my boy."

"Your boy...I hope he lives long enough. He won't if he keeps making enemies with powerful people," Gabriel said as the two shook hands. "I understand he's not much of a gambler either."

"You heard that, huh? What else have you been hearing?"

"Lots of things. We'd better talk. But not on the phone." Gabriel smiled.

"Not on the phone?"

"No, I wouldn't say much on the phone these days. Chariot's interested in your thoughts on his granddaughter."

The men walked to the back of the house and were going inside before Julian stopped them both. "He can listen all day. I don't know anything about that."

"How about Junior? What's he know?"

"Nothing. About this or anything else."

"You sure, Julian? It's going to go real bad if he's behind this. You'll look silly to Baron if it wasn't you but your boy who put the squeeze on Chariot. Then again, if you did, Chariot isn't going to think it's silly at all."

"Chariot won't think it's too funny you working for me either. You better hope this comes off with me smelling like a rose."

"I don't know about a rose, but I can pick a winner as good as the next guy. And what I just saw of Chariot tells me that he ain't it. Something's wrong with him."

"What do you mean?"

"He's either sick or half in the bag on the regular. I just came from his place and you'd think he was having a stroke."

"Probably the kid missing has messed up his head."

"Could be."

"So, you throwing over your old bookie?"

"Like I said, I gotta go with the winner."

"Glad to hear it." DeSeti slapped Gabe's shoulder and steered him into the house. "Let's have a drink."

"I never turn down a free drink. But remember, I don't see much of a win in this for you if your boy is trying to break into the big leagues behind snatching that kid."

Julian looked around the back of his own home as if he might be watched. "So, Chariot wants you to tap my phone?"

"Sure does."

"Okay, let me make it easier for you. Tap Junior's instead. If that little shit is holding out on me I'll break it off in him myself."

"Wise choice."

"How come Chariot's got a hardon for me? He ought to be after Baron."

"He is. He wants him tapped too."

"Okay. Good. That's the right move. Feed me whatever you get on Baron, too."

"That's why I'm here. Oh, and to get my money."

21

Hours slipped away as the manifold of monitors cast their soft light around The Book's office. Somewhere in the shadows on the dark side of twilight, a fleeting screen from Santa Anita brought Donna from the trance that took in terabytes of data with such apparent ease. She stopped the scrolling screen and looked with a bemused expression at a revelation. As she stared, the numbers expanded and glowed in a disjointed rhythm.

"Hey, Dad? Take a look at this. I've found something, or rather, I see something. I think. I mean, I know I see it, but...come look at this."

Donna pushed away from the desk and got up. She stretched but looked back at the screen. The numbers were still signaling her. She moved further away and looked again. The numbers were glowing. "Is that monitor calibrated?"

"I suppose."

"Do you have any recognition software running behind these feeds? What's making those numbers react?"

Donnie was back at his desk and looked at the screen under Donna's scrutiny. Then he looked at his daughter. He followed a quick glance back and forth again by settling in his chair and concentrating fully on the monitor. "I don't see anything. What do you mean by reacting?"

Donna was watching but moved across the room as though slightly repulsed by what she saw. "They're kind of glowing. Radiating is a good word for it. Not all of them. Just a few."

"I'm not seeing it."

She came back to the desk in a rush. Her finger jutted into the screen too hard, and it shook under the assault. "You don't see that number right there? The pulsating?"

"I see the number, but it's the same as every other number."

Donna now stared at her father with the same intensity she had reserved for the monitor. "Stop playing. You don't see that number? That number right there. It has a higher resolution than the rest."

"Not to me. But I believe it does to you. I believe it because I used to see the same thing. I don't any longer."

Donnie began making notes on what Donna was seeing. "This one?" he said as he pointed to the number she'd indicated.

"Yes."

"Which others?"

Donna pointed quickly without speaking.

"You know what this is, kiddo? It's a special. There's a balance here—fragile—but it's there."

Donna strutted away across the room. "It's like a damn dog whistle. No one else can see it. I'm a freak. Again."

"No, you're not. It's a gift."

"For what? So I can make money for fat-cat gamblers? Some gift."

"You use it in your firm. That's not gambling."

"All business is gambling," she said as she pushed further into the room and away from the task. "What a waste."

"There is one thing you can use it for."

"What's that?"

"Bringing Alexis home."

Donna laid her head back over her shoulders and looked at the ceiling in dreadful resigned homage to her father's failing curse. It had led her daughter to be kidnapped. She felt forced to watch as an unwilling, but completely immersed player. Lexy's return was being dangled in front of her on a string that employed the curse of her father, but now it came from within herself. It rent her, spirit and soul.

"Come back to the desk," her father cajoled. "Look again. Tell me what you see."

"I don't need to. You know that. I've seen it once. What do you need to know?"

Donna reeled off the numbers that had conspired to show her a pattern no one else could see. Her father worked some of his own equations, most in his head. But for the first time since he was a child, Donnie Chariot used a pad of paper to collect and discern the final tally, and even then he wasn't certain his end of the calculation was correct.

22

Junior DeSeti slammed the trunk of the big Lincoln as Baron slid in across the back seat next to Julian. In a moment, driver, car, and passengers were meandering through the maze leading away from JFK airport. Another car carrying more luggage and bodyguards trailed behind.

Julian tapped the driver's seat in front of him. "This is my son. Junior, meet Baron. King of Las Vegas."

"How's it going?"

"Quite well, but your father exaggerates. I'm sure Steve Wynn would dispute that title. I'm a simple businessman."

"Hardly. You know, you came in earlier than last year," Julian said in an attempt at small talk.

"Did I?"

"Last year you came in Friday, the day before the race."

"I didn't know you took such a keen interest in my travel."

"You only come to town for the big race. I try to put together a good show for you. I needed to make longer hotel accommodations this time. That's all."

"I trust I haven't put you out."

"It's always a pleasure, Baron. You have a suite at the Plaza. I've compiled a list of shows you might enjoy seeing while you're in town. There's—"

"What I'd like to see is Donnie Chariot. Ask him to come to the Plaza. Tomorrow will be fine."

Julian hesitated. "Chariot? I'm sure that can be arranged."

"Does he know I'm in town?"

"Not from me if he does."

"Good. He's been doing very well again. I don't want him distracted tonight."

"What happens tonight?"

"He'll be working up the odds. I don't want to trouble him over my appearance. Being a man of honor, he would no doubt feel compelled to have me to his home or sponsor me for a dinner."

"I was going to take you to dinner myself."

"Thank you, no. I'll settle in and have dinner at the hotel. I have several friends in New York from the old days. We get together on the rare occasions I'm east. Tomorrow will suffice for Mr. Chariot."

Julian went fishing. "You think he'll be happy to see you?"

"Donnie Chariot? I should hope so. There's no reason to assume otherwise."

"No?" Julian trolled. "A few weeks ago in Vegas, you didn't have a very high opinion of him."

"A gambler's memory is only as good as the last race. The possibilities beyond the next clang of the gate erases all recollection of races that didn't go your way."

"You're a very kind sort, Baron."

"Nonsense. Kindness has no place in business. Kindness is weakness. Remember that."

"So... the change in The Book's fortune is due to the fact that other races crowd out the losses he forced on us?"

"Forced on me, Julian. You forget yourself. And yes. He seems to have turned this nonsense around. There's still a matter of what happened at Churchill, I grant you, but now that he's regained his footing, I have confidence that he'll eliminate that concern in short order."

"And loose ends? Aren't there a few details to be tidied up before Donnie Chariot is ready to break bread with you?"

Baron reined in the conversation and pivoted in the back seat of the big car.

"What would they be?"

DeSeti smiled, which made Baron uncomfortable. "I can't say. That is, I don't know. Not exactly."

"Julian, you know my disdain for loose ends."

"I do know that about you."

"And your point is?"

"That I'm prepared to help you remedy any that might be hanging around Chariot."

"There are loose ends around Donnie Chariot?"

"There may be."

"Stop talking in riddles. Speak plainly."

"I'm thinking someone—and I assume it to be you—has gotten leverage on Chariot and brought him around. If he's dropped his Dutch book, good. What I've said is that I don't know, exactly, but if you need anything done, anything else, you only have to ask."

Baron turned away and looked out the window. He caught a glimpse of the East River before the car dove beneath it and entered the Midtown Tunnel.

· · ·

Behind Baron, above the East River to the edge of Queens, Donna had recounted what the numbers had suggested. While her father labored some with his figuring, Donna moved in another direction. She was perched on the edge of the couch with a laptop rocking on her knees to the gentle prodding of its keys. She was tracking. A huntress hunting.

The prey wasn't the ambiguous number no one else could see. She was on the trail of something much more tangible in the age of digitalized fingerprints. Donna was tracking an IP address. The experience at the track and the recent revelation of her own skill confirmed to her that Alexis was behind the drop of cash that primed the race at Belmont. Now she hoped she might track the next weight-shifting bet back to her daughter.

As Donnie worked his numbers with an uncomfortable and unaccustomed pencil, Donna tapped away at the vault of the dark web. In a few minutes, she was up at his desk, the laptop dangling from one hand.

"I need more power. This thing will take an hour to get me where I want to go. I'm guessing your computers have some monsters behind them somewhere."

Donnie took a moment to be torn from his work. He looked up from beneath a frazzled brow. "How's that?"

"I need more computing power. The drive in my laptop won't cut it. In order to run what's crossing this desk, I'd bet there's a dedicated set of mainframes somewhere humming along just for you."

"A bet," Donnie said, as near a question as was possible without his voice actually rising.

"Dad. Your computers. They must have a private network, right? You're not pulling all this through a router from the phone company."

"There's cables that run…." Donnie pushed back from his desk and pointed to a colorful collection of neatly bundled wires disappearing into the floor. "Those cables. I think they go to the basement."

"If they're in the basement, they can stay there, but that's good. Which one of these can I use?"

"All of them."

"I only need one."

Donna set her laptop on the floor and pulled up her chair again. In an instant a wide monitor flashed to black with a single blinking icon reminiscent of the earliest days of computers. While the language did not look so terribly different, it was more specific and much more powerful. It treated all manner of security like an onion before a laser-guided peeler. Layers of security fell away in rapid succession without tripping a signal or leaving a trace that there'd been a breach.

With the massive computing power of her father's mainframes in the basement, it was only minutes before she had rows and reams of IP addresses scrolling by at breakneck speed. Meanwhile the gift or curse came into its own, like a muscle growing stronger with use. She entered a specific set—her own IP address which Lexy's iPad routinely shared. Then she handed it over to the dark web to work its unique black magic in conjunction and collusion with her own rather mystical skills to locate the most recent IP address associated with that iPad.

"What have you got there?" Donnie asked as he pointed to the wide screen.

"Addresses. IP addresses. Where inputs are coming from. What computers. We're going to track Lexy if she bumps the numbers for that race—the one you call 'a special' at Santa Anita."

"You think that's what she'll do?"

"Not normally, no. She never looked at races or odds or any of this stuff before all this happened." Then Donna corrected herself. "At least as far as I knew, but no doubt you taught her plenty."

"I probably mentioned a few things between ice cream cones at the park."

"Belmont Park. I know. Anyway, somebody has got her started in earnest. They probably made a little money on that race the other day. I'm thinking they'll have her looking for the same thing we just found. If she sees it, like we have—"

"Like *you* have."

"They'll have her bump it at race time. Unless they're going to drive to California overnight so she can see the tote board at Santa Anita, they'll have to do it over the web. If they use Lexy's iPad, we should be able to narrow down where she is."

"That was about three pretty strong 'ifs' in a row," Donnie said. "If she sees it. If they use her iPad. If—"

"Have you got something else?" Donna said as she continued stalking through the high grass of the dark web's savannah.

The expression on her father's face changed like a high cloud over the moon. Skepticism morphed through concern to an odd nervousness that fumbled to find a foundation.

"Does that work? That is, can you tell where she is from that?"

"I'm not certain, but we're going to give it a helluva try."

"What's your plan if you locate her?"

Donna's fingers went still and the keys quiet. "We're going to go get her."

23

"You said we could go to the park." Alexis was berating Mrs. Glass with an enthusiasm left unbridled by the knowledge that she could manage her caretaker by managing horse races.

"I don't know that I said any such thing."

"Well, you did." Alexis punctuated the declaration by tossing her iPad across the bed. The device was her most valuable possession, made even more so since the door to her posh prison cell in the Grand Hyatt Hotel closed behind her, but she feigned otherwise. Pushing it further away with her foot, accentuated her resolve. For her part, Mrs. Glass was being outwitted and reeling under the pressure of a seven-year-old savant.

"I'll make a deal with you."

"No more deals."

"Here now. What kind of way is that to act?"

Alexis pulled her feet up and rolled over on the bed leaving her back to the question and the asker.

"Okay then," Mrs. Glass said slowly as she got up from the foot of the bed and brushed the comforter flat. "If you don't want to call your mother, we don't have to."

Resolve in children has the shelf life of an ice cream cone in the sun. Lexy's personal conviction in the matter of Mrs. Glass vanished at the sound of the word *mother*. It was an unfair ploy, perhaps even a hollow negotiating ruse, but for Glass, it had the desired effect.

Alexis spun from her fetal position and was up on her knees clutching at Mrs. Glass's waist and words.

"Deal! Deal! I'll be good. Let's call!"

"Now, doesn't that feel better? Who wants to be down in the mouth all the while? What's the point in it?"

"Let's call," Alexis was near shouting as she bounded from the bed. "I'll get your phone."

"Hold on. I didn't say just now."

Alexis was already at the bottom of the big purse. By touch, she knew keys from wallet from makeup and medicine. She yanked out the phone.

"My, but aren't you the grabby one? You know better than to go rummaging about in other people's things. My purse is no place for you. You know that."

"I was trying to help."

"You don't need to try so hard. I'm a fair hand at finding my own phone. Thank you very much."

"Let's call. Let's call."

"Don't get your hopes up."

Mrs. Glass cued up a call. Alexis reached for the phone, but Glass pulled it away. "I'll turn her over as soon as I know who it is. I'd be a poor nanny who let you talk to strangers. What kind of person would that make me out to be?"

The phone kept ringing. And again. And once more.

"See there?" Mrs. Glass scolded. "All that fuss and she's too busy to answer the phone. Just as I told you. You got yourself worked into a tizzy on no account."

The phone had rung several more times. Mrs. Glass held it down and disconnected.

"Awww, we could have left a message," Alexis said as she began to tear up.

"We'll try again later. I told you we might not raise her. Didn't I tell you?"

"Yes."

"Okay then. What shall we do? How about a bite to eat? What's your pleasure?"

Tears were coming in earnest. "I'm not hungry," Alexis said as she plopped down and rolled back into her ball to the far side of the bed.

"Stop this foolishness. I told you she like as not would be busy. You built yourself up for a fall, you did."

"I want to talk to my mom."

"Well, you can't. Not just now."

"I want to talk to my mother!"

"Settle down, for—"

"*I want to talk to her!*"

"Good lord! Hold on there." Mrs. Glass paced away from the crying and screaming. She had the phone out a second time. "You collect yourself. Find us a good race so we can earn our keep while we wait for your mother to wrap up her work. Then she'll be home. Lickety-split. The sooner the better, suits me."

Mrs. Glass went in her room through the shared door and closed it on the racket and Alexis without apology. She was calling as soon as the door closed. In the Chariot mansion, Donnie's phone was ringing in his jacket pocket.

The Book saw Mrs. Glass's name on the ID. He looked sideways at Donna who was deeply entrenched in her cyber-hunt.

"Yes?" he said as a soft answer.

"The girl is crying her face off for her mother. She wants to talk to her. Pronto. Can you manage that?"

"I can," Donnie said slowly. "We'll be brief. Please put her on."

Donna came away from the computer when she heard her father's words.

Mrs. Glass opened the door and carried the phone to Lexy's bed. "I've got your mother on the line."

"No you don't."

"I swear it. You can only chat a sec. She's busy. Don't saddle her with all your nonsense. We're getting on fine. You'll see her soon and tell her all about it."

Everything was near frozen in Chariot's office as Donna held her hands up, slow and shaky, to take the phone.

"It's Alexis," Donnie said as a caution. "Don't question her as to where she is. They're listening and it will only raise issues. Can you do that, kiddo?"

Donna nodded quickly and shook loose tears that were already welling up as she took the phone.

"Lexy?"

"Mom?"

"Hi, sweetheart. Are you okay?"

"I'm good. How are you?"

"I'm real good now that I got to talk to you."

"What are you doing?"

"I'm working, honey." Donna hunched over the phone, pressing it hard against her face as though to get closer to her daughter. "What have you been doing?"

"Playing a little. Mostly watching movies. I have pizza a lot. Mrs. Glass says you said it was okay. Is that okay? If you don't want me to eat so much pizza, I won't."

"No, that's fine. Do what Mrs. Glass tells you. Stay with her. Don't go off with anybody else. Can you do that?"

"Yes."

"Are you...have you...are you doing anything special today?"

Donna cringed at her own words as Alexis asked her caretaker.

"Are we doing anything special today?"

"I'll have to check my itinerary," Mrs. Glass smirked.

"We have to check something first."

"Are you feeling okay?"

"When are you coming home?"

"Me? Umm...I think real soon."

"But when?"

"I'm not sure, honey…umm…you know the big horse race? It's called the Belmont Stakes. It's just a few days away. I'll be home then."

"Can we go?"

"Maybe. I'll try."

"We went there the other day to see the horses. I picked the winners."

"You did? Good for you. Was it fun?"

"Kind of. I didn't get to see the horses that much."

"Are you going—I mean, you keep go—keep picking winners. And I'll try to do the same and when we're back together I'll take you to see the horses and we can stay all day."

"When?"

"As soon as we can. You keep picking the winners for now. Can you do that?"

"I guess so."

"Good."

"Okay, hot stuff," Mrs. Glass interrupted. "It's time to say good-bye there."

"I have to go now. Can I call you again?"

"Absolutely. Any time."

"Will you answer?"

"I'll try very hard. I love you, honey. Be good. You'll be home soon. I promise."

"I love you, Mommy."

"Love you, too."

Mrs. Glass took the phone and hung up without a word.

"That was real sweet. You gonna keep a rein on yourself now?"

"Yes, ma'am."

"Good. You want to pick out a race for poor Mrs. Glass now?"

"My mom told me to. We're going to watch the horses when she gets home."

"Now you're talking," Mrs. Glass said as she scooped up the iPad and spun it through the air like a playing card onto the bed near Alexis. Glass rubbed her hands together, heating up. "Let's get to it."

• • •

"Can your friend trace that?"

"I'll get him right on it," Donnie said, taking his phone back from his daughter. "Will that impact what you're trying to do?"

"No." She motioned to the screen as though it was currently in the way. "This is deep geolocation. It tracks Lexy's IP address. Dark web stuff."

"I don't understand a thing you just said."

"It doesn't matter. It won't be perfect. Might not even work. Maybe it will be close and help with the trace on the call or vice versa." Donna returned to the screen she'd been engaging, hoping it would provide a distraction. It didn't. "Jesus Christ, Dad. Someone has my baby...."

Donna didn't collapse in tears. They were running unchecked to be sure, but she stayed focused on the monitor, though she didn't ask anything of it and had yet to move. "They took my girl and I can't do anything about it."

"Yes, you can. We set those odds and find those special races. She'll be home safe."

"We don't know that."

Donnie got up and hugged his daughter from the side. If asked then and there, against ten thousand dollars, neither could have recalled the last time they'd hugged, and the poor recollection had nothing to do with Donnie's disease.

"Of course, we do," he said as he rubbed her arms and pulled her tight. "She's safe and healthy with someone we know. We saw her at the track. Now you've talked to her. She's fine and we're nearly there. Let's push on to the end. C'mon, kiddo. Let's finish strong."

"Finish strong?" Donna said as she broke the embrace. "It's not a race, Dad."

"It sort of is. And we're coming into the top of the stretch."

If there was an answer, it took the form of Donna pulling herself painfully back to the computer. She brushed fresh tears from her cheeks and locked her eyes on the screen. If this was a race, as her father suggested, Donna would take the attitude of a headstrong charger who had the bit between her teeth. There would be no reining her in now, and at the wire, when this was over, it was even money that someone was going to get run over, stomped, bit, and kicked.

When Donna, changing her lead as she rounded to the top of the stretch, began typing madly, Donnie excused himself with no fanfare. "I'm going to reach out to Gabriel."

Outside the office, Donnie looked up and down the wide hallway of the mansion. Not yet content with the depth of privacy, he plumbed further until he found himself in a small anteroom that on other days in the estate's life would have served as the music room. He closed the wide double doors and walked to the furthest corner, pulling out his phone yet again.

He dialed a familiar number, scarcely looking.

"That was a dangerous thing to do. What's going on there?"

He waited, listening, but had little interest in the response.

24

Back in The Book's office, Donna found herself drawn to the window. Captured in its frame, Nicky was pacing at the front gate between the big shepherds. Donna discovered she was in the midst of unabashedly examining him for traits that would prove helpful in the return of her daughter. He looked strong—that would be helpful. Good balance—more a boxer than dancer, but a plus. There were likely other traits her father had recognized, or he wouldn't have hired him. Loyalty would have been paramount. The other things her father required of men made Nicky less attractive as a man, but more attractive as a rescuer of little girls. Still, the last thought that dashed through her mind as a car approached was that Nicky was handsome.

The visitor was Gabriel. Donna returned to the desk and her manipulating of the dark web as Nicky escorted the seasoned detective up the stone steps.

Though she anticipated the knock on her father's office door, she wasn't pleased with the interruption and was quick to pounce.

"Miss Chariot?" Nicky said as he stepped in with Gabriel in tow and noticed The Book was not in his office. "Where's your father?"

"Shouldn't you know that, not me? Perhaps you should review your job description."

"Yes, ma'am."

"He just stepped out. He lives in this room, so I suspect he'll return momentarily."

"You mind if I wait?" Gabriel asked.

"Suit yourself."

Gabriel stuck his hands in his pockets and began reading the titles of books that lined the walls. For his part, Nicky examined the books with him, absorbing Gabriel's whispered comments on various titles.

"Were you able to trace that call?" Donna asked without looking up.

"Manhattan. We've been scouring the big hotels along 42nd to start."

"We had that much the other day. The second call didn't help narrow it down?"

"What second call?"

Donna's fingers stopped their searching.

"We received a call—an hour ago. Maybe less. My father was trying to reach you."

Gabriel reached for his phone and scrolled through any messages or missed calls. "I don't see anything."

She was up and headed toward the door. "Jesus, he probably forgot before he got out of the room." She stopped and returned to the desk as she waved Nicky toward the door. "Go find him. Do your job. He's probably howling at the goddamn moon somewhere."

Nicky did as commanded, but when he opened the door Donnie spilled in.

"Thank you, Nicky," The Book said as he saw Gabriel just beyond. "I've been trying to call you. Answer your phone."

"Hasn't rang."

"We had another call."

"That's what I heard," Gabriel said as he pointed to Donna who had her head back down in her work.

"Can you trace it?"

"I can try it. The process triangulates off nearby towers. It'd be great on some wheat field in Kansas, but in a city like New York, it's not that precise."

"Donna's working an angle that might help. What did you call it, Donnie?"

The familial nickname went down sideways, but she'd take it for now. It wasn't worth the time or energy to rebuff him. "Geolocation. I have Lexy's normal IP address. I'm cross-referencing for where she logs on now. That should tell us where she is."

Gabriel threw out a question. "How do you know she's on at all?"

Donnie wasn't quite sure. "She's a kid. Playing games, I suppose—"

"We know for sure," Donna corrected her father. "She's been watching the races at Belmont, probably others as well. I've got software in the dark web that can find her. I'm getting close."

"How close are you now?"

"Midtown."

"Same as the phone trace," Gabriel said as he crossed the room to Donnie. "Make you a drink, Book?"

"Yes. Thank you."

Nicky went to the desk and was stealing a glance over Donna's shoulder. "42nd Street?" he said as he looked at a strange map on one of the screens dangling from the strings attached to Donna's fingers. "Is that for sure?"

"Looks like. I've got a couple block square. Bryant Park...down to Lexington. Christ, up to 46th."

"That's a lot of ground."

"Grand Central is right there. That'd be handy if they wanted to move her."

"They'd use drivers," Nicky said. "That's what I'd do. Safer. Discreet. Less video than the train station."

Gabriel was savoring his drink. "Those hotels are monsters. Thousands of private residences too."

Donnie was quiet, but Nicky slid closer to the desk. "Still worth trying," he said to everyone then quietly to Donna. "We've got men checking the hotels. If she's there, we'll find her."

Donna had not stopped her rush to the wire. "Make that north to 43rd. Lexington to Vanderbilt. What's there?"

"The Grand Hyatt," Nicky answered for everyone. "I've got guys in the area right now."

Donna looked up for the first time in several minutes, right in Nicky's face. There was sweat on her forehead. "You've got someone checking the Hyatt?"

"I'm on it," Nicky said as he pulled his phone out. "If they're not literally in the Hyatt, they will be in ten minutes."

"Thank you, Nick," Donna said. "A voice of reason in the wilderness."

"You want me to head that way, boss?" Nicky asked The Book as he listened to his call ringing on the other end.

Donnie felt himself slipping. "Go find Frank."

"I'll see what I can muster," Gabriel said as he pulled his own phone and stepped into the hallway ahead of Nicky.

With the others vanishing, father and daughter were alone again.

"It's a big city, Donna."

"I know, but it's getting smaller. I'm trying to see the router or the network of the Hyatt. If Lexy's iPad is on that network, we've got her."

Donnie put his hands over hers on the keyboard. "We can't do that. If we try a rescue, it could go very badly. Very badly. People could get hurt. Alexis could—"

"I can't hold back. Win, place, or show. I have to try." Donna entered the last of her commands.

"Another day or two. After the Belmont."

"We can't trust them. They're criminals."

"What if," Donnie stammered, "what if...how about I have Gabriel bring in the police? He has friends who can do this professionally."

Frank walked in with Nicky in tow.

"Whatcha need, Mr. Chariot?"

"Donna's developed what might be a lead on where Alexis may be. Ask Gabriel to come in. We'll turn this over to the police."

"The police?"

"Yes. Get Gabriel."

Nicky was out the door in a flash.

"I've got her!" Donna jumped. "She's on the Hyatt's guest network!"

"The cops are going to ask a lot of questions, boss. It could get worse."

"For who?" Donna snapped. "You two? Your cronies? They can put you all in jail—under the jail—as long as I get Lexy back."

"I don't want to talk out of turn—" Frank began.

"Then don't," Donna tried to cut him off.

"—but cops aren't necessarily the best at handling this type of thing. They're gonna want to bring in tanks and SWAT teams. Guns make people nervous. Just saying."

"I'm going, Dad. Have your rent-a-cop Gabriel call in the cavalry."

Frank kept at it. "Maybe I could go down there with Nicky and Gabriel and case the joint. If I see her, I'll snatch her back. If that's what you want, Book."

"No, I'd rather play it out. That was the deal. That's our obligation."

"Obligation?" Donna screamed as she shot away from the desk. "Jesus, what's wrong with you?"

"They said they'd release her after Belmont. If we don't hold up our end, why should they adhere to their word?"

"Holy shit! Because they're criminals!"

Donna headed for the door. Nicky almost ran into her as he shot around the corner into the office.

"Gabriel's gone. He got in his car and drove off."

"He's headed to midtown," Frank said. "How about me and Nicky head that way too? If you bring the cops in, we'll be there to pick up the pieces. If you don't, we're there to try to snatch the kid back."

Donnie didn't answer.

His daughter answered for him. "I'm headed downtown."

"Maybe you should stay on that thing," Frank suggested as he pointed to the computer bank. "In case she starts to move."

"I'm going."

"I talked to our guys," Nicky said. "They're on 42nd, headed to the Hyatt."

Donnie was calling Gabriel. There was no answer. "He's probably already bringing in the police."

"Boss, he wouldn't do that without your say so."

"Is anyone going with me?" Donna said again but didn't wait for an answer as she went out the door.

Nicky jumped at the chance. "You don't know our guys. I'll introduce you."

Nicky and Donna were gone. Frank looked to Donnie for orders, but they were slow in coming.

"Boss? You want I should go with her?" A moment passed. "Boss?"

"No. Let her go. Wait. Go with her. Don't let them take my girl."

•   •   •

Before Donna, Frank, and Nicky had cleared the gate with Nicky behind the wheel of Frank's car, inside the mansion, Donnie had tried Gabriel three more times. The response was the same. For his part, Gabriel had been busy making his own calls. First he phoned his uniformed flunkies to descend on the Grand Hyatt and round up the men Nick had sent. Then he called Julian DeSeti.

"Where are you?"

"Manhattan. I just tucked Baron in at the Plaza. Why?"

"Chariot's kid is at the Grand Hyatt. I already talked to my guys. They're picking up Chariot's people and clearing the area. No one should be in the way. You still want her?"

"I do."

"You're closer than me. Frank and his girlfriend are probably ten minutes behind me. You better drop down to midtown fast and get some help."

"I have Junior with me. Is the kid still with the cook?"

"I think so."

"Good. We won't need any help if she is. We'll be there in ten minutes. Maybe less. Get me their room number before I walk in the door."

Gabriel's minions tried to corner every associate of the hotel they could, to learn what room an older lady and a little girl might be in, but the exchanges deteriorated at the sight of a badge. The hotel workers were also less inclined to help a pushy cop when Nick's team had asked nicely behind a discreet press of currency into a grateful hand.

Predictably, an older lady traveling with a young girl who lived off room service and did not tip, stood out. They may or may not be in at the moment, but when they were, the disgruntled tip-less restaurant staff said they were making their deliveries to room 3431.

Mrs. Glass's phone was ringing. "Yes, sir?"

"Are you at the Hyatt?"

"I am. Where else would—"

"I need you to leave. Right away. No questions. Go to Grand Central and take the subway. Any one. Any direction. Get away from 42nd. Call me when you get off."

"How far do I go?"

"It doesn't matter. One stop. Find a new hotel. Stay off the street and call me. Do you understand?"

"Yes, but—"

The phone clicked. The caller had been Donnie Chariot.

25

Outside the hotel, one unmarked and two marked police cars were loading a few of the men who had recently enjoyed Nicky's free coffee in the Chariot mansion's basement. As those cars drove off, the DeSetis hustled up the sidewalk and passed beneath the overhanging classic Sun Garden restaurant of the Grand Hyatt. They took the escalator up to the main floor and looked around the mammoth atrium. As if on cue, the room number Julian had demanded came through in a text.

Eschewing the front desk, Julian made for the long bank of elevators as he issued final orders to his son. "Stay down here. Frumpy middle-aged lady. Looks sixty-five. A little plump with gray hair. Dragging around a seven-year-old girl. There can't be many pairs like that in here. Don't screw this up."

"There's like, a thousand rooms in this place. This is stupid."

"Shut your mouth. And keep your eyes open for Chariot's boys. Looks like New York's finest just swept the place pretty good, but if you see Frank, try not to piss your pants."

Junior was fuming, but settled at the far end of the expanse. By moving only slightly he could see the elevators plus the stairs and the escalators leading to and from the entrance. He had his phone in his hand with his father's number keyed up. Under his jacket was a compact Glock 9mm pistol.

When Julian stepped off the elevator on the 34th floor, Mrs. Glass was waiting in the wide hallway with a small suitcase. Alexis was beside her holding one strap of an oversized backpack that rested on the floor.

Julian was quick. Quicker than Mrs. Glass, but not quick enough to piece everything together. "Well, hello! You're all ready to go. Very good." He took the bag from Glass, stepped back into the elevator, and held the door. "Shall we?"

"I suppose so," Mrs. Glass said as she relaxed and stepped aboard the heavily paneled car with Alexis in tow. "He doesn't trust me to find my way to Grand Central. Isn't but one door down. My, he's a bother."

Julian touched the lobby button and his phone at almost the same time.

"I doubt that works in these things," Mrs. Glass said as both she and Alexis watched the numbers above the door flash and go dark again and again as the elevator dropped.

"We're on our way down. Bring the car up," Julian said to his son before he hung up. He smiled at Alexis and held up his phone. "It worked."

The elevator slowed and stopped halfway to the lobby. Julian's smile vanished. The door opened and a couple of tourists stepped on, full of small-town excitement. They were near giddy running their fingers over a digital map of Manhattan and whispering openly to each other as they pointed to the etched mirrors and polished brass railing around them in the elevator car.

An eight-floor drop was the extent of the next ride and the elevator slowed again. Julian sighed.

"We in a rush?" Mrs. Glass asked.

"Oh, no," Julian moaned. "Some. My son's bringing the car around front. Midtown traffic. They'll toss him from the cabbie lane. He'll have to cruise around the block until we catch him."

"What's he driving?" Mrs. Glass asked through a slanted smirk as she bumped Alexis with her elbow. "I bet it's no sports car. Maybe 'bet' is a bad choice of words."

"That's all been straightened out."

"Sure it has." Glass cast an obvious look at Alexis before fixing her gaze again on the descending numbers. "Her grandfather isn't one to be trifled with. Don't I know it."

The door opened and no one was there. Julian punched the lobby button again and repeatedly pressed the button to close the door. It didn't advance his cause. The door closed when it was ready and continued its drop to the main floor, but it tortured Julian with one more stop.

This time a couple of conference attendees got on dressed in their casual business attire carrying prerequisite stenciled gift bags weighed down with manuals and the like. At the elevator's leisure and Julian's dying dismay, the door appeared to mockingly hesitate before closing. Only then did the car continue the organized fall to the lobby.

The conference goers were last on and first off. The tourist couple stepped off next and looked up into the vast lobby. Nearly jostled by DeSeti, they stepped to the side and consulted their map against the agenda for a day.

The phone was still in Julian's hand when it rang. It was Gabriel.

"Have you got her?"

"I do. Where are you?"

"Just coming onto 42nd. Where're you going to take her?"

"Wouldn't you like to know?"

"I don't give a shit what you do with her, but I will get paid. Plus a bonus. I came thru."

"Yes, you did," Julian said as he steered Mrs. Glass and Alexis across the lobby to the escalators and down to the main doors.

"Wherever you're going, you better get gone. Chariot's been trying to call me since I left the mansion. He might be going crazy—"

"He's always been crazy."

"—but he's not stupid. By now he's put it together and has Frank and that young buck right on my ass."

"Good to know. I'll catch up with you later."

"Make sure you do."

The street that held the Grand Hyatt back was the standard New York City fare of hustle and bustle. Yellow cabs were lined up to take riders to JFK, LaGuardia, uptown, and downtown. Bellhops carried suitcases to the curb where eager cabbies loaded them in exchange for hopeful tips yet to come. Horns blew, hands waved and gestured all manner of communications. It was everything the tourists who had shared Lexy's elevator hoped it would be.

While Julian scanned the street in front of the Hyatt and beyond the steady flow of cabs for his Mercedes, Mrs. Glass took her small suitcase from him and stepped away with Alexis up the wide sidewalk to Grand Central Station.

"Hold on," Julian said as he pointed up the street in the opposite direction. "The car's coming around."

Mrs. Glass kept walking. "I was told to take the subway."

"There's been a change. We have the car now."

"He told me the subway. One stop. I gotta do it."

"What stop?"

"He said it don't matter."

"That's crazy. I'll have a car here in a minute."

"Nice of you to stop and help out, carrying my bag down and all, but he'd have called if he changed his mind about the subway."

Mrs. Glass continued stepping away toward the 42nd Street entrance to the station. Julian was left alone in a crowd. He was quickly being swallowed by the sidewalk traffic. Junior's horn blowing would have been lost in the raucous throng had he not lowered the passenger window and yelled for his father.

"Hey! Where are they? What happened?"

Other horns were already encouraging the younger DeSeti to move on.

Julian yelled from the sidewalk as he began to jog away to Mrs. Glass. "Pull up to Grand Central."

"What?" Junior screamed back—half in defiance and half as a legitimate question.

Julian flailed his arms toward the end of the block to direct his son's attention and relieve his own frustration. "They're going in the station." When Julian sped up his run, the combination of yelling and waving drew attention.

Several cars back from the Hyatt on 42nd Street, Nicky saw him. "Is that Julian DeSeti?"

Frank had seen him too. "Sure is. What's he doing?"

Julian's hand tipped when Donna followed his waving back to Junior and the Mercedes, then ahead to a middle-aged lady walking away hand-in-hand with a little girl.

"There's Lexy," Donna said, almost matter-of-factly. If there was any excitement in her voice, it was drowned out by the rush of her jumping out of the car. She was in the street ahead of the slamming door and was gone before Frank could follow suit.

"This ain't gonna be good," he said as he lumbered out of the car leaving Nicky stuck in both the car and traffic.

At the other end of the block, Junior had caught up to Mrs. Glass at the same time as his father. Junior had none of the reserve of the senior DeSeti and jumped from the car. His father was trying to explain the supposed change to his intended quarry when Junior discreetly pulled his pistol and stuffed it in Mrs. Glass's ribs.

"Get in that car, bitch."

Before she could answer yes, no, or maybe, Junior had her arm and was lifting her toward the car. Alexis came as part of the package. In the crush to the car, both DeSetis caught sight of Donna running through the traffic toward them. Mrs. Glass and Alexis saw her too.

"*Mommy!*"

"*Lexy!*"

Junior had the door open and shoved Glass in, prompted by the gun. He caught Alexis up in his free hand as he barked at his father. "You drive."

Julian dashed around the car and hopped behind the wheel while Junior tried to stuff Alexis into the back. She grabbed the door frame screaming.

Donna was nearly on them but as Junior grabbed Alexis with both hands, Donna saw the gun. It froze her.

"Just let her go," Donna pleaded and took a tentative step.

"*Mommy!*"

Frank caught up as Alexis disappeared into the back seat. He passed Donna and was already at the car, never seeing the gun until Junior's hand came back out from the car. The muzzle blast into his chest was so close Frank's shirt puffed up and deflated like an exploding balloon. He landed one punch as he grappled with Junior before he slumped to the street at Donna's feet. Junior was shaken by Frank's fist, but dove in the car on top of Glass and Lexy and yanked the door closed.

"Get us outa here!"

Donna saw the blood oozing from Frank's chest. The blood grabbed the throat of her mind. She saw flashes of another man dangling by his arms in a dark room, blood dripping from his chin. The man's eyes were crusted over with dried blood. Where his nose had been, was little more than pale white cartilage, blood, and bone.

Her own blood fled from her face as she neared fainting. She staggered and went down to her knees over Frank. Her hands reached out to steady herself and found Frank's bloody chest. As she inadvertently leaned on him, he moaned, and opened his eyes.

"Get me up...."

Donna snapped back to an adrenaline rush. "Help! *Help!* Get an ambulance!"

"No, LD. Get me...out of here...."

"*Someone, help!*"

"No cops. She'll be in the middle...he'll kill her."

Nicky was at Frank's side having stopped his car in a growing puddle of his friend's blood.

"Jesus...Frank! What the—"

"Get me...the car...."

"You need a doctor—"

"Nick...they'll kill the kid...get Chariot...."

Nicky looked hard at his mentor. Frank blinked slowly and made the slightest shaking motion with his head. It was a clear no. Both men understood as sirens grew louder nearby.

The faceless bleeding man hanging in Donna's nightmares appeared again. He moved from her mind's eye and materialized in the back seat of Nicky's car only a few feet from Donna's face. He turned and looked straight at her through the rear passenger window with black holes for eyes and bloody teeth behind a lipless mouth. His jaw dropped as though to speak.

Donna fell backward from Frank onto the street.

"Grab his arm. Help me get him up," she heard Nicky say.

With one hand propping his partner up, Nicky reached back for the door of their car. Donna followed him as the door opened. The bloody man was gone.

"Get him in," Nicky directed.

Donna looked with anxious eyes from the back seat to Frank. Neither place held the remotest comfort. "He needs a doctor."

"He needs to get off the street. Hurry."

Frank pushed with his feet and was sitting on the sill of the open door. He pushed again as Nicky heaved and Frank went into the car—half on the seat, half on the floor.

Nicky left the door open and ran around to take the wheel. "Get in. Help him!"

The best Donna could do was fold Frank's feet into the car. She was instantly in on top of him. Acceleration of the car was enough to close the door as Nicky shot down 42nd Street.

"Tell him…slow down…" Frank mumbled.

"Slow down!" Donna relayed.

"Nick…north… north of 130th…."

"What? Why?"

"Dump…car…."

"We need a doctor, big guy."

"Too late…north…I'll be dead…when we get there."

"Don't say stupid shit."

"Dump car. Take the subway. Get Donna out...split up...change two, three times—"

"Shut up, Frank! I ain't dumping you in the projects!"

"Get a train to Queens." Frank looked at Donna for the first time. He was pale and fainting. The voice was instantly weaker. "Get to your father. He'll know...he'll know what to do."

Donna's eyes were darting and she couldn't answer.

"He's sick, LD," Frank pleaded. "Help him...."

She nodded slightly and tried to pull the big man closer to her. His hands were failing, but he tried to ease her away with his wrist, careful not to get blood on her blouse. "You'll get bloody," Frank's voice dropped to a whisper between blue lips. "No matter what you do...."

"I know," she breathed, an inch from his face.

Frank's eyes were still open, but he couldn't see. His chest stopped oozing blood or breathing.

"Nick?"

"How's he doing? Hold on there, Frank."

"Nick? He's gone."

• • •

In another car, there was screaming and crying, but no one dying.

"What the hell are you thinking?" Julian DeSeti was shouting at the rearview mirror. "Jesus, you just shot Frank in front of three hundred people!"

"To hell with that asshole! He won't mess with me again."

"*What?* Are you high? You shot him on the busiest street in New York! *In broad daylight, you moron!*"

"He thinks he can play me like he does his bitch girlfriend Nicky. That shithead's next! And I want that fucking *car back!*"

"Mr. DeSeti?" Mrs. Glass said with surprising calm. "I didn't see nothin'. I don't know nothin'. And this kid don't know nothin' neither."

"*Shut up!*" Junior snapped, the gun jumping up to Glass's face.

Alexis screamed and willfully went beneath Glass's protective hand and was pulled tight under her arm.

"Let us out. Anywhere. We got no stake in this."

"You do now!"

"Shut up, Junior," Julian ordered. "You're scaring the kid."

"No, you shut up, old man! You're the one got us in this!"

"I didn't shoot somebody in the middle of Manhattan. Instead of them, I should put *you* out in the street!"

Junior waved his gun with brash menace. "You try that. See how it works out for you."

Father and son locked eyes in the rearview. Junior broke the fragile stalemate. "You wanted her. Here she is."

"I didn't want to shoot somebody for her."

"I'm just making my bones. There's a trail of bodies following you. Don't think I don't know."

"Not like this. I never whacked no little kid."

"Neither have I! Frank was trying to kill me. It was self-defense."

"Hardly."

"He's a big guy. He's all right."

"You better hope so. If not, there's two more sitting next to you you'll have to deal with. Plus The Book's daughter."

"I probably just winged him."

"He looked like he was hit pretty good to me."

"You'd know."

"Damn right, and so won't Chariot. He's not going to like you shooting up his help—"

"Or you kidnapping his grandkid."

"I didn't kidnap anybody." Julian adjusted the mirror and looked at Mrs. Glass as he drove. "Did I, Mrs. Glass?"

She was slow to answer. "No. Like I said, I ain't seen nothing."

"Damn right you haven't," Junior snapped then spoke to the mirror again. "Where're we headed? You must've had a plan walking into the Hyatt."

"I did, but that was before you started shooting up Manhattan. We're going north."

"The Bronx?"

"We need to get out of the city until I can sort out your nonsense." Julian was driving sharply but obeying every law. "I'm leaving Baron unattended. That's not exactly how I wanted this to go, but he'll play ball once he learns we've got his leverage on Chariot."

Mrs. Glass's eyes were darting. "Say, Mr. DeSeti? Like I said, just let us out anywhere and you won't hear a peep out of me."

"Now, what would Baron think of me if I were to put you out in the street like that?" It was Julian's turn to search for answers in the wake of his own restless eyes. Chumming the waters with having Baron's advantage presently in the backseat of his car and forcing the bait on his hook with a bloody body in the distant rearview mirror, Julian pressed his immediate violent advantage. "You know, thinking back fifteen minutes, it seems like no one was holding you in the Hyatt. I guess that means you're working pretty closely with someone. Now, that's good. That's good. But, as I was saying, if I was to abandon you to any old street corner of the city—with you and your boss sharing this special bond of trust, so to speak—that would paint me in a very dismal light. Certainly in Baron's eyes. Wouldn't you agree?"

"I get on with the boss all right, but I don't know nobody name Baron."

"Right…sure you don't. Nice and cozy relationship you have there. What's it cost him for you to be your own jailer, or does he pay you in chips from Vegas?"

"I get the same pay as always, but I don't have to make meals or clean up. That's a bonus right there."

"Same pay as always? Baron has you on the payroll?"

"I told you—" Glass started to quip, then reeled in her tone considerably. "I told you, I don't know nobody named Baron. What's a baron anyway? Isn't that like a king or a prince or something? I think I'd remember if I met a prince."

Junior had been listening and leaned into the conversation happening in the rearview mirror. "You don't know Baron?"

"Nope. Am I supposed to?"

"Chariot works for him."

"Chariot works for hisself," Mrs. Glass said. "You can believe that. He don't do nothing for nobody but hisself. Anybody who thinks Chariot is working for him is a fool."

Junior leaned up over the front seat until he was nearly in his father's face. "You hearing this?"

"I heard her," Julian said. Then he pushed his son—gun and all—out of his way and spoke to the mirror again. "Mrs. Glass, I've always been straight with you. Am I right?"

"Far as I know."

"Will you be straight with me? A hundred percent. No nonsense now. Will you answer one simple question for me? Just as honest as you possibly can?"

"Will you let me and the kid go?"

"Absolutely."

Junior began to balk until his father's waving hand shut him up.

"Fire away," Mrs. Glass said as Alexis pulled her head free.

The car was quiet. Alexis was emboldened by her caretaker and glared at Junior and his gun. When the car stopped at a red light, Julian abandoned the mirror and put his arm up on the seat. He squirmed and turned most of the way around until he could see Mrs. Glass square.

"Mrs. Glass—as honest as you can state it—who put you up at the Hyatt?"

"Whaddaya mean?"

"Who's picking up the tab?"

"I dunno. Chariot, I suppose."

"Which Chariot? Donnie or Li'l Donnie?"

"Her name's Donna. She'll go off on you if you call her LD."

"Was it her that put you up to this?"

The younger DeSeti couldn't hold his tongue. "She's not going to have her own daughter snatched. You think I'm high? You must be stoned."

"What better way to muscle aside her father and take over his book." Julian was now thinking out loud. "She runs a big-time accounting firm. Numbers are numbers. It's never made sense. Baron knows Chariot is going around the bend so he's trying to leverage The Book's daughter."

"What?" Junior said as one of the few totally honest statements he'd made in recent months.

Julian literally slapped the seat in celebration. "Baron's deal is with Donna. The kidnapping could all be a ruse."

"What are you talking about? Kidnapping?" Glass said. "We was on vacation until you started shooting up the street. Chariot will have your eyes for that. You'll see. Or then again, maybe you won't."

"Christ, which Chariot will have my eyes?" Julian said in total despair.

"The old man, but don't think Li'l Donnie isn't in league with the devil. She's as wicked as her father. You'll see. You poked a bees' nest. I wouldn't be you two for all the tea in China."

• • •

Donna's blouse was still wet from a crude rinsing in a filthy subterranean restroom. She and Nicky were being rocked back and forth to the sound of the train barreling toward Queens. The Bronx and Frank's car, with his body in the trunk and the keys in the ignition, abandoned in one of the sketchiest sections of the borough, was miles behind them. Nicky knew that at the minimum it would carry some joyriders to anywhere and confuse the cops with a fresh location and unknown fingerprints. At best, the car might be run through a chop shop. Somewhere in that process, the disposal of Frank's body would become someone else's problem. Though it had been Frank's call, it didn't make it go down any easier.

Nicky's face was in his hands when he felt Donna's arm across his back. "Sorry seems so trite."

"Trite. Is that French or something for absolute total bullshit?" he said through his fingers.

"Something like that."

"I left him in the trunk of a car. Friends don't do that."

"It's what he wanted. He knows these things."

"I'm no damn good for doing that."

"That's not true." Donna took his face from his hands and held it. "I've known Frank my entire life," she said through a voice that cracked, caught up in an unwillingness to use the past tense. "He's been in the…well, in the people business his whole life. He once told me he could read a man's intentions in two minutes—if he'd pay or welch. He knows people and told me you were a good guy. That's about the highest praise anybody can get."

"You're making up shit to make me feel better."

She released his face and brushed at her tears, trying not to draw attention. "You think you're the only one hurting? He raised me as much as my father. He's been in my life forever." She had more to say, but it all trailed off, drowned out by the train.

"I'm gonna kill that sonofabitch," Nicky whispered.

"Oh, yes," Donna said as she rubbed Nicky's shoulders. "We'll find him. He'll answer for plenty, and the questions will cut deep."

The train rolled on until they both looked at the approach of the next station.

"Did he really say that about me? You know, being a good guy?"

"He did, and more." Donna smiled slightly. "He thought we'd make a cute couple. That's what he called us. A cute couple."

Nicky smiled back. "He told me I'd be lucky to have someone like you in my life."

"Who'd have thought Frank would ever play matchmaker?" But her smile faded. She couldn't stop fresh tears. "When my dad was too busy—he was always too busy—Frank taught me how to throw a ball. We used to play catch."

They traded shoulders and Donna buried her face in Nicky's chest. In two more stops, tears were surreptitiously brushed from each other's faces when they split up as their teacher had told them. When they saw each other again at the mansion, they hugged gently and examined one another for more tears or sad eyes that needed attention.

26

Exercise riders in blue jeans and flak jackets were putting Belmont Stakes wannabees through early morning workouts. Taking a rest day, champions, favorites, and contenders for the last race of the Triple Crown would be confined to hot walks or strolls around the barns. The race was only a day away. The Kentucky Derby winner was led around the stables to walk off some energy, stay loose, and to let his handlers inspect every motion. He'd run here before, but never at a mile and a half. The sand wouldn't be a problem—the distance, maybe. The Belmont Stakes was called the "Test of a Champion" for a reason.

In the end, the race might come down to a last-minute passing rain shower, a loose shoe, a slip out of the gate, or a bump—unintentional or maybe not—from another horse equally bent on winning the big silver bowl that went to the winner. More variables than anyone could count would determine the winning mount's place in history. But still, Donnie and Donna Chariot would be tasked with determining the opening odds for the betting action and placing numbers where dollars would follow. It all had to play out to the satisfaction of gamblers, connections, the New York Racing Association, and the back side of Vegas. There was more than power, prestige and breeding fees at stake. Somewhere northwest of the exercise riders, a little girl was eating a Happy Meal on the floor and watching a newscast being broadcast in French.

The unusual language reached out to Junior as he passed through the room. "Whatcha watching, kid? Soccer?"

Alexis didn't answer.

"I said, whatcha watching?"

"Leave her be," Mrs. Glass mumbled from her imposed seat on a couch across the simple room.

"I asked a question. I want an answer."

"She ain't fussing. What do you care?"

"She ought to answer when she's spoken to. It's not right."

"I wouldn't answer you either. You're nobody. After what you did to Frank and what your father did grabbing that little girl, I wouldn't give five cents for either one of you. Mr. Chariot is gonna kick you so hard he'll break his leg off right in your ass."

"That old bastard isn't going to do shit. I hear he's going crazy too—a stroke or something."

"You got the crazy part right. And mind your language."

"You mind your mouth, bitch."

Glass wasn't wilting. "You know better. Even you ain't that stupid or stoned. That's why you sleep with a gun. I also seen you don't go to the bathroom without it. But then you ain't allowed to go to the privy without your daddy's say-so—or do you go in the pisser to shoot up? I've seen your kind before—usually holding a piece of cardboard on a corner. Yeah, you're real tough. I know I'm scared. You scared, Lexy?"

"Scared stiff."

Mrs. Glass laughed. "Ha! That's funny, that is. It only took a seven-year-old a day to figure out how tough you are."

"And it only took me one minute to figure out you're the weak link in this chain. Keep it up, old lady. You'll be buried in the Jersey swamps before this is done."

The thought of the swamps of Jersey gave Glass pause. She had a counter ready in short order. "If you was to do that, you'd miss out on something pretty special."

Now it was Junior's turn to laugh. "Oh, no! Your best days were at least forty years ago. My old man wouldn't even want what you're offering."

"Not me, you dope head. The kid."

"You're sicker than I am."

"Not that, you disgusting—You're a sicko just thinking of it. I mean, the kid has a special trick she does to pick horses. Learned it from her grandfather. Didn't you, Missy?"

"*Oui.*"

"She won't do it for you—would you, Lexy? But she might for me if I was inclined to ask her nice."

Junior dropped coarsely into a chair. He parked one foot up on the seat and perched his arm on his raised knee. The gun dangled loosely and served as a dangerous pointer as he talked.

"You sound like every person who's just figured out they were expendable. Everybody's got a big plan—a reason they should be kept around. Go ahead. Make your spiel. Try and tie yourself to the kid so you get to live another five minutes."

The intentionally titillating reference to life and death brought Alexis away from her news show, but the move wasn't physical. Her eyes stayed riveted on the small screen, but her ears no longer occupied themselves with translating the French of the reporters. Any decoding taking place now was strictly focused on those in the room with her.

Mrs. Glass had made it clear that she could hardly be called a friend. Most times she wasn't even a friendly face. Since Alexis had been picked up at school, she'd never been comfortable with her supposed babysitter.

Though Glass was coarse, this other character was worse. This "Junior" person was a bully. He argued with everyone, even the man he called his dad. And the arguing was the least of it. Though it had happened so fast she didn't see much, she'd heard the gunshot. The screaming breakdown of it that seemed to take place on the hour since the group settled into a nondescript small house was giving her bad dreams. It appeared Julian DeSeti had had enough of his son. He'd stormed out. Alexis would rather have gone off with him than stay in the house with Glass and Junior.

Before Mr. DeSeti appeared at the big hotel, Alexis had been heeding her mother's words and not thinking of a way to slip away from Glass. That was before she knew Glass was a liar. Now she knew her mother wasn't away and was looking for her along with Lexy's friends from the driveway of her grandfather's house. She watched the talking head relay the news in French and listened to the arguing behind her, but focused on escape.

"It ain't a spiel. It's the truth," Glass was saying. "The kid is some kind of brainiac. You see what she's watching?"

"Soccer," Junior said again.

"It's French news. She watches all them foreign stations from the city. She speaks all them languages. So she claims."

"How many languages you speak, kid?" Junior asked.

"Just English," Lexy said without turning. "She's crazy."

"That's what I thought," Junior laughed. "Trying to save your old ass."

"Kid? Don't hang me out there like that. Go ahead. Speak some French or something. Go on now."

Alexis turned slightly, stared back silently, and remembered a lie about her mother being out of town.

"Oh, you're a wicked one, you are," Glass snapped at her. "You're like your grandfather—mean as a snake. Greedy."

Junior's gun was rocking back and forth, barely hanging on his trigger finger. "Straight up, kid. Your grandfather—he's a genius with horses and numbers. You know that?"

"Yes."

"He's also a prick, like the old lady said. Do you know that, too?"

"No."

"Well, he is. Believe that. He stole my car."

"No, he didn't. He wouldn't do that. He's rich. He can buy any car he wants."

Glass jumped in. "That's true. He's rich because he's greedy, like I said. But the kid is right, he didn't steal that car. I heard he won it from you fair and square."

Junior's grip tightened on the gun. "Keep talking, bitch."

"I heard that, too," Alexis said, although she hadn't.

"Both of you just keep running your mouths. See what happens."

"You can't do anything until you ask your daddy," Alexis snickered, but Junior snatched the last of the chuckle from her throat. He had her almost off the ground by one arm. Before she could scream or even realize what had happened, he tossed her across the floor.

"Here now!" Mrs. Glass objected and rushed between the pair. "There's no call for that. She's playing. She's just young."

"She's not going to get any older if she pops off again."

"You don't want to hurt nobody. Least of all this girl. Show him, Lexy. Show him what you can do with the horses."

"No," Alexis said as she rubbed her arm. "He's mean."

"Say something else smart and you'll find out how mean I can get."

Mrs. Glass bent and cupped Lexy's face with her hands. She was whispering. "Listen. This might be your best shot. You get hold of a computer and maybe you can send a message to your grandpa. Know what I mean? Play along and see what you can muster." Then a bit louder. "You up for it, Missy?"

Alexis shook her head yes. A light was on in her eye.

"You got a computer, DeSeti?" Mrs. Glass asked.

"Do I look like a got a computer?"

"An iPad maybe? The kid is right handy with an iPad."

"Can't help you."

"Where's our bags? She's got an iPad of her own."

"Still in my father's car. Looks like you're shit outa luck."

Lexy was ahead of him—miles ahead. "You can get on the internet with your phone."

"No shit, Sherlock. But you got as much chance of getting your grubby little mitts on my phone as you do getting this gun." Junior lifted the pistol for effect and punctuation.

"You can watch. I don't need the phone part. You can turn the phone function off. If you know how."

"I know how, smart ass." He didn't and it showed in his voice.

"Yeah, right. If you say so."

"I do."

"Okay."

Junior had been led to the edge. He'd jump off under his own volition. Alexis was content to let the venom from her last bite work. Mrs. Glass, not as sharp as her purported pupil, didn't recognize the value of patience and pushed.

"You're missing out. Maybe you don't need a few dollars, but I—'"

"Money is the least of your problems, lady."

"Well, then you oughta see it work just to say you did. Damned amazing. Really is. She's like a wizard or—"

"Or a witch. You a witch, kid?"

Lexy waited a beat, cast her face down then looked out from beneath her faint eyebrows. She smiled as eerily as she could. "Maybe."

"That might be," Junior laughed out loud. "Your grandfather's the devil. Probably something in the blood."

"That's it right there," Mrs. Glass said, trying to save her place at the table and maybe her life. "Chariot goes through a racing form like a hot knife through butter. He picks winners faster than a lion spots a limp."

"He's still a sonofabitch."

"That'd be true too. He ain't never shared one tip on a pony. Not true about his fry here. She's shared many a tip with me that took us straight to the pay window. Tell him that's true, kid."

Alexis mimicked. "That's true, kid."

"See there?" Glass continued, laying it on thicker and heavier as she went. "Pencil in a few picks from Einstein here and you can tell your old man to take a long walk off a short pier. You'll be the shot caller. If you parlayed what this kid can do, the whole gambling world would be eating out of your hand. Why if you—"

"Christ! Shut up!" Junior took a breath. "Jesus, your voice goes through my head like a nail. Everybody just shut up."

It only took five seconds for Junior to break his own order. "Kid? Are you like your grandfather?"

"Just like him."

"You better hope not."

"Why?"

"I don't like him."

Alexis smiled. "That's too bad."

"That's right—for him," Junior said as he pointed his gun at Alexis. She wasn't rattled. "Not really. It's bad for you."

"How do you figure that, kid? I got this," he said as he waved his pistol.

"Yeah, but you also have a limp."

"A limp?"

"Yep. And my grandfather's the lion."

Junior had to think it through a second. "Is that supposed to scare me?"

"It would if you were smart." Then she quickly added. "And I think you are very smart."

Junior smiled and lowered the gun. "Is that so?"

"Yep. Smart enough to turn your phone off long enough to bring up the card at Belmont. Let me see if there's any perfect races for you."

"A perfect race, huh?"

"Once in a while."

Mrs. Glass elbowed her way back in, but was cautious. "That's what she does. Let her give it a go. You won't be sorry."

Junior was up and exchanged the pistol for the phone in his pocket. "If anybody's gonna be sorry, it's you," he said to Glass. "If either of you try to make a call, email, or a text, I'm gonna put a bullet right in your head."

"She won't do nothing. She's a good girl. Ain't you?"

"The best," Alexis smiled again.

"What are you, running for office?"

Junior slid a finger across his phone a few times. "You know, I heard your grandfather never reneged on a bet or went back on his word.

Never. I still hate him, but if you're like him, tell me you won't go stupid on me and try to send up a flare and I'll roll the dice on you."

"I won't."

Junior brought up his web browser and handed the phone to Alexis. "Christ, I've reached a new low." He moved around behind her. "I'm watching. If you're like your grandfather, you gotta keep your word."

Alexis had already heard the bell and the crashing open of the starting gates. Her fingers bolted and were sprinting.

"Yep. Let's see who's running."

In the flash of screens between the browser and the card for the day's races, she opened the compass app. Her sleight of hand would have made a magician proud. She turned her hand over to acclimate the GPS locator and scratched the back of her wrist where no itch existed.

A super slow-mo camera couldn't have caught her stolen glance at the screen and the swipe that closed the GPS coordinates. The nanosecond blink of the GPS coordinates was all Alexis needed. The six-digit numbers were instantly etched in her mind. A purposeful balk was the last movement and provided the perfect cover.

The racing card for Belmont was left open.

"Hand it over," Junior said. "I seen that. What else you looking at?"

"The DRF." Alexis handed the phone over.

Junior swiped aside Belmont's card. What remained was the Daily Racing Form. He looked, but saw nothing else and handed the phone back.

"Stay away from the phone part. If you try to text, I'll break your arm."

Alexis leafed through the day's racing lineup. Everything she saw—past performances, weights, jockeys, weather, track conditions, competition, and connections—were remembered with one look. Like her grandfather and her mother, reams of data—the business end of a firehose—now went into a thimble and never spilled a drop. She handed the phone back to Junior, but left the pages open for inspection.

"What's the matter, Merlin?" Junior prodded. "You lose the magic touch?"

"Naw. She's funnin' you," Glass grinned and played. "Take it back, kid. Unleash the lightning on those nags. Show him what you got. Go on. Show him."

Junior dangled the phone between two fingers as though teasing her. "You want it? Or was this all bullshit from the start?"

"It's real," Alexis said as she crossed the room swinging her arms back and forth in the exaggerated posture of a disinterested player. "But you can't afford it."

"Can't afford what?"

"The bump."

"What bump?"

"We'd have to move the odds on the five horse in the fourth race. Based on the size of the pool, it'd cost about five thousand dollars."

Junior put the phone in his jacket pocket. "You're touched in the head."

"No, hold up. I seen her do it. We—"

"You two are trying to play me."

"No, she ain't. She can pick 'em!"

"Shut up!"

"She said the fourth race. Give her—"

Junior snapped the pistol into Glass's face. Any relaxing preoccupation with horse racing was gone. "Shut the fuck up!"

"Give her walking money for the first race," Glass said quickly through a veil of hands that would have done nothing to stop a 9mm bullet. "She'll have the five grand by the fourth. If she don't, you ain't out nothing."

The gun stayed trained on Glass's head. Junior was sweating and there was a slight tremble in his hand that graduated until the end of the barrel shook.

Glass was looking at the muzzle quivering near her face. Junior's own eyes left what he thought would be a trembling victim and were now locked on the gun shaking in his hand.

"You're jonesin', son."

"Shut. Your. Mouth."

"You hide it pretty good. I bet your old man doesn't even know."

Junior stretched his hand further toward Glass's face.

"Two hundred dollars," Alexis blurted. "I can get to five thousand by the fourth race with two hundred dollars."

"What?" Junior said, pulling away slightly from Glass.

"If we put two hundred down on the three horse in the first, roll the payout onto the six horse in the second, and rolled again onto an easy exacta in the third race, by the time the riders for the fourth are getting a leg up, we'll have the five thousand."

"You're going to turn two hundred into five thousand in three races?"

"I seen her do it," Glass said. "I got forty bucks in my purse—more in the lining of my suitcase. I'll put it in the kitty toward the two hundred."

The three people in the room exchanged glances like gunfighters. Junior was skeptical. Glass was hopeful. Only Alexis was certain. She had seen the numbers and that was all she needed.

"You're both full of shit."

"Nope. I told you. Two hundred."

"Then what? You just say, 'oops' when this goes south on you?"

"No 'oops.' It's there."

Junior was relenting. "I'll bite," he said as he exchanged the gun for his phone. The Belmont card was still up. He looked it over as he moved to drop down beside his miniature bookie. "For a couple a hundred, it'll be worth it to watch you try to cry your way out of this when it collapses on your head."

"I won't cry."

"You don't cry?"

"Not anymore." Alexis looked at him a little too hard, nearly tipping her hand before she purposely softened up. "I gave it up for Lent."

"Shit," Junior laughed. "Lent."

"Lent was three or four months ago," Glass said as she almost literally scratched her head.

"That's funny, kid. We might get along after all." The smile faded, but the tension had eased. "As long as you don't get cute. *Capisci?*"

"Capisco perfettamente. Avete il denaro?"

The screen of the phone was swiped a few times until Junior had his Off Track Betting account opened. He laid the phone flat on the palm of his outstretched hand. *"Qui. Sai come fare una scommessa?"*

Alexis took the phone. *"Senza dubbio."*

"Hey hey hey!" Glass interrupted. "Knock off the mumble-jumble. I might want to play along."

"We're going to use his OTB account," Alexis explained. "Hopefully he has enough money in it to float the first wager."

Mrs. Glass laughed for them both. "Right? Don't sign nothin'. He'll like as not try to stiff you."

"That's real funny." Junior walked away from Alexis and snatched up Glass's purse. He dumped it on the floor and began kicking through the pile.

He hadn't taken his first step before Alexis had his phone working overtime. She was peeling the OTB site beneath Junior's account. He had more than enough money for the fourth race bump as it was, but Alexis had to not only ensure her greedy pair of gamblers would visit the payout window, but she also had to muster up a notice that she was nearby, alive and well, and positioning herself for rescue. There wasn't a single sure thing in any part of the plan. The alert would take some doing and it had to come through the OTB site as Junior would likely be looking over her shoulder before she finished.

She started inputting minor wagers for the first race. Some bets were small, others in the hundreds. The mathematic juggling taxed her and tested a constant process that was difficult to maintain. To align the number eight horse's action, there was impact to both the horse's total and the total pool for the race. From the onset, her goal was the wager pools and totals that would contain the numbers of the Chariot mansion's address, 3-2-9.

Lexy knew what a sequence of these digits would trigger in her grandfather. Her fingers were flying. There was no room for mistakes. As the numbers began to appear on the tote board, a longing punter perhaps a thousand miles away laid his two dollars down at a betting window, unintentionally, but effectively forcing Alexis to quickly reset.

Junior was on one knee in the disheveled mess that was the contents of Glass's purse. He was rifling the cash from her wallet like the junkie he was. "Thanks for the donation, Grandma. Anything else funny you want to say?"

"Keep it, but you'll do good to remember who gave you the seed money to prime the pump. Forty dollars of the two hundred she needs is mine."

"Not anymore," Junior said with an accompanying twitch.

"Hey, kid?" Glass asked. "What share of that two hundred is my forty bucks?"

Alexis didn't look up and her fingers continued racing. "What share? You mean, what percent?"

"Yeah. Percent. That's it."

"Twenty percent," Alexis said, still not looking up.

"Okay. Then twenty percent of what she brings down belongs to me."

"Christ, do you ever shut up?"

Glass would have quieted, but sensed Alexis was doing something that might help them both out of the frying pan she was sitting in. Getting shed of the addict with a gun would be the blessing of her life, but one miscue exiting the fry pan would lead directly to the fire.

Glass pressed the issue one more time and held Junior's attention on her with her seeming inane confidence. "How do you expect me to keep still when my money's driving the score? I'm all in. All in. Especially when I know for a fact it's a sure-fire winner. The way I got it figured see—"

"*Shut up!*"

In the rapid-fire shouting, chased by the intimidating but fleeting silence, Junior saw Alexis working the phone. Her finger's race captured his immediate though slipshod attention and he staggered toward her, his face and hands now sweating heavily. "What are you doing there? Hand it over."

She complied, confident that her arranged threes, twos, and nines, facing out as a digitized SOS, would flash in her grandfather's eyes and whisper that she was behind them. When Junior looked at the screen, all he saw was Belmont's racing card over his own OTB account, just as it had been when he'd descended on Glass's purse. He took a deep breath and looked the phone over—front and back—as though something could possibly be seen on the aluminum back cover. He handed it back to Alexis yet again. "I need a laugh. Go ahead and place that bet. Two hundred. No more."

To Junior DeSeti, Lexy's efforts were invisible, but back in the Chariot mansion, her manipulations reached out across her grandfather's desk and slapped his face.

27

"Donna? Lexy's here."

"Here?" Donna bounced up off the couch toward the windows. "Where here?"

Donnie was pointing at one of his many screens. "Right here. That has to be her."

Donna dismissed her father's suggestion out of hand. She scarcely ventured a glance at her father's target before she launched. "Lexy's been kidnapped. And Frank's been murdered. No one's taking a timeout to look at a claiming race. Maybe before, but that was a fluke. The stakes are higher now.

"We're done, Dad. I'm done. We've been doing everything your way and now Frank's dead and the people that killed him have my daughter. I'm calling the FBI. *Real* police. Doing things your—"

"No police."

"*Frank is dead!* Jesus, they shot him right in front of me! A foot from Lexy. Your granddaughter."

"Where are you going to tell them to start looking?"

"I don't know! That's their job. They're professionals, not like that friend of yours who's probably more criminal than cop."

"Who are you talking about?"

"That other thug who's been hanging around. He was with Frank a lot. You said his name was Gabriel. Like a goddamn angel. You said he was a cop, but I sincerely doubt it. Gabriel. If he's a friend of yours, he's more devil than angel."

"Gabriel's here? Nicky, is Gabriel here? Ask him to come in."

Nicky was pulled from the far wall by The Book's voice. He'd been leaning heavily, relying on the stout wall to fill in for knees still weak over what had happened to Frank and also from what he'd done with his body. Nicky's attempt to disappear ended when Chariot called his name.

"He's not here, boss. He left before we did and he's not picking up his phone."

It was clear Donnie was lost in thought or, as Donna and Nicky were both deeming a likely option—just lost. In another moment, he pointed again to the betting pools on the first race at Belmont Park. "Did you even look at that? I know you did. You can try to play it off as just a glance, but I also know that's all it takes. I have it too, remember?"

"You remember…" Donna's cruel words dripped venom.

"You could write every one of those numbers down in ten seconds if you had to. If your life depended on it. Or someone else's life depended on it."

"How dare you be so flippant? She's a baby. My little girl."

"And my granddaughter! And she has it too. Goddamn it! You know she does. And she's reaching out right this minute. Look!"

"You're so full of shit. There's nothing there. You never could let yourself see things as normal. Always an equation. A theorem. For once, just be normal."

"Normal? What the hell is normal when you've got what we have bashing through our brains every second?"

"I don't have any of that sickness you have. Neither does Lexy."

"Oh, yes you do. You've already shown it. Lexy has it too."

"She's smart and has a good memory—"

"Photographic."

"A very good memory—"

"She has more than that. And so do you."

"Maybe, but I don't waste it on gambling and bookmaking for a bunch of criminals."

"Horse racing is entertainment."

"Tell that to the horses."

"You love racing. You have since you were little. Alexis loves it, too."

"She doesn't love it when a horse breaks down and she has to watch their broken legs flailing like—"

"No one likes that."

"But they keep pumping them full of dope and sending them out on the track."

"I have nothing to do with that."

"You're the engine that drives the train, Dad. Take away the gambling and they'll be jogging horses at county fairs for ribbons in a week."

"When did you become a bleeding-heart liberal? You used to be a lot tougher."

"No, you don't." Donna was shaking her finger across her father's desk in his face. "I see what you're doing. The same shit you used to do with Mom. Move the conversation wherever you want. Not this time. Alexis is with killers. Your friends. Ex-friends. Whatever—"

"You should remember that."

"Remember what?"

"That they're killers. No cops. I'm telling you we don't need them. She'll tell us where she is and how to get her home. But you have to look. I can't. I can't see it anymore." Donnie spun a big monitor around into his daughter's face. "She's talking to us. Right there. What's she saying?"

"This is more of your bullshit games! I'm calling the FBI." Donna whipped her phone up and started to dial 911.

Donnie snatched the phone from her hand and threw it as hard as he could against the wall near Nicky. The racket stopped everyone.

"*Look!*" Donnie was shaking but pointed again at the monitor. "I can't see beyond her first message."

"Good!" Donna screamed at him. "I wish you would have lost it thirty years ago! You probably would have if you hadn't worked so hard to nurture it. You practiced all those damn games to get better at it. Like you were racking a wine."

"I was trying to not go crazy!"

"So you drove the rest of us crazy instead!"

"I never harmed your mother—"

"You didn't have to! She killed herself rather than stay married to you!"

"That's not true," Donnie said, suddenly on his heels and lost again.

"It is! You should have let all this lunacy go a long time ago. Tried being a husband or, I don't know, maybe something real exotic, like a dad."

Donnie feigned exasperation. "Here it comes. I was a terrible father. I didn't play Barbies with you. Didn't throw you a ball—"

"You were a monster! You tortured people! You cut people until they screamed what you wanted to hear as they bled to death on our basement floor!"

"I don't remem—"

"Oh, bullshit! *Bullshit!* You haven't forgotten. No one can forget that sick shit. I know I haven't, and believe me, I've tried. I've tried everything. Years of therapy. Gallons of gin. It doesn't work."

"I don't remember any—"

"No!" Donna moved around the desk and was threatening. "Goddamn it! If I have to remember, you have to remember!"

Donnie lowered his eyes. "In the basement?"

"How the hell can you forget what went on—what you did down there?"

Nicky came up behind her. "Donna? Cut him some slack. If he doesn't remember, he doesn't remember."

"He's lying. He lies about everything. He always has. He's vicious. You don't know him. I was there when—"

Donnie suddenly slapped the monitor. "Will you please stop your crying and look? She's probably trying to tell you where she is."

"She'd call or text if she could do that."

"Not with a gun to her head."

That shook Donna from her rant. The shouting echoed away, and her father's deeply paneled walls heard nothing but quiet.

Nicky touched her shoulder. "Maybe, you know, maybe there's something there. You raised a really special kid. Give it a look. What's the harm?"

Donna's eyes were locked with Nicky's. There was a gentle pleading in them and she felt a change behind her own.

"I don't have to. Most of the pools contain the series three twenty-nine. He's right. I saw it before."

When Donna allowed her gaze to shift to the screen, her father spoke softly.

"I froze it when I thought there was something there. You see it?"

Her face couldn't hide the recognition. "Of course. Could be an anomaly. It's just numbers."

"Yes, but what numbers?"

"I see them. Still could be random. It doesn't mean anything."

"Yes, it does. It means she's in on that race."

Nicky maneuvered to see the frozen screen though the meaning of the numbers were lost on him. Donna's finger lazily pointed out the stacked row of dollars in each horse's pool of bets. Several included the series—three, two, nine.

"Three hundred and twenty-nine? A lot of totals have a three twenty-nine in them," Nicky questioned. "I don't get it. What's it mean?"

Donnie Chariot sat down, content amid his own loss to let his daughter explain.

"Three twenty-nine," she said. "That's the address to this house. Its street number. Like a shout out. A signal to this address. That maybe she's sending a message. If it's her—"

"It's her," Donnie said as he began scouring other screens haphazardly. "Help me look. She'll do it. She's good. Better than me. You'll see."

Nicky's skepticism was obvious. Donna would have liked to join him in his suspicions, but she knew her father—with all his faults, demons, and past—was probably quite right. Alexis did share the trait. Her father was right about something else too. Alexis was better than he was. Finding her message would be no easy task.

• • •

"Well, smart ass," Junior was saying to Alexis. "You forget how to place a bet?"

"She don't forget nothing. Ever. Damnedest thing I—"

A look from Junior choked the words off in Glass's throat.

"Better get moving, Einstein," Junior picked. "They're probably at the post."

Junior was right. Moments before the bell rang that signaled the start of the first of the day's races at the Big Sandy, Alexis touched the screen on Junior's phone and laid down the bet that was to build the pot for the big payoff in the fourth race. What her supposed guardian and the gun-toting addict thought was her first bet of the day was in truth number thirty-six. It had taken thirty-five other wagers across six claimers to line up the signal that she hoped had caught her grandfather's eye.

"Can I open another page?" Alexis asked.

"Why?"

"So we can see the race."

"Oh, yeah. Hurry up."

Alexis had it already done but was busy making more clandestine maneuvers on Belmont's tote board for the second race. Her adept sleight of hand was wizardry, but it came with risks. Her second performance would be tougher. She'd massage pool totals again and lean heavily on what she knew of her grandfather. It's what she didn't know that could be her undoing. Her grandfather was losing his grip on the deft skill he had built his life on and along with it, reality.

"Let's see," Junior said, reaching for his phone and stuffing the gun in his pants.

Alexis left the OTB site and Belmont's tote board open. She handed over the phone with a video stream up just as the gate flew open for the first race.

"Where's my money?"

"*Our* money," Glass quipped.

"It just left the three hole," Alexis smiled.

"You look pretty sure of yourself." Junior looked at the small screen. "The nag got a name?"

"Ruffcutt."

"That makes sense. Sounds like a loser."

"You'll see."

Glass tried to, but couldn't, and Junior wasn't making it any easier. "Turn it up at least." Every few seconds she pestered. "Well? Where's he at? What's he doing? What's happening?"

"Shut. Your. Mouth. I'm watching a race here."

"I got money on that horse too."

"You ain't got shit. Shut your face."

Alexis wasn't even trying to watch. She had confidence in Ruffcutt, but even more in her handicapping. Plus she was busy. She had seen the early tote board flash to the second race almost as soon as the bell rang for Ruffcutt's getaway. Her mind was running calculations.

"He's in traffic," Junior snarled.

"He'll break at the ⅜ths pole," Lexy said clearly.

Junior kept watching and Alexis kept deciphering her manipulations.

"Still penned in."

"He hasn't hit the ⅜ths yet."

"How do you know?"

"Claiming horses won't run like that. The pace would be too fast." Somewhere in her head, a sweep second hand was ticking of fifths of seconds. "He'll hit it…now."

On cue, Ruffcutt's jock made his move. The horse slipped through a crease between fading pace setters.

"He shot the gap!" Junior jumped. His eyes cleared for a moment and he could see through the craving for heroin.

"Where is he?" Glass said as she slipped to the edge of the couch.

"I dunno," Junior stumbled. "Fourth or fifth, but his ass is on fire!"

While the other two-thirds of the room were lighting up in anticipation, behind the blank stare on Alexis's face, neural transmitters were firing by the millions. With every tap on Ruffcutt's flank from his jockey's crop, Alexis pushed herself as well, harder and further than she had ever been before. On one side of the elastic ledger bursting in her consciousness were the GPS coordinates she'd pinched in that stolen glance at Junior's phone. On the other, was the tote board for the 2nd race at Belmont Park. She laid in bets yet to come behind her eyes until the board's numbers began to tick off, flicker, and glow as they matched the GPS coordinates. The top row of numbers would become the location of the phone. Find the phone? Find Junior DeSeti. Find Junior DeSeti? Find her. Then she'd be home again. She didn't have the luxury of considering if her grandfather would follow the alert of her three-twenty-nine. It was taking everything she had to align the coordinates onto the manufactured prism that was the betting totals.

Even when the numbers flashed complete compliance, she would have to recall the steps and make innumerable corrections after Ruffcutt took the purse from the first race. There was much to do and little time. Juggling an addict whose physical and psychological desires would quickly overcome the adrenalin rush of Ruffcutt's win, only tossed another layer on the impossible.

"He's closing…he's there. A neck…he's gonna take it! Yes! *Yes!*"

Junior jumped and Glass came off the couch. With a less tensioned short history, the two gamblers might have hugged. In between Junior pumping his fist, Alexis slipped the phone from his hand in exchange for a low "high five." Before she turned away and long prior to the dying clamor, she was manipulating the numbers for the second race.

"I told you," Glass gloated.

"Okay," Junior said as he settled back to earth. "What's the payout?"

"The results aren't final," Alexis said in an effort to buy more time though she knew Ruffcutt's take to the penny.

Junior rubbed his hands together feverishly and began to hover over his little bookie. "What's next? Are we going to let it ride?"

"I need a few minutes," Alexis said, now openly calculating on the phone.

Junior snapped his fingers. "Let's go. Let's go! There's money to be made."

"Give the kid some space."

Alexis echoed in an attempt to literally move Junior away from her maneuvers, "Yeah, give me some space."

For her trouble, Junior slapped her on the back of her head. "What I'll give you is a boot in the ass. How'd that be?"

"She did good. Let her be."

"You shut up. I'm keeping my partner focused."

"Partner? You didn't bring nothing to the table save a few bucks. And a sizeable share of that was mine."

"Shut. Up."

"She don't need you. You ain't nothing but a meth head that ain't lost his teeth yet. It'll happen. If you live long enough."

The gun snapped from Junior's waist with remarkable precision, given that its owner was in increasing decline. The vacuum left by the fading adrenaline of Ruffcutt's win left his body hurting. "You're the one who should be concerned with living." As he pointed the pistol, Junior's aim suddenly relaxed and he laughed. "Lose my teeth?"

"I don't stutter."

"You dumb bitch. Get back on that couch and shut your face before I put another hole in it."

Junior turned to Alexis. Her fingers were a blur, moving like a cascade over smooth stones.

"What's my payout?"

"Can't you see she's working the next race? Good thing your old man's got money."

"How about I just put you out of my misery?" the gun said as it came up yet again.

"Ignore her," Alexis said as she feverishly worked the tiny screen and pushed the phone to its technical limit. "She's not very clever."

"Hey! I been sticking up for you."

"You needn't bother. I can take care of myself."

"Glad to hear it. You're gonna need to if you hook up with the likes of this one. He's trouble. No crack head ever amounted to much."

"He's not addicted to crack. Or meth—"

"Thank you—"

"It's heroin."

"Ha!" Glass snorted. "She's got your number."

"Watch your mouth," Junior warned, but it was subdued.

"I watched a documentary on heroin users in Europe. It's a real problem."

"Pretty good problem here."

"Not if you have money, like Mr. DeSeti does. As long as you can get it. He'll be fine. Until he isn't."

"Get to work on that next race."

"Thank you. I will," Alexis said as she drifted away to the corner of the room, the phone heating up in her hand.

• • •

In the Chariot mansion, Donnie and Donna were both seated at the desk, captured by the changing numbers on the monitors flickering in front of them. Nicky was behind them and though he shared their concern he didn't share their ability and had no idea what he might have pretended to be looking for. As he leaned forward onto the desk in an awkward attempt to increase his focus and somehow his aptitude, his arm unwittingly brushed against Donna's shoulder. Without her eyes or mind straying from the screens, Donna's hand mirrored Nicky's absent movement, reached for his arm, and stroked it gently. The touch brought him away from his wasted efforts at the monitors. He looked at Donna and slipped his hand over hers. She stayed with the monitors, but a finger entwined itself with his.

"I'm not seeing—"

"You will," Nicky encouraged with another pat on her hand as she gripped tighter.

Numbers trickled onto the screens as father and daughter vied to solve a puzzle with no edges, no corners, no pattern, and no rules.

"That had to be her, right? Three twenty-nine," Donnie asked no one in particular.

"It's her. Keep looking."

Almost immediately Donna unraveled the enigma. "It's GPS. She's trying to give us coordinates."

"Where?" Donnie asked as he did everything but run his fingers over the screen.

Donna pointed. "Look at the first numbers on the board. They change, but watch. The first set keeps coming back to forty and ninety-seven. Watch."

The set changed, but as Donna predicted, the first series returned to forty and ninety-seven.

"I see it," her father said as he counted off pairs of numbers to the right. "If these are coordinates, this pair is the degrees for west," he said as she pointed to a set. "And they're doing the same thing. They change, but they come back to seventy-three."

Even Nicky could see some of the puzzle now. "The next pair. They keep coming back to ninety-three. See it? Is that something?"

"It sure is," Donnie answered as he watched the changing numbers. He picked up a pen and began scribbling down the numbers that kept bouncing back in three sets of two numbers across the tote board.

"I've got them," Donna said and she did. "I need an app or a program that will plot a set of coordinates. Which one of these has clean access to the net?" Donna asked as she looked over her father's myriad of keyboards and screens.

Nicky touched the search engine on his phone and set it in front of her.

"Will this work?"

"Perfect."

In seconds Donna had located a site and input the numbers. In a blink, a world map appeared and began to close in tight on the eastern seaboard of the United States. The screen drew down tighter to New York City and Manhattan, then drifted north and slightly west. Then it closed in further and stopped—its pointer exactly on the parameters of the numbers Alexis had sent.

"North Jersey," Donna said as she pushed up and away from the phone and the desk.

Nicky pointed at the small screen as he picked up the phone and slipped it in his pocket. "Palisades. I know it."

He headed toward the door with Donna on his heels, but she stopped and went back to the big desk.

"Wait."

Without a word she began opening and closing the drawers of her father's desk.

"What is it?" Donnie asked.

Donna's answer was to reach in the last drawer and retrieve a small revolver.

"Hold on—" her father began as Donna moved away.

"I don't normally forget things like which drawer," Donna said. "I must have been traumatized. Imagine that."

"Donna, you don't want that thing." Nicky added another layer of caution. "Somebody could get hurt—"

"You're goddamn right," Donna said as she flipped open the cylinder to ensure the gun was loaded.

"Don't take that. Please. Let me make a few calls. I'll get Gabriel. We need professionals. If Alexis is there, they'll get her out."

"I've been trying to reach Gabriel since Manhattan," Nicky said. "He doesn't pick up."

"He will for me."

"You can tell him where to find us," Donna said as the gun went into her purse. "Let's go, Nick."

"Donna wait—"

"Give him the coordinates. That'll put him right on top of us. If you reach him, fine. Have him call Nick. We're going to get my girl."

"Let me make a call first." Donnie Chariot was dialing. "Wait a few—"

"We're headed to Palisades, Dad. Call me on the road. And tell your supposed cop friends to not shoot us. We're the good guys. As I recall, it's always been difficult to tell which is which in this house."

Though Nicky led the way out of Chariot's office, it was clear this was Donna's show. It was also clear that regardless of how he got paid—providing he lived—he was working for the younger Donnie now. There would likely be a reckoning for that at some juncture, but it wasn't going to be now. He'd stay close to protect her and hope that she would protect him after all the chips had fallen.

As he hustled down the wide hall of the mansion, he stole a glance at Donna. Her eyes were tight, her jaw was locked. She was beautiful in her determination. Whatever was happening between them, in the length of the foyer Nicky weighed their upbringing, education, and career choices, and found himself wanting. When the crisis passed, he'd go back to being a driver for her father, if that. Should things end badly, she'd never be able to stand the sight of him. Even if he could somehow come out the hero, the chasm between them would likely prove too large to be eclipsed, even by the saving of her child.

28

Behind them, Donnie Chariot was calling Mrs. Glass. On the living room floor of the small safe house, in the rifled contents of her purse, Mrs. Glass's phone began to ring.

"Don't even think of answering that," Junior ordered as he crossed the floor and bent to pick it up. He looked at the number, then at Alexis. "Seems like your grandfather is looking for you. Or maybe he wants to talk to the old lady here. Is old man Chariot sweet on you, Grandma?"

"Mind your mouth."

Junior answered the phone, but didn't speak.

"Hello? Mrs. Glass?" Chariot asked. "What's happened?"

Silence.

"Mrs. Glass? Who's there? Who is this?"

Junior smiled, looked from Glass to Alexis and held the pistol barrel to his lips as if it were his finger. The move only served to toss down the gauntlet.

"*It's Junior DeSeti, Mr. Chariot!*" Glass screamed. "*Junior DeSeti!*"

The phone went to the floor and Junior went to the couch. Glass leaned away and held up her hands to ward off the swinging pistol, but her arms faded after a few crisp and weighted blows. Unprotected, her face caught several sharp strikes before Alexis ran into Junior from behind.

"Leave her alone!"

Chariot heard her yelling through the phone. "Alexis? *Lexy!*"

Junior spun from Glass, gun in hand, waist high. It clipped Alexis in the mouth and sent her sprawling across the floor. Glass saw the little girl collapse and was on DeSeti from behind just as Alexis had been. She had a hold of his waist and buried her teeth in his forearm.

Alexis realized she was on the floor near the phone and snatched it up.

"Run, Lexi! *Run!*" Glass yelled through bleeding, broken teeth.

"Don't move! I'll shoot you dead!"

Distracted by Lexi again, Junior was open to one last assault. Glass punched her fist up from behind between Junior's legs. It was a hard shot to his balls and he instantly sagged.

"*Run, Lexi!*"

Junior scarcely aimed. He didn't need to. Glass was still holding him by the crotch and, as he was driven to his knees by weakness and numbing pain, he had only to blindly put the pistol beneath his opposite arm and fire. The bullet went straight into the top of Mrs. Glass's head. She was dead before her body slumped to the floor and rolled up the back of Junior's legs.

Already weakened by the punch to his groin, Glass's bulk on the back of his legs took him down further. Her literal dead weight and the effect of the punch combined to hold him there for a moment and gave Alexis time to run for the door yelling over her grandfather's voice into the phone.

"*Grandpa? I'm winning at Belmont. Can you see it?*"

"*I see it, honey! Stay on the rail! Horses are closing fast. Understand?*"

"*Keep on the rail,*" Lexy answered as she hit the door. "*I can do it.*"

"*Are you okay?*"

Behind her, Junior was dragging himself out from beneath Mrs. Glass's body.

Ahead, Alexis was fighting the lock on the door and dropped the phone just as Julian DeSeti burst the door open into her and unintentionally flung her to the side. She recovered, but Julian caught her easily as she tried to dash by.

"Whoa now! What's going on here?"

Junior lunged across the room, snatched Alexis by the collar, and jerked her away from his father. He stuffed his pistol in his pants and grabbed the phone from his father's feet.

"*Are you okay, Lexy?*" Chariot was still pleading through the phone.

"Hell no she's not okay!" Junior hollered. "Did you hear that gunshot? The next one's going in the kid's eye. I want four million cash and gold. And I want my fucking car back, you cocksucker! You hear me?"

Only then did Julian look beyond his son and the little girl and see Glass's body slumped in a still-growing pool of blood. He immediately went to Alexis and turned her away from the carnage.

"Come with me. I'm so sorry. I'll get you out of here."

"I'm okay. I have to stay on the rail. I mean, keep my horse on the rail."

"Has he got you placing bets? No more. You're done. It's okay. I'll take you home."

"Home?"

"You're not takin' that little gold mine anywhere!" Junior barked at his father.

"Where's Mrs. Glass?" Chariot's voice came over the phone. "What's happened there?"

"What happened is your maid and the kid are with us!" Junior screamed as he sweated out Glass's numbing punch and his aching for a fix. "That's what happened. Except one's not breathing anymore. And you're gonna hand over that four million unless you want the little one to join her. Take your time raising the money, Chariot, because between now and then the kid here is going to be working for me."

Chariot was calm. "The only thing that little girl is going to do for you is get you killed."

"Four million, Chariot. You've got the phone number. Call me when you've got the money. *And I want that car!*" Junior disconnected and threw the phone on the couch.

His father was still holding Lexy's face into his side. "What have you done?"

"What you don't have the guts to do!"

"You're trying to run a ransom scam on Chariot? Four million? Is that what you're after?"

"Why not? What were you going to do?"

"You strung out addict. Chariot doesn't care about four million dollars any more than he does that cook over there. He could probably have that in an hour, you dumb shit. Then what?"

"I'll trade the kid for the cash."

"And then?"

"What? Live like a king."

"On four mill? You'll shoot most of it into your arm, but you won't live long enough to overdose. Chariot will cut you into little pieces."

Junior waved his gun. "He can try."

"Oh, he'll try. And he'll do it."

"Then I'll hold the kid."

"How? You killed the only good babysitter we could have trusted."

Junior began to pace as Julian walked his charge to a chair, turned it away from the couch and sat Alexis down. He crouched down next to her to keep her from looking at Glass.

"So what was *your* big plan, Daddy? This was your idea."

The senior DeSeti snapped a finger at Glass's body. "That wasn't my idea! All I wanted to do was get in the middle. Leverage Baron for thirty seconds. Only long enough to let him know we can run this town. Christ, we'd have made four million the first quarter."

"Then do it! Leverage, whatever."

"Not now, you idiot! We'll never pull it off. You saw to that. If we'd have laid it off to Baron, Chariot would never have even known we stepped in. He'd blame Baron."

"So let him blame him now!"

"You just blew it up by trying to squeeze him. Jesus, kidnap his grandchild? This world isn't gonna be big enough for you to hide."

"I'll kill him then."

"Shit. I can't believe you're my son."

"Why not whack him if he's such a problem? I drive right through his front gate every week. No problem."

"When he wants you to."

"He has almost no security."

"You think so?"

"All he has is that punk, Nicky, and Frank," Junior laughed. "And that dynamic duo has been cut in half."

"You keep making my case. No one can get near Chariot unless they're supposed to. Go ahead and walk through that gate unannounced. You'll never leave."

"You're scared of him."

"Not scared. It's called good sense."

"You're scared." Junior was saying it, but he was the one starting to shake, not from fear, but withdrawal.

"You're a mess. I raised a doper."

"You're yellow."

Julian had heard enough. "I was making my bones when you were dragging around on your mother's tit." Then Alexis's presence brought him back. "That's enough. Hush up."

"The kid works for me now. She can really pick a horse. In fact, she's loafing. Get over here," Junior said, his voice and hand trembling as he held out his phone. "Bring up the next race."

"Cut it out. She's not doing that."

"She'll do what I say to do!"

Alexis spoke for the first time in several minutes as she turned and looked up at Julian, but pointed to his son. "He's mean."

"And dumb as a box of rocks."

"Keep talking, old man. I got two bodies already today. Three don't make no difference. Might make Chariot number four, if I can get back through the city in time."

"Mrs. Glass is hurt bad, huh?" Lexy said.

"She'll be all right. We'll send someone to see to her." Julian took Alexis's hand. "Let's go, miss."

"You ain't taking her nowhere."

"Come along. What's your name again?"

"Alexis."

"Let's us two go for a ride, Alexis. I'm taking you home."

"No you're not," Junior threatened.

"You gonna shoot your own father?" Julian said calmly.

"Not just now. She's first," Junior said as he shifted the pistol to Alexis.

Julian stepped in front of the pistol and eased up tight against the muzzle. "Listen to me. I'm going to try to save your ass. The 'why,' escapes me at the moment. Maybe just for your mother's sake." He pointed behind his son at Glass. "Get that mess cleaned up, then call me. We'll find you a spot to hang your hat until I can sort this out."

Junior wasn't ready to capitulate just yet. "I don't need no help, but she's not getting out of my sight! She's a money maker. She can pick horses. We can make a fortune off her."

"I'm not showing you any horses," Alexis blurted. "Never again."

Junior grabbed for her, but his father pushed him away, ignoring the pistol.

"Stop it, you goddamn fool!"

"If we're not going to use her then she's out. She's a witness. I'll get rid of her and Chariot too."

"Put the gun down, son."

"Catch another body. Four. Five. Makes no difference now."

"Put it away."

Junior balked, but his addiction was rising up and clawing at his face. "You want her? Hope she don't come for us in twenty years, but she's yours. Little Miss Sunshine gets a pass, but Chariot's done. He's done! If he's as dangerous as you say, he's dead."

"To you, he's more dangerous dead than alive, and that's saying something after what you've done."

"You don't make any sense, old man."

"He's the brains behind Vegas. Julian. Son. Listen to me. Can you understand that?" The senior DeSeti hadn't called his son by their shared named in memory. "If something happens to Chariot, the weight of the world will fall on our family."

Junior's voice softened at the sound of his name though his words were still full of bite as he forced his pistol into his waistband. "Who's gonna say it was us that did him?"

"Considering you shot his number two on the main drag of a city of eight million people, my guess is somebody would piece it together."

"Maybe Frank ain't dead."

Julian looked away from his son to Alexis who had been soaking up both the talk and the sight of death. "We'll finish this later." He took Lexy's shoulders and turned her again away from the gore of both the room and the conversation and eased her toward the door.

"Am I going to my grandpa's now?"

"Almost," Julian said as he looked at his son. "We got to make a stop first."

"Then my grandpa's?"

"Why not."

Junior leaned close to his father and whispered. "Where you going?"

"I'll call. Try not to be high as a kite. I'll need you thinking straight for a change, not like this," Julian said as he motioned toward Glass with his eyes. "And clean this up before you leave."

"I'll take care of it."

"I take little comfort in that."

"I said, I'll do it!"

Julian was easing Alexis beyond the door. "I'll call you."

The door closed in the same motion as Junior tore off his blazer. He wadded it up to make the symbolic throw of frustration into a chair, but stopped when he felt a bunch in the pocket. After fighting and fumbling with the jacket, Junior retrieved a small black leather eyeglass case. Now however, it contained his heroin kit.

In a moment his sleeve was up. The cooking was completed as he sat in a chair near Glass's body. In another minute the needle found a well-used vein on his forearm and Junior's body slowly melted into the chair as he slipped off to chase the dragon.

29

Nicky and Donna were headed north on the Palisades Parkway with Nicky at the wheel and Donna watching the GPS coordinates click by on her phone. She leaned over to make a show of looking at the speedometer. "Faster. C'mon. Go!" She meant what she said, but she left her hand on Nicky's thigh when she sat up straight.

"The troopers love this section," Nicky answered the directive. "If we get stopped, it'll cost us a ton of time. We'll get to her."

"Is that the extent of the plan? 'We'll get to her?' Is that all you've got?"

"Excuse me?"

"Forget it." Donna patted his leg and checked her phone for the umpteenth time. "I'm sorry. I'm scared. I'm scared for her."

"You've got reason, but we have an advantage."

"Which is?"

"They don't know we're coming."

Donna let a small smile escape her lips. "And we don't know where we're going."

"Sure we do," Nicky said as he motioned at her phone.

"I hope it isn't on the 10th floor of a guarded high-rise. This thing doesn't read out the vertical."

"I know that area pretty well. All residential. My best guesstimate is that DeSeti has a safe house up there. Have you ever met Junior DeSeti? I mean, before 42nd Street?"

"I don't think so. Why?"

"He knows me. Real well. If I go to his door, it'll be nasty quick."

"So, we're going to knock on the door? We're back to your plan?"

"What do you got?"

"I'm not sure, but seems like we should employ a little more subterfuge than that."

"I'm listening."

Donna thought for a moment and equations began running wild in her mind. Percentages of successful entry. Retrieval ratio analysis. Quantitative variables. She shook her head in an ongoing lost battle to clear her mind.

"You okay?" Nicky said.

"Yeah."

"You come up with something?"

She hesitated.

"C'mon," Nicky teased. "Let's hear it."

"I'm going to knock on the door."

"Brilliant. Wish I'd thought of that."

If the mission were any less grave, they both might have laughed. What Nicky didn't know was that their plan—simple as it was—had come up at the lightning end of Donna's calculations as the best option to save Alexis. Still, beyond the mathematics and the odds, there was something Donna did not know. For while she thought through the process of the rescue ahead, the focus of it all was crossing her on the opposite side of the median. Alexis was headed south and back across the city to the borough of Queens, gently buckled into the front seat of Julian DeSeti's Mercedes.

• • •

"I hear you like horses," Julian was asking his passenger as Nicky's car sped by in the opposite direction.

"Yep. They're beautiful. I used to go to the track all the time."

"Which track?"

"All of them."

"All of them. That's a lot a tracks."

"Yep."

"Got a favorite?"

"I've got three."

"Three favorites? You can't have three favorites. Like a race. There's only one favorite."

"Nope. I've got three. Belmont—because it's my home track. You have to support the home team."

"That's good. I'm glad you like Belmont, because that's where we're stopping. You don't mind, do you?"

"No. I don't mind. I've already got one winner off Sandy today. I'd look at the rest of the favorites for you, but they'll be winding down when we get there."

"Thank you, but I'm good. Speaking of favorites, what's your other favorite tracks?"

"Churchill Downs for the history and Tampa Downs in February for the weather."

"By God, you do have three favorites."

"Told you. I don't fib."

"Not even a little?"

"Not even a little. I never welch on a bet and I always keep my word."

"I believe that's true, Miss. I believe that's true."

●　●　●

Twenty minutes later, Donna was at the door to a small, neat cottage tucked away behind a cloak of shade trees. She had considered a walk-by first, but gave way to a straight frontal assault, knowing that looking like you belonged was as important as stealth. Nicky had given up the wheel a quarter mile away and was creeping through the Hudson Valley forest like a Lenape Indian might have done two hundred years before.

He came into the tree line behind the house and watched for movement inside. He watched Donna discreetly check her GPS readings for the last time as she walked up the empty driveway to the front door. Not finding DeSeti's Mercedes seemed a plus. Alexis had likely been given over to others which decreased the chance that Junior would be there.

Donna pretended to ring the doorbell and stood back for effect in the event someone was watching. Rather than knocking, she looked in the windows on either side of the door. From her new vantage point— her hand shielding her face from glare, nose pressed against a windowpane—she could see into the edge of the living room and one of Mrs. Glass's feet. The foot was at an awkward angle to the floor and suggested the person who owned the foot might be sitting on the floor.

Regardless, someone was home, so Donna rang the bell in earnest, all while watching the foot. It was clear the foot was a woman's. That would be a plus, either to appeal to maternal instinct or to physically overpower. To sway the advantage further, Donna took the gun from her bag and held it discreetly behind her purse.

When the foot didn't respond to the bell, Donna pressed the button a second time and watched. Still nothing.

In the back of the house, Nicky glanced at his watch and stepped out from the cover of the trees. He'd given his partner enough time. By now Donna would be inside regardless of if the entry was easy or hard. He watched, listened, adjusted, and waited. There was no movement and no sound. He couldn't wait much longer. A good citizen's call to the police wouldn't do, but a bullet from a DeSeti bodyguard would be worse.

Out front, Donna still got nothing from the foot. "Sound sleeper," she said out loud to herself. In the unwelcomed respite, Donna checked the GPS on her phone. If everything she'd assumed up to this point was correct, Lexy's coordinates were less than twenty feet away. Mrs. Rip Van Winkle aside, Donna was going to get in this house and search for her daughter.

She casually looked over her shoulder to check the street. The protective shield of trees was doing its job. Donna held the revolver and her purse tight as she braced to slam into the door. It was a pure gamble that she had enough heft in a hundred-twenty-five pound projectile to even breach the door, but she was banking on adrenalin, old locks, and a tired casing to help.

As she took hold of the latch and prepared to launch herself, the mechanism gave way under her hand. The door wasn't locked.

Finding an unlocked door was one thing. Opening it and stepping through proved something entirely different. Walking into this house would be the first time she had knowingly broken the law. Even though doing so was a necessary element leading to the rescue of her daughter, if a seven-year-old had made a one-digit mistake sending a cryptic message through a racetrack's tote board—the whole thing was suddenly implausible—Donna would likely end up waking a lady from a nap and making a run from the police.

"Oh, Christ…" she muttered as she held the pistol behind her purse and stepped quietly inside. The door stayed open for a hasty retreat. If the babysitter had fallen asleep, it might be possible Donna could kidnap Alexis back without a sound. In the three painstakingly slow steps it took to get into the living room and see Mrs. Glass, any thought of a carefree escape vanished. It was replaced by a tightness in her throat that refreshed the fear in her heart when she'd watched her daughter taken away over a dead man in Manhattan. The foot Donna had seen from the window was, of course, attached to Mrs. Glass. She was sitting on the floor against the couch in a pool of her own blood.

As foreboding as that sight was, into the room further, another, potentially more frightening picture waited. Junior DeSeti was sitting, snoring slightly, slumped down in an overstuffed chair, a hypodermic dangling from his arm. On his lap lay his gun and kit, but the cooking spoon had fallen to the floor. Junior was dead out. On the floor, Mrs. Glass was just dead.

Alexis had done a masterful job. There were no mistakes in her message, and it had all worked. That was of little consequence to Donna as she stood between killer and killed. Alexis had certainly been here in this room when she sent the coordinates, but between the two alternatives in the room, Donna was marginally happy she wasn't here now. Her absence would be remedied in short order, Donna thought, but the priority was to pull the fangs from the drugged-up viper dreaming in the chair.

She didn't make a sound as she crept close and stopped in the shadow of a sleeping human Vesuvius. She reached down with one hand, moving like cold syrup toward the gun. The other hand held her father's revolver an inch from Junior's face. If he opened his eyes the last thing he'd see would be a muzzle flash.

But the heroin had him swaddled and cradled. His position nearer the supplier in the chain from heroin manufacturer to addict gave him access to a high that would last. Donna could have screamed and no one in the living room of the DeSeti safe house would have twitched.

With Junior's gun in one hand and her father's in the other, Donna backed out of the room and went to the rear of the house.

Nicky was crouching out of sight alongside the back door with a hand under his jacket holding his gun. When the door moved an inch, he grabbed the handle and jerked it open, propelling himself and his pistol into Donna's face. Both of her guns were pressed into Nicky's ribs.

Donna moved the barrel of her father's gun to her lips as though she'd done it a thousand times. "Shhhh…the baby's sleeping."

"Alexis?" Nicky whispered.

"No. I assume it's Baby DeSeti."

Donna motioned with the gun and Nicky followed her back to the living room.

"Is that DeSeti?"

"Yep."

Junior hadn't moved, but instead, Nicky's eyes went to Glass.

"Shit…."

"Yeah, shit. Watch this piece of it," Donna said. "I'm going to look for Alexis."

"Wait," Nicky answered, still whispering. "You watch him. I'll look. He won't be here alone. Someone will be with Alexis."

"Hurry."

Donna was examining Junior's kit when Nicky came back into the room a few minutes later.

"She's not here."

Anyone else would have asked a half dozen clarifying questions to pacify their own mind. "Are you sure?" "Did you check every room?" "Did you look in the closets?" "Under the beds?" But not Donna. Her stare asked those and others and heard the answers already written on Nicky's face.

"Okay," she said soft and slow as she pointed at Junior with his own pistol. "Somehow, this asshole is coming with us. She was here. She sent the GPS. And she's all right or she'd be laying alongside the cook."

"We can interrogate him right here. There's no need—"

"He's going to my father."

"Donna, we—"

"I'll take him by myself, if you want out."

"I don't want out, I want in," Nicky said as he took her hand, gun and all. "I want in."

Donna's head bobbed a slight acknowledgement. It was clear to them both that this was not going to be easy.

"I think I'd like that too, but first this piece of shit—"

"Is going to your father's. I know. We're taking a chance though. You've probably already calculated the odds on success of transporting a drugged up killer through the biggest city in the United States."

"Matter of fact, I—"

"Figured that. I'll tie him up."

"With what?"

Nicky went to a floor lamp and laid it over on the floor. He pulled the plug from the wall, stepped on the base, and ripped the wire free. He came back winding the wire up around a hand.

"Frank taught me that. He said the old standby used to be phone cords, but cell phones ruined it. Ready?"

"Ready."

Nicky slipped the wire around one of Junior's sleeping wrists, but left it loose. He took the needle from Junior's arm and went to toss it across the room.

"I'll take that," Donna said.

"For—"

"I've got the rest of his stuff." She tucked a gun under her arm and pulled Junior's eyeglass case from her back pocket, took the syringe, and put it in. When the kit and the gun were back where they'd been, she motioned to Nicky with the barrel of her father's revolver. "Do what you've got to do."

"If this sonofabitch gets away, start shooting and keep shooting."

Donna adjusted the guns in her hands.

"When he's down, turn his eyes away and lean on his face with your knee. Block his eyes until I can tie them off."

Donna trained both guns on Junior. "Do it."

"He's going to the floor," Nicky said and followed it by doing just that.

The slam was an equal balance of fluid and force. By the time Junior was awake enough to struggle, Nicky had his hands laced up tight behind his back with his feet. Donna had her full weight on Junior's head until Nicky ripped another cord from a second lamp and wrapped it tight around their prisoner's neck and eyes.

Donna pressed her revolver's muzzle hard into DeSeti's cheekbone next to her own knee. "Where is she?"

"Who?"

Donna chocked the gun. "Last chance, asshole."

"Pull that trigger and you'll never get her back."

Nicky touched her hand. "That'll do for now. Let's go."

It took a few breaths, but Donna relaxed and carefully lowered the hammer. "You're going to wish you'd told me."

Junior's slurred curses wore thin quickly. Nicky found the solution when he ripped off one of Junior's loafers, tore the accompanying sock loose, and stuffed it in the offending mouth. The mumbling was reduced to nothing in favor of trying to sufficiently breathe.

With no conversation, Donna and Nicky half carried, half dragged the stupefied addict into the garage.

"Put your foot on his neck," Nicky suggested as he hit the garage door opener and ducked out beneath the slowly rising door.

When the trunk popped open as the car stopped its backing up, Donna looked toward the living quarters. "What about Glass?"

"Too late for her. Grab his feet."

"It's a trail that will bring a lot of questions right to Queens," she said, half coded, but making no move to lift Junior.

"Good point. I'll get her. Stand on his neck again."

It was no time before Nicky returned, unceremoniously dragging the corpse of Mrs. Glass and dumping her body in the trunk. He tried to adjust the body over, but was thwarted by the literal dead weight.

Gravity pulled more blood from Glass's head. It ran into her lifeless eyes without objection. With one foot on Junior's neck, Donna reached into the trunk to help, but froze when the bleeding man of her dreams took Glass's place.

Donna recoiled at the sight of the bloody black holes for eyes and bare teeth of his face. "Get back!" she screamed and reached to slam the trunk.

Nicky thought she was yelling at him until he saw the terror on her face.

"It's all right. I can move her."

"It's him! Close the trunk. *Close it!*"

"We need to put DeSeti—"

Donna pulled Junior's automatic and fired three times in rapid succession into Glass's corpse.

Nicky dove away and Junior shook at Donna's feet. The reports careened in the near empty garage, magnifying the sound. In the ringing left in their ears, Donna heard the tingling ping of the ejected brass casings as they bounced across the concrete floor. The noises combined to wake her from her daylight nightmare.

She was shaking, staring at the bloodless holes she put in Glass's body. Nicky moved with great care. It was clear Donna was scared near death. Nicky saw it, felt it, and wanted to help. Perhaps it was the vacuum created by the carnage of blood, guns, and circumstance, but somehow, Nicky was in love with this woman who needed something—someone—so desperately.

He reached for the pistol slowly. "It's okay. Look at me. Look at me." She did and saw the thing she had unknowingly longed for. "You got him. He's dead."

Her eyes stayed on him. She wanted to believe the words she heard him say.

"Did you hear me?" Nicky repeated. "He's dead. He's gone. He won't bother you anymore."

Donna felt the gun being slipped from her hand and a weight being lifted from her shoulders. Both arms followed the pistol, draped over Nicky, and squeezed. It wasn't the collapse of a frail, broken woman. The holding was acceptance and recognition of a requited love. It was carried by a man with an understanding of the life she'd led that had her standing over a bound killer, an arm's length from a bullet riddled body, yet still willing to love her.

"He's gone."

"Is he?" Donna said as she relaxed her embrace and lifted her head.

"If he comes back, I'll help you bury him. All right?"

"Yes."

There was no anchoring kiss, but another, gentler hug, and stroking of Donna's back to erase years of anguish. In the moment, Nicky had his face in her hair, whispering. "What did they do to you?" He didn't expect an answer, but when they slipped out of one another's arms, he saw in her eyes that eventually, an answer would come.

"Ready?"

Donna nodded.

"Take his feet."

The two of them had an easier time with Junior and he went in, on and alongside his earlier target.

"Get cozy with your girlfriend there, but try to keep your pants on," Nicky said to Junior as he prepared to slam the trunk lid.

"Is there enough air in there? He needs to be alive," Donna said with enough hesitation and disdain that anyone who heard would have recognized the concern for Junior's life was fragile.

Nicky pulled Junior's pistol from his own waist. He eased the trunk down partway and put the gun against the inside of the lid, checked around the interior of the garage then looked at Donna. "Step back. Plug your ears and look away."

"Kinda late for that," Donna said through an embarrassed grin.

Nick smiled back, but she did what he said and heard the muffled gunshot. When she saw the spent shell casing bouncing across the floor, she pointed to it and others.

"Do we need those?"

"No, it's his gun."

When Nicky tried to slam the trunk, Junior stuck his knees up. They took a sharp blow, but stopped the attempt.

"Knock it off, dickhead!" Nicky yelled then punctuated the order by rapping the pistol barrel down hard several times on the offending kneecaps.

Junior recoiled and the trunk slammed closed.

30

The single bullet hole in the trunk's lid proved sufficient. Miles later Junior was alive, but whether he knew it or not at the time, he was far from all right. His transgressions against the House of Chariot had left him perched precariously close to the edge of oblivion. Donnie Chariot had tossed others into the abyss of eternity and now, though he could not recall most of the men who'd passed through his basement, he harbored no qualms about dispatching another, especially one who had interfered with his plans.

For her part, Donna might always struggle with the past where it intertwined with her father, but in the present, her love for Alexis and a growing sentiment for Nicky, might be enough to sustain her through anything unsightly, gruesome, or deadly.

Nicky held no reservations of any kind. He hated Junior and would gladly put a bullet in his head for a myriad of reasons, not the least of which was that he'd seen Junior kill Frank and had been unable to stop him. That episode was playing through Nicky's mind when he opened the trunk.

"Everybody out. Are you done groping Mrs. Glass, DeSeti? Zip up your fly. I hope you've come down from your high enough to answer a few questions. If you can't, there's ways to sober you up—no black coffee involved."

Junior was unceremoniously set on the floor of the garage next to the trunk.

"What about her?" Donna said as she motioned to the body of Mrs. Glass.

"I'll take care of her later. I better get the boss. He'll know what to do with this piece of shit." Nicky punctuated the sentence with an easy toe to the ribs of Junior.

"Pick him up," Donna directed. "I already know."

"We're taking him in the house?"

Donna answered slowly. "To the basement."

Nicky had Junior under the arms and lifted nearly all his weight. "I've only been down there a few times. Frank introduced me to a few guys who work for your father."

"You're ahead of me. I haven't been down there in twenty-five years."

"It's nice. There's a bar. I'll buy you a drink," Nicky winked around his cumbersome package.

"I used to serve drinks at that bar when I was Lexy's age."

"Sounds like fun."

"Maybe it was. There's another room off the bar. It was called The Locker. That room's not so fun. That's where we're going. You hear that, DeSeti? You're going into Chariot's Locker. Ever heard of it? If I were you, I'd have the location of where my girl is served up to fall right out of your face when that sock comes loose."

Junior was lucid enough to understand. He tried to fight against his handlers and the electric cord. Donna was getting the worst of it from his feet as the trio navigated the basement doorway to the stairs. She dropped his feet and drove the palm of her hand up hard under his nose. Junior flinched, groaned, and spouted blood from both nostrils.

"How'd that feel?" She stuck a finger beneath the wire around Junior's head and stabbed him in an eye until the blur of the wire gave way to black and lightning. "Where is she? *Where is she*?" Donna pulled her finger from Junior's eye and stepped back. "To hell with it. Throw that sonofabitch down the stairs. I'm not carrying him another inch."

"Get your father. I've got this piece of shit. Here," Nicky said as he pulled Junior's pistol from his waist. "He may want to give this to Gabriel. That's the gun that killed Frank and Glass."

Donna disappeared as Nicky began to drag Junior down to the basement. After two steps Junior felt his feet drop against a riser. He suddenly had a little leverage and pushed as though his life depended on it, as he'd correctly assumed it did.

The combination of Nicky pulling backward and Junior's shove sent them careening down the stairs. Though the fall only tightened the wire on Junior's hands and feet, it did snap the hog-tie between the two. All Junior's weight landed on Nicky and bounced his head off the floor, effectively knocking him out cold.

Bracing for a fight, Junior head-butted his abductor in the mouth for good measure. Only then did he realize it wasn't needed. Nicky wasn't in any condition to answer the bell.

It had been one fluid motion from the top of stairs to near freedom for Junior. He squirmed his arms down around his feet and up in front of himself. The stifling sock and wire around his eyes were the first to go. His teeth bit and pulled at the lamp cord until it gave way, then he tore at the binding on his ankles. In seconds he was loose and up.

Junior tore at Nicky's jacket until he was able to rip the big automatic from its holster. He put the muzzle in Nicky's mouth, but with nanoseconds to spare, looked up at the ceiling and considered the guns just beyond. Instead of drawing attention, he stomped Nicky's face a few times and pistol whipped him with abandon. Leaving Nicky unconscious and bleeding, Junior ran back up the stairs two at a time.

He'd never been in this part of the Chariot mansion and hadn't been able to see clearly through his wire blindfold. When he stumbled on the exit from the house to the garage, he heard Donna talking to her father and coming closer.

"This is the gun he used to kill Frank."

"Frank's dead?"

In a crushing rush Junior flung open the garage entry and bolted by the car with the bullet hole, and Mrs. Glass, in the trunk. Beyond it, he saw his Corvette.

The Chariots heard the ruckus and came running, but DeSeti had already cleared the garage through the still open overhead door. Junior ran toward the gate and triggered several motion detecting floodlights and also the attention of the guard dogs who exploded against their chains.

Donna passed the basement steps and saw Nicky's feet splayed across the floor below. While her father, alerted by the dogs, ran into the garage holding DeSeti's pistol, Donna jumped down the stairs. Nicky was still out and she wasn't able to wake him, though she felt a pulse and saw him breathe.

Outside, mindful of the dogs and shunning the light like a vampire, Junior jumped into the shadows of the guest house as Donnie, hidden from the blinding eyes of the floodlights, pressed against the wall inside the open garage door.

"DeSeti!" Donnie yelled. "This isn't necessary! The contents of my safe against the little girl."

Junior didn't make a sound as he adjusted his view down the sights of Nicky's pistol, scanning the garage opening toward the voice. The pistol stayed ready, but Junior joined the shouting from the shadows. "What's the terms?"

"Is she all right?"

"Far as I know, but she won't stay that way if anything happens to me."

"I can appreciate that, but if she's harmed it would be very bad—"

"Don't start crying—"

"—for you."

DeSeti was forced to try to think. He was hurting from the treatment inflicted by Donna and Nicky, but more so from his addiction. He was sweating and his hands were shaking. He needed a fix badly. "She's fine."

"Where is she?"

"Can't say."

"Can't or won't? There's a difference."

Junior hesitated, but tossed an answer into the light. "My friends have her."

"I doubt you have any friends, but I'd ask you to call them. Have her brought here and you can take everything in the safe. That's my word."

"That easy?"

"Exactly that easy."

"I'm missing a few things. Your daughter's boyfriend took my phone."

"Use mine."

"And a guarantee. What guarantee do I have you'll pay off if she wheels through that gate?"

"My word."

"Now, that's funny."

"You know I always pay."

"Gamble with your family's lives often, do you?"

"Every day of my existence. Anything else?"

"My car."

"You can use it to carry away the gold that's in my safe."

In the quiet, Donna had heard her father's parley and slipped from the house. She came up beside him, clutching his revolver.

"How about that guarantee?" Junior yelled.

Donnie's answer was to step out into the light with his arms outstretched, Junior's pistol dangling from one finger. "Here you are." He methodically dropped the magazine from the gun, kicked it away, and ejected the chambered round. It pinged and bounced around his feet while he made a show of tossing the gun like a Frisbee far into the darkness. "I'm not armed. You'll need me to open that safe, however," Chariot said as he stepped further into the crisscrossing lights. "I'm an old man. You could take me out with one punch, steal a car, and go. But you'd be better off leaving with all my money. It's yours. The money for the girl. What'll it be?"

Junior stepped from the darkness, his gun leading the way. "Very nice. That's a start. How much you got in that safe, Chariot?"

Donna pressed tighter against the wall in the garage while her father answered.

"More than you and your father handle in years. It's all yours." Chariot took a few steps toward the voice. "But I'll need that little girl back. I have a phone in my jacket. I'm reaching for it. Don't get anxious on me."

Donnie did just that as Junior walked right up to him, his gun trained on Donnie's face. The phone was held out, but Junior ignored it.

"Change of plans. Let's us go open that safe. I'll take the money up front."

"That won't do. When she's—"

"I don't give a shit, Chariot. Your options just got tossed in the grass. You're going to open that safe or I start putting holes in you." The declaration was punctuated by Junior pressing the muzzle of Nicky's automatic tight against the bridge of Donnie's nose.

"You're clever enough to know I'll never open it under threat. If you pull that trigger, you'll never get in that safe. The girl for the money. That's the only way."

Junior pulled himself up tight alongside the gun and Chariot's face. "I've been thinking about killing you since you stole my car."

"Now's your chance," Donnie said and spread out his arms again. "Or you could take that money."

"You want to die right here?"

"I'm already dying. You'd be doing me a favor."

"Happy to help. Now, move!" Junior said as he spun Donnie around and marched him across the pavement with the gun creasing the base of his skull. "Holler for Li'l Donnie and tell her if she tries anything, I'll blow your head off."

"I'm afraid you overestimate the value of her filial love. I suspect you and your father are in similar straits. My daughter wouldn't care if you shot me right now. You should take the money, DeSeti. If you kill me, there goes the money—and also, Baron will massacre you and your entire family."

"Shut up."

"Ask your father what will happen if you kill me."

"Shut up!"

"You better ask—"

Junior jerked Chariot to a stop. "I'm sick of your mouth. Maybe I just kill you and your pets and walk out that gate."

"You'd be in Riker's by tomorrow. All these lights have cameras. But jail would only be a temporary reprieve. It'll take a few days for Baron to reach you in there, but he'll kill you wherever you are."

Junior shoved Donnie again, this time into the garage. As soon as they cleared the door, Donna shoved her pistol into Junior's neck from the shadow. "Drop it or you're in hell."

No one flinched. Junior heard his tormentor's voice again and felt the pinch of the gun's front sight in his neck.

"Use your head for once. If he dies, you die."

Junior was aching more than ever for his drug, but tried to be defiant as he kept his pistol on Donnie. "I don't think you can do it."

The Book smiled. "Would you like to bet?"

"You don't look good, DeSeti. You need a fix. I've got your kit. Put the gun down and I'll give it to you."

"You're a condescending bitch. You know that? You raised a nasty daughter, Chariot."

"She does possess some of my more admirable traits."

"Where's my daughter?"

"You better ask nicer than that," Junior said, continuing to hold his pistol tight against the back of Donnie's head. "I'm not so helpless and you're not so tough now that I'm not tied up." Junior touched the blood on his face. "I'm pretty sure I owe you a punch in the mouth. Maybe more."

"Whatever you say. Where is she?"

"Hey, how's your boyfriend?"

"He's hurt pretty bad. Happy?"

"You know it."

"He likes hurting people, Dad. Did he tell you he killed Mrs. Glass?"

"You don't know that," Junior protested.

The Book touched his chin—thoughtful as a judge—but temporarily lost as to who Glass was and why it mattered.

"Where?" Donna asked again, pressing home the question with the muzzle.

"Get that gun out of my neck and I'll tell you."

"Never happen."

"Okay. I sold her to a ring of pedophiles. She should be getting put on a boat for—"

Donna stabbed him hard with the barrel of her gun. "Shut up! *Shut up!*"

"Pull that trigger, she's dead!"

"Stop!" Donnie cautioned in front of Junior's sweating hand and the barrel of a gun. "I want my daughter back, DeSeti. You want to live a wealthy man. There's a resolution. Both of you—lower your guns. Make that call. When she comes through the gate, I open the safe. We all get what we want and no one need get hurt."

"How about that famous word of yours, Chariot? Your psycho daughter inherit that?"

"Ask her."

"How about it? The street says your father has never welched on a bet and his word is better than gold. I want that special Chariot word from both of you bitches. Then I'll make that phone call."

"Sure," Donna said from behind the sights of her dad's revolver.

"Not a lot of room for discussion, is there? Give me your word. You too, Book."

"Done," Donna said. "Tell him, Dad."

"You have my word."

Junior DeSeti answered by flipping the pistol in his hand away from Donnie's head and stuffing it in his waist band.

Both Chariots held looks of surprise, but for different reasons. "Commendable," Donnie said as he turned, rubbing the impression from the base of his skull. "I'm confident we can—"

"You stupid bastard." Donna pushed her revolver in Junior's face. "Get your ass on the ground."

"Wow...so that's how it is," DeSeti said.

Donna was smirking. "That how it is."

"No," Donnie said. "That's not how it is. Donna, you gave your word."

"To a piece of shit who killed Glass and Frank, kidnapped my daughter—"

"Those are other matters. We'll manage those now that we know Mr. DeSeti to be a man of his word. It is important to maintain—"

"What? That bullshit code? Honor among thieves?"

"It's more important than that."

"Not to me."

"The deal's off, Chariot," Junior snapped, but raised his hands. "No call. No kid."

"You'll make that call," Donna said with no attempt to veil the threat. "Tell him, Dad."

"I believe he will. But we must keep our word. Put the gun down." At that, Donnie touched the revolver to ease it down.

"You *have* lost your mind!"

Donna wasn't complying and it made Donnie more confused. "These things will adjust themselves. They'll work out. One covers the—"

"Work out? He's an animal! He shot Glass."

Glass's name didn't register though Donnie understood enough to know it should. "This Glass's death, that does change things somewhat. Negotiations require a certain discipline. Restraint."

"I never killed anyone."

"He killed Frank, too. Remember that."

Frank's name rang a truer bell. "Frank," Chariot said as the puzzle came into temporary focus. "This puts our discussion at a severe risk."

Junior couldn't continue. "She's lying! I'll go get the girl right now." His mind was now aching for the drug as bad as his body. "Go get the money—all of it. And I'll take my car too. I drive out of here with the money and my car or you never see that kid again. That's the deal."

"Don't trust him, Dad. He's an addict who kills women."

"You think I kill women, do you? You scared? Here. You want my gun?" Junior pulled the pistol from his waist slowly, with two extended fingers. "It's yours." He threw it onto the driveway, but his hands came back in a flash. One grabbed Donna's gun and the other punched her in the face.

Donna was staggered, but DeSeti's rightful attention was on the gun. He forced the business end away as Donna held on but crumpled. Her father threw both hands into the clawing fight for the gun. Junior kept one hand in the mêlée and belted Donnie hard under the chin with the other. The Book sank. Now Junior had both Chariots reeling.

With her father stymied, Junior wrenched the gun from Donna and belted her in the mouth with a fist weighted by a gun. She went down to the pavement and Junior dropped down with her. He whipped her in the face with the revolver until she stopped flailing then reached out and delivered the same to Donnie. When the Book went flat, Junior stuffed the gun in his pants and took Donna by the throat.

"Good night, bitch. So you know, I'm going kill your father and your boyfriend if he's breathing. I can make more money with your kid. I'll give her the needle and turn her on. She'll stay with me forever chasing the dragon." He punctuated each word with a tighter, strangling grip. He was wide eyed and sweating. "Maybe I'll marry her or just—"

Whatever words Junior had intended to say were knocked back down his throat along with several teeth by the spade end of Mr. Abreu's shovel. Junior collapsed on Donna with a sickening moan and an accompanying snoring wheeze through a broken face. The old gangster had him by the scruff of the neck and yanked the revolver from DeSeti's pants. Abreu tossed Junior off his long-ago hide-and-go-seek playmate, sending him sprawling face first on the pavement.

"You okay, LD?" Mr. Abreu asked as he knelt, still holding the shovel and the revolver, each cocked should the lesser DeSeti come to.

Donna thrashed at her own throat and Mr. Abreu until she regained her bearings. When her mind cleared, she found she was clutching the hand of an old friend.

"Mr. Abreu. Are you all right?" she said as a reflex.

"I'm well, kiddo. Actually, very damn well. Not much call for a good shovel to the bean these days. Felt good to let the old devil in me stretch his legs a little."

"Yeah?"

"Yeah. Your father's business is pretty boring these days. He's a changed man, you know."

"I know."

"I hope so. He has his demons, like we all do. But you remember, Donnie," Mr. Abreu said as he gently tapped her forehead with a ruddy finger. "Every saint has a past, as wicked as it can be, and every sinner has a future—maybe full of blessings. You follow, kiddo?"

"Yes."

"Okay. Get your wits while I tend to The Book."

The gardener soon had both Chariots, each still shaken, on their feet. He steadied the pair into each other. As they exchanged checks for injuries and soft assurances, Abreu went to DeSeti.

Junior had just begun to move. A boney knee dropping into the small of his back squelched anything sudden. Abreu yanked his belt from his faded trousers like uncoiling a whip. A world champion calf roper would have been proud of how the old man looped first one wrist than another, before bringing DeSeti's bare foot into the fold with his rickety knee.

"Give me a hand with this, LD," Mr. Abreu said as he roughly began to pick Junior up by one arm. "Seems as though some dog took a shit in our driveway."

"I got him," her father answered for her. "Go get Frank."

Donna didn't release her father's arm. "Dad, Frank's gone."

"He was with you."

"No. Nicky was with me. Frank's dead," Donna stammered as she tried to focus the breaking lens of her father's mind. "Nicky's...he's in the basement. He's hurt."

The Book was driven out of misplaced answers by Junior's limp body being thrust at him.

"Grab ahold, Book," Abreu said as he sought out Donna's eyes. "Run check your boy."

It took an exchange of equally pained looks before Donna resigned her father to the care of the old gardener and ran ahead through the garage.

By the time Abreu and The Book navigated the basement steps with Junior DeSeti, Donna had Nicky sitting on the floor, leaning against the wall. She was pressing a damp bar towel against the back of his head. Her hand and the towel were already bloody. Donnie Chariot stepped in a small pool of the stuff at the base of the steps as he lugged his share of the weight.

"Mind your step, Book," Abreu said. "That gets greasy, if you recall."

Chariot looked down at his footprints in Nicky's blood. "Indeed. Mrs. Glass will be on my ass, without a doubt."

More looks bounced around the basement. Having missed the early flailing thoughts in the driveway and with a ringing in his ears that overrode any warning, Nicky's thoughts stumbled out of his mouth as unencumbered as Chariot's.

"Mrs. Glass isn't going to clean that up, boss. That sonofabitch shot her. Just like he shot Frank."

"Nicky, he knows. Sit still. You're bleeding all over."

Mr. Abreu steered his boss with Junior instead of words. He jerked his side of Junior and pulled Donnie away from responding to Nicky with another lost thought. "You want him in The Locker, boss?" Abreu asked without breaking stride toward a steel door at the far end of the basement.

Donnie nodded and pointed toward the same door with his chin.

Behind the men, Donna pulled the bloody cloth away from Nicky's scalp. She could see a deep gash. "You're going to need stitches. I think Abreu can do it. Mr. Abreu? Do you have something for Nick? He's hurting and could benefit from a stitch or two."

"I don't need stitches." Nicky made a move as though he might stand, but didn't get far. His head ended up in his hands. "I can barely see."

"I'll fetch a few things after The Book's settled."

Before Donna could get up from the floor, Nicky had her by the arm. He pointed weakly toward the opposite end of the room and the steel door. "The Locker?"

Donna stared at the door as Abreu produced a thick brass key that would have been more at home unlocking a cell door. The heavy door opened and Abreu, DeSeti, and the Book eased into the darkness inside.

When she didn't answer, Nicky looked at her and saw an ashen profile. "Donna? Hey."

Her face turned toward him slowly and he saw eyes that were filling with tears. Memories were being loosed that had been held in feeble check for twenty-five years.

"What's in there?" Nicky said in a whisper that betrayed something between wonder and fright.

Donna balked again as the tears overcame their ramparts and streamed down her cheeks. The tears collected and were dripping unmolested from her chin before she answered. "You'll see. And then you'll wish you hadn't. But there'll be nothing you can do."

At The Locker, the door closed behind Donnie Chariot without a sound.

31

Julian DeSeti's Mercedes pulled in near one of the sprawling stables inside Belmont Park. Adjacent to the barn, walking rings and shower stations that had been in near constant use all day were finally quiet as darkness covered the complex. The biggest day on the track's racing calendar was tomorrow. Apart from those equine athletes that had appeared in the first two legs of the Triple Crown, few of the runners would have paraded on a track in front of a crowd as large as the one anticipated for the Belmont Stakes. The bustle and noise would unnerve a few, but propel others.

Julian DeSeti was looking to the crowd for something different. He hoped the boisterous throng would cloak an exchange that would secure his place in the gambling side of the *Sport of Kings* for as long as he wished. What he'd do with the unending windfall was less relevant than the amount itself, which was all but immaterial. The victory was in the power and esteem that came with positioning himself as Baron's second. He'd no longer hold his hat in hand when he went to Vegas. Baron would remain king, but even kings are mortal. This would be made evident as soon as Julian was thoroughly entrenched.

"When are we going to my grandfather's?" Lexy asked as she half followed, was half led, toward a small house between barns.

"He's going to meet us here."

She stopped and turned back to the Mercedes. "I should get my backpack. I want to check the card for tomorrow."

Julian held her up. "We'll only be here a short while. The service is real spotty anyway. Besides, your grandfather will be right along."

Alexis heard at least one lie sandwiched between two likely others. She'd traversed Belmont with her iPad many times walking beside The Book checking weather and results at various tracks. "When?"

"I'm not sure," Julian said honestly as he encouraged her along. "That's up to him, but it won't be long."

"If it turns into a while, can we get my iPad? I can play games at least."

"I'll get it myself," Julian said as he held the door open to one of the permanent houses that dotted Belmont Park. "We have to wait for your grandfather here. So he'll know where to find us."

"Can I go see the horses? I'll watch for his car. He'd know I'd be with the horses if he couldn't find me in the house."

Julian thought for a few moments about the chance Lexy might be seen. "I have to make some quick calls and I want to show you our digs. If your grandfather can't come right away, we'll go see the horses. How's that sound?"

Alexis was way ahead of him though he was leading her through the house. If this turned into another hotel room or another shooting, she'd bolt. She knew Belmont Park too well. If her grandfather didn't come for her, she'd slip off to the barns, maybe even the train station and beyond. Nothing had felt right since Mrs. Glass had picked her up from school. Mr. DeSeti was nice enough, but most adults started out that way. She followed Julian on through the house, but her escape plans were already taking shape.

"Is there a computer here? I'd like to see the racing card. I'm trying to pad my college fund," she said as she looked around what might have passed for a dormitory or boarding house.

Julian laughed. "I suspect your grandfather has got your college fund all taken care of. I have an office here, but no computer. I usually bring my laptop," he said as they wandered down a long hall. "Most of these offices are for trainers. Sometimes people working the track stay over. Once in a while a jock. Nothing fancy, but it keeps them out of the weather."

"Probably nothing to eat then. Jockeys are always starving themselves. We should order a pizza."

"That's an idea."

"Got a TV?"

"Right in my office."

Julian was at a double dead-bolted, heavy door. "This is us." He caught her looking at the multiple locks. "A lot of people come and go. I keep some business records here. I can't have them wandering away."

The room was small, but clean. There was a couch and the promised television. A metal desk was set against the wall but gave little sign of having seen much business recently. Several old racing forms were scattered across the desk's top. Beneath it was a miniature refrigerator that would have been equally at home in a dorm room.

"Small, but it has a private bathroom." Julian pointed to a narrow door in the corner. "Right through there if you want to wash your hands while I order that pizza."

Alexis knew a grownup request cloaked in a suggestion when she heard one. Without a word she went to work on her hands a few feet away. On the wall near the unadorned sink she could see the outline of a poor patch job where a window had once been. When she came back, she saw evidence of similar construction on the wall above the desk.

"Did you take the windows out? If I was you, I'd watch the horses while you work."

"Burglars."

"Safety first," Alexis said as she grabbed the remote and jumped up on the coach.

Julian opened the fridge and retrieved a bottle of water, twisted the top enough to be loose and handed it to his guest.

As Alexis toyed with the remote, Julian worked his phone, hoping Alexis was listening as intently as she pretended not to be.

"It's Julian. At the track. My office. How soon can you be here?"

"Who's that? Is that my grandfather? Let me talk to him," Alexis asked, well above a whisper. When Julian didn't respond. She issued a directive. "Ask him to bring a pizza."

"Hey, stop and get a pizza. She's hungry."

"Half broccoli and half green peppers," Alexis shouted toward the phone as she jumped off the couch. "Tell him I want broccoli and peppers."

"She wants half broccoli and half green peppers. Perfect. See you then."

Alexis was already fading back to the couch.

"That was your grandfather. He's in a meeting and has a few things to finish then he'll be over to pick you up."

"Couldn't you drop me off there?"

"I've got some things to do myself. I'm doing both of you a favor getting you back through the city."

Alexis wasn't certain what was going on, but she was certain her grandfather wasn't on the other end of that call. He would have wanted to talk to her and besides, the pair had sworn off green peppers for life. She began flipping through channels.

"He'll be an hour or so. Can you hold out that long?"

"I'm good."

"I've got to make a few more calls. You okay watching TV until he shows?"

"Yep," she said as she intently searched channels.

"Don't go outside, okay? It's dark. I don't want you to miss him. Fair enough?"

"Yep."

Julian made his way into the far reaches of the house checking doors and windows as he went to help ensure his guest would remain one. The pass also confirmed no one was curled up in a corner sleeping off a pre-dawn exercise ride.

Down the hall, Julian perched on the arm of a chair in the living room and found some relief in the turned-up volume coming from the

TV in his office. In a moment he had Baron, still comfortably ensconced at the Plaza, deeply engaged on the phone.

"What do you mean, you have the girl? What girl?"

"The Chariot kid," Julian chattered. "The Book's granddaughter."

"For what? What are you talking about?"

"You had her. Now I do. You held the cards. Now I've got them."

"Are you drunk, Julian?"

"No hard feelings, Baron. Let's just say I saw your play and I raised you. The game is still on, but now we share the pot. Fair enough?"

Across the East River, Baron was staring blankly at his elegant, but temporary hotel desk. He pressed the phone tighter against his face as though it might ensure understanding.

"Julian. Please listen closely. I have no idea—"

"Baron. It's okay. I'm with you. I agree with you."

"Agree with what?"

"Putting pressure on Chariot. It was the right call. It's working. We both know he's been dropping the ball."

"I don't know what you think you know, but Donnie Chariot is far from your chief concern. You should be managing that son of yours. I've heard what happened a dozen blocks from where I'm sitting."

"Yes, that was an unfortunate turn—"

"Unfortunate? I'm not prone to hyperbole, but it is a tad worse than 'unfortunate.' The Book placed a great deal of stock in Frank. I wouldn't care to go by the name DeSeti at any time in the near future in this city. Might I suggest you bury your boy away somewhere deep before Chariot does?"

"I'm not concerned about Junior. He's out of town. Upstate—"

"I don't want to know more. This conversation is—"

"Thanks for your concern."

"My concern rests with my business interests."

"Exactly," Julian said as he ratcheted up the conversation, but chanced a glance up the hall. "It all plays into your move just fine. You grabbing the kid was brilliant. I understand my play will cost me something, but—"

"You keep referring to an event that has a rather heavy and dark veil of kidnapping over it."

"Not kidnapping—leverage."

"Leverage. I see. My recommendation is that your best course of action includes explaining the distinction of your definition to the FBI just prior to entering their witness protection program. This being my counsel as, if you're saying you've taken Chariot's only grandchild, there are no odds long enough to support you or anyone in your family being alive this time next week. Being on the list of people Donnie Chariot is displeased with has never been good for one's health."

"Then I suggest you're a sick man, Baron. Remember, this was your party to start with. I only cut in and stole your dancing partner."

"And I submit that your ability to make sense is not increasing with the duration of this conversation. I have nothing to do with what you or your family has done. We may not share the same circles, and I assure you, this most recent escapade will likely indemnify we never do, but you must know, despite my business proclivities, I would in no way bring a child into play. There are countless methods at my disposal to bring pressure to bear should it be required. Some of those come to mind just now and I suspect The Book will employ several against you with all possible haste."

"You want me to believe it wasn't you behind taking Chariot's granddaughter?"

"On the lives of my own grandchildren."

DeSeti was stilled for the first time in several minutes. He checked the hallway again.

Baron waited, but instantly felt the shift. "Julian, listen closely. In the strongest possible terms, I propose you contact Chariot and arrange to take his granddaughter home as soon as possible. If things are as you say, you must distance yourself from the seamy side of what has occurred. I understand this is difficult to entertain, but you must lay this at the feet of your son. He'll be taken to task for killing Frank despite your intercession. There's no distance you can put between your boy and Chariot that will guard your son's life. None."

Julian heard his own voice, but knew it was bluster. "Then I'll have to take The Book out. To protect my boy."

"I can't allow that."

"And I can't allow my boy to be killed by that butcher!"

"Those days were long ago and the time to consider another tack vanished when your son decided to kill a man and snatch a child from 42nd Street.

"Julian. Make the best of what rests in your hands. You can be the redeemer in Chariot's eyes. Return the girl."

"How do I know you're not running a game on me right now?"

"I don't kidnap children. Return the child."

There was only a slight gap for the thought to form and fall into. "For my boy. I'll return her if he backs off my boy."

It was Baron's turn to pause. "He might take that, but it is tenuous at—"

"You better hope he takes it because if he doesn't, I'll put every dollar I have on the street for his head!"

"This train has advanced too far down the track to be braked by threats."

"Fine. No threats then. But if he doesn't take it, you'll be the first to know. You're going to make the offer."

"Not likely. I don't care for any part of this."

"Too late. You know I have the girl. Plus, it's difficult to believe you didn't have a hand in this. Who else would try something like this and who else but you stands to profit if Chariot starts producing again?"

"And who stands to lose the most if this scheme goes awry, as it already surely has?"

"We're all gamblers in this business, Baron. So, as you seem very concerned with The Book's happiness, you should set about hedging a few bets to make it so."

"I see the threat you said was behind us is clearly just below the surface."

"Hedging my own bets. That's all. You said I can be Chariot's redeemer. Well, you be his savior. This may still benefit us both. If

Chariot thinks you negotiated for his kid's release, he's going to owe you and if history serves, Chariot never owes for long. Just remember that if he puts you on a pedestal, who made it possible."

"That far-flung notion is absolutely no consolation to me."

"Make that call, Baron. Then call me back. I know what his honor means to him. Tell him he can have the kid back in her own bed in half an hour based on his solemn word that my boy is left alone. Is that understood?"

"It is."

"And you're vouching for the arrangement and the exchange. If Chariot reneges, all bets are off. Maybe not right away, but his daughter and this kid—I'll find them. Maybe he'll whack me too, but those girls of his will still be dead."

"You and your threats."

"Not threats—promises. Make the call."

Julian ended the call, stood, and immediately leaned heavily against the wall. The call he thought would be his making instead left him staggered. In the rambling shambles of his plan, he decided he'd better lay his hands on his son and also make a longer-range plan for holding his trump card against Chariot and indirectly, Baron. Trying to think a few steps ahead, Julian went back to his office and Alexis.

"You okay here for a little while? I need to see some people."

"Whatever."

"There's more to drink in the fridge. Stay out of the beer. Your grandfather should be along any minute. Wait right here for him."

"He's bringing pizza?"

"That's what he said. There's a couple blankets under the towels in the bathroom if you get chilly. I'll be back in a few minutes."

Julian stepped out and closed the door. Between snippets of voices and laugh tracks, compliments of surfing channels, Alexis heard both dead bolts turn and lock. In a minute she faintly heard the Mercedes start and pull off. If she could have heard inside the car, she would have known Julian was trying to reach his son. If she'd been riding along, she would have ridden by the DeSeti home looking for Junior then traveled back across the bridge into the city. Soon she would have traveled all the way up to the Palisades safe house which had been witness to Mrs. Glass's killing. With each mile and move, she would have seen the creases tighten around Julian's worried eyes.

32

Any sound in The Locker was muffled to near extinction by padded, thick insulated walls and a two-door entrance on either end of a tiny vestibule just inside the initial steel door. Junior's straining moans as he was stretched and ratcheted between the floor and ceiling were reduced to gentle sighs by the soundproofing. His ankles were belted and chained in a three-foot-wide pit less than a foot deep. At the bottom was a rusted drain. His arms were over his head and excessively strapped and tied to a chain block-and-tackle pulley rooted in the rafters. The controlling chain of the hoist went to the wall and a simple latch-locking slip device. Junior was securely held, but not stretched tight. That would come later.

On the floor, circling the shallow pit, were a dozen or more two-inch holes that held several removable lengths of tubular steel, perforated every now and again with half inch holes. The lengths were at least seven feet high. Against the wall were a number of various lengths of rough rebar, the kind used to reinforce concrete. When the upright lengths were placed in the floor, the rebar could be slid through the holes on the uprights horizontally, forming a series of tight braces that crisscrossed the pit and rendered the unfortunate body inside, immobile.

Around the adjustable web of rusty steel uprights and cross members, a platform of wood unfolded with steps and landings that embraced the steel at various levels. The rough stage conveniently placed hands or tools at whatever part of the helpless, imprisoned person was presently under examination. The coarse timber of the platform, with its steps and ascending levels, gave the contraption the appearance of a perverted hangman's gallows, wrapped in dust and veiled in cobwebs.

Junior DeSeti dangled within this macabre labyrinth, slowly swaying back and forth to some semblance of consciousness. His broken mouth and shattered teeth, compliments of Mr. Abreu's shovel, still bled, but the trail down his neck had mostly dried. Above him, two banks of fluorescent fixtures hummed ahead of a harsh light. On a wall hung a few short ropes and an ancient riding crop. Beneath them rested a cluttered table, bolted to the floor. The table's top was covered in dust and contained a wide assortment of cutting tools and pliers, all held down by more cobwebs. A neglected sharpening stone slept unused amongst the many tools. Next to the table, an old garden hose, suffering dry rot, was rusted to an even older spigot and lay curled in an antique concrete basin.

"He'll be around in short order," Abreu said as he reached through the blocking uprights and horizontal rebar and pinched Junior's side. "I may have been a bit heavy-handed with the shovel. You see what lack of practice does now, don't you?"

"Indeed."

"Those were heady days—keeping the books balanced."

"How's that?"

"Balancing the books."

"I don't follow," Donnie said honestly as he drew a straight razor across a stone several times at the table then looked closely at its edge.

"That's what we called it back in the day. Oh, you were always a leg up with your numbers. Anyone could see it, but I always felt this was your true calling. If someone's fingers were sticky, you just—" Abreu made a quick motion as if his own fingers were a pair of scissors, "—snipped them off. Seeing that *tarado* walking around without a thumb cured a lot of *vaqueros* of stealing. One snip saved much money and a great many more fingers, I tell you."

"I don't…I really…."

"It's okay, Book. I remember for us both. What about this one? You say the word, I kill this one for nothing."

"He's…was he stealing?"

"Worse! He ran over my flowers!"

Donnie laughed despite the seriousness of current affairs. "I don't know that posy destruction constitutes a capital offense."

"This boy…he *muy malo*. I see it in his aura. Very bad."

"Yes. I agree. But he has something I want."

"He's a beggar. What could he—"

"He took my daughter."

"Li'l Donnie? No—"

"Oh, yes, and he's about to tell us where she is. His lips are bleeding. I'd start there, but he'll need them to talk. Pin his head and neck first. Then wake him up."

Abreu slid pieces of rebar in front and behind Junior's body. He moved an upright to gain maximum leverage and forced more rods under junior's chin, around his head and at the base of his neck. By the time Abreu flushed Junior with the rusty water in the rotting, stiff hose, Chariot was standing at the table with a glistening razor in his hand.

DeSeti came to spitting water and chipped teeth. Abreu lit him up with the hose once more for good measure and in defense of his flowers.

"Hello, DeSeti," Donnie said plainly. "You have something that belongs to me. I need to know where it is. Right now. I'll send someone. If she's there and well, you live. Lie? And I'll start cutting and ask again. We'll continue until your memory improves. You won't die, but you'll pray for it. Do we have an understanding?"

"Fuck you. Touch me and you'll never see her again. I guarantee it."

"Suit yourself."

Only then was Junior aware enough to realize he could not move. His hands were blue and numb from holding his weight and his face was wracked with pain from his broken teeth. His head had been cut and torn by the pressing bars, but it all faded to nothing when Chariot came up the gallows steps.

With no urgency, Chariot touched the razor against the side of Junior's nose while beneath it, pleading words spilled out in a torrent. Above the blade, Junior's eyes were so wide his pupils were encased in white. As the blade began to bite, Junior's words were drowned out by his scream.

There was no hesitant cut like a fast hand testing a hot plate. The first slice went deep through the cartilage like soft butter. The blade became an easy pry bar and laid the fleshy part of the nose forward until Junior's gasps snorted blood out the front of his face like a harpooned whale through its blow hole.

Junior's distorted eyes craned to see his ruined nose. The horror of the dangling cartilage drove his cries back down his throat and took him to the brink of passing out, but Donnie grabbed his face.

"Not so fast. You have something to tell me first."

"I don't know...."

Donnie laid the blade alongside Junior's head and gently brushed his ear with the dull side of the knife. "Hear that?"

Junior's darting eyes were the only answer Donnie would wait for. He sliced deep and hard. In two strokes the ear fell off onto Junior's feet in the pit.

"How about now?" Chariot asked as he cocked his head to the side as though listening intently.

The scream that exploded from Junior's battered face sent a shower of blood into Donnie's. As his victim struggled to thrash, Donnie walked casually down the few steps, took the hose from Abreu's hand without stopping and went to the sink. As he began to rinse his face, Abreu stepped up and took the hose back. He held it and turned down the flow so his boss could wash more comfortably and completely.

"Thank you," Chariot said softly.

Donnie finished and looked around. "Inquire of Mrs. Glass if we might garner some towels and perhaps a bar of soap."

"She's not with us," Mr. Abreu said as he closed his eyes a moment. In the process, he inadvertently moved the hose and missed the sink, slightly dampening Chariot's shoes. Both men ignored the slight.

"Ask my wife," Donnie said as he wiped his hands on his pants. "She'll consider it beneath her, but ask anyhow." Donnie smiled. "Then duck."

"I'll ask," Abreu said as he turned the water off.

"Before you do, would you cauterize that ear?"

"Happy to," Abreu said as he legitimately smiled. "I'll go out to the garden shed and get a torch." Without asking if Donnie would be all right for a few minutes without him, Abreu headed for the door. Behind him, Donnie nodded the slightest acknowledgement as he looked rather curiously at Junior DeSeti dangling before him.

"Your memory getting any better, young fella? Listen to me with your good ear. Where's my daughter?"

33

Outside The Locker, Mr. Abreu found Donna and Nicky sitting at the bar nursing drinks with a towel full of ice on Nicky's head. Her hand moved from the ice pack to Nicky's shoulder as the old gardener went behind the bar and rummaged for more towels.

"He thinks your mother is upstairs."

Nicky was quiet, but Donna pressed.

"Has he learned where Lexy is?"

"Not yet."

"Will this one talk?"

"Everything he knows."

"Good."

"Can you give him these?" Abreu said as he set several bar towels in front of Donna. "I need to go to the garden shed."

"Not a chance," Donna said as she pushed them away as though they smelled bad.

"You?" Abreu said as he redirected the towels to Nicky. For his part, Nicky looked at Donna for an answer.

She took a long pull on her drink. "You'll never be the same if you walk in that room."

"He ain't a child," Abreu said.

"No he isn't. That would make it worse. Believe me," she said as she drained her drink. "I'd know."

Minus any revelations concerning the past or the present, Abreu rummaged under the bar and tossed a small vintage leather travel bag up on the bar. "There's things there for your head. I don't think drugs go bad. Should still be suture thread and those fancy curved needles." Abreu walked around the bar, leaving the towels to Nicky's inattentive care, but he pointed at them. "One for you, the rest go to the boss."

Once up on the ground floor of the mansion, Abreu heard a phone ringing in the master's office.

"Yeah?" he answered, hoping only slightly he'd hit the right digital button on Donnie Chariot's cell phone.

"Mr. Abreu? This is Baron. I see your duties have been expanded beyond the immaculate grounds to include answering the telephone."

"He's busy. I'll tell him call you."

"I'm afraid that won't do. Please tell him I must talk to him forthwith. Concerning his granddaughter. I'm certain you are well aware."

"This will take a while. He's real busy."

"I'm happy to wait, Abreu. If I may inquire, are you at the mansion?"

"I am."

"And again, indulge me please. Who might be there with you?"

"No idea. Hold on."

Baron cringed, but without any true surprise. He knew the aged henchman's loyalty would never waver. For Abreu to offer more information would have proved a disappointment.

• • •

Inside The Locker, Junior DeSeti had physically given up his struggle against the steel rods and chains that confined him. His head was numb from constraint and pain. Blood seemed to trickle from him everywhere.

"Where is my daughter? I asked nice. The next time I'll ask with the razor, and you know how well you fare beneath it." Donnie paused and lowered his hands. "Let's try again, shall we? Where is she?"

"I don't—"

"Wrong answer." The tip of the blade pressed against Junior's right eye.

"I don't know *exactly*! Not exactly! My father took her. I don't know where to."

"Where did he take her from?" Donnie made a delicate cut across Junior's eyelid. There was little blood and no cry followed. Chariot persisted. "Where?"

"Upstate…Jersey…a safe house off Palisades."

"More specific."

"*I don't know!*"

"You haven't the time to learn how poorly an answer such as that reflects on you."

"*I don't know the address*! Ask your daughter. She was there."

"My daughter was there. Very good. That's a start. We know where she was. The sixty-four-thousand-dollar question is, where is she now? Tell me, where is my baby?"

The door opened and stymied an answer that would have left both Junior and Chariot wanting. It was Nicky, carrying the bar towels.

"Thank you, Frank," Donnie chirped, blade in hand. "Just set them on the table."

All Nicky's energy was diverted to his eyes. Within them came a case of tunnel vision that exceeded anything blinders on a racehorse could have hoped for. The walls around Donnie Chariot and Junior DeSeti could have melted into gold and run across his feet and Nicky wouldn't have noticed. He was captured by the sight of the apparatus as surely as DeSeti was captured within it. The rusty bars were directional finders—arrows pointing in toward their captive—and the uprights, bars of a cage that did nothing to conceal the animal within.

The towels were taken to the table and tenderly set on the pliers and dust-covered blades as if the table and all its contents were fragile and ready for collapse. Chariot had watched Nicky over a slight smile.

"That'll do. Please ask Mr. Abreu to step in, would you?"

"Of course…."

DeSeti heard the new voice and reached for it with his own. "Help me," he pleaded not much above a whisper. "He's killing me…."

"Oh, he can see that plain enough. He's a smart man. But—are you?" Chariot laid the blade over Junior's eyelid again. "Well, are you?"

"Help me…."

"Mr. Chariot? What—"

"That's fine, Frank. Get Abreu if you please."

"I—"

"Tell him I'll be ready for the next man momentarily. Give him a hand please. Time is critical."

"Help…" DeSeti began to plead to the voice he was prevented by the rebar from seeing. "Please, help me…."

"Hush up! There's only one thing I want coming out of that mouth of yours and I judge you have about three seconds to say it before I cut your tongue out! Where is she?"

"*Help me!*"

"Help you? That's very selfish. My girl is missing and you want help? Hardly."

The edge of the knife disappeared into DeSeti's eye. There was no shyness in the cut of the blade. It buried itself as though it had done the procedure a thousand times. If there was pain, it was minimal—overrun by the bright flashes of lightning that were ricocheting around inside Junior's head. On the outside, vitreous fluid from the eyeball ran down Junior's cheek and washed away his blood. If he intended to say more, it was lost as his mind gave up his body and he fainted, less so from pain than the knowledge of what had just happened.

"Jesus…" Nicky muttered as Mr. Abreu came into The Locker.

"Book? You got a call," Abreu said as he casually passed Nicky, held the phone up, and then set it on the table near the towels.

Chariot glanced at him annoyed and waved him off.

"It's Baron. Says it's important. About the kid."

As Chariot descended the short stairs and went to the sink, Abreu motioned to Nicky and on to the door. "You should step out. This is big-boy talk."

Chariot was splashing his face and seized up as he watched the blood run from his hands and circle the drain in front of him. The mesmerizing pattern and the cold water brought him back from where he'd been.

"Nicky," Chariot said as he reached for a towel and dried his face and hands. "You can stay." Chariot picked up the phone and pointed with it to Junior. "Mind that ear, Mr. Abreu. Show Nicky how it's done please."

Leery of telephones since the early days when FBI agents donned telephone repair work clothes and climbed the poles outside the mansion, Donnie spoke softly with guarded words.

"I want you to know," Baron was saying. "I had nothing to do with what's occurred."

"I know."

"You do?" Baron said, genuinely shocked.

"Indeed."

"Spoken with such assurance leads me to believe you know who is responsible."

"Right again."

"And I am well removed from the equation?"

"You are."

"That is good to know. Very good to know. That said, is there anything I can offer in assistance?"

Donnie looked over his shoulder at DeSeti, dangling in the apparatus. On the platform next to him, Mr. Abreu was applying heat from the propane torch to a wide knife blade and explaining to Nicky the ins and outs of cauterizing an open wound.

"Perhaps we should meet," Donnie said. "The 'who' is something I've known from the outset. The 'why' is something it's time for us to discuss."

"All right. Where?"

Donnie shuffled his feet and leaned on the dusty table. "Where? Yes, 'where....' That's become a concern for me. You mentioned my missing package to Abreu. I know 'who' and I know 'why,' but I no longer know 'where.'" He looked at his men pressing the hot knife to the side of Junior's head to stem the flow of blood. "But I'm working on that as we speak."

Baron heard Junior come to life and scream. "I see you are. Any good fortune?"

"It's coming around. Would you be able to stop by?"

"I'll head in your direction, but I don't believe the mansion would be my first choice at present as you already have a guest. I'll be nearby. Call me when you're ready and tell me where you wish to meet. Regarding the 'where' and your package, I believe I can assist with that concern."

"Is there a carrying fee?"

"Donnie...we're two old friends—"

"It's business. I understand."

"There's a place in North Jersey I believe may require some attention. We have a mutual friend. He maintains a little place I'm aware of—"

"Is it off the Palisades?"

Baron smiled. "Well done. I see your interview has been fruitful."

"Some. But we've already read that book. Not a page turner. Nothing in it worthwhile."

"I've heard mention of another book worth reading. Your home track. An office maybe. Do you know of it?"

"No. I do not." Chariot looked back across The Locker at Junior DeSeti. "But I'll find out."

34

A few miles away, Alexis was bumping against the door of Julian DeSeti's Belmont Park office. With its double dead bolts, the solid door wasn't budging, and the encouragement of a seven-year-old's narrow shoulder wasn't going to change that. She kicked the door—not her best effort—as though no door had been thoroughly tested unless it had been booted a couple of times.

When the door proved uncooperative, Alexis turned back to the room and began an investigation. The first stop was the walls where the windows had been. She ran her hands over the patches of rough spackling that did little to hide the outline of the absent windows. She rapped her knuckles on the wall. Solid. Though the coat of matching paint on top of the shiftless work was lipstick on a pig, breeching the heavy external wall was unlikely. The lightly constructed interior walls might prove something different.

She was in the bathroom going over its forgotten window when the plan grew teeth. As she looked over the partitioning walls, in her mind's eye she could make out the labyrinth of wiring and plumbing incumbent in a bathroom. More hurdles, she reasoned, and abandoned the bathroom for the one-room workspace.

Her mind went to the droning television and followed its power cord to the wall. There she transitioned to her mind again and followed the wiring hidden in the wall. What she knew about electrical systems wouldn't fill a very big book, but she thought it best to avoid the hazard. The wall on either side of the uncooperative door looked to be blank and the odds maker in her saw less risk and an increased payout.

She tapped the wall listening for voids and looking for hastily covered nails and screws. Finding a good spot to mine, she cocked her foot and kicked the wall like an old-time football player launching a field goal try. Nothing happened. A few more attempts resulted in noise, but no crashing breakthrough. She needed a tool.

Back in the bathroom, a cheap towel rod came off the wall without a fight. Working it less like a hammer and more like a punch and chisel, she began to see chinks in the sheetrock's armor. With the first good cracks she reverted back to her kicking, but this time turned around and fired her heel backward with a much more concentrated effort. In less than a minute she was through the inside layer of sheetrock.

• • •

Donnie supplanted Nicky and Abreu on the wooden platform. He had the razor in his hand. "Thank you, gentleman. Would you please step out? I need to further my discussion with young DeSeti here."

"You want me to…to help?" Nicky asked as tentatively as he might volunteer to walk a high wire in the circus.

Abreu swatted his arm. "If he did, he'd ask."

Both men washed in the sink and left carrying towels, wiping their hands and faces as they went out the door.

Donnie leaned in close to Junior DeSeti's char-blackened ear. "I understand your father has a permanent room at Belmont. True? Yes or no would serve you nicely."

"You psycho bastard—"

Donnie felt the edge of his knife ripple across Junior's teeth as it cut cleanly along the bottom of Junior's lower lip and nearly dissected it from his face.

"You're a slow learner, DeSeti," Chariot said as he pressed the bloody blade against Junior's remaining eye. "Where's your father's office?"

"*Stop!*" The word came out from beneath Junior's sliced lip as much as over it. "Gate Five. End of first barn, right on Count Fleet. First place on right."

"If it's not, you know what will happen. With that in mind, are there any changes?"

"Clubhouse turn," Junior spit blood as he fell away, fainting again.

Donnie was already headed down the stairs. He washed more thoroughly, dried his face and hands, and picked up his phone. He closed the door behind him and saw Abreu, Nicky, and Donna at the bar. He didn't stop as he issued his last order. "Cauterize and clean him up."

"Dad. Dad!"

"*What?*" Donnie snapped as he kept walking.

"What'd you learn? Where is she?"

"I don't know yet. I'll be back in a half hour. Keep him breathing."

As Chariot was clearing the basement steps, he hit the recent calls on his phone and dialed up Baron.

"Meet me at the Park. Gate Five Road. Take the first right to the barns and the first right again onto Count Fleet Road. Look for my car."

"Thank you for your confidence, Book, but what you have to say or do there is outside of my bailiwick. I don't—"

"There'll be none of that. You won't see anyone. But there is something I need to tell you—and something I need to give you—to protect your Vegas interests. Every dime. Be there as soon as you can."

"All right. All right. I understand."

Donnie disconnected.

Beneath that conversation, in the basement, Donna abandoned her drink when her father entered the stairway. "I need something to eat. You, Mr. Abreu?"

"I'd take a little something."

"Nick?"

He sent the briefest of glances back to The Locker. "No. I'm not hungry."

"I told you. That'll take your appetite away," Donna said as she moved toward the stairs in her father's shadow. "Come give me a hand."

Nicky fell in behind her, but when they reached the first floor Donna stopped and listened for the sound of the front door of the mansion closing.

"Follow him," she ordered. "Hurry. He's up to something."

"He wouldn't like—"

"I'll like it less if you don't."

"Donna. He's a...a serious—"

"You mean dangerous, but that's my daughter. If you don't follow him, I will."

When Nicky still hesitated, Donna stepped right through him. "I'll do it."

He grabbed her arm, but she wrenched it away with an intensity that caught him off-guard.

"I'll go," he said and didn't wait for more discussion.

•   •   •

Lexy's heart was pounding from breaking through the sheetrock, but also from fear that she might look up from her improvised mouse hole and see Julian DeSeti staring down at her. He wasn't and she wouldn't wait for him to show up. She scrambled across the pieces of broken wall and dust then up and through the kitchen. Once outside, she avoided the quiet streets of the sprawling barn complex and ran into the nighttime shadowy arms of the barns themselves.

As she crept along the never-ending length of a stable she could smell the pleasant scent of clean hay, grain, and horses. Occasionally she would hear a horse move in its stall or flare its nostrils to her own scent. She'd never risk cutting through a stall—these were mostly stallions—high-strung, gifted athletes, full of competitiveness, aggression, and testosterone. If *American Pharoah* was here, she might chance it as she heard the Triple Crown champion's temperament was as gentle as a kitten. The rest of the racers, though remarkable and stunning, likely couldn't be trusted to keep a secret if she dashed through their bedchamber. Besides, with millions of dollars on the hoof and at stake in the races, security was everywhere. Alexis was fortunate the guards and all-night grooms didn't share the horses' keen sense of smell.

The night before the famous Belmont Stakes, the park was alive and busy despite the hour. Cars and trucks came and went, each splashing their headlights across the sides of the barns and the grounds as they turned near the buildings. Security rolled by slowly and voices were coming from the long narrow barn at her back. She couldn't make out everything. The grooms were cognizant of letting the horses rest and spoke low.

All the movement, lights, and voices kept her pinned in the shadows. Finding a hideout wasn't going to be easy, and trying to go the length of the park to the train terminal all but impossible on the most protected night in Belmont's racing season. Even if she made it to the platforms, the trains wouldn't be running again until early morning. A turning car, its lights racing down the length of the barn toward her, forced her to dart from her shadowed safety.

She crossed the grass at a brisk walk but held herself short of a run. If she was seen, a run would give her away without question. A walk would leave doubt that perhaps she belonged. With outrageous luck, the voyeur might mistake her and her stature for a jockey.

Her quiet but deliberate steps served her well enough, and she crossed away from the house and the road. Rather than try for the storage and rinsing stations, she slid beneath a low white rail fence and settled in behind a fat tree. She was close to yet another barn in what seemed an unending array of buildings. Here she was protected from the lights of cars but could still see the house she'd escaped from. Her perch also afforded her time to sort out her next move. Well before dawn, the entire park would be teeming with people. Then she could slip in and around as easily as if she was invisible.

Alexis could see into the nearest barn, compliments of a few doors and windows left open to the warm June night air. Sporadic lights in the center hall filtered through stalls inside allowing the expensive tenants to be checked on often. She settled into watching wealthy connections inspecting their prizes then wandering off to parties. After the fancy cars pulled away, she listened as late-night grooms laughed at the moneyed men and women and the silliness of their pre-race rituals. It seemed the rest of the night might be consumed with such entertainment until a Mercedes pulled up near the house with a girl-sized hole kicked through a wall inside. It was Julian DeSeti and he got out of his car carrying a pizza.

Julian found his keys unnecessary as Alexis had sprinted out the door and left it unlocked behind her. It might have taken him two minutes to survey the child-sized hole in the wall, search his office, and dart back outside. As he wandered aimlessly around the house, Alexis pressed tighter to the tree and tried to be small. Like an infant animal tucked in tall grass, she'd be safe as long as her resolve held her perfectly still. When Julian's cell phone flashlight came on, she made herself smaller still.

The light led Julian's eye into the dark spots around the house. Then it tried to stretch to the first barn and drew Julian in that direction. Alexis slid around the tree and kept it between herself and the light. Ahead of her, a horse snorted and stomped, and looked on as well.

But Julian's small light was garnering attention beyond Alexis and the stallion who'd leap from gate number five in eighteen hours. A groom saw the light bounce down the wall of the barn and into the stall of his charger. Alexis saw him come out with two friends. They were too far away to understand clearly, but rather quickly they seemed to join Julian in a search for something on the ground—something small—perhaps a wallet or another phone. In less than a minute the ruse was abandoned and Julian went back toward the house. He looked around outside for a few more moments. In his pitiful attempt, he looked right at Alexis and her tree, saw nothing but shadows, jumped in his car, and drove off.

Nicky recognized after only a few turns that his boss was headed to Belmont Park. He lay back enough to stay out of sight, but was well aided by the heavy New York traffic surrounding the park the night before The Belmont Stakes. In a matter of minutes he followed The Book through Gate Five. When he saw the brake and backup lights blink from the Bentley, he knew Donnie had stopped.

Chariot had parked nearer the first barn than the house that held DeSeti's office and, once, his granddaughter. His slow walk up to the house gave Nicky time to park and cross the street to his own tree where he could watch. From her new perch, Alexis saw headlights, but not the long approach of her grandfather to the house.

The door was still slightly ajar, but Donnie knocked anyway. A few lights were on, but there was no answer as he eased open the door. Behind him, Baron was rolling to a stop.

"Nice night," Baron said from the back seat of his chauffeured ride as the car came to a stop.

"For some, maybe," Donnie answered from the open door. "This look like the place?"

"I've never been here. Is Julian around?"

"No answer yet. The door was open. C'mon in."

"I'll pass, thank you. Talk to him and I'll pick up the pieces."

Donnie didn't answer and walked in the house. Just as he was ready to call out for his granddaughter, he saw the broken sheetrock on the floor and the hole through the wall. The door to Julian's office had been left open like the front door. Inside on the desk was the pizza. It was still warm.

Nicky was watching Baron who was watching the door for Donnie. At the next barn over, disguised by her tree, Alexis had seen Baron's car stop and was casually watching it and listening to nighttime grooms trade stories. She saw the interior light come on and a man get out. It wasn't Mr. DeSeti, but that was all she knew or could tell.

"What are you afraid of?" Donnie was saying from the doorway. "I told you. He's not here. No one is, which is why I need you to look at something."

"I trust it's not a body."

"The opposite. The absence of one."

In a moment, Baron was standing with Chariot looking at the mouse-hole.

"You think so?" Baron asked without specifics.

Chariot nodded. "Yes."

"Very resourceful."

"Indeed."

"Minus his bargaining chip, Julian will run. He'll know you're on the hunt."

"Likely."

"Let us go elsewhere, Donnie. Should someone discover us here, the questions could prove difficult."

Chariot looked around inside the house as if Alexis might be hiding. "She couldn't have gone far. She's little."

"Perhaps she's still with Julian. He may have been waiting on this side, as we are."

"Doubtful. He left both doors unlocked, and the pizza is undisturbed. No struggle and no missing slices. She dug out while he was gone. He found this just as we did."

"Now, they're both on the run."

"Correct."

Content she wasn't in the house, Donnie went outside and Baron followed obediently. Chariot repeated his looking around outside the house as he had inside despite the darkness. Baron flipped his cell phone light on as Julian had and walked around the house showing the way. After one pass, they started to cross the lawn toward the first barn.

Baron was earnestly looking, but stated the obvious. "You understand we're in the middle of a four-hundred-acre horse track adjacent to a city of eight million souls."

"She'll be nearby. Probably looking at tomorrow's runners. Looking for an edge."

"She's a little girl, Donnie. She's probably crying in a corner."

"Did you see what she did to get out of that room? She's a Chariot. And she has the Gift."

That brought Baron up short. "Perhaps, but—"

Donnie turned quick and faced him, drawing up so tight Baron was taken aback further. "She's not crying," Donnie said coldly.

"I believe you're right. I see I was mistaken. Let's check the barns."

"Let's," Donnie said as he spun and led the way.

They had only gone fifty feet when Alexis nearly tackled her grandfather out of the darkness. Her relief was matched by his shock and momentary alarm.

"*Grandpa*! There's some bad men! They shot Mrs.—"

"Whoa! Whoa!" Chariot said as he knelt quickly and cradled his granddaughter. "Are you hurt?"

"No, but Mrs. Glass is hurt bad!"

"Okay," Chariot said as he hugged her tight again and kissed her face repeatedly. In his hugs, he felt her all over as if roughly checking for broken bones. "I'll check on her. Are you certain you're all right?"

"I'm okay. I busted out of a room! I broke some of the wall. I might be in trouble for that, but I didn't belong there. Did you see my messages on the tote board?"

"I did!"

"Amazing," Baron said as a highly interested observer. "She is a special child."

"Damn right she is."

"We should leave straightaway."

By his movement, Donnie agreed. He had Alexis by the hand and was moving quickly toward his car.

"I need to ask you to do something for me, kiddo. It's not easy. Are you up to breaking through one more wall?"

"It was hard."

"This isn't a real wall, but I'm asking you to be pretty tough. I think you're up to the task."

"I can do it. Then can we go home?"

"We sure can."

"And come back tomorrow to watch the Stakes?"

"Indeed."

Donnie Chariot stopped in front of the house he'd just searched, knelt down again with his granddaughter, but pointed to Baron. "This is a good friend of mine. Not like that other man. I need you to go with him to a very fancy hotel. He's going to take care of you tonight."

Alexis's eyes asked what Baron said out loud.

"What?"

"I'm very sorry, but there are a lot of things your mother and I have to do before the big race tomorrow."

"I can help," Lexy began to plead.

"Tomorrow you can help do all kinds of things, but—"

"I'm very clever. You know I am."

"I do know that. If you—Tonight, you can help best by going with Baron."

"I want to go to your house and see Mommy."

"I understand. Tomorrow she will meet you right here at the track and we'll have a wonderful day."

"Excuse me, Book," Baron interrupted. "Perhaps we could discuss this a moment."

Before Donnie could agree or find exception, Nicky stepped out of the shadows and crossed the road.

"Hey, Boss, you need a hand?"

"Hi, Nicky," Lexy said matter-of-factly.

Donnie's disjointed plan was developing snags before it could either roll out or come unwound. "What are you doing here?" he said as he stood.

"Your daughter. She made me tail you. You know how she is. I didn't have a choice."

"Does she pay you? Go back to the house."

"Can I go with Nicky, Grandpa? I can go with Nicky back to the house. You and Mommy can work and—"

"No. *No!* You need to go with Baron and Frank needs to leave."

"What? Boss, I'm sorry, but if we don't bring Lexy home, Donna will scratch our eyes out. She's going be so happy you found her she'll—"

"Lexy? There's a pizza in the house here. It's on the desk in that room you were in. Will you go get it?"

She looked at the house and balked. "I don't like it in there."

"That's a fair statement. I don't blame you. Take Frank with you and show him what you did. This is a very brave girl, men. We've got to keep her that way."

"Take Nicky with me?"

"Yes, yes. Show him how you broke out."

Alexis turned to Nicky, happy to be doing anything but going to another hotel with another stranger. "You want to see?"

He took her hand, but was staring at Donnie. "Sure I do, kiddo. Sure I do."

The pair were just out of earshot when Baron launched. "That's Nicky, right? Not Frank."

"I know that."

"You called him Frank."

"Simple mistake. Now, I need you to take—"

"Where is Frank, Donnie? Right now."

"Back at the house. Why?"

"No, Book. He's dead. I fear you're not yourself. Come with me now. I'll drop you off at your—"

"No! *Goddammit!* You think I don't know I'm sick? That's what this entire affair has been about!"

"Donnie, I don't understand. Please. Let me take you home."

"There was never a kidnapping. She was never in danger—at least not until those DeSetis got involved."

"What are you saying?"

"I had Glass take Lexy to the Hyatt in midtown. That would be my leverage to bring Donna into the business. She wouldn't do it for me, but she'd do it to protect her daughter."

"Jesus Christ, Donnie…you're not well. Come—"

"You're right! I'm not well. I can't set the odds. Or make the calls. None of it. You thought I was running a second book to lay off against. It was never that way. I had to do this. If I didn't do it, you would have! You'd have gotten around to it eventually. Whatever it took to get me to produce those numbers."

"There are other ways. You should have come to me."

"With what? That I'm losing my mind? That I can't remember anything for days on end? That whatever this is in my head is being turned off? I feel it. I can see it. Like a spigot slowly being turned off. The flow turns to a trickle. Then it stops."

"You've been doing fine. Not a number has missed in over a thousand races—ten thousand horses."

"It wasn't me. It was Donna. She's doing it. She's the one you need now. Not me. You see? I can't do it any longer. It...it's slipping away. I can't, but Donna can. This was the only way I could protect my girls."

"I would never have involved a child."

"Maybe not you, but how about the next man up? What if someone like DeSeti was running Vegas? Where would he draw the line? The only way I could shield Donna was to involve her—preserve the main book. And the only way she'd work the book was if it saved Lexy. I had to pull her in."

"Kidnap your own grandchild?"

"It wasn't kidnapping! I had her taken to the nicest hotel in Manhattan with her babysitter. I talked to Glass every day. It got Donna involved with the book and everything was working."

Baron snapped his head to look around Chariot. Donnie followed the move and spun around.

Alexis was holding the pizza box in front of her. Nicky was just behind with both hands on Lexy's shoulders to steady both himself and the little girl under the weight of what they'd just heard.

35

The ice in Donna's third whiskey was drooling a water ring on the bar. Abreu had been in and out of The Locker twice and on the gardener's last pass, he left the bottle on top of the bar after he freshened her drink and headed back upstairs. She hadn't stopped him pouring or turned away the bottle. Fearful of blowing Nicky's surveillance, she had resisted calling or texting though her resolve was melting under the weight of the booze.

The decision to go into The Locker was made in a combustible cauldron of repressed yesterdays, frustration, anger, and alcohol. The conflagration burned white hot from her bar stool through the first door. At the second, heavily insulated one, dried blood drops on the floor blew a cooling breeze over the fire. When she took the doorknob in her hand, it began to rain. When she stepped inside and saw the apparatus, winter came. Bitter winds visited the passion she'd mustered at the bar and left her icy and hollow—her body and mind seemingly frozen in place.

Abreu had modified the rods and uprights. DeSeti no longer dangled over the drain, but was sitting in a dusty steel chair, his hands now restrained behind him. He'd been hosed down and even sported a rudimentary bandage where his ear had been. Another bloodstained gauze ran around his head and face, covering his nose and ruptured eye. Rods were fitted tightly over his lap, back, head, and neck. The position was more comfortable than hanging, though the improvement would seem marginal and evaporate in the next few minutes. As it was, he saw little except the movement of Donna tenuously crossing the floor, hands trembling.

"Help me...."

Donna didn't answer though her eyes were locked on him, mesmerized like a traveler gawking at a car accident. The apparatus didn't change, but in her mind were flashes of another man, equally bloodied and worse, fixed to the chair. She was at the table watching the repeating transformation of the men bleeding in the same chair, twenty-five years apart. Hypnotized by the memory, she was seeing herself standing in The Locker. Like the changing man in the chair, Donna flashed away from the present to herself at seven years old, standing at the table. The flickers in time continued, picking up a frenetic pace until the little girl reached onto the table and picked up Donnie Chariot's razor.

She walked to the man in the chair and delicately laid the razor across one of his eyes. Slowly, but with no grimace or disinclination, she dragged the shiny blade across the tightly closed eye. A line of blood appeared as neatly as if the knife had drawn it like a deep red pen. The girl peeled the eyelid up with the tip of the blade and flicked it away leaving a naked darting eye flailing in an increasing reservoir of blood.

As neatly as before, the little girl pushed the razor into the white of the eye and deeply scored the pupil. A clear fluid oozed out and down the man's face as around them both, the world went dark.

36

Though the men stood in a faded pale light from a distant streetlight, Baron, Chariot, and Nicky each had seen and heard the facts quite clearly. Confusion might remain about the whys and wherefores, but there was no longer any doubt as to who was behind the kidnapping. Despite her unique abilities, Alexis could not piece the puzzle together. The love she had for her grandfather wouldn't allow her to quantify anything further and made an answer impossible.

Nicky wasn't searching for answers. He'd heard enough. "I'll take Lexy back to the big house."

"Not if you care about her. Or care about Donna," Chariot said, stopping the younger man with his voice instead of his hand. "This has to play out."

"No, it doesn't! I have tremendous respect for you, but this is six kinds of wrong."

"It's necessary—"

"No, it isn't!" Nicky snapped before collecting himself for Lexy's sake. "She's a little girl."

"Who needs protecting!"

"Yes, from you!"

"Nonsense. This protects her. Her *and* her mother."

"Like it protected Frank? And Glass?"

"Frank? Yes, yes," Chariot said. "Go ask Frank. You trust him. Ask him if this wasn't the right play."

"Ask him? He's dead, Mr. Chariot. Frank's dead. Because of what you did. He's dead."

Donnie searched the eyes locked on him. "I'm right, Baron. You know it. Tell him."

Baron was slow to start. "I could not bring myself to agree with the tactic, but I can't deny the thought process behind it. The service you provide is very valuable to myself and a great many others. Some…some would take exception to an interruption of that service. Guaranteeing continuity would be advantageous to all involved. I imagine one would find this young lady—through her mother and you, Donnie—somewhere on that list."

Nicky's arms circled Alexis. "Continuity? You put her through this for 'continuity'?"

"Not me, *per se*," Baron added. "But The Book has a valid point. You must know the character of many of the men in our business. Frank certainly knew. I'm certain he provided instruction—"

"He would have never gone along with this. Never."

"Perhaps. Perhaps not."

Chariot stepped closer to Nicky and Alexis and away from Baron, in a literal step to show an intention that was only the bastard child of his immediate misfortune. "You're right, Nicky. Frank wouldn't have gone along with this, but he would understand it and back my play. He'd do anything to protect her."

"I know! I saw him give his life—"

"Then back his play!"

"This isn't a game! These are lives. Real people. Real people getting hurt."

Alexis had heard much, understood some, but couldn't manipulate sentiments, conniving greed, and consequences as easily as she could numbers. When the blank space in her reasoning tipped its hand, as no more than an unqualified null set, she realized where her own lacking rested and projected the same onto her grandfather.

"Are you in trouble, Grandpa?"

The Book dropped to his knees. "No, honey. We're all fine."

"If we're all fine, why are people yelling? And shooting guns? Mrs. Glass was strict, but she liked horses and I think she's hurt really bad. I like Mr. Frank a lot. Is he dead?"

"Nobody's hurt. There's just some things we all need to do—"

"Nobody's hurt? I saw Mrs. Glass and—"

"There's things we all have to do. And that includes you. You have the biggest job of all."

"Boss? Don't put this on her."

Chariot ignored Nicky's directive, but took a cue from him. Donnie would put this on Alexis and she'd shoulder it as her mother wouldn't. Alexis would do what any good Chariot would. She'd always do the work first—and in a density so profound, others would have long since staggered and fallen under its weight. In the crush of the task, she would find a singular pleasure no one without the Gift could realize. And in her embrace of the aptitude she shared with her lineage, Donnie determined that Alexis would never open the family to extortion as he felt her mother had done by dismissing her gift.

"Honey, what's three hundred seventy-three times fifty seven?"

"Right now?"

"Yes."

"Twenty-one thousand, two hundred sixty-one. Is that an important number?"

"I think all numbers are important. Like you do. Like your mother does. Do you think twenty-one thousand, two hundred sixty-one is an important number, Baron?"

"I do now. Astounding."

Nicky was staring, but Donnie spoke only to his granddaughter. "Tomorrow, you and your mother are going to move into my house."

"We are?"

"Indeed. I should've never let you leave. We'll work on this ability of yours. You can be better, stronger than me or your mother. I'm sure of it."

"Is this the best place for her?" Nicky said weakly. "I mean, shouldn't she work for the government or something?"

Chariot and Baron laughed together outright. "You really want her to be miserable, don't you?"

"No, but, you know, maybe she could solve some major issues. Medical things. Cure cancer. I don't know."

Donnie was through laughing. "That's the only thing you've said that's right. You don't know."

"And you do?"

Chariot slipped the pizza from his granddaughter and handed it to Baron. "Take this over to your car. Alexis, honey? Would you go with my friend and make sure he only gets one slice? Watch him close. He might want to go for two."

"I'm not too hungry. Besides, half has peppers."

"Peppers? We've sworn off peppers."

"That's how I knew it wasn't you on the phone. That's why I broke the wall."

Baron held the pizza in one hand and extended the other to Lexy. "Perhaps we could take the peppers off."

"They leave pepper juice."

"They leave pepper juice," Donnie echoed.

"We shall share the half not impacted by the pepper juice."

"Okay. You won't leave, Grandpa?"

"I won't leave, kiddo. Sit with Baron and enjoy the pizza. I need to talk to Nicky a minute."

Baron put his free hand on Lexy's shoulder and asked for clarification regarding pepper juice's impact on all things. She didn't object, but watched her grandfather all the way to Baron's car.

"If there was another way," Donnie was saying to Nicky. "Don't you think I'd have chosen it?"

"It's not my place to question—"

"But you will."

"Well, yeah. Jesus, you're putting Donna through hell."

"A hell I control."

"Not DeSeti. You don't control that psycho sonofabitch."

"I do now. Did you look at him closely before you followed me?"

"I saw him, but that doesn't help Donna any. Or Lexy."

"I regret DeSeti's involvement. I also regret that I have yet to think through how that came about, which is a reoccurring concern I have of late. Which points to the very root of this entire sordid business."

"Alzheimer's?"

"Did Donna tell you that?"

"She did, but she didn't have to. I knew something was wrong. Frank told me the rest."

"Frank's a fine man. Very loyal—"

"Very dead."

Donnie looked at Nicky hard and fought to bring recent events into focus.

"You don't remember that, do you, boss? And I told you not more than five minutes ago."

Donnie turned and walked toward the barns. "Come with me."

Alexis started to move, but Baron gently touched her arm. "He's not leaving you. He likes to walk when he talks. I'm certain he'll be right along."

Nicky and Chariot were at the barns before either spoke. "I grant you, I often don't recall recent things I've been told, perhaps even things I've said or even seen. Several months ago it was just the numbers. They ceased to jump out at me so readily.

"It was actually quite a relief at first. The constant, interminable ciphering of everything I saw. Even if I saw nothing. My mind would be racing—solving equations that didn't exist. Then, seemingly overnight, it all stopped.

"The change didn't bring any peace, however. It brought mistakes. Oh, sometimes it works out." Donnie smiled, "That's why they run the races, isn't it?"

The grooms recognized Chariot walking up the aisle of the stable and drifted out of his way. Donnie stopped to pet a three-year-old stallion. "Oh, you're a fine-looking boy, aren't you? Tomorrow you can become part of history for all time. Do you know that?"

The horse nipped at Donnie's hand. "You'll not be surprised to learn that isn't the first time someone has attempted to bite the hand that feeds them. Happened twenty-five years ago. It was an awful time.

"I'm about to share something with you, Nicky. Something very personal. It cost me my wife, nearly Little Donnie, and almost my own life I suppose. It's up to you if you discuss this with Donna, but my recommendation is you avoid it. I fear she'd come to resent you for knowing all the dirty little secrets of our family. Instead, I think she'd enjoy making a life with you. You care for her, I can see that. You protect Lexy as if she was your own. And you know of my business so my girl wouldn't go crazy hiding things from you. Crazy...like her mother.

"Years ago when Donna was small, probably Lexy's age, maybe younger, I had come into my own with Vegas. I'd been managing my own book here in New York for years. It was doing well and I managed everything, just to keep my mind busy. I set odds, took wagers, collected—everything. Sometimes things got rough. Maybe somebody skims or another guy doesn't want to pay. That would have cut the nuts off any book.

"So, I didn't let it happen. Not once. Not even close. The book got stronger as a result. I got stronger. Then my wife got wind of some 'interviews' I conducted in The Locker. She saw things. It scared her. It also scarred her. I didn't know how badly.

"Vegas realized what I could do for them—how this talent of mine translated into big money. My wife didn't know how big the book became. She had no idea what was happening with me, and I didn't know what I'd done to her. She came to question my need to work the puzzles day and night to give my mind something to do.

"The curse was tearing me up. I couldn't control it with a sudoku game. I started running a Dutch Book on the side—working all the angles to stay sane. I was pretty cocky back then, sure of myself, but I was walking on the edge of my own razor.

"It was hard on my wife. I never raised my hand to her, but my mind," Donnie said emphatically as he nearly grabbed his head from either side. "My mind was making us both crazy. She couldn't keep up.

"Anyway, Vegas got wind of my Dutch book. I thought I was too big, too important, too valuable to touch, and I was right. But Little Donnie…Li'l Donnie wasn't valuable. She wasn't valuable to anybody but her mother and me. So they took her."

Chariot stopped and looked a horse over closely as though genuinely considering an impact on his morning line for race day. Nicky stepped into the opening in the story. "Donna was kidnapped?"

If there was a mental note taken from the horse's stall, Donnie wasn't sharing. He moved on and barely took notice of the cream of America's thoroughbreds he was walking by.

"They snatched her off the street. They didn't hurt her—as much as you can't hurt a little girl whose been kidnapped. For extra effect, they called my wife. She lost it. At least she came to me before she called the police—of course screaming it was all my fault—which it was.

"I had Gabriel on the payroll even then. I remember he came by in full uniform and talked my wife off the ledge, but I'd already teed her up with what I'd created with The Locker. She only knew enough to think everybody in the business had a Locker. She was possessed with visions of Li'l Donnie chained to the wall in a dungeon somewhere. It was a horrible time."

The Book stopped to stroke the muscled neck of another champion. Nicky stared, fighting back questions and a rush of anger that Chariot had not been able to protect another little girl.

"But you got her out. Broke her out or whatever. Rescued her."

"Not really," Donnie said as he moved off again. "I'd like to take the credit. Maybe I did more than I remember. I had Frank round up several guys from different crews. He and Abreu brought them all into The Locker and had them watch—to help with their memories. The truth came out in short order, but I continued to cut. Frank made a call—got the terms—and Li'l Donnie was brought home. It was all pretty simple."

"And she was okay?"

"Until she got home."

That made no sense. "What happened when she got home?"

"Her mother was drugged up so she could rest. Maybe it was an excuse. I don't know. I don't think she even knew Donna was home.

"I was moving in and out of The Locker directing Frank and Abreu regarding men or what remained of them. Donna went into the basement looking for me. Instead she found someone who'd terrorized her during the kidnapping. When I came in, she had my razor in her little hand...."

37

The ace Julian DeSeti thought he'd kept in the hole had shimmied out another hole in the middle of Belmont Park. He had no idea where she was. His son was missing, and he presumed him to be dead. On that account, Julian was nearly right. Out of options with a dangerous man after him who rumor had it was losing his sanity, Julian walked in the Midtown South Precinct of the New York Police Department. A pair of manacles bolted to the floor received Gabriel's kick.

"What the hell are you doing walking in here and asking for me?"

"We're in trouble."

"Did you say 'we?' I'm not in any trouble."

"You don't think so? Standing close to Chariot is not a safe place to be. You should know that by now."

"He don't have anything on me. Christ, he doesn't even know what he did five minutes ago."

"He's slipping fast, I agree. Baron knows it too. I guess that's why he brought you in on all this—to watch Chariot."

"Baron didn't bring me into this. Chariot did."

"When?"

"While you and that punk kid of yours was busy counting pocket change, Chariot's been counting millions. He knew his gears were slipping and he knew what Baron's crew would do when the odds really shit the bed. The people in Baron's circle love their grandchildren, but they'd eat 'em before they'd lose money and shitty morning lines are how they lose money.

"Chariot does what a building full of computers and a hundred people can't do. He saved Vegas millions, *billions*, and *made* millions for his trouble. When the wheels started to come off, he had to bring his kid in to keep Vegas happy and himself alive—probably his daughter too. So he cooked up the kidnapping. I was only there to pacify Donna and ease her into the business. Then you and that dickhead son of yours screwed the pooch. Probably get you both killed now. Well, not me, DeSeti. Not me."

"What are you going to do? I need protection."

"Protection? That's a joke. Chariot will butcher you like a pig for screwing up his plan, but mostly for putting your hands on his granddaughter. You must not know the family history. He don't like people touching his family. He's funny like that."

"If he gets near me, I'll—"

"No you won't. You'll already be dead."

"Okay. I blew it! I tried to make a play and came up short. I need help. I can't find my boy."

"Probably dead. I heard he thought the Grand Hyatt was the OK Corral and 42nd Street, Tombstone. Well, it ain't, but he'll get his tombstone all right, and probably one for you too."

"Give me a hand here, Gabriel! You help me and I'll help you."

"You can't do nothing for me, but get me in a jam. You better go."

"I can give you Chariot!"

"Nobody touches Chariot," Gabriel snapped. "Not until Baron says, 'Touch.' Savvy?"

Julian didn't have an answer apart from a slight nodding of his head.

"He's toast anyway," Gabriel continued. "Chariot's off his feed, as they say around the track."

"You'll still need proof to convict him. I could—"

"A conviction? A conviction comes after a trial and who said anything about a trial? He'll end up in the East River when this is over. Right beside you."

Julian was done. "That's not a river at all," he said as he drifted, shoulders weighed down, dragging toward the door. "Did you know that? It's...technically, it's an estuary."

"It's a graveyard."

"Thanks for the help. I don't suppose money—"

"No."

Julian stopped with his hand on the doorknob. "For the record, you're no babe in the woods here. The District Attorney wouldn't take much prompting to indict—"

"Are you looking for a quicker way to get in that river?"

"Estuary."

"Whatever. Don't go there, Julian, and I'm saying that as an old business acquaintance. Don't."

DeSeti nodded again. "Sure thing. I know. Forget it. Can I ask something though?"

"No—"

"How are you getting around all this? All that's been done?"

Gabriel's smile revealed the faith he had in his own hole card. "I've got a badge, remember?"

DeSeti straightened his back and rubbed a kink out of his neck. He was beaten, but might be able to land one good punch before he hit the canvas. "That badge bulletproof?"

His answer was Gabriel's pistol jumping from its holster and parking its muzzle under Julian's left eye and driving him to the wall. "I'll put one through your face right here and now."

"No you won't—"

The gun bit deeper and pressed Julian's face tighter against the wall.

"—too many questions. You don't like questions and the answers don't suit you."

"Too hell with you, DeSeti." The pistol fell away with a sharp punch for good measure. "You're already dead. I'll leave you to Chariot and mop up the last man standing."

"Maybe."

"Yeah, maybe."

"I feel a vacation coming on. Maybe I'll go to the old country. Maybe I'll write to the DA from there. Maybe I'll do a lot of things."

"Did you order a headstone and accidently have today's date carved on it? Are you that stupid?"

"Are you?"

Gabriel was exasperated. "Here's what's gonna happen. Where's your boy? I'll do what I can for him on the body in Manhattan. You go take your vacation. And keep going."

"You won't do anything for my boy."

"If I don't, you can pick up your pen and start writing."

There weren't many choices floating around the room. There hadn't been from the onset.

"He doesn't pick up his phone. I think he's already left town. Maybe he's flying."

"You hope. I'll check JFK and LaGuardia. Where was he last?"

"We have a place off the Palisades."

38

Donnie Chariot was kneeling on the door sill in the soft interior lights of Baron's chauffeured Lincoln. Lexy sat on the back seat in the open door. Baron was across the rear seat with the pizza between them. The thought of kidnapping a child disgusted him, but at this point, he wasn't doing anything more than a favor for a friend. In spite of, or despite that friend, this time tomorrow he'd have exactly what he wanted as he'd laid in hedge bets all over the table. There were few ways Baron could lose.

"Are you okay with this?" Donnie asked his granddaughter. "I mean, I know it's not what you really want to do, but you can do this for me?"

"Yes," Lexy said minus any resolve.

Nicky leaned over his boss. "And no kicking walls down and bailing out. But you do have to show me how you did that. Pretty impressive. Deal?"

The slightest smile came on Lexy's face. "Deal."

Donnie was taking off his Rolex. "What time are you going to the track?" he asked Baron.

"We will be taking our breakfast at the Plaza. I suspect we shall arrive at my box by 10 a.m."

Lexy spun on the seat and spoke to her new babysitter gently. "First race isn't until one o'clock."

"So it is. Then you and I shall meander the grounds and ply the horses on the state of their current condition. Perhaps we can pick up a tip or two."

"I don't think we can get near the horses on Stakes day."

"I know a few people there. Unless…that is, if you wish to stay at the hotel."

"No thank you."

"Let's breakfast at the Plaza then. We'll be at the track by ten, peruse the stables." Baron leaned smiling devilishly across the seat to Lexy. "Perhaps we can spot an unscrupulous veterinarian, a tender step, or a patched hoof, and cause a handsome scandal."

Lexy smiled a little wider as she felt her grandfather's heavy gold watch slip over her hand and onto her thin arm. "Okay, Donna, now you take this so you'll know what time it is."

"I'm Alexis."

"I know that, kiddo. I know that." Donnie stood up but leaned into the car and gave his granddaughter a hug and a kiss. "I'm proud of you, you know that?"

"Yep."

"Take care of my girl," Donnie said with very tight eyes.

Baron shook his head very deliberately yes.

"Nicky?" Lexy asked. "I know she's busy now, but you and Grandpa will bring my mom to the races tomorrow? We'll be there at ten."

"We'll bring her to your box at the end of the first race."

"But I'll be there at ten."

"Your mom, me, your grandpa have to get things ready for you to move into the big house. Anyway, time goes fast at the track. We'll be there."

"Okay. You're sure, right?"

"She'll be there."

"Don't lose my watch," Donnie said as he tapped the face of it.

"I won't."

A minute later Chariot and Nicky were crossing through the dark for their cars.

"Take it slow going home. I'm tired," Donnie said. "I better follow you."

"What happens when we get there?"

"Where?"

"Home. With Donna."

"That's up to you I guess. You can tell her I'm a bastard, but she knows that. You could tell her I sent Alexis to the Grand Hyatt with Mrs. Glass. She'll probably shoot me with my own gun. But if you go that route, she's apt to get hurt or Donna too."

"Alexis?"

"Yes, yes, dammit! That's not always the illness. I've been doing that since she was born. She looks just like her mother did."

They were at the cars. "If Donna and I are going somewhere—with your permission—I hate the feeling of starting it off with a lie."

"I understand. Lying bothers me too. That wasn't always my policy, but I'd do it all day to protect those girls. You'd do it too. The part you have to believe is that it was better for me to do it—and control it—than let what happened to Donna happen again."

"Until you couldn't control it."

"True. It had to be Gabriel and DeSeti. No one else could have put it together. Gabriel was in from the start. He was going to steer Donna off the scent."

"You mentioned that."

"I did?"

"Forget it."

Donnie smiled as he got in his Bentley. "That's funny. 'Forget it.' That's the problem. Don't lose me. Think it over, kiddo. Tell me before we walk in the house. I'd like to have my left up if she's going to be swinging."

Ahead of them, Baron was escorting Alexis to The Plaza. Once there, he set her up in grand style in an adjoining room meant for his security. They were moved to another room with strict instructions to closely monitor the hall for the little escape artist. Baron wasn't certain if a Chariot's unbreakable word had yet extended to the smallest one, but it had. The Plaza would easily hold the little girl in an oversized bed with a pizza box at the foot and a $70,000 diamond-encrusted gold watch held on her arm by a sleeping hand.

• • •

By the time Nicky and Chariot entered the mansion, Nicky had come down on the side of keeping his mouth shut. He was convinced that Donnie's move was the wrong one for the right reasons. He also had a better appreciation and understanding for Donna's bite. A traumatic abduction, on top of an out-of-control, turbocharged mind, coupled with what she'd seen and done in The Locker—it was a wonder she was as sane as she was. He was looking around the first floor for her, carrying gentle hugs and a lifetime promise to protect her and her daughter, but couldn't find her. His last stop was her father's office where he walked in on Mr. Abreu talking softly to their mutual boss.

Nicky's hands were held out, palms up, asking the universal quiet question.

"Wait here," Chariot directed as he pushed by in the direction of the basement.

Donnie walked in The Locker to find his daughter kneeling on the scaffold, torch in one hand, razor in the other.

"What are you doing?"

Donna looked up only for a second before returning to Junior's knee. "Following in your footsteps, Daddy. And making sure this piece of shit never walks again."

Chariot came closer. "I think he's dead."

"He's not dead. He'd like to be, but he's not. I traded him a shot of his heroin for where Lexy is. It's a different approach, but it seems to be working. He said his father has her."

Abreu slipped into the doorway behind the Book while Nicky stayed out of sight in the dead space between the insulated doors.

"If you know that," Chariot said as he took another cautious step. "Why are you still cutting him?"

Donna came up throwing. The propane torch, still lit, narrowly missed Donnie and careened with an echoing clank around the room. The razor was in her hand, pointing like a bloody finger at her father as she screamed. *"Because I can't cut you!"*

Around the corner, Nicky slumped against the wall. His heart was breaking for her. He wanted to rush in—her knight in shining armor—and sweep her away from the gore and all the pain that tore at her. He'd tell her all he knew and they'd abandon New York to the gamblers and money changers, grab Alexis, and run.

Unknowingly, he had turned to the inner door to push through with the breaking of his word—a cardinal sin in the House of Chariot—but he felt Abreu's thick hand on his chest holding him back and out of sight.

"Wait," Abreu said to Nicky, but inadvertently he brought both of the Chariots' attention to him from each other. The old gardener had to follow the suit he'd played. "Boss, remember Baron? He's helping. You should tell Li'l Donnie."

"Tell me what?"

Chariot's face was vacant except for a furrowed brow that hid a mind searching the recent past.

After a slight but strong push to ensure Nicky's feet were locked, Abreu rather shyly explained what Donnie could not. "Baron has arranged to get the little one back. Tomorrow. At the track."

Donna came off the platform like a shot and directed the question more to her father than Abreu. "Where is she now?"

There was no guarantee in Donnie's voice that he even knew what he was answering. "I don't know."

"That's a lie!" Donna snapped again. "Why can't you tell the truth? Just once!"

"Because if I told the truth, you wouldn't believe me."

"Try me," Donna said, flashing the blade for punctuation, but Donnie had already slipped into the abyss.

Donna moved her eyes, the question, and the knife to Abreu. He stepped away from both the door and the question and crossed the site of so much terror. He picked up the torch and put out the flame. "I don't know either. I really don't, kiddo. If I did, I'd tell you."

"Same old thing. You'd say whatever he told you to say."

"That's right. I would. If it meant protecting you and the little one. I would."

"I wouldn't," Nicky said as he stepped into The Locker and away from the shelter of Donnie Chariot's lie. He crossed the floor, oblivious to the remnants of DeSeti's torture, Abreu, and his boss. He saw only Donna. He walked by Donnie and the slightest look of desperate exasperation came over The Book's face then disappeared down the same hole with other memories.

Nicky steered Donna to the sink, slipped the razor from her hand, and tossed it on the bench. He turned the water on a gentle flow and with her hands in his, took up a battered bar of soap and began to wash the blood from her fingers.

"I love you, Donna Chariot. It's not important how you feel about me. But I need you to know I love you before I say anything else. Do you believe me when I say that?"

Her shoulders relaxed as she allowed him to carefully wash away the blood. "Yes. Yes, I do."

"I don't know if you've ever been loved, Donna. I really don't. Or if how I feel about you is enough for you to trust me. Is it? Do you trust me?"

"Yes," and the blood circled the drain, faded, and vanished.

"We're going to walk out of here now. You and me. And tomorrow...tomorrow we're going to the track at the end of the first race. We're going to pick up Alexis from Baron. He had nothing to do with her being taken, I swear on my life, but he can get her back. It's that easy. It's that hard. And that's just the way it is."

Donna felt his hands wrap hers in a clean towel. He dried them gently, then dabbed her face and neck free of any traces of the night. He moved as though cleaning the face of a child.

"Okay," was all she said. Her head fell on his shoulder as his arm circled hers. They walked by Donnie and Mr. Abreu without a word and left The Locker, the blood, and the memories circling and succumbing to the drain. In moments they were driving away from the manor. They never saw the horde of flashing lights or heard the cry of the police sirens descend behind them.

Nick decided for them that it was best to forego staying at either's apartment and checked into the best room available at The Hilton at nearby JFK. They showered together gently and fell under a real, but subdued passion. The frenzy of first-time lovers was tempered by recent events, replaced by a calm that came with knowing the commitment would endure beyond the heat of early kisses.

39

The next morning dawned with a promise to ninety thousand spectators, fans, and fanatics who would witness the "Test of the Champion." The finest thoroughbreds in the world were waking to test their mettle against the mile and a half that was The Belmont Stakes. Also attending on a promise were one little girl and her mother, looking to be reunited in the fray.

Baron had kept his part of the bargain and Alexis had kept hers—there were no tunnels out of the Plaza behind them as they finished a light breakfast. With the subtle doors Baron could open around the track, he added to his promises kept by taking the girl by the hand through several barns. Despite the pleasant access to her favorite athletes, Lexy often checked the big watch dangling from her hand.

Before the call for "Riders up!" went out for the first race, Lexy and guardians were comfortable in their box seats on the wire. Though she had the best view of the track in the house, Lexy spent every minute squirming and craning her neck up and around, searching the crowd. She didn't know for certain, but hoped her mother and grandfather were doing the same.

"Where's their box?" Donna asked from beneath a hand shading her eyes. She lacked a festive hat—though it wasn't her style—as Nicky had been unwilling to stop at her apartment for fresh clothes. So she searched the crowd in the same outfit that had run rough shod over The Locker and lay discarded on a chair in their hotel room the night before.

"On the wire. Millionaires' Row," Nicky said pointing.

It was only another breath before she saw her daughter. "She's here!"

"What'd I tell you?" Nicky said as he was rewarded with a kiss on the cheek. Donna took a step, but he stopped her with a clutch at the elbow. "After the first race. That was the deal."

Overcome, Donna waved both arms when she thought Alexis was looking her way, but she was hidden by the masquerade of the crowd and her daughter's eyes continued their search.

"Your father's not in the box," Nicky said watching.

"Probably exhausted. I should have stayed and helped him with the morning lines."

"Do you want a program?" Nicky asked, though his eyes never left Baron's box.

"No. I don't bet. You?"

"Sometimes. Only to make the races more interesting. Maybe I'll do it more often since I just woke up next to the best handicapper in the world."

"Forget it. When today's behind us, I'm out of the business. These people can rot. You said we'd go away. Say what you will about Chariots, but we never renege. And we hold others to the same standard."

"I know you do."

"I should call my father, I suppose."

The bell for the first race rang, dispelling any notion of a phone call. The starting gates exploded and the horses bolted. In less than two minutes the race would be a memory. More people would be disappointed than cashing out, but as surely as the horses were conditioned to run at the bell, Donna started again for her daughter.

"C'mon. It's only seven furlongs. It'll be over before we get through the crowd."

As the new couple weaved through the still collecting early race fans, above them at either end of the mammoth grandstand, teams of uniform police and plainclothes detectives were scanning the crowd, just as Donna had done. Gabriel was at the mouth of a net that was closing, two women officers at his side, and two pieces of neatly folded paper in his hand.

The contenders for the first race's purse were thundering down the stretch, reaching for the wire. Cheers came up to greet the thoroughbreds as they crossed the line and brought Lexy's attention from the stands to the track. Most of the polite racket was venting from race-goers thrilled to see the day's events begin in earnest. No one took notice when Baron stood as the mass had risen to welcome the end of the first race. In fact, Baron had stood to clear the way for Donna and Nicky to enter the private box.

Lexy's eyes followed the horses into the clubhouse turn as they eased into slowing canters. She took a moment to focus when her eyes were suddenly full of her mother standing right next to her.

Their cries and impassioned hugs were mirrored by a display a few aisles over in the winning connections' box. While that box emptied in an exuberant trek to the winner's circle, Baron's box filled with Donna and Nicky, and they settled into their seats, with Lexy nestled firmly on her mother's lap.

Baron saw and felt Donna clutch his arm. "Thank you. Thank you so much!"

"You're most welcome."

Donna returned 100% of her attention to her daughter. The kisses didn't stop, and hugs were sprouting from the place Donna had normally kept her fears and memories. Lexy gently touched the cuts and bruises DeSeti had left on Donna's face. When tears began to come from mother and daughter, they bathed the last of Donna's transformation.

"I thought it might come to this," Nicky said as he handed over tissues.

Donna wiped her eyes and nose and encouraged Lexy to pour out every detail of her long adventure. For the pair, they were all alone and not in the middle of 90,000 people.

The second race of the day came and went without notice as they continued to catch up every detail. The bell for the third race signaled the story of gunfire on 42nd Street and the first hesitation, compliments of Mr. Frank being shot.

This wasn't the place for that conversation and Donna knew that somewhere around race four on the card, Mrs. Glass's death would surface. She steered it all away.

"Let's go on home, honey. We can talk more there. It'll be more—"

"But it's Stakes day! Oh, my gosh! I wait for The Belmont Stakes all year!" Alexis suddenly had energy to look around. "Hey...where's Grandpa? He said he'd meet me here. He wouldn't lie to me. I know it. I have his watch," she said as her arm went up and the watch settled at her elbow.

"I...well, it's really crowded...and the traffic's terrible. Maybe he's having trouble getting through. It's still early."

Nicky was already dialing. He waited, but no one picked up. He tried again. "No answer."

Baron leaned forward to speak around the Chariots to Nicky. "Excuse me, did I hear you say The Book had not picked up?"

"Yes, sir."

Baron tapped his program across the palm of his hand. "That's unlike him."

The concern brought Donna from her daughter's recollections. "He was probably working late on the morning lines."

"Perhaps."

She motioned to his program with a smile. "No racing form?"

Baron returned the smile. "I don't gamble."

"You're like my father."

"Yes, I know. We prefer certainty. We crave it, don't we? A sure thing."

"No sport in that," Donna smiled again.

Baron leaned back in his seat and made a sweeping gesture with his program at the Big Sandy. "All this? I enjoy the animals a great deal. The people? Much less. Occasionally, I may feel the twinge of 'sport.' The allure of the yearly chase for the Crown. The Pegasus. Meydan, Dubia. Ah, those glorious purses. But in large part, I see only business." He turned in the seat and rested his arm on the backrest. "Which brings me to you. The 'sure thing.' I'd like to make a proposal—a suggestion— a job offering. However you prefer to define it."

"I have a job."

Baron shook his head. "Not really. You only disguise yourself— cloak yourself with a toy. It bores you to tears. There's no challenge for you."

She hugged Lexy. "I'm not looking for challenges any longer."

"Then relief. I offer relief."

That gave Donna pause. "Honey," she said to Lexy. "Explain to Nicky what horse will win the next race. Can you do that while I talk to Baron?"

Lexy picked up her program and slid from lap to seat without a word. She leafed to the next race and began to chatter about past performance and trainers.

Now it was Donna who turned in her seat to better address her daughter's benefactor. "What do you mean 'relief?' Relief from what?"

"I imagine you know. I imagine you're a considerable distance ahead of me in this entire conversation. You've weighed the input against the costs. ROI. Probabilities. Odds for failure, success. Impact on yourself." He leaned to look at Lexy. "On your daughter."

The last suggestion caused Donna to bristle. "I am eternally grateful for what you've done, but let's get right to the rat killing."

"You are your father's daughter."

"Indeed."

"If you wish."

"I do."

"I'd very much value you continuing to work with your father on my business interests."

"I'm sorry. That's not going—"

"As a measure of…your appreciation," Baron said as he leaned and looked at Alexis again.

An uneasy quiet settled over the pair that no one else could hear. Much was said and unsaid in the stillness. The colorful mass around them continued to laugh, chat, and gawk. The horses continued to run, and Alexis continued her lesson with Nicky.

A full minute slipped by unnoticed and left no change with its passing. Their silent world waited. If there be loss, Donna decided she would rather drive than be driven.

"Anything else you want. Anything. I swear. A Chariot's word."

Baron's palms turned up. "My needs are few."

Donna looked away and let her eyes settle unfocused across the wide track in front of her. To her side, beyond her daughter, Nicky was watching and listening as best he could over a lesson that would have been profitable on any other race day. "I can't do that," she said. "I'm sorry."

"That's rather a disappointment."

"I'm very sorry. You don't understand. I've spent most of my life trying to get away from that business, that house, and my father."

"Are you certain the escape is from all three?"

"They're inseparable."

"As are you."

She came back to him, squared off. "What do you mean?"

"You're still his daughter. That's very evident. She'll always be his grandchild."

"More's the pity."

"And the risk." Baron raised his hands. "Not from me. Though some think otherwise, I do not command the world." He cast out a genuine disarming smile at Alexis like bait.

Donna's own look followed his and wrapped around Alexis and Nicky before they settled back on Baron. "We're leaving the city. That thing that makes us unique can also make us disappear."

"Of that I have no doubt."

Donna smiled, but it was clearly strained. "I'll buy you the most powerful mainframe they make. Two of them. Three! I swear it."

"Thank you. I much prefer one Chariot over a bank of computers."

Donna took his hand. "I understand, but I can't."

"And there we are then," he said as he slipped his hand free and in turn painted hers with compassion. "I wish you the very best. I sincerely do."

A resounding sigh escorted the sounds of Belmont Park back to her ears. "Thank you. Thank you so much."

"May I ask, what of your father? Somehow, I don't see him adapting to a new life at this stage."

"He always lands on his feet." It sounded more callous than she'd intended.

The aisle was suddenly under a deluge of suits and uniforms. "Donna Chariot? I have a warrant for your arrest."

The speaker was Gabriel and he was backed by a small mob of officers who had positioned themselves around the box.

Donna's face asked, "What?" but her mouth couldn't move. Her arms however, reached for Lexy and pulled her onto her lap.

Nicky looked over his shoulder at the uniforms then said what she couldn't. "What's this all about?"

"Nicolas Colletta?" Gabriel said as he held up the papers in his hand. "I've got one for you, too. Let's go."

"This is crazy," Nicky said through an anxious cringe. "What's the charge?"

"Top of the list is murder. We got two bodies with your name on them. Add racketeering, gambling, assault—a whole list for you, tough guy. Let's go."

"That's nonsense," Donna said, recovering and launching her counter.

"We got a witness, Miss. He gave a statement. Best he could anyway."

"Then he's a liar!"

"Maybe, but since we found this witness bleeding to death in your father's basement chained to the floor, I'd say he has a pretty good case. We located the murder weapon in the front lawn. Don't make me ask you again," Gabriel threatened. "You can walk out of here on your own or get carried kicking and screaming. Your choice."

"Where's my father?"

"You worried about him all of a sudden? He's tucked away in a cell on Riker's Island. Been there all night while we were looking for you two. I'm about ready to stop being polite." Gabriel looked closer at both Nicky and Donna's faces. Each showed the beating Junior DeSeti had administered. "Looks to me like the two of you have been fighting the world. All that ends now."

Nicky was flippant. "You should have seen the other guy."

"I have. Looks like he was put through a meat grinder. He says you two did it. When he dies, you'll catch body number three."

"This isn't—"

"You comin'?"

"I was looking for—"

"Take the kid," Gabriel said to the matrons in tow. "She'll be in the custody of the City since all her family's gonna be in jail. Hopefully forever."

"Wait," Donna said as she tightened her grip on her daughter. "Wait!"

"Mommy? What's happening?"

Nicky was up, but the cops were pouring over the railing. Baron's security looked to him and he motioned for them to stand down.

"Detective, excuse me, please," Baron asked politely. "May I read the warrants?" At the opposite end of the row, Nicky was bent over his chair getting handcuffed.

"You ain't mentioned. Lucky for you. But you should pay attention to who you go to the races with. This pair is going to jail. People might get the idea you're a criminal too."

"What people think of me is none of my business."

"Same as these warrants then."

"I'm an attorney—licensed to practice in this state and countless others."

"You her counsel?"

Baron looked at Donna. If there was a wait it was a short one.

"Yes," she said for them both.

"This has got stink all over it," Gabriel said to Baron. "You should get out of the way and catch the next flight to Vegas."

"May I see the warrants?"

"I wouldn't if I were you."

"You're not."

Gabriel pushed the papers at Baron. The entire group froze as he read through the papers. When he finished, he put the papers in his program and folded his hands over it and his lap. "I'll surrender my client tomorrow morning at—"

"Are you sure you read them papers? Those are for murder. These two are going with me. I'm done asking. Now, I'm telling you, counselor. Their next stop is arraignment and Riker's. Talk to the judge."

Baron snapped toward his newest client. "Go along quietly, Miss Chariot. Do not say word one. Do you understand? Not a word."

"And Nicky?"

"I am returning a favor to your father. You are my concern."

"We're an *exacta*."

There wasn't time for discussion. "Fine. Nicolas, do not say a word. Nothing about the warrant, the case, the ride, treatment, the weather. Nothing. Not a single word. Can I make myself any clearer?"

"I understand."

Donna's attention was already on Alexis. "I have to go with these people for a little while."

"You just got here! Why?"

"There's been a mistake—a big one. You have to—" The words died in her throat as the matrons stepped forward. "These ladies will take you—"

"I'll go with Grandpa. Where is he? I want to go with Grandpa!"

"Take her," Gabriel directed the women.

Donna was caught. She couldn't pull in a breath. Reason whispered that a fight to protect her daughter would be fruitless. On the other side of the closing cage was the maternal instinct of a tigress. She was as stretched as if she'd been on a medieval rack, and the pain was equal.

Donna looked at Baron, her eyes welling up with exasperated, unspoken pleas. Without a word of recognition, he tossed up a bulwark to her tears.

"That won't be necessary, ladies. I am the child's godfather. She can remain in my care."

The matrons stopped and looked back to Gabriel for direction.

"Godfather ain't blood."

"Where did you stay last night, Alexis?" Baron asked quickly.

"With you," she said, cowering tightly into her mother.

"That's precedence. We have a familial relationship. There are numerous instances of case law to support this."

Gabriel stiffened. "I don't know if you're who or what you say you are. Take the kid."

"Are you certain you want to use that tone with me, Gabriel?"

Stifled by his name, the detective instantly deferred to the women. "I ain't got no warrant for the kid. What do you usually do?"

"Do you know this man?" a woman asked Donna.

"Yes."

"Sweetie, do you know this man?" the same woman asked Alexis.

"Yes."

"Do you want your child remanded to his custody?"

"Will you take her to my father's?"

"Whatever you wish."

"Yes, I give him custody."

The women melted into the throng. "We're done," they said as they squeezed by Gabriel.

"Lexy, you go with Baron again," Donna pleaded. "Only for a little while."

"I'll have a bail hearing as soon as possible and a motion to dismiss on its heels. You should be home by tomorrow."

"Tomorrow. I'll be home tomorrow," she told Alexis. "You finish watching the races now and pick a winner for me, okay?"

"No…you just got here."

"I know and I'm so sorry. I am so very sorry, honey." The apology was punctuated by as long a hug as the police would allow.

"We're out," Gabriel said. "C'mon."

A cop who had vaulted the railing pushed Nicky in front of Donna and beyond Baron.

"Good-bye, Nicky," Alexis said. "Will you come to the house tomorrow, too?"

"You bet I will."

"Bet," Gabriel snickered. "That's funny. Your next bet will be how long Dannemora lets you stay a virgin. Move your ass. Get him out of here."

As Nicky started his escort up the steps, hands cuffed behind his back for his insolence, Gabriel pulled out his handcuffs for Donna. "For your protection and my own," he smiled.

"Hardly warranted," Baron offered as he took Lexy's hand without looking then cast a quick glance in her direction for Gabriel to see. "And unnecessary given the circumstances."

"Like I said, she's under arrest for homicide. I'm only trying to protect myself."

"I see that very clearly. Very clearly."

The cuffs were put on Donna's wrists behind her back. At least they were shielded from sight when Donna dropped down to Alexis. "Can I have a kiss?"

Lexy complied and Donna kissed her repeatedly. She saw Baron's hand gently holding her daughter's. When Gabriel pulled Donna to her feet, she leaned heavily into Baron and whispered in his ear. "I'll do it. I'll do it all. Please get me home."

DAVID-MICHAEL HARDING 299

40

Five Months Later

The big desk in Donnie Chariot's office held a new bank of computer monitors and a coloring book. The monitors were larger than before and the screens scrolled by faster. Thicker brightly colored cables that matched the crayons in Lexy's hand, fell from multiple keyboards and monitors. They were all bound neatly and disappeared through the floor. Everything sent out was deeply encrypted by monstrous mainframes that labored deep in the basement in heavily air-conditioned comfort.

"Dinner in half an hour," Nicky said as he floated in.

Donna looked up from the desk and smiled. Nicky had a light air in his step. Married life suited him. She leaned back and rested one hand on her slightly distended stomach. It remained to be seen if fatherhood would as well, but if Alexis provided any indication through past performance data, her husband would finish in the money.

When Nick settled in at a long bureau across the wide office, Donna heard an electronic automated money counter whirl. "Set that aside for the restaurant," she said.

Lexy didn't look up from the corner of her grandfather's desk she was sharing with her mother. "That was $17,400 you just gave—"

"Stop that. Mind your coloring," Donna said, absent any real threat. "You'll be well-rounded if I have to sand the edges off you with a broomstick."

Nick laughed. "I got you! They were twenties, not hundreds."

"That's cheating," Lexy protested as her head came up. "Mom, Nicky's cheating."

"Color!"

"What a cheater. I don't care. Twenties would be—"

"Don't!" Donna said as she snapped a luxurious fountain pen to the desk. "I mean it. Color. Then write. I want to see a hundred words tonight."

"I have math homework."

It was Donna's turn to laugh. "Don't give me that. Math homework...after dinner you write. Longhand. Cursive. No computer."

Lexy returned to her coloring. In a few seconds she posed a simple question any child might ask. "What did you whip up for dessert?"

"My decadent chocolate cream pie," Nicky said. "Elegant in its simplicity."

"Did you beat the batter a lot to make it super fluffy?"

"I did."

"Like, 3,480 times?"

Donna shot up from the desk as best she could with her condition out in front of her. "Okay, we're done here. Let's go. You two are incorrigible! Get your gloves. We have time for a game of catch before dinner."

"What?" husband and daughter said in unison.

"Batter strokes, my foot! How much was Nicky's last count if it was twenties?"

Lexy shrugged. "Beats me."

"Cute. Three thousand, four hundred, eighty." Donna came around the desk. "Both of you. Get your gloves. One of you hooligans grab mine, please."

Alexis ran from the desk and bumped past Nicky who was reaching over her for his wife. He hugged her carefully and put a hand on her stomach. "How's my babies?"

"Fine. A little tired."

They took a few slow steps toward the doorway. "I know you've thought about it," Nicky said. "But Baron getting us out so quickly, yet he can't do anything for your father. Isn't that odd?"

"He pretty much had a knife in his hand when the cops kicked the door in. He admitted everything and the gun was DeSeti's. That's what hung that sonofabitch."

"I know, but Baron—"

"We can't prove anything and maybe it wouldn't be good for us if we could. I'm very happy. Very happy."

"Me too," Nick said as he kissed her cheek. "But no restaurant. Not yet."

"We can afford it."

"Someday. Now I want to be here for all my girls. Open a restaurant in this town and you have no life. Thanks for supporting the dream though. We'll put that money in the Foundation instead."

"It's packed."

"We'll back off when they have a cure. Will you go see him tomorrow?"

"I don't think so. He's gone down so fast. They think it was the shock and stress of prison. He never understood where he was or why." Donna continued to walk, but leaned heavily on her husband. "He doesn't know me anymore."

He kissed the top of her head. "I know."

Donna stopped and slipped from beneath his arm. "You go ahead. Forget my glove. I'll sit on the steps and watch. Go on. I'll be right there."

Nick obliged as Donna went back to her father's desk. She picked up the fancy pen, but was instantly interrupted by her daughter at the door holding hers and her mother's baseball gloves. "Hurry up!"

"Go on out! I'll meet you in the front yard. Practice with Nicky until I get there."

The gloves sagged as though instantly heavy, but Lexy vanished into the hallway and beyond to the weighted oak doors, down the stone steps, and out into the yard.

Donna watched through the massive windows and heard the muffled voices of those she loved as they began to toss a softball back and forth between alternating words of encouragement and instruction. Beyond them, Mr. Abreu was raking leaves. To her, the scene was ready for Norman Rockwell's brush.

Without sitting down, Donna pushed aside a spreadsheet. Beneath it was her father's leather bound sudoku book opened to a fresh puzzle. She stared at it and tilted her head, thinking. As though in a rush, she began to write in numbers. In a moment the puzzle was solved.

Donna picked up the book and closed it around the fountain pen. She slipped open a drawer of the big desk to tuck the book safely away. In the drawer was her father's revolver. She moved it slightly, touched it gently, as though it was a precious artifact.

She took a deep breath and smiled. Finally engaged enough to keep her mind at bay, she let out a long sigh. This was the happiest moment of her life. The smile lingered as the sudoku book was nestled beside the gun in the desk that was now hers. She slid the drawer closed and headed for another game in the front yard, still smiling.

41

Marcy Correctional Facility

The buildings looked like a prison from most angles. Certain places inside looked more like the hospital it was. Only the sickest of New York State's convicts were sent to Marcy and the sickness needn't be physical. Marcy housed a psychiatric prison inside a prison. It was a dangerous place where what the inmates saw was not always what was there. In Marcy, industrial Linoleum square tiles, often in alternating colors, took the place of dirty bare concrete floors. Some windows had heavy steel mesh instead of bars. Most gun towers had been replaced by concertina wire. But it was still a fortified maximum-security prison.

Deep inside, two dozen inmates wandered around a recreation room. Wheelchairs were common and rolled up to grated windows for a time then skated away to tables and conversation or cards. Chairs and benches were collected around a pair of televisions in opposite ends of the room playing different channels in an often-failed attempt to keep disagreements to a minimum.

One wheelchair stayed at the windows. The man in the chair had long greasy hair, covering the places where his ears had once been. The scarring on the sides of his head trickled around his face to where his lips should be but weren't. He flicked his tongue like a snake in an attempt to keep his teeth moist. The Phantom of the Opera would have grimaced at the sight of him except for a last trick played out by heartless staff.

A pair of cheap novelty glasses—the kind with a big plastic nose attached beneath the frame—was on his face. Minus ears to hold the bows up, a dirty white shoe lace ran through his hair and tied the ninety-nine cent glasses to his face. The mis-colored flesh toned nose covered a split gash where his nose had been. The empty lenses were black electrical tape crudely wrapped around the frame. Behind the tape, his eyes were gone. Not sick, diseased, discolored, or damaged. His eyes were gone.

Donnie Chariot came into this room having traded his tailored suits for green prison garb with elastic waist pants. Over his left breast was an iron-on tag with his name and prison number. An identical one was on the outside waistband of his pants.

He walked unsteady around the room—lost. The televisions held no interest for him. There was nothing in the card games for him. He could no longer understand the suits and worse, for a man that had once commanded his level of mastery over numbers, The Book could no longer count. Not even the spots on cards.

Donnie began to drag a chair across the floor to the windows. The noise annoyed some, but even in their private stupors, many knew who this was, or had been. He'd be left alone—protected by reputation and words of warning slipped into the system like commissary money that appeared from nowhere.

The chair came to rest next to the Phantom with the toy glasses in the wheelchair. Chariot looked at him, closer than most. Uninhibited by memories of a scary movie or any memories at all, he lingered, inches from the Phantom's face. Donnie's eyes dropped to the name tag on the Phantom's shirt. It read, "DeSeti, Julian Jr.", but Donnie had forgotten how to read and even if he heard the name, it would have meant nothing.

"Jesus H. Christ," he said slowly as if the pace was necessary for emphasis. "What happened to you?"

DeSeti twitched slightly. "Is someone there?"

"Hell yes, someone's here."

"I can't hear good. What did you say?"

Junior's voice was lisping and awkward—disabled by poor hearing and a lipless mouth.

Donnie was almost yelling. "I said, what the hell happened to you, friend?"

DeSeti laughed a spitting rasp. With no lips to curl back or smile, it was a guess that it was a laugh at all. "You shoulda seen the other guy."

Chariot snorted a smile. "No thanks."

"What?"

"I said, *no thanks.*"

"Whatever," Junior said as he sat in his sightless cage.

"If ever being ugly was a crime, you're it. That why you're in here?"

"No, I caught six bodies. Three of them for killing people who said I was ugly. How about you? How come you're in this shithole?"

Donnie Chariot tried to think. He searched his thoughts and memory and uncovered nothing. The only discoveries were blank spaces and darkness. He felt along the wall of his mind for a light switch, but found nothing to help him. It was all gone. He was alone except for the Phantom in front of him.

"You know, kiddo, I don't have a clue. Not one damn clue."

THE END

ABOUT THE AUTHOR

David-Michael Harding is a past PEN International Award winning author. He is a former semi-pro football player and criminal investigator. His writing is passionate and hard hitting. A native New Yorker, he now resides in Tampa, Florida.

NOTE FROM DAVID-MICHAEL HARDING

Word-of-mouth is crucial for any author to succeed. If you enjoyed *Breakage*, please leave a review online—anywhere you are able. Even if it's just a sentence or two. It would make all the difference and would be very much appreciated.

Thanks!

David Michael Harding

We hope you enjoyed reading this title from:

BLACK ✾ ROSE
writing™

www.blackrosewriting.com

Subscribe to our mailing list – *The Rosevine* – and receive **FREE** books, daily deals, and stay current with news about upcoming releases and our hottest authors.
Scan the QR code below to sign up.

Already a subscriber? Please accept a sincere thank you for being a fan of Black Rose Writing authors.

View other Black Rose Writing titles at
www.blackrosewriting.com/books and use promo code
PRINT to receive a **20% discount** when purchasing.

Printed in the USA
CPSIA information can be obtained
at www.ICGtesting.com
JSHW021203120824
67774JS00012B/6